COBALT CHRISTMAS
A COBALT ROGUE STORY

ALEXANDER ENGEL-HODGKINSON

COBALT CHRISTMAS: A COBALT ROGUE STORY

COBALT CHRISTMAS: A COBALT ROGUE STORY

Copyright © 2018 by Alexander Engel-Hodgkinson

ISBN 978-1-989331-08-8

Cover Art by Alexander Engel-Hodgkinson

Published by
Dark Brothers Incorporated

PARENTAL ADVISORY

'Cobalt Christmas' contains extreme violent content including terror and menace throughout; frequent strong profanity, graphic crude and sexual content, and other themes intended for mature readers ages 17 and up.

Author's Comment

Ah, Christmas. It's a time of joy and cheer, where spoiled children complain about the colours of their new iPhones, and terrorists take over Nakatomi Plazas. I used to wonder what a 'Cobalt Rogue' Christmas story would be like if I actually wrote one, but I couldn't imagine it being anything like those terrible Hallmark TV specials. Even if he was surrounded by nothing but holiday spirit and an overabundance of joy and cheer, Damian would still find a way to mess it all up. Perhaps if 'Die Hard' or almost every Shane Black film ever made had their stockings stuffed with cyberpunk layers and dark anime-inspired stories and dream-like (or nightmare-like) elements, one would have a general idea of how a 'Cobalt Rogue' Christmas would be.

So I figured I would just write one.

COBALT CHRISTMAS: A COBALT ROGUE STORY

COBALT CHRISTMAS: A COBALT ROGUE STORY

Chapter 000
A Quick Withdrawal

Wynnarz International Bank, Cryo City—Thursday, December 21st, 2031

The jolly tune of Billy Gilman's *Jingle Bell Rock* echoed through the bank's majestic, dark marble interior. The halls were empty. The offices in the back were deserted, probed by the fluctuating saturations of red and blue lights flashing in through panoramic windows overlooking the street.

The security room wasn't isolated from the holiday spirit bubbling up from Gilman's lyrics, either. Two men sitting in swivel chairs busied themselves with the surveillance footage on the wall of thirty monitors in front of them. On one of the monitors, a news broadcast chattered on about the hostage situation. With plastic reindeer antlers on their balaclava-wearing heads, they seemed, at first glance, to be a pair that no one could possibly take seriously. Their silenced machine pistols sat idly on the console board under the screens. One of the men leaned back in his chair, sipping a cold mug of coffee while his partner took a Kleenex and wiped a crimson spatter off one of the monitors.

"Blitzen, you goddamn trigger-happy son of a bitch," the second man said as he wiped the rest of the blood off the screen.

"Hey, hey, now," the other man, 'Blitzen,' chuckled, "'Donner,' my man, gimme a break here, will ya? My trigger finger's got tons o' uses. Like shooting things that move. Or pushing buttons. Or holding mugs of coffee like this one." He paused to sip from the mug. Then he glanced over at the trio of dead security guards piled up in the far corner of the room by the door. Their white collar shirts stained a few different shades of red, all mixed in. Smiling at the grisly sight, Blitzen said, "It's the gift that keeps on giving." He took another sip.

Donner dropped the reddened tissue into a garbage bin under the console and sat down with a grunt. He ignored his companion and spoke into a CB radio: "Vault. 'Dasher,' 'Cupid.' Status?"

COBALT CHRISTMAS: A COBALT ROGUE STORY

*

In the basement, a two-man crew—also wearing fake reindeer antlers—worked an electric drill that was in the process of cutting through the massive vault door. A terrible metallic shriek filled the air as sparks sprayed out of the entry point in the vault. The large drill bit progressively ate through the door. One of the operators took a few steps away from the drill to answer the call. "We're on the last lock. Won't be much longer now."

The other operator pulled his jacket sleeve over a faded heart tattoo on his left wrist and muttered bitterly, "Get a heart tattoo and suddenly you're goddamn 'Cupid.'"

Donner said, "Good. Head office—Dancer. How's our manager doing?"

The question made 'Dancer' a little nervous. He glanced over at the headless corpse slumped in an overstuffed leather chair with its brains and skull fragments caking the desk it sat behind. He fidgeted with the MP5K in his hands. "Uh... *manager*?"

Donner said curtly, "He's dead, isn't he?"

"Oops."

"What about the senior manager?"

Dancer looked across the room at the senior manager, whose body sat slumped against the same wall that had been caked with his brains, as opposed to a desk. "Senior manager?"

"You weren't supposed to kill them yet!" With a growl, Donner said, "We should've named *you* 'Blitzen,' you inept... *fuck*!" He banged the console with the bottom of the radio. "For fuck's sake!"

"Easy, tiger," Blitzen said.

Donner jabbed an angry index finger at him. "Not another word from *you*, Mr. 'My Finger Slipped Long Enough to Shoot the Guards Forty-Seven Times.'"

Blitzen shrugged his right shoulder while tipping more of the mug's contents down his throat.

Donner composed himself, then spoke into the radio again. "Lobby—Prancer. Vixen. Comet. Status?" Donner held his breath, prepared for the worst.

*

COBALT CHRISTMAS: A COBALT ROGUE STORY

In the lobby, Prancer had all of the hostages rounded up in front of the windows on the other side of the teller desks, and was himself leaning against a frosted glass partition with his machine pistol raised. Most of the tellers were shuffled into a corner behind the desks, overlooked by Vixen's watchful eye as well as his enthusiastic machine pistol. Comet stood by the doors in the blind spot of any snipers outside. The red and blue lights that strobed the walls of the lobby were, of course, from the cherry flashers of a small army of police that had the whole corner surrounded.

Like their companions, these guys also wore balaclavas and antlers.

Vixen answered Donner's call: "All good here. Not a creature is stirring. Not even a mouse."

"Has the negotiator called you back?"

"Not yet."

"Well, keep me posted."

"Bah humbug."

"Say again?"

"Will do."

"That's more like it," Donner said. "Bus—Rudolph. Status?"

"All good," came the swift reply.

Donner breathed a sigh and leaned back in his chair, eyeing the security feeds. "So far, it's going okay. Could be better."

"It's going fine," Blitzen said.

"Yeah, but it could go *better*. S'all I'm saying."

"Could be worse."

"Andrew—I mean, uh, 'Dancer,' wasn't supposed to kill the managers yet. Don't know where he got the idea to shoot them *before* we left."

"Me neither."

Donner glared at Blitzen. "He's been talking to *you* too much."

Blitzen chuckled.

In the lobby, Comet glanced through the glass revolving doors at the police barricade outside.

Vixen perched himself on a teller's desk, tapping the side of his gun against his thigh while keeping it pointed at the tellers. He dragged on a cigarette. Leered at one of the young female tellers. He pointed his gun at her, making the lot of them flinch. "You. Blondie. What's your name?"

The young teller pointed at herself and stammered, "M-m-me...?"

"Yeah, you. What's your name?"

"Maria."

"You scared, Maria?"

"Yes, sir."

"Drop the 'sir.' Don't call me 'sir.' It's unnecessary."

"S-sorry, s—" she slapped her hand over her mouth. Eyes wide.

Vixen smirked. "Aw, lighten up, princess. I ain't gonna kill ya. I don't *plan* on it, anyway." He took another puff. Breathed in. Blew smoke in her direction, making her cough. "It's nothin' personal. Nothin's personal unless you make it personal. That's how I see it." He leaned forward a few inches. "You ain't makin' this personal, are you?"

"N-no, def-def-definitely not," she stuttered.

"Good." Another drag. The cigarette nearly shrunk to a useless butt. "Wanna know somethin' funny?"

"S-sure..."

"Now, don't tell anybody this, or I might hafta kill you," Vixen said as he lowered his voice, leaning even closer, "but I used to work for the bank."

"Really?"

"Oh, yeah," he said. "I was a repo man. Anybody behind on their car payments might've had to familiarize themselves with my work when they woke up one fateful morning to find out their car's not in their driveway no more. What's even funnier is that they almost *always* filed a police report for auto theft. But it ain't theft; it's just reclamation of property. They signed the agreement. They knew the rules. They knew what would happen. If I had to follow those rules, so should they, right?" He blinked, giving Maria an expectant look. He flicked his gun muzzle in her direction, making her jump. "*Right?*"

"R-right!" she piped up.

"You even listening to a single fuckin' word I'm saying?"

"Of course!"

"You better be."

"I am."

"Good, cuz I'm not finished. Now where was I?" He sucked in the last toxins in his current cigarette and flicked it across the lobby. "Oh, yeah. 'Vixen the repo man.' I was good at it, too. Never had a single confrontation on my record. Always worked around the target's schedule to avoid that kinda unnecessary drama." A frown cut into his masked face. Disturbingly noticeable, even under the balaclava's thick fabric. "That is, till *one* day when some prick filed a police report for theft after I repo'd his car."

"B-but didn't that s-s-sort of thing... you know... n-not matter?" Maria's heart lurched when Vixen looked at her. She sputtered, "B-because you were just doing y-y-your job!"

Vixen grinned. "Aha, you *were* listening! Yeah, usually, that's the case. But not *this* time. Turns out that rotten son of a bitch had a whole collection of license plates and he kept switching registrations and VINs and all that shit with his real one, and goddamn my luck, on the day I went looking for a particular one, he'd made the switch to the exact one I was lookin' for without knowing the consequences in doing so. I swear that's how it went down. He was up to some shady shit. So I took his car over to the impound lot, and during the ensuing legal procedures, that slippery cocksucker managed to sneak back into the impound lot and switch everything back to his own. So of course, *I* stole the goddamn thing. Right?"

"R-right."

"WRONG!" he roared, punching the glass out of a nearby partition. All the tellers made startled yips. Vixen shoved his gun in Maria's face. "You weren't paying attention at all!" He blasted the ceiling lights above them with his pistol.

Maria and her fellow tellers screamed and covered their faces in their arms as ceramic shards rained down on them. Maria shrieked, "I'm sorry! I'm sorry! I'm sorry!"

"Goddamn lying bitch!" He kicked her against one of the teller's chairs. It was enough to calm him down... for the moment. "I didn't get arrested in the end, but I *did* lose my job. No warning or anything; I got fucking fired. So naturally *I* was now unable to pay my bills. Now *my* shit was getting repossessed, and it's all thanks to this here goddamn bank."

Maria did her best to listen, cowering and trembling and sobbing in the farthest corner away from Vixen.

Donner's voice called out from the radio: "What's with the shooting?"

Vixen answered, "Relax. Just a few lights."

"I can see that. Knock it off. If you keep actin' all gung-ho, it'll make the cops think we're ready to pop the hostages. Then they'll storm the fucking place. We don't need that shit right now. We're not ready."

"Alright, alright. Out."

Maria didn't dare move. When Vixen's eyes shifted to her, she stiffened. Held her breath.

"Hey," Vixen said to her.

She pushed against a cabinet in an attempt to get further away.

"C'mon back here. I didn't mean it..."

He reached for her.

BRRRIINNGG!

The office phone next to him rang. Vixen paused, as if weighing his options... grab the girl... answer the phone... grab the girl...

He answered the phone. "What?"

The negotiator responded coolly, "What are you doing, Mr. Vixen? I thought we had an agreement."

"Hold your goddamn horses. Nobody's dying right now."

"C'mon, talk to me. What were those shots?"

"Just a couple 'o warnings."

"Did you hurt anybody?"

"Mmmmmmmm not *too* badly," Vixen said, grinning from ear to ear as he leered at Maria. Pieces of the ceiling light covers had cut slits all over her arms. He liked the way her cuts bled. "Just make sure you keep that route clear for when the bus arrives. And no goddamn funny business!"

""The route's open. We're not trying anything. Can you at least let go of *one* hostage?"

"You want us to let a hostage go?"

"Just one, man. All we ask."

Vixen put the receiver against his vest. Spoke into the CB radio. "They want a hostage free. Those slow-ass bastards done yet?"

"Almost," Dasher shouted over their machine's shrill droning. "Another minute or so. We're almost through."

"Christ, it's taking too long."

Donner said, "Stall 'em a little longer."

"Ah, for fuck's sake." Vixen put the receiver back up to his ear. "You ain't in a position to make demands. You hear me, you negotiator wannabe piece of shit? You ain't in a position to negotiate! *We're* in charge!"

"Alright," the negotiator said quickly. "We're just trying to establish that—"

"Establish?" Vixen guffawed. "You know what you can establish? We can establish that I have enough hairs in my asshole to catch my shit like a bug in a spider's web. We can establish that we can do whatever the fuck we want, *whenever* the fuck we want to do it! You trying to take control? You *can't* take control! You can't even call this 'stealing.' This ain't a bank robbery. We're just making a quick withdrawal. We'll be out in a jiffy!"

Vixen put the receiver to his chest again and addressed Donner, "Hey, get Dancer to move his ass in case he didn't catch the hint already."

Donner said, "Dancer?"

Dancer, in the process of crossing the second floor, said, "I'm almost there." He walked briskly down the center of a cube farm, now deserted with papers and office supplies scattered by the chaos of the group's hostile takeover. When he reached the end of the row, he turned left, toward the front. More glass partitions whisked by him as he jogged to the end of the corridor. He arrived at an open door, slapping its pine surface as he jumped into the boardroom and scurried around the long conference table to the shaded windows.

"Sure, sure. Just a sec." Vixen snapped his fingers at Prancer. "Now."

Prancer nodded and jabbed a middle-aged man forward with the muzzle of his rifle. "Get a move on."

The middle-aged hostage sobbed. "No... no! Please!"

"Move!" Prancer jabbed him toward the doors.

Watching the sobbing hostage get jostled to the main entrance where the cops could get a clear view through the glass doors, Vixen said into the receiver, "Okay, Mr. Negotiator. I fold. We'll give ya one hostage. Just because I'm feeling a little holiday spirit."

"That's good," the negotiator said. "Thank you."

"Good, eh?"

"It's a start."

Vixen put the receiver to his chest again. Spoke into the radio, "Dancer?"

"I'm all set up," came the reply.

"Good." Vixen returned the receiver to his ear as he gave Prancer the thumbs-up. "You still there?"

"Yes, I'm here," the negotiator said.

"We're sending him out now."

"Please," the hostage whimpered. "I don't—"

Prancer kicked him out the first set of doors. The hostage pivoted and hit the marble floor. "Get a goddamn move on." Prancer grabbed a fistful of the hostage's coat collar and hoisted him up to his feet and shoved him against the front door. Pressed his face to the glass and jabbed his cheekbone with a pistol. He made sure the cops outside could see it clear as day. "You make a move, I blow him away!"

The cops remained crouched behind their flashy vehicular barricade. More cops, including the Captain and the hostage negotiator, stood around a table in the department store directly across the four-lane street from the bank. They watched in tense participation. The Captain squeezed his radio, snipers on standby.

Prancer gave the hostage another kick out the front door and then immediately ducked behind a cash machine. The hostage tumbled down the front steps into the hands of two crisis elites decked out in full riot gear, holding up bulletproof shields as they swarmed the screaming hostage.

"No!" the hostage cried. "Please, stop! You don't under—"

They didn't heed his warnings, instead hoisting him up, keeping the shields between them and the bank's entrance, pulling the struggling hostage toward the barricade. "Civilian secured! Civilian secured!" one of the elites chanted into a radio.

The other elite tried his damnedest to console the screaming, flailing hostage. "Sir! Sir! *Sir*! It's gonna be alright! It's gonna be..."

Prancer locked the front door latch and scurried back into the lobby, keeping his head down.

"It's a bomb!" the hostage shrieked. "Bomb! Bomb! There's a bomb... under..."

The Captain scrunched his eyebrows together, watching the hostage wriggle desperately in the elites' durable grips. "What's going on? What's he saying?" He said into the radio, "Crisis Bravo, why is he struggling?"

Inside the bank's surveillance room, Blitzen clapped his hands and laughed as he watched the scene unfold on one of the monitors. "He's trying to warn them!" He held up a cell phone in an overly dramatic fashion, guffawing maniacally. "They're doomed! DOOMED! HAHAHAHAHAHAHAHAAAA!"

Donner gave him an amused look.

"Listen! Listen to me," the hostage screamed into the protective visor of one of his crisis elite escorts. "There's a bomb attached to my chest. U-under my sweater."

"*What*?!" the elite exclaimed.

"Please—"

The elite tore the hostage's sweater open, revealing the vest of C4 explosives with an old flip-style cell phone stuck in the middle, wired and ready. "Jesus Christ!" He barked into the radio, "We need bomb squad *NOW!*" He pointed at his partner. "Get outta here!"

"What about you?"

"Forget it, kid! You got more to lose than I do." The elite started fumbling with the lock on the vest, shaking the crying hostage in the process.

Surveillance room. Blitzen started imitating explosions like an excited child hovering over his army play set. "Three... two..."

Donner in the CB radio: "Take cover, boys!"

In the lobby, Vixen shouted, "Thar she blows!" and rolled off the desk to join the tellers.

Prancer barrelled through the second set of plate glass doors.

Comet shouted at the hostages, "DOWN, DOWN!" as he hugged the floor. They screamed and copied his every move, all kissing marble.

Blitzen hit DIAL on the phone. Leaned back in the chair with a smirk. Fired up a cigarette. "Boom."

The crisis elite barked at his younger partner, "*Go*, goddamn it!"
The elite's partner took a tentative step back. "Uh..."
The elder elite struggled with the locks on the whimpering hostage's vest. Suddenly the flip phone blipped. The elite looked at the hostage. The hostage stared into the elite's visor; at his own terrified reflection. The partner took off running for the barricade. Everything stopped for three... last... beats.
The ringtone shouted, *"PHONE CAAAAAAA—"*
KABLAM!
A concussive blast tore the hostage and elder elite in half and scattered their flaming portions in all directions, across the intersection. The younger elite went sailing over the barricade, screaming. The trees lining the main street's median had their branches sheared off and their fake leaves ignited. The elder elite's upper torso crashed into the barricade. Metal shrieked as debris shredded through cars and shields. Tires burst. Windows blew. Cops screamed as shrapnel cut them down. A tidal wave of fire rushed through the streets, scorching vehicles and men; stripping signage and paint off storefronts. Overhead signs shattered and crackled into brilliant neon sprays like rogue firecrackers. Holographic screens hovering above the street flickered dead before disintegrating into dust.
The bank's plate glass walls and doors exploded into billions of tiny particles that showered the lobby and its screaming hostage occupants. Smoke and debris flooded the place in seconds. The lobby trio—Comet, Prancer, and Vixen—kept their palms over their ears and their heads down. The lights flickered violently above them as the building's very foundations shook around them.
In seconds, it was over. The lobby, now filled with smoke and caked in sparkling layers of broken glass, was silent only for another moment before the emergency sprinklers came on. Outside, a huge fireball blossomed like a rose in the middle of the intersection and curled into the night air. Light debris and snow fluttered down into

the smoky shroud that filled the street.

This changed everything.

Chapter 001
Couch Potatoes

Cryo City—Elsewhere

In a twelve-storey apartment building in the uptown part of District 12-E, in an all-inclusive two-bedroom domicile on the eighth floor, *they* spent their evening doing what they did almost every evening they could. Lounging on a foldout couch with heated TV dinners on their laps, the couple stared tiredly at their panoramic flat screen TV as the news droned on about current events. A loose bed sheet draped over their legs did nothing against the draft coming in from the closed windows.

The woman, a fiery-haired hellion whose soft, gentle features were betrayed only by her bright, diamond-hard blue eyes. Her athletic body was tall and slender, with breasts that, one would think, would always get in the way, and shapely thighs that could kill a careless man. A loose tank top and panties were her usual casual wear, and tonight was no exception to that unspoken rule. Her name was Jenny Knight; a young woman whose tempting allure matched her surprisingly short and vicious fuse. Fittingly, she possessed superhuman strength and pyrokinetic abilities.

The man was an oddity of sorts; despite his age being in the early twenties like his better half, he appeared to be more in his mid-to-late teens; a high school senior with the evident wear-and-tear qualities of a seasoned marine. His cobalt eyes shone with an unnatural glimmer—cold, calculating, intellectual, angry... and hollow, like his consciousness was a thousand yards away. A nest of messy blue hair covered his head, sticking out in straight, uneven spikes, creating a dramatic shadow over his glowing eyes. His rough, unsettling appearance and menacing hint of a scowl didn't detract from his own strange beauty that drew more than his fair share of wandering eyes. His name was Damian Warkowski; a young man with a faint Russian accent and the damaged mentality of an elite operative whose experience far exceeded the healthy boundaries of any ordinary retiree. A Dehue—an advanced form of human with psychokinetic and reality-bending abilities, Damian's power to manipulate energy and matter with his telekinesis were damn-near unmatched in strength and complexity. He wore a T-shirt and colourful spaceship-patterned pyjama pants that didn't suit his personality in the slightest to combat against the winter draft. He was the only one of the pair who felt the cold, since Jenny's pyrokinesis protected her from feeling the discomfort of cold weather.

As coverage of the upcoming Santa Claus parade came up and a shot of cheerleaders in skimpy green-and-red outfits with fake pointy ears danced across the screen, Jenny nuzzled her cheek against her man's face and said with a smile, "Imagine *me* in one of those costumes?"

Damian smirked, eyes glued to the TV. "Yep. I could imagine you *out* of one, too."

She laughed. "Oh, of course you could."

He shoved a greasy slab of microwave steak in his mouth and chewed, ignoring the grease dribbling down his chin.

Jenny's thumb wiped the grease off his face, and she scraped it off her thumb along the rim of his dinner tray. Can't you eat without getting shit everywhere?"

"No, I'm too retarded for that," he said sarcastically.

She set her empty tray aside and snuggled up against him, resting her head on his shoulder. "No, no, baby. You're not retarded. You're just stupid sometimes."

"Thanks," he replied nonchalantly, "that means a lot coming from you."

She giggled and kissed his shoulder. "I was only kidding."

"I know." He stuffed the last of the mashed potatoes into his mouth and chewed noisily.

A female newscaster's voice interrupted Santa's cheerleaders: "Sorry to interrupt you there, Sherry, but I just received word from Cheryl, who's on the scene of a bank robbery in progress. Cheryl?"

The picture cut to a woman in thick winter wear hiding behind a white van with their channel's logo emblazoned on the side. "Thank you, Shannon... I'm standing here in front of the Wynnarz International Bank where a hostage situation is currently taking place. We're not sure how many are in there but numbers are estimated to be around twenty or thirty. As for hostage-takers, it has been speculated that there may be up to seven or eight..."

Damian yawned exaggeratedly. "Boring." He flicked to a different channel where cowboys blasted their pistols at yipping Indians and yipping Indians threw spears and launched arrows at cowboys. The picture was saturated yellow, and it was very clearly a low-budget film from a bygone era. "A slight improvement," Damian said as he watched an Indian tomahawk cave in the right eye of a screaming cowboy.

"Damian," Jenny said curtly.

"What?"

"Change it."

"Why?"

"Just change it. I'm not in the mood to argue tonight."

He switched the channel to a candy-coloured collage—a soft-filtered slideshow of tropical scenery; of sandy beaches and blue skies; of palm trees swaying in the breeze. Pink and blue skyscrapers overlooked sparkling ocean waves, themselves standing mightily under the sky's warm sunset clouds. Tall, skinny women in skimpy two-piece swimwear lounged on red-and-white-striped lawn chairs; their oil-tanned skin shimmering gold and brown under the sun. Upbeat vaporwave music played in the background as a young woman's soothing voice spoke over the subtle crackling of the average-at-best sound quality: "Bask in the comforting warmth of Flowrami City's eternal summer at our exotic resorts. Behold our fantastical tourist attractions known worldwide for their brilliant architecture and wondrous designs. Enjoy the daily commute of sexy women and sizzling men on the prowl to sate their lust with experienced newcomers and hot new locals. The nightlife is like nothing you've ever seen before. The catering and the food are to die for. Come down to Flowrami City and prepare yourself for a one-of-a-kind experience. *You won't regret it.*"

"I hate this commercial," Jenny muttered.

"Why?" Damian asked as he finished his TV dinner and set it down on a folding table.

"I'm just so tired of seeing it. It's like looking through a window at a better place, but being unable to do anything more because you're in detention, or something."

"Huh."

"You know?"

"Yeah."

"I'm tired of it. I'm tired of all this goddamn snow."

"Me, too." Beat. He smirked, anticipating her inevitable reaction to *the big reveal*. "What if you could get away from it all?"

She cocked an eyebrow. Instant suspicion. "What're you getting at?"

He concentrated on remembering where he put his bag—the kitchen table behind them. It turned black as his telekinetic energy took hold and pulled two first-class plane tickets and a tour guide book out of its front pockets. Protected by a translucent black ball, the tickets and guide drifted across the apartment to the couch until they came within reach. Damian snatched them out of the bubble, which then dispersed like cigarette smoke. He waved them in his girlfriend's face and sang, "Look what I got."

Jenny did her best to avoid them as they brushed around her face like houseflies. With a frustrated grunt, she took them and gave them a good look. Her eyes bulged when the realization hit. "These...!"

"Uh-huh," he said proudly.

"These are..."

"Yeah, baby. Ten days in paradise, and then it's back home on a seafaring cruise. Bet you never thought we would celebrate the New Year on sandy beaches, huh?"

Her head turned sharply toward him. Her scowl returned. "And just *how* did you pay for these?"

Oh, shit, he thought. "Uh," he said aloud, "I won them."

"By 'won them,' you mean you spent more money than you were supposed to on them, don't you?"

"Oh, come on, baby."

"Don't 'oh, come on, baby' me, sweetheart," she replied tersely. "We can barely afford maintenance on your car; how the fuck're we supposed to afford a first-class flight to Flowrami City and ten days *basking in the comforting warmth of eternal summer* and another..." she paused to look at the tour guide "...four days on a luxury cruise across the Orion Sea when the flight alone would and *should* empty our entire bank account?"

"Remember the Reaper job?"

"What Reaper job?"

"Jack Reaper. Had to track him down last week for the

assassination attempt he tried to pull on the mayor. His brother hired me."

"Reaper's brother or...?"

"The mayor's, dumbass."

"Okay," she said, unperturbed by his verbal abuses. "What about it?"

"The Reaper job helped."

"How much?"

"Twenty-five."

"Hundred?"

"Thousand. Twenty-five thousand."

"Okay, that covers *the flight*," she said, sharp enough to cut him if he wasn't careful. "How're we supposed to afford everything else?"

"Will you relax? I got it covered."

"I'm relaxed," she said. "I'm totally calm. But I'm still curious. How do the rest of the inevitable expenses fit into your brilliant plan, genius?"

"It all costs less than fifty grand for two. Holiday discount."

"And the other half...?"

"More like 'the last ten percent.' Everything else is just about covered."

"I want a number, Damian, not an estimated percentage."

He scowled. Fired up a cigarette. "Forty-five set aside."

"And you got all of this from doing jobs?"

"I saved a little each time."

She heaved a deep sigh and rested her head on his chest. "Whatever."

"You excited?"

"I guess."

"Well, get more excited, because they're non-refundable, and we're catching that flight on the 27th."

"Fine."

Damian's scowl darkened. Frustrated by her reaction. "God forbid I spoil my girl..."

"It's not that, honey. I'm just worried about how it'll affect us financially."

"I'll work it out. I always do."

"*Almost* always work it out."

"Right," he said. His mouth an annoyed straight line. "Almost always." He changed the channel again. A cowboy took his dying father's rifle and aimed it at an Indian fleeing on horseback. He fired, hit the Indian square between the shoulder blades.

"Change it back to the news."

"Why?"

"Might be one of those things Sergeant Hill will call you for."

"It's just a routine bank heist/hostage situation. We get one of those every week. No biggie."

"Change it anyway."

He looked at her. "But I'm watching cowboys and Indians."

She tilted her head up. Her bright blue eyes staring into his. "Just do it, for me."

He gave in quickly. He usually did. "Fine. Whatever."

The news went on about the hostage/heist situation.

With a sly smirk, Damian grabbed her shapely hips. She looked at him. "Can I help you?"

"Just imagine the sandy beaches," he said as he nibbled on her neck. "You, me, and a beautiful sunset." His lips brushed further up her neck, planting little kisses. "Tangled up on a soft towel by a sparkling sea..."

Her heart fluttered as he started down her neck to her collarbone. Her head automatically tilted away to give him more room to do his thing. A shuddering sigh. "Ugh, are you serious?"

"You want me to stop?" he asked as his strong hands slid up her sides under her shirt.

She smiled, touching his arms as they wrapped around her middle, just under her breasts, and pulled her closer to him. "Did I say that? I don't remember saying that."

He kept kissing her neck, feeling her breath get heavier as he caressed her body. She started up like an engine in pristine condition. "I've barely touched you."

She moaned, "That's what you think." She turned her head back to give his lips a hungry kiss. "Mmm."

His hands cupped her breasts and squeezed gently, playfully; firm enough to get her to moan into his mouth. He thumbed her hardening nipples, making her squeak.

She took his hands from around her and rolled over on top of him, straddling him. She pinned his wrists above his head, smiling when he lifted his head up to kiss her clothed breasts hanging over him. "Why don't you marry them already?" she joked.

"I prefer the full package."

"Oh, yeah?"

"Oh, yeah. And I'm gonna..." He jerked his hands out of her grasp and pulled the sides of her shirt up to her pits "...open it up!"

She laughed and playfully slapped his chest before crossing her arms, pinching the bottom sides of her shirt and pulling it up and over her head.

He gazed upon her teardrop-shaped breasts following her slightest movements with equal bouncy slowness. Excitement rushed through him every time he saw her naked. The TV glow behind her made her hair shimmer red-orange and gave her light skin a bluish shine. The colours of her aura a perfect contrast between warm and cool colours. Her brilliant blue eyes, the pink hue in her cheeks, the tender lust in her small smile...

He kissed her again. She slowly grinded her crotch against the rising lump in his pants. Gave them both a push in the right direction.

They tackled each other in a wild passionate frenzy.

Chapter 002
Call to Action

The department store was gutted by the explosion. The windows carpeted the floors. The ceiling tiles were all but gone, revealing a complicated web of damaged wiring and flimsy steel framing. A few unlucky officers lay sprawled on the floor, twisted out of shape, bloody, acupunctured by the window glass that blew into their fronts before they had time to duck. The ones that survived the impact, including the Captain and the negotiator, slowly and painfully lifted themselves up to their feet.

"Fucking Christ," the Captain grumbled as he dusted himself off and checked himself for any wounds. "Head count. How many down?"

The negotiator looked at the unfortunate corpses on the floor. "Perkins, Troy, and Janson, for starters."

"Anyone else?"

The negotiator looked at all the other cops as they brushed themselves off and began salvaging the machinery that had been swept off the tables from the blast. "Looks like we've only lost those three."

The Captain looked at the corpses and shook his head regretfully. He took his hat off and put it to his chest. The other cops followed suit. "What a goddamn waste. Martin. Oliver. Petersen. Please move these poor bastards to the side till this is over."

As Martin, Oliver, and Petersen started moving the bodies into the far end of the room, the negotiator looked around and barked, "Where's that phone? Guys, find me that phone. We gotta re-establish—"

"Fuck the phone," the Captain said.

The negotiator looked at him. Eyebrow arched. "Sir?"

The Captain fired up a cigarette. "There's no point in trying to re-establish communication with these bastards. They're clearly not willing to cooperate."

"Sir, please," the negotiator pleaded, "maybe we can still work things—"

"Did you *not* just see what happened?" the Captain snapped angrily. "Were you blacked out for the past five minutes? They're playing our asses for fools."

"I understand and respect that, sir."

"We just lost three good men, and that's just in this room. Christ knows how many more we've just lost out there!" With his cigarette between the middle and index fingers on his right hand, he pointed at the negotiator. He adopted a softer tone, knowing that taking his frustration out on a man two decades younger than him would solve nothing. "Now, Daniels, I see where you're coming from. I respect your decision. You're a diplomat; that's why you're a negotiator. But our diplomacy with those psychopaths died with that hostage. The time for diplomacy is officially over." He sucked on his cigarette. "Now is the time for action."

"With all due respect, sir," Daniels said, "what 'action' might that be? We can't just charge in. We don't know how many there are. Hell, if the tracker's got it right, they have an outside guy."

"I know."

"They'll slaughter our guys and kill more hostages."

"I know."

"So... sir... what, exactly, are you thinking?"

The Captain's mouth curled upward in a wry smile. "I never said *anything* about sending in *our* guys..."

His statement drew some varied reactions from the other cops; a mix of horror, hope, relief, and glee among them. The negotiator knew full well what that meant. "Sir... are you sure that's wise?"

"Of course not. It never is with him. He's a goddamn hurricane. A menace-for-hire. His price is steep, but it's either his steep price or our sudden drop into despair. Which sounds more appealing to you, Daniels?"

"Do you even need to ask, sir?" Daniels nonetheless maintained a gloomy expression. "It's just... risky. Almost *too* risky."

"Then perhaps *we* can be of some assistance," a new voice cut into the room.

All eyes turned to the trio of newcomers as they entered through the splintered doorway. A man in his sixties with mildly grizzled features and greying brown hair addressed the Captain. He was flanked by two heavily armed men in chrome-plated battle suits. The man in the middle said, "Captain Carver?"

"That's right," Carver said as he took another drag. "I presume you're the outdated cavalry."

"If by 'outdated,' you mean 'underfunded,' then you'd be correct." The man stepped forward and extended his hand. "My name is Colonel James Fairman. I'm the commander of an elite police unit that specializes in infiltration and extermination. Quick and clean and to-the-point extermination. That's Afrókrema's speciality, sir."

"I know who you are, Colonel," Carver said with mild disdain. "Commissioner Montgomery has told me *all* about you and your band of merry men."

"Then you're aware of what we can do?"

"And what you *have* done..."

Fairman's mouth hung open for a moment as he thought of how to respond. He maintained a cool composure. "A... minor mishap, sir. Since our transfer and subsequent cuts to our budget, we've been able to maintain a modest unit within the department and an agreeable morale. All of our questionable men have been terminated from our ranks. I assure you, we are the better alternative to the man you seem to be considering." He furrowed his brows together. "With all due respect, sir... you're not *seriously* considering bringing in an outside party to handle a police matter, are you?"

The Captain scoffed at Fairman's audacity. "You talk a good game, Fairman."

Fairman smiled.

"But then again, you always *were* a slimy prick," the Captain added for the sole purpose of wiping that smile off Fairman's face— and it worked. "I'm not interested in hiring a unit that's on everybody's shit list right now. And besides... *this* guy's cheaper by a significant margin." Carver looked at a nearby cop, who picked up his ash tray off the ground and handed it to him. Instead of taking it, Carver crushed his cigarette in it and motioned for the cop to place it on the table.

Fairman said, "Sir, we can save those hostages without any unnecessary carnage."

"So can *he*," Carver said, grinning at Fairman. "He just chooses not to."

"Then why bring him in if we're one in the same?"

"Because you're *not* 'one in the same.' Our boy's a straight-shooting hell-raiser, and you... well, you're an inept fool." He let Fairman stew and gestured toward another cop who had just salvaged the phone. "That phone in working order?"

Fairman could only watch in disbelief as the cop brought Carver the portable phone. Carver stared at the phone for a moment. Then he asked, annoyed, "What the hell is the extension to Sergeant Hill's office?"

Damian and Jenny's Apartment

The explosion was caught live. It lit up the TV screen to a two-person audience that was no longer present. Bed sheets and rumpled clothing were strewn about the otherwise empty foldout bed. Empty, grimy TV dinner containers set on the folding table beside the couch. The only other source of light besides the TV was the dull yellow coming in from the open bathroom doorway. With the light came a steady, hard banging rhythm in the walls...

He had her sitting naked on the counter beside the sink, her back pressed against the mirror. Her legs wrapped around his waist, pulling him deeper between her thighs with every thrust. They panted and moaned together as their bodies, slicked with sweat and other fluids, writhed against one another. His hands took turns pulling her hips toward him and squeezing her breasts. Every time he slid inside her tight, wet warmth, the up-and-down jiggle of her breasts made him hungrier for her. He liked to surprise her; flicking her nipples with his thumbs and giving her crotch a playful slap to send another pleasurable shock through her body.

He touched her cheek, rubbed his thumb around her mouth, tracing over her lips. She took his thumb in her mouth and sucked on it. That only made him quicken the pace, pounding her body against the mirror until it cracked. Her frazzled hair, rosy cheeks, lustful smile... her mouth open so he could see her tongue roll around his thumb. As if her pleasurable moans weren't enough. "If only you could see yourself right now," he breathed. "You look so fucking good."

"Mhm?" she hummed. Her legs tightened around him. Her

hands on the counter behind her kept her from falling back. He yanked her away from the mirror and over the side of the counter just far enough for him to squeeze her bottom and push his hardness as far in as he could penetrate. A bit more hard grinding against her and...

"Fuck!" she screamed. He felt a rush inside her; it coursed over his member and then spurted out, splashing his abdomen and thighs. "Fuck, baby," she moaned in pleasure and embarrassment. Heaving; out of breath.

He looked down at her. Watched her breathe. Watched her breasts rise and fall. Watched the shimmering patterns of light on her flat, sweat-soaked stomach flutter with her shivering movements. He smiled. She smiled back. That lust in her glowing blue eyes. "I'm not done with you yet." He grabbed her hips and lifted her off the counter.

"Whoop!" she exclaimed in surprise. She giggled, keeping her legs around his middle, her arms strung over his shoulders. They twirled across the bathroom tiles slippery with their juices and slammed into the opposite wall. She screamed in pleasure as his body rammed her into the wall.

Damian could feel her tighten around him. He started moving again. She cried out and dug her nails in his back.

Brrriinngg!

Then the goddamn phone rang. Damian sighed and ignored it. Kept on pushing himself inside her.

"Get it," Jenny gasped. "Get it."

"Fuck 'em," he said.

Brrrrringg!

"Baby. Ahh... baby... i-it could be Hill."

"Don't care."

Brrriiinngg!

She pushed him back and put her feet on the floor. Laid her palms flat on his heaving chest and looked him square in the eye. "Pick it up. Then we'll be able to afford that vacation."

Damian groaned. "Fuck, come on."

Her eyes shot down any argument he could ever throw at her.

"*Govno*," he muttered as he exited the bathroom and telekinetically summoned the portable phone from across the room. Enveloped in a black aura, the portable hovered into his outstretched hand. He answered it. "Donovan here."

Sergeant Hill's voice crackled through the phone: "Captain's got a job for you."

Damian said, "What the fuck's he want with me?"

"Bank job. Bunch o' psychos got themselves some hostages."

"Saw that on the news. Looks like Wynnarz is on the losing team now."

"Very funny. I'm assuming you saw the explosion."

"What explosion?"

"They released a hostage. Little did we know that the hostage had a bomb vest strapped to him. Cleared out the whole goddamn intersection."

"They came prepared."

"Professionals. All of Santa's reindeer are accounted for."

"Reindeer?"

"That's the theme of their codenames."

Jenny started running a bath. Damian looked at the half-open door and barely caught a glimpse of her perfect backside behind the door. "Nice."

"Captain requested you personally."

"And what if I'm too busy?"

"It's fifty grand a head."

Damian's eyebrows went up. Total surprise. "Give me twenty minutes."

Jenny made an exaggerated "*Ahem*!"

Damian sighed. "Fifteen."

"On the corner across from the bank, you'll see a department store. Enter that department store through the back and identify yourself. They'll be waiting for you."

Damian hung up and sent the portable back on its base. He returned to the bathroom, pushed the door open, and found his woman with her back to him, bent over the side of the tub. She was dipping her hand in the water to test the temperature. He spanked her, made her giggle. He positioned himself behind her, hands on her bottom cheeks, and teased her with his persistent hardness. "We've got five minutes."

"Five minutes," she moaned. "I'll make sure you're done in three."

He chuckled. Don't count on it.

COBALT CHRISTMAS: A COBALT ROGUE STORY

*

Six minutes later, Damian was fully dressed; tactical gear layered under casual wear, a black jacket with white trimmings over both layers, and fingerless gloves. Despite his ability to manipulate matter and create his own fully functional weapons with pure telekinetic energy, Damian made it a point to keep two real pistols holstered under his armpits. A necessary precaution should he use too much power too fast and 'burn out.'

As he was putting on his combat boots, Jenny approached him in her fuzzy red bathrobe and hugged him from behind. "Make sure you find out whether or not they've got FATE rounds before you jump in there."

"Yes, dear," he said sarcastically.

"Hey." She turned him around and planted a firm kiss on his lips. "You better come back to me in one piece."

He smiled. "I'll consider it."

She smiled back. "Good. Now get out there."

He undid all seven locks they'd installed when they first moved in, and opened the door.

"I love you," she said.

"Love you too," he replied, and shut the door behind him.

He passed a couple doors on his way down the hall and hit the down button for the elevator. He whistled the main theme from *Rambo: First Blood Part II* while he waited.

An old woman's head poked out from the fourth door on his left, on the far side of his own apartment entrance. "That you, Blue?"

"Just me, Mrs. Gammy."

The sweet old lady leaned further into the hall. "Off to make another delivery, huh?"

"Uh... sure. Yeah."

"Can I ask you a question?"

"Sure."

"What are you and Jenny doing for Christmas dinner?"

Damian shrugged. "Maybe going someplace fancy. Why?"

"Well, uh, we got a lot of food we were gonna make for the family, but the family's not coming. Way too much for old Arn and I to eat on our own. I was wondering if you and Jenny would like to have Christmas dinner with us a few days early."

He smiled at the kind old lady. "Sounds good. When?"

"Tomorrow?"

"Sure. Don't think I'm doing anything tomorrow."

"Your place or ours?"

"Ours. Then maybe you can see your damn cat again."

She chuckled. "Felix's taken a liking to you."

"Just Jenny. He doesn't like me very much."

Ding. The elevator door opened. "Gotta go," Damian said.

"Okay. See you tomorrow, kiddo."

He got out in the underground parking garage and headed over to his car, a gleaming 1968 Ford Mustang Shelby Cobra GT 500 KR. Cobalt blue with white racing stripes running from bumper to fender. Specially modified by an old friend to fit his every need. An armoured beast of a sports car, something Damian took a moment to admire before every drive. Like a ritual that had to be carried out every time.

He got in behind the wheel and started up the engine. Its new upgrades gave it a retro-futuristic look: a touch screen GPS on the dashboard, a small row of six buttons installed above the horn in the wheel—each able to activate one of the car's combat features. Dim strips of neon blue lined the interior. The bulletproof windows were tinted black. The all-terrain tires fitted with spiked treads that could just as easily eviscerate a human being as flatten them into the road.

As the car roared to life, Damian gave the wheel a loving pat as if it were a pet dog. Then he peeled out of his parking space and sped off out of the garage to...

The Department Store

In the back, just like Hill said. He saw that the closest row of parking spaces had been taken up by police cruisers. A few armoured cops with shotguns and assault rifles hung around, watching him like hawks. The more experienced guys recognized the car right away. A few rookies were among them, asking, "Who the hell is that?"

"That, son, is a man you don't *ever* fuck with," a middle-aged cop said.

Damian locked the car up and headed for the back entrance. A few guards parted ways, made a path for him to the door. One of them was even gracious enough to open it. He passed through without a word. His combat boots pounded the concrete floor, announcing his presence to everyone inside. Cops pressed themselves against walls to let him pass.

He entered the gutted 'operations room,' being sure to hit a lingering Colonel Fairman's shoulder on his way in. "Move it, pencil neck."

Fairman glared at the back of his head as Damian addressed the Captain. "You called?"

Carver looked up from a blueprint of the bank and said, "Technically, I had your agent call you."

"Hill isn't my agent."

"Well, whatever. Come have a look at this."

Fairman butted in, "Sir, I *really* feel the need to protest..."

"You're still here?" Carver asked.

Fairman ignored the jab and continued, "I can't stress enough the sensitive nature of this situation. There are innocent lives at stake. How good could this maniac possibly be when it comes to saving hostages?"

"I've saved a few hostages in my line of work," Damian said. "What've *you* done lately?"

One of Fairman's men stepped forward. He was big, and he looked nasty, covered in scars and carved out of stone. "I'm already tired of this little shit."

"You wanna do something about it?" Damian asked. He was eager to snap this big mouth like a twig.

Fairman placed a hand on his man's shoulder. "Let it go for now, Lerner."

Lerner hesitated.

"Yeah, Lerner," Damian said with an air of condescension. "Let it go."

Lerner growled in his throat, but otherwise obeyed the Colonel.

Fairman looked across the room at Carver and said, "Well, Captain... if you need us, you know how to reach us. Good luck. Let's go, boys." He turned and left, with his two men following suit.

"Thought they'd never leave," Carver said.

"That makes two of us," Damian said. "So what've we got?"

"Hill briefed you, yeah?"

"Said all of Santa's reindeer were accounted for, and that they had hostages."

"Just about the gist of it. However, we managed to intercept their frequency. They're using old CB radios. Not exactly the smartest move they've made, but it works in our favour. Rudolph isn't here."

"So where is he?"

"He's in a getaway bus somewhere within a three-kilometre radius."

"Shouldn't be too hard to find, then."

"It wasn't."

"So what's the hurry?" Damian asked sarcastically.

"He's parked somewhere in a school bus depot. Like finding a quarter with two heads in a bucket full of normal quarters."

"I'll find him."

"How?"

"I'll use the shadows."

"Really creepy when you do that."

"Good mode of transportation, though."

"I'll order the search party to stand down, then."

"Much obliged."

"What about the rest of 'em?"

Damian smiled. "One thing at a time, Carver."

"I just want to know the plan before you go all gung-ho."

"I'll take out the driver and replace him. I'll pick up the others; drive to their hideout, and bam! I turn off the lights, ambush them, and leave in one piece, and they are as solid as *okroshka*."

"One more thing."

Damian turned.

Carver tossed a small device the size of a 2B eraser at him.

Damian caught it, inspected its smooth, black metal finish. "A tracker?"

"I'm sure I don't need to spell it out for ya."

Damian shook his head.

"Then good luck to you."

Bus Depot

Like a phantom from a child's worst nightmares, Damian used

the darkness to teleport from one shadow to another. Even with the perimeter lights, there were plenty of shadows between the parked school buses to make good use of.

His appearance simplified, turning into an inky, all-black figure with cobalt blue eyes and a sinister smile. He sank into the darkness under a bus and came out of the shadow of the bus beside it, and so on; poking his head into the aisles between the seats in case Rudolph was occupying one of them.

Eighteen buses later, Damian found him. His full features returned as the black aura around him faded. He no longer looked like a demonic nightmare. Just a vicious mercenary out for blood.

He stood up to his full height.

Rudolph sat behind the wheel, listening to something on his headset, munching on a sandwich.

Damian snuck up behind him, placed a hand on Rudolph's shoulder. Before the startled driver could fully understand, Damian had already punched his fist through his chest and pulled his half-eaten sandwich through the cavity.

SPAK!

Rudolph choked, looked down at the hole in his chest. Eyes wide in disbelief. He looked up at Damian, who smiled and waved his bloody sandwich in his face. "Surprise, motherfucker."

Rudolph squeaked, and then pivoted out of his seat.

Damian lifted the fake antlers and the balaclava off Rudolph's head. Then he threw open the door and kicked Rudolph down the stairs and out into the parking lot. He tossed his sandwich out after him and shut the door. He sat down and said into his own radio, "Got the driver."

"Good work," Carver said. "Now what?"

"I'll sit tight till I'm given the signal to move in."

"You'll gonna wait for them to...?"

"Yeah, pretty much."

"What about the hostages?"

"I'll save whichever ones they drag along with them. In the meantime, don't do anything. Call your guys off the street and hide in case they try something else."

As soon as Damian said that, Dancer had everything all set up in the boardroom: an M60 machine gun on a tripod, which he promptly unleashed on the cops in the street.

"They're firing on us!" Carver growled.

"Then I hope your guys can run," Damian said over the radio. "Signing off now. I'll be in touch."

Dancer's bullets shredded everything in his sights—cops, cars, trucks, vans, signs, storefronts, even the sidewalk. He sprayed the entire three-metre ammo belt into the intersection with child-like glee, never shifting his aim away from a vehicle until it burst spectacularly into flames. He didn't even spare the gutted department store. Carver and the other cops fled the scene, losing a few in their desperate retreat for a safer room as bullets ripped through the ceiling.

By the time the belt ran out, the intersection was a blazing pit carpeted with debris and corpses. The vehicular barricade the police had set up was already a wall of fire in the wake of the exploding hostage, belching columns of rolling smoke into the night sky. Now everything else behind that barricade had been destroyed. Not a single vehicle remained, nor a human being left alive.

The sirens of incoming reinforcements wailed in the distance.

Dancer whooped and laughed maniacally, unable to contain his excitement. "Fucking *love* these new toys! Yeah!"

Vixen peeked up from behind the counter. After assessing the damage outside, he stood to his full height and whistled. "That's a clean, burning hell, I tells ya what!" He laughed.

Prancer and Comet joined their companion, beholding the destruction they caused. "Christ," Prancer said.

Comet spoke into the radio, "That goddamn vault open yet?"

Dasher and Cupid had just gotten the door open when the call came in. Dasher picked up the radio and replied, "Just got it. It's payday, fellas."

"Merry Christmas, boys!" Cupid shouted from the vault as he started shovelling cash into his bag.

In the security room, Donner and Blitzen high-fived. Blitzen finished his coffee as Donner barked instructions into the radio: "Alright, let's pack it up, boys. Dancer, get your shit ready and meet us at the rendezvous point. Prancer, Comet, help the guys in the basement load the cash. Vixen, start herding some hostages to the dock. Not all of 'em; about three or four will do. Rudolph, you know what to do—meet Dancer at the rendezvous and wait for us there. If we're not there by quarter after ten, go on without us. Everyone got that?"

A swarm of replies came in, confirming they got it.

Rendezvous, shit, Damian thought. His mind raced. "Where the fuck is the rendezvous?" He started looking around the cab, sifting through all of the real Rudolph's papers and fast food containers. He found a map and looked it over. X marks the spot, just four blocks south of the bank in permanent marker, with a squiggly line running across the map and ending with an arrow pointed at a location on the outskirts of town across the lake. Seemed like the marked route was a little too scenic for a getaway to a private air strip, but hey, whatever works.

He grinned, breathed a sigh of relief as he tossed the map aside. He started up the engine. "Here we go."

Chapter 003
The Getaway

Mertopher's Alley

Damian parked behind a hardware store and waited in the dark. He switched on the radio and tuned it to a station that wasn't rambling on about the robbery. The *Zerodome Runners* game, where men dressed up in bizarre outfits and fought to the death in equally bizarre, anti-gravitational environments, was being described in rapid detail by the announcer.

"McFarlane's got the ax, he's swingin'—oh! *Right* through him! Daniels is down! His head is in two! It's floating—oh, man, if only you folks listening in could see this; his brains are going out in every direction in glorious slow-mo! This being his fourth kill tonight, McFarlane's out for blood! And his thirst ain't quenched yet; he's flyin' straight for Kimberly from Cloverfield. Kimberly's ready with his spear gun, he's aimin'... he shoots! He misses McFarlane by an inch! McFarlane's on him—"

Bang-bang!

A rap at the bus doors caused Damian to whirl, Colt pistol drawn toward—

—Dancer with most of his gear in a bag, and his M60 resting against his shoulder. He shifted his weight nervously and banged the door again. "C'mon, lemme in before someone sees me!"

Damian withdrew his pistol and let Dancer in. Dancer hopped up the stairs, breathing hard, and threw everything into the nearest seat behind the disguised getaway driver. "Hot damn, that was fun."

"Yeah?" Damian said, turning the radio down.

"You shoulda been there, man. Shoulda been there. It was fucking wild. I must've killed a hundred of 'em. And that explosion? Fuck! They never knew what hit 'em!"

"Cool," Damian said.

Dancer sat down beside his things and heaved a drawn-out sigh. "What time is it?"

Damian glanced at the digital clock console. "Ten after."

"Five more minutes," Dancer said anxiously. "Just five more minutes. You think they'll make it?"

"Sure."

"What if they don't?"

"Stick to the plan. We go to the air strip."

"Then what?"

Damian shrugged and lit himself a cigarette.

"I didn't know you smoke..."

"Quit long time ago."

"You okay?"

"Yeah."

"You seem different, man."

"I always smoked before I drove," Damian said carefully. "You've just never seen me do it, because I stopped doing it. For a while, anyway."

"Oh. Guess that makes sense."

"Calms me down."

"Yeah, I can see that."

The radio announcer went on: "Skullblazer's got McFarlane in his sights. Here it is, ladies and gentlemen: the ultimate rematch!"

"Those things'll kill you," Dancer said.

"What're you, a Mormon?"

"No, no."

"Hm," Damian grunted. He leaned forward, tapping a fast rhythm on the steering wheel with his thumbs.

"You scared?"

"No. You?"

"No." He scoffed. "Hell no. I'm pumped. If we fly clear, we're rich, man."

"*If* we fly clear."

"You're really bumming me out. You sure you're okay?"

"Good enough to drive."

"Why is there a hole in the back of the seat?"

Shit.

Damian slowly turned around and looked Dancer straight in the eyes.

The rest of the crew made it to the rendezvous. One at a time they surfaced, climbed out from beneath a manhole cover. Three of them were carrying one hostage each, draped over their shoulders with their hands and feet bound, their mouths gagged with rags.

Donner banged on the door.

Damian let them in and silently counted them as they filed onto the bus, and worked up a tally: two down, seven to go, and three hostages to save.

Donner lingered as the others took their seats. He placed his hand on Damian's jacket, which he'd draped over the driver seat to hide the hole. "Where's Dancer?"

"Guess he didn't make it," Damian said.

Donner nodded slowly. "Alright. Let's get going."

Damian waited for Donner to take a seat three rows down before pulling the bus out of the alley and down the road. A police cruiser flew by, going in the direction of the bank. Then another. And another. Damian turned up the radio.

"Skullblazer and McFarlane are still going at it! Beaten! Bloody! Mere zombified shreds of their former selves! They're no longer men; they're animals! Skullblazer's caught in McFarlane's choke hold. It looks like the end is near for Skullblazer!"

His passengers stayed quiet, and kept low.

For the most part, traffic was low. The only vehicles he saw were pedestrian cars. Damian didn't see another cruiser. Carver was watching over him, keeping the streets clear. Good, but might raise questions. They were driving a school bus in the late evening, after all. Not exactly the most conspicuous vehicle to be driving after a bank heist.

Stupid assholes, Damian thought. *This wasn't worth the trouble. These morons would've practically caught themselves.*

"New plans," Donner said from directly behind him. "You know where the pier in Waterport is?"

"Lots of piers in Waterport."

"Very funny, smartass. Pier 7, warehouse 5. Go there."

Damian nodded, and took the next turn.

Damian parked the bus in the warehouse, which was mostly empty save for a black minivan sitting on the side.

They unloaded the money, their gear, and the hostages off the bus, tossed all but the hostages in the back of the minivan. The hostages were grouped together: two tellers, one of whom was

Maria, and an unlucky customer.

"Finally," Blitzen said, "I can take these stupid fucking antlers off."

"Stay in character," Donner said. "They stay on."

"What?"

Damian stood back as the two confronted each other. He crossed his arms and sighed, leaned his shoulder against the passenger side of the minivan.

"Antlers stay on," Donner said.

"What's it matter? We're in the clear."

Are these idiots serious? Damian could only watch, wanting to laugh at their petty argument.

"The antlers stay on," Donner growled, slow enough for anyone to understand.

"That's fucking stupid—"

"Come on," Prancer said, "Forget it."

Vixen stepped in between them. "We got bigger fish to fry right now, guys. Fuck, if it means so much to you, we'll keep the antlers on. It's fucking stupid, but—"

"Bullshit," Blitzen said, "You takin' his side?"

"*BUT,*" Vixen emphasized, glaring at Vixen, "if it keeps us from re-enacting the ending to *Reservoir Dogs*, we'll keep the fucking antlers on till we get to the final location."

Comet had been eyeing the hostages since they'd put them in the corner. "What about them? We can't fit them all in that tiny minivan."

"Hell with 'em," Donner said.

Blitzen racked the slide on his pistol. "I'll take care of them."

""Whoa. Whoa. Whoa. Whoa." Vixen leaped between Blitzen and the hostages.

"Out of my way."

"I don't give a shit what you do to those two, but the girl is mine."

Maria moaned in fear.

"Are you twelve?"

Vixen shrugged. "I like her."

"We can't take this bitch with us."

"Hey, if anything, she might be worth somethin' to us."

"You just want to fuck her."

"That too."

"Donner?"

Donner said, "Leave them."

Blitzen exclaimed, "What!?"

Vixen snickered.

Donner said, "*All* three of them."

It was Vixen's turn to protest.

"Enough," Donner barked. "We're wasting time. Rudolph, get the van started."

Damian went round to the driver side and climbed behind the wheel.

"Let's go," Donner said. "The rest of you in the van, *now!*"

"Fuck," Blitzen snarled as he stomped to the minivan.

As the guys loaded themselves into the minivan, Vixen approached Maria, knelt down on one knee, and held her chin in his hand. He looked into her fearful, teary eyes and said, "Sorry, babe. Wasn't meant to be." He stood up and hopped into the passenger seat.

Now everyone was in the minivan except for Donner, who lingered outside of it. All the seats were taken.

Damian started up the engine. Something didn't feel right...

"What's the holdup?" Vixen asked through the window.

"I'll get in the back," Donner said as he stepped behind the minivan. Damian watched him in the rearview mirror as he threw up the back door, and then started pulling all the money out and tossing them as far away from the minivan as he could throw.

"Hey, what the fuck!" Damian shouted.

By the time the others realized what was happening, Donner was jogging away from the minivan.

Vixen and Cupid threw open the doors—

Donner dived to the floor. Pressed his thumb down on a detonator and covered his ears, hugging the concrete.

KABOOM!

The minivan blew apart, blasting its seven passengers in every direction. The warehouse's factory windows disintegrated. A fireball curled into the rafters.

Damian shouted in agony, feeling the flames tear away at his flesh and claw through his insides. A little thing like this wouldn't kill him, but it would certainly hurt like a son of a bitch. He snarled, writhing, kicking the dash. The flames engulfed him, eating away at him. His body burned as quickly as it healed. The seatbelt pinned him down until he tore the damn thing off.

He booted the door off and pivoted after it onto the floor, still coated in fire. He rolled around, back and forth, emanating little telekinetic blasts outward to put the fire out. Eventually, he was a smouldering, walking corpse.

The hostages stared at him, horrified.

Damian, on his hands and knees, rasping and coughing as his lungs healed. His black-red skin slowly reverted back to its original peach colour. His cobalt blue hair sprouted from his head, all the spikes shifting back into their usual place.

He groaned and cracked his neck. "Fuck..."

With pain came fury. His heart pounded, raging like a war machine.

Damian listened to the crackles of the flames in the minivan; the terrified, muffled cries of the hostages in the corner... the sound of a sputtering engine outside. Engine...

A boat starting up. Or trying to.

"You're not getting away, you motherfucker." Damian rushed to the school bus and snatched the tracker. Then he raced outside, kicked down the door onto the dock—

BRRAAAACCKKK!

Bullets raked across the warehouse wall and Damian took two to the chest, one in the shoulder. He staggered.

Donner stood in a motorboat, yanking the ignition cord with one hand and handling an MP5A3 in the other. He released another three-round burst at Damian, who took the shots in his stomach. Only made him angrier.

"FUCK YOU!" An energy pistol formed in Damian's hand. He returned fire with it, but he was disoriented from his wounds and the ringing in his ears. He blasted the small wharf beside Donner's boat to flying splinters.

Donner yanked the cord again, firing his submachine gun erratically. His aim was all over the place.

Damian's healing factor was already pushing the bullets out. He aimed, fired.

BLAM!

The energy round whistled across the gap between them and

splattered Donner across the boat's dash and windshield. He went down with a gaping hole in his chest, pulling the ignition cord as he fell. Ironically, the engine roared to life.

Damian scoffed and approached the destroyed wharf. He hopped onto the boat and looked over his latest kill.

Donner was splayed out over their bags of stolen money and a small stash of weapons.

Damian looked at the tracking device in his hands and dropped it onto the floor. They ought to be here soon.

He moved to shut off the engine—

BOOM!

Next thing Damian knew, his guts were coiling over the motor. "What... the...?" Blood rushed up his throat. He gagged on it, vomited all over his own guts. He turned...

Donner was sitting up against the dash with a shotgun in his hands. The cavity in his chest was getting smaller as pieces of him from everywhere slithered back into place.

A healing factor! Damian cursed his own stupidity right before Donner's shotgun barked again, slammed him against the vibrating engine.

"You stupid son of a bitch," Donner spat blood and wiped the rest off his chin. "Lookin' awful familiar—"

Damian spat a gory projectile all over Donner's pants. Donner looked at it, then glared at him. Damian, weakened by the shotgun blasts despite his healing factor, struggled to muster up enough strength to raise his gun.

BLAM!

Right before Donner's shotgun sent his entire arm spinning into the water. "Persistent son of a bitch, aren't you?"

The good old red stuff flooded Damian's mouth and dribbled down his chin, streaming down what was left of his front. "Part of my charm," he gurgled.

Donner chuckled. "A sense of humour. Nice." He didn't bother wasting another shot on his Dehue opponent. Instead, he brained him with the butt of his shotgun and threw him over the rear of the boat into the water. Damian's intestines were still strung on the deck. "Charm your way outta this." Donner grabbed one of his entrails and started to reel Damian back in, pulling him toward the outboard motor's spinning propellers.

Damian knew exactly what the fucker was up to. The propellers got closer, and Damian braced himself for a world of pain. *This is gonna hurt...*

And it did. A lot.

Donner wasn't completely satisfied by the propeller's brutal work on Damian's body until the intestine in his hands snapped loose. By then the water had been saturated dark red, polluted by Damian's remains. Donner tossed the intestine overboard and made his getaway to the open waters. The blood trail he left behind only lasted halfway.

Chapter 004
Air Raid

Cryo City—Pier 7

Carver was on the scene with his most trusted men. The hostages were safe with big, soft blankets wrapped around them. The fire in the minivan had been put out, and investigators scoured the entire site for anything that looked out of the ordinary with their cameras. Carver was more interested in the wharf. The remains of Damian's body were in the process of being gathered by a pair of divers under Carver's close watch.

"Found the other leg," one of them announced.

"Any luck finding his head?" Carver asked solemnly. "His torso? Anything?"

"Nothing else here but a bloody mist."

"The rest might've floated off," Carver suggested.

One of the divers shook his head. "No, sir. The rest of him is just... *gone*."

Carver furrowed his brows. "What do you mean, 'gone?'"

Kartovski's Airstrip

Donner brought the boat in quiet and roped it on the dock. He still had the mask and antlers on to hide his identity. Two men armed with submachine guns strapped over their shoulders met him and helped him unload the money. They escorted him off the dock, through the checkpoint entrance guarded by two MP knockoffs armed with assault rifles, and inside the fenced perimeter without a word.

"This way," one of them finally said, making a gesture for the hangar located between towering oak trees. An L-shaped landing strip ran across the gap between the entrance and the men. A fuel station and a jeep were located on the far side of the hangar, out of the way. Directly beneath the trees beside the hangar was a barracks for the small army under the airstrip owner's employ. In the elevated southeast corner of the perimeter, a four-storey lighthouse stood at the top of a steep cliff face; a warning for boaters driving blind in the night.

Donner's boat bobbed up and down on the water, bouncing off the side of the dock as the lake's gentle waves rolled beneath it. A hand emerged from beneath and reached over the side. Damian's head surfaced. He groaned quietly and pulled himself up and into the motorboat. He gasped in pain, still not quite well enough to do much else except lie on his back and stare at the stars in the sky. It took half the trip for the lower half of his body to grow back, and it took everything he had to hold on to the back of the boat as Donner stole across the freezing lake.

Damian curled up on the floor, shivering violently. His skin tinged a light blue, his lips an even deeper blue. "F-f-f-f-f-fuuuuck," he moaned through chattering teeth. He wrapped himself in a thick energy blanket. It shimmered as it warmed him.

It would take him a while yet to recover from the cold.

They escorted Donner through the hangar. His getaway jet sat idly in the middle, ready for takeoff. They brought him to a door with a glass panel, opened it, and then had him follow them through a narrow corridor with half-glass partition walls on both sides, dimly lit, but the rooms behind the windows were dark and empty. At the end of the hall was another glass-paneled door with the owner's name on it: Ivan Kartovski. There was a light behind it, glowing like a campfire behind the frosted glass.

One of the escorts rapped his knuckles against it.

"Come in," Kartovski's deep, Russian-accented voice called.

The second escort opened the door and allowed Donner entry.

Kartovski sat in front of a wide strip of windows behind a large oak desk with a single lamp lighting the small room. He was large and ugly with a receding hairline revealing a field of scabs on his wrinkled head. Dressed in a dirty white button shirt with suspenders to keep his pants from falling down whenever he walked. His left eye was clearly a biomechanical prosthetic, made obvious by its unnatural green shine as opposed to the natural brown of his right eye. He was seated in his wooden swivel chair with his elbows on the arm rests; his hands busied themselves with lighting a cigar.

"Really? With the mask? What is this?"

"Can't risk anybody seeing my face," Donner said as he

dropped one of his two bags of money on the floor.

"It is just you, correct?"

"Just like I said." Donner heaved the second bag onto the desk, knocking over a few trinkets and pens. "Your share."

"Two million?"

"As instructed. Is the plane ready to go?"

"Am I safe to assume you were not followed?"

"Lost 'em long ago."

Kartovski's eyes watched Donner carefully. He stood up, bit down on the cigar, and unzipped the bag. He dug his fat hands all the way to the bottom.

Donner scoffed and said sarcastically, "The phone books are all pressed to the sides instead of the bottom."

After confirming that all the cash was there, and that it was real, Kartovski smiled and said, "Your plane was just filled up to maximum capacity an hour ago."

"Perfect."

"Will you still be needing a pilot?"

"Seeing as how I didn't have time for flying lessons since our last meeting... yeah. I'm gonna need a pilot."

Kartovski nodded. "Good. He's ready, too. I believe he's in the lounge."

Donner nodded and lifted his bag off the floor. "Be seein' you."

"I should hope not," Kartovski said with a grin.

Donner left the office. The guards immediately flanked him again and followed him down the corridor. "Take me to the lounge, boys."

The motorboat was empty. Damian was nowhere to be found. Neither was the motor.

He carried it off the dock like a lumberjack carries a chainsaw, hiding in the shadows and brush. He crouched down and peeked through a bush at the checkpoint gate. Two guards, one on either side. One of them sat in a glass booth reading a porn magazine. Easy fodder.

He made a fist, stuck out his index finger and raised his thumb, pointed it at the guard standing opposite the booth. A small energy blade appeared from his index fingertip. He folded his thumb down, sent the blade zipping through the guard's throat.

The guard choked as he slid down the chain link fence, gurgling quietly.

The guard in the booth looked up. He did a double-take when he saw his dead comrade slumped against the fence. "What the—"

KSSHH!

Damian's hands burst through the glass pane behind him and pulled him backwards out of his chair and through the window. He twisted the guard's head around with a sickening *snap* before he could scream.

Damian could sense it before he could see it. He looked up at the security camera mounted above the gate with its lens fixed on him. He gave it the finger.

The siren started to wail. A security officer on the PA system started announcing, "Intruder alert! Intruder on the premises! North gate! North gate!"

In the lounge, Donner, his escorts, and the pilot seated at a table with a cup of yogurt were startled by the announcement.

The escorts dropped the money bags and leaped back, going for the weapons slung over their shoulders. "You motherfucker!"

"You brought visitors!"

Donner became a blur; he drew his pistol and cut them both down in a second. Then he turned to the frightened pilot and growled, "Get up. We're taking off."

The pilot stared at him, clutching his yogurt in frozen fear.

"Get up!" Donner slapped the yogurt cup out of his hands and hoisted the man to his feet, gun muzzle pressed against his cheek. "Out!"

Kartovski's voice roared over the PA system, "Do not let either of our visitors escape this facility alive! Kill them both!"

"Guess the deal's off," Donner grumbled. "Get the money!"

The pilot quickly lifted two bags off the floor. Donner looked at the other two bags and grinded his teeth in frustration. Sacrifices had to be made if he wanted to escape. He pushed the pilot into the corridor. "Move!"

Two guards appeared in his path. "Stop!"

"No!" the pilot shrieked. "No, please don't shoot!"

Donner shot at them over the pilot's shoulder. One of them

went down. The other had the sense to take cover around the corner.

"*Ublyudok*!" Kartovski roared behind Donner. "You said you weren't followed!"

Donner whirled around and fired a five-round beat at Kartovski, who dropped behind the partition wall as the windows popped around him. "You got your money, you fat fuck!" Donner turned again just as the second guard came out. He cut him down. The guard's gun sprayed the wall as his head punched through the exit door's window pane.

Donner rushed the pilot to the end of the corridor, shooting at Kartovski's office to keep him down. Clicked empty. He hastily reloaded, but too late.

Kartovski stood in the shredded doorway of his office with a magnum aimed at Donner. He had the drop on him.

Then the windows shattered behind him. An engine roared. Donner watched confused as Kartovski whirled to face his new intruder and screamed in terror.

Damian gutted him with the boat engine's propellers, splattering Kartovski all over the place. Through his stomach, then worked his way up to his scabby head, splitting him in half.

Kartovski's mangled corpse collapsed.

Donner's face went white under the mask. His eyes wide as saucers. "You again!"

Damian stood there with the sputtering motor in his hands, covered head to toe in Kartovski's blood. His facial expression seemed vacant. "Surprise, motherfucker."

Donner emptied his magazine into Damian's chest as he backed up and slammed the pilot into the door. "Open it!" he yelled at the pilot. He reloaded.

Damian stepped over Kartovski, telekinetically powering the motor in his hands. He stomped down the hall toward Donner. An unstoppable force.

Donner pounded him with bullets. "Get back! Back, goddamn it!"

Damian absorbed the bullets, grunting, wincing. Never stopping.

The pilot threw open the door. Both he and Donner scrambled toward the jet, going through an aisle of crates situated on skids.

Kartovski's soldiers entered the hangar, assault rifles

stuttering. Bullets clapped all around Donner and the pilot like hail.

Damian kicked the door down, earning the soldiers' attention as they shifted their aim to him. "Come on, you cunts!" Damian yelled as an energy submachine gun appeared in his right hand. His left hand held the motor by the handle, letting its propellers scrape the floor.

A wave of bullets ripped across the hangar interior, blowing through crates and biting into Damian's torso.

Donner and the pilot clambered up the stairs into the jet, bullets whizzing by them. Donner returned fire and hit one before ducking inside the jet and pulling up the door. "Get this plane in the air!" He shoved the pilot into the cockpit. "Hurry up!"

Damian's submachine gun rattled. He swung it back and forth, leveling the entire squad in a wild spray of blood and gore, each energy bullet as powerful as a .50 caliber round. He discarded the gun, held up the motor with both hands and jogged between the crates.

Another militant leaped out from behind a crate with a knife. Damian's foot caught him in the chest, sent him staggering back. He sliced the propellers through the militant's throat.

Two more emerged from behind a fuel tank on the other side of the plane. Their submachine guns spat bullets into the jet between the wheels.

Damian took one in the shoulder. The rest missed. He returned fire with a Model 500, his favourite. Didn't aim for *them*, but for the fuel tank behind them.

BOOM!

The tank ruptured, fireballs blossomed rapidly, decimating the far wall. Flaming militants spun through the air, crashed through shelves, low-hanging light fixtures, partitions...

The force of the explosion tossed the jet plane into the air for a split second, nearly flipped the whole thing on its top. Debris punctured its side and scraped the wing. The pilot screamed as he swerved to avoid the worst of it. Donner flinched as a chunk of metal pierced through the window and burned into the seat across from him. "Whoa! Jesus..."

Another militant descended from above a stack of crates, brandishing a pair of combat knives. "YAAHHH!"

Damian threw up the propellers for the militant to land on. The militant squealed as the motor tunneled through his chest. Damian grabbed his neck and ripped him in half, tossed him to the side. He stepped over the militant's legs, charging toward the jet.

The engines screamed. The jet started to roll out of the hangar.

Damian exited the aisle and dashed toward the front end of the burning hangar.

BRRRAACCKK!

Machine gunfire from the overhead catwalks. A flurry of bullets stitched across the concrete floor in pursuit of the rampaging Dehue. A dozen of them crawled around up there, constantly moving to try and get a better shot at Damian.

A jeep slewed into view. A passenger opened fire over the windshield while a third militant started to make good use of his machine gun mount, spraying Damian's surroundings.

Damian took cover behind a shrink-wrapped steel desk on a skid. Sparks and plastic shreds filled the air as the desk shielded the machine gunner's target.

Damian glanced over his shoulder. He was ahead of the jet, but not for long.

The militants above couldn't see him; their catwalks ran out just shy of allowing them view over a steel partition wall that stood between them and Damian. That didn't stop them from trying to shoot him through it.

Another militant started charging across the hanger away from the fire spreading from the ruptured fuel tank toward him, pistol spitting rounds at him. Damian flinched as a bullet glanced off a drawer a few inches from his head. He tossed the motor aside and clapped his hands together, compressing energy. His hands drifted apart. A glowing, black-blue orb expanded between his palms. Damian grunted as a bullet burned through his wrist. He stood up and thrust his hand toward the jeep. The ball shot out of his hand at lightning speed and destroyed the jeep in a fiery conflagration. Blue flames curled into the rafters.

"Freeze!" the other militant barked, pistol trained on Damian's head from a two-foot range.

Damian looked at him and scoffed. The jet was bearing down on them, engines spinning at full strength.

"Get down, goddamn you!" the militant ordered.

Another explosion in the hangar's rear distracted the militant.

A blade appeared in Damian's fist. He disarmed the militant at the wrist and threw his foot up into the bastard's chest, launching him over the approaching jet's wing into one of the turbofan engines' intake. It sucked him in and exploded.

Damian leaped out of the way of flying debris as the jet's wing passed over his head.

The jet rocked back and forth, threatening to career off course, throwing Donner against the wall of the cabin.

"We can't take off!" the pilot yelled.

"Like hell we can't!" Donner replied, threatening him with his pistol. "Get this thing up!"

"That's fucking impossible!"

The pilot was right and Donner was rational enough to know it. "Fuck! *FUUUUUUCK*!"

The jet coasted out of the hangar. The entire rear section of the hangar went up in flames, blowing debris to the front. Militants fell screaming from the rafters as everything started to come down. The stacks of crates ignited in a series of concussive blasts, scattering debris and weaponry. Ammo crates crackled violently as every bullet they contained exploded outward, screeching and zipping like firecrackers, cutting out lights, peppering the corrugated walls, chopping down partitions and a group of militants trying to escape the fire.

Damian dashed in pursuit of the jet, ducking to avoid machine gunfire. The wing was just up ahead. He jumped up and plunged his blade through the wing's rudder and held on tight.

The rest of the militants surrounded the plane in jeeps that zigzagged from one side to the other, constantly passing beneath the jet as it taxied onto the runway, all while their machine guns spattered its sides with bullets.

Damian squinted and grit his teeth as a dozen rounds of hot lead raked across the wing he held on to. A jeep fishtailed beneath his feet. The machine gunner in the back took aim.

Damian turned, blasted them with the revolver, taking out the gunner first, then the two in front with enough energy to blast craters in the tarmac under the jeep. With the driver dead, the shredded jeep veered off to the side, clipping the back of another incoming jeep.

Damian pushed against the wind as he hauled himself onto the wing. The flaming engine was a few yards behind him. And then—

Another jeep positioned itself behind him. The machine gunner unleashed hell into Damian's back. Stray bullets pounded the wing as the rest of them seared through Damian's flesh and guts. The pain, hot and burning in his stomach, filling his chest, unbearable. Weakening him. Melting his insides. Damian howled in gurgling agony but didn't let go of the plane. He bit his bottom lip hard enough to bleed, swallowing blood that caught in his throat. Pulled himself further up, slipped his fingers through the small niche, gripping the rudder. Now that he had the rudder, he pulled his blade out and hurled it at the attacking jeep.

The blade extended as it spun, becoming a disc that sliced the jeep in half front to back. Both halves split apart, burst into flames.

Donner went over to his gear bag and pulled out an MP5K. "Cruise us! I'm gonna kill every last one of these motherfuckers!" A few windows popped around him. He ducked instinctively.

He kicked open the door—

Damian leaped across the flaming wing and tackled him to the floor. "Got you, motherfucker!"

Donner punched him, trying to wrest his gun free from Damian's grip. The two of them rolled across the floor. The MP5K sputtered, cutting holes through the money bags and punching dents across the control console in the cockpit, earning more of the pilot's terrified screams.

Damian lifted him and slammed him back on the floor, disorienting him long enough for him to tear the mask and antlers off Donner's head, revealing a shock of blonde hair, hazelnut eyes, and hollow cheeks. For any other guy, Donner would be a stranger. To Damian, he was a ghost from Christmas past. "*You* again!"

"Excuse me if we've never been formally introduced—and will remain so." Donner lashed out. Damian caught his fist. "Oh."

"I killed you," Damian sneered.

"Did you, though?"

"I've seen your fucking face."

Donner's forehead connected with Damian's chin. Damian felt his teeth cut into his tongue, drawing blood. *Fuck!*

They rolled down the cabin with the hot air current rushing out the open door; punching, kicking, swearing.

Damian seized control of the MP5K and squeezed the trigger, riddling Donner with holes until it ran dry. Then he smacked the side of his head with the empty gun; left side, right side, left—

Donner parried and rabbit-punched him in the stomach. It hurt Damian enough for him to mentally note that a healing factor wasn't the only superhuman advantage Donner had.

Damian slugged him, then cracked the MP5K against his cranium. Kicked him hard enough to send him flipping ass over tea kettle to the back of the cabin.

A jeep parked itself at the end of the runway up ahead. Behind them: the perimeter fence and a steep drop into the lake. The pilot shrieked his last as the machine gunner filled the cabin with hot lead. The jeep's passenger stood up from his seat and leaned over the windshield frame with a China Lake launcher aimed for the incoming plane.

A squad of tactical police motorboats raced across the water along the airstrip, shining their searchlights across the compound. "This is the police!" a cop on a loudspeaker announced. "We have you surrounded! Lay down your weapons! Turn off your vehicles and surrender! You have nowhere to go!"

Police choppers roared over the airstrip. Door gunners hosed down the jeeps, causing them to spin out of control. A few jerked in a different direction hard enough to capsize. One exploded as it tried to take shelter under the jet's belly, its flaming wreck torn apart by the jet's landing gear.

The jet lurched violently, screeching across the tarmac, tossing its combating passengers from side to side.

Police cruisers swarmed in from the east. The machine gunner at the end of the runway opened up on them, causing them to swerve uncontrollably in a vain attempt to escape the attack.

The grenadier in the jeep's passenger seat readjusted his aim toward the incoming cruisers and fired.

KABLAM!

One of the cruisers exploded. Cars slewed around it. Cops leaped out of their cruisers and took cover behind them.

The grenadier reloaded and fired at the plane. His grenade whistled through the shattered opening in the windscreen and hit the floor.

BOOMM!

COBALT CHRISTMAS: A COBALT ROGUE STORY

A flash-fire filled the cabin, engulfing Damian and Donner. The plane's body ruptured as the explosion concussively ripped it in two. The entire plane went up in a spectacular fireball, launching panels and debris into the night sky, consuming the last surviving jeep that had taken refuge under it before the blazing airframe fell on it, grinding it into the tarmac. Skidding fast to the end of the runway, straight for the jeep.

"Move it!" the grenadier screamed, only to discover the driver slumped back with a hole in his seat. "Oh, shit!"

The machine gunner bailed, flying through the air. The grenadier froze up. All he could do was scream.

The plane rammed the jeep head-on and obliterated it. Both vehicles ripped through the perimeter fence and vaulted over the side of the cliff, dived for the dark waters below.

It collided with the jagged rocks at the base of the cliff and came apart.

Damian and Donner survived every painful second of it.

Carver stepped out of a cruiser and looked over the edge at the smouldering wreckage on the rocks. The lake's foamy waves crashed mercilessly against it with a cruel rhythm. His breath plumed as he heaved a sigh. "What a goddamn mess."

Chapter 005
Debriefing

Cryo City—Friday, December 22nd, 2031

The rest of the early morning was cold and bitter. A snow flurry began to descent on the city, hell-bent on blanketing its streets in silvery whiteness.

In the 28th Precinct station, in the private office of Sergeant Donald Hill, Damian sat in a chair with a blanket wrapped around him and a hot cup of coffee in his hands. Jenny stood beside him with her hands on his shoulders, watching Sergeant Hill pour a fresh pot of coffee into his personal 'I Heart Cryo City' mug. Hill was of an average build, wearing a brown leather shoulder holster over a cream-coloured button shirt with the sleeves rolled up to his elbows, and he neglected to tuck it into his blue jeans. His black raven hair was combed to the left, and his jaw was lined with the old-fashioned six-o'-clock shadow. His eyes were always in an angry squint, even when he was happy.

"You want one, Cap?"

Captain Carver stood behind Hill's desk with his hands clasped behind his back. "No, thank you, Sergeant."

Hill applied his preferred amount of cream and sugar before returning to his seat behind his desk. "Okay." He sighed and looked at the couple. "You guys're something else."

No one said a word.

Hill opened the file on his desk. "Now, this list is speculation only for now until we can get an official tally." He cleared his throat and read the list of statistics: "'Three dead hostages, Nine dead robbers. Sixty-four dead cops, twenty-three injured cops, two dozen dead at the airstrip...' uh." He looked up at Damian. "Three of which you mutilated with a motorboat propeller."

"The steering wheel was too small," Damian said sarcastically.

Jenny rolled her eyes.

"A little excessive, don't you think?"

"More like poetic justice."

"Listen," Hill said, leaning forward, netting his fingers together on his desk, "I know it's difficult for you to control your violent impulses, but you have to understand something: I don't care what you do when you work for other clients, but when you work for *us*, you need to practice a little restraint."

"What the fuck are you bitching about?" Damian asked heatedly.

"We can't have you going around ripping heads off and mutilating people with boat propellers like you're Jason goddamn Voorhees when a bullet would do just fine. Or maybe I should phrase this more delicately... just because we hire you to catch a gang of bank robbers doesn't mean we're giving you a license to kill. The key word here is 'catch.'"

"Go fuck yourself," Damian snarled, lurching forward, only for Jenny to pull him back into his chair.

"Shh," she said.

Damian continued, "I saved the hostages."

"You gutted two of the bank robbers and blew up the rest. Not a single prisoner. Not one."

"*I* didn't blow the fucking thing."

"No? You telling me they torched themselves?"

"Their leader drew first blood. I didn't start that one."

"Alright, your statement... statement," Hill said as he flipped through the pages. "Ah. You said their leader blew up the van, you got out and pursued him as he made a getaway in the motorboat after pulling you into the boat propellers—ooh, ouch."

"Yeah, that fucking hurt."

Hill continued, "You held on to the boat as he made his way to the airstrip, which you were aware of... how?"

"They had a map with the locations marked down."

Hill gave him a doubtful look.

Carver said, "My men *did* find such a map on the bus."

Hill nodded in acknowledgement. "Okay, then. So our guys weren't exactly top-tier professionals. It happens. You said this guy was immortal?"

"He was definitely immortal."

"How do you know?"

"Didn't you read the goddamn report? It's in there."

"All it says is that you confronted him on the boat, then on the plane as he tried to make his getaway."

Carver checked his watch and went around to the cooler by the door.

"It's fucking in there."

"No, it isn't."

"Well, he is. He's immortal. He heals. I painted that motorboat with the inside of his chest, for fuck's sake."

"Was that before, or after he cast you out like fishing bait?"

"Before. That's why he was able to do that in the first place. I didn't expect him to get back up."

Carver filled a paper cup with water and tossed back a pill, washed it down.

Damian glanced at the clock.

"One would think someone in your profession would know to expect the unexpected."

"Kiss my ass, shrimp dick."

Hill scoffed and added, "You *did* get Kartovski, a known smuggler for terrorists and thieves." He grabbed a few photos clipped to the folder showing different angles of Kartovski's remains. He added as he started looking through the small wad of photos, "I would've preferred to see him tried in court, but I'll admit, there *was* a little satisfaction to be had in looking at what you left of him on the floor of his office—and the walls... and the ceiling... and the windows." He tilted his head when he saw the last one. "And inside the A/C, apparently."

Damian sipped his coffee, quietly grateful for Jenny's calming shoulder rub.

"This situation is gonna have political consequences, you know," Carver said.

"Throwing me under the bus again?"

"We don't have a choice," Hill said. "What would the public think if they found out their police force hires mercenaries to do their dirty work?"

"Not to mention the polls," Carver added. "It's better to say an outside party intervened. It maintains the city's trust in the department and it keeps the mayor off our backs. Makes him look good."

"I'm so happy for you," Damian said with bitter sarcasm.

"You're starting to become a hazard," Hill said. "We call you to do these jobs to keep police fatalities low and the civilian fatalities lower. This clusterfuck is a major slip-up, kid. You're starting to overstay your welcome. You're on the same road that Colonel James Fairman took."

"Don't compare me to that piece of shit," Damian spat. "I didn't lose fifty hostages in a warehouse inferno over a bad hunch."

"My point is that you're starting to take the same stupid risks, and we need you to ease up on the crazy risk-taking, or we might have to call off our deal."

"What deal?"

"That's not funny, Damian." Hill leaned back in his chair. "Only reason we're allowing you to work under your current identity is because you've been useful so far." He chuckled. "'Matt Donovan.' Where did you get that name from? Some pulp novel?"

"Something like that," Damian said.

"Well, 'Mr. Donovan,' I'm gonna let you in on a little secret: there's this asshole named Damian Warkowski, AKA the 'Dead Blue.' Wanted internationally, guilty of almost every crime known to man, including mass murder, destruction of property, mischief, theft, espionage, terrorism on a global scale; except, arguably, for rape and sodomy. Believed to have died a year ago when he tried to raid a government genetics laboratory in Central Congoria. Members of his faction mostly wiped out, with the rest of 'em scattered to the wind."

"What do you mean 'arguably?' I never raped or sodomized anybody."

"Remember the Konnerd incident?"

"Barely."

"The Harley Brothers. Pair of pyrokinetic rapists. They would rape whole families and then burn down their homes with their broken victims trapped inside. They burned down a warehouse full of people. You just mentioned it."

"Oh, yeah. What about them? I didn't rape them."

"What do you call shoving one of your telekinetic *Dragon Ball Z* shotguns up one of their asses and pulling the fucking trigger?"

"Poetic justice," Damian said.

Hill stared at him. Then he chortled, burst into a laughing fit. "Oh, Christ. You kill me."

"Maybe later."

Hill scoffed. "Back to the point: you cross the line again, and you'll be back on the wanted posters. No more good-paying jobs and no more 'Jim Donovan.' According to the world, you died raiding a chemical plant. Funny how insignificant an ending that seems for someone as big as you. The phrase 'Damian Warkowski Returns from the Grave' won't be a joke anymore; it'll be a headline on every paper from here to Cloverfield and around the world twice over. And my friend, you might find that we can be quite... *inhospitable* toward terrorists."

The look on Hill's face was enough to anger him, but then he had to talk. Damian could feel Jenny holding him down as much as she was rubbing his shoulders, trying her best to silently console him. So instead of just killing the two of them here, Damian smiled and said, "Then there would be nothing left to protect you from me."

"Maybe, maybe not." Hill shrugged. "Bottom line: try to keep your impulses under control next time we call you in for a job. Maybe surprise us and apprehend someone *alive* next time."

Carver folded his arms across his chest, leaning against the wall. "We like you, Damian. We like you both. You've proven to be very useful to us, and despite the extreme collateral damage, you've helped our department more than any normal people could possibly be expected to. You've proven to be more efficient when you're working as a team. Frankly, I'm glad to have you two on our side."

"Don't insult me with your lame backtracking," Damian snapped. "You both fuckheads, and the minute you drop me, I'll take great pleasure in slowly twisting your heads off your shoulders."

"Fair enough," Hill said.

"Will that be all? Can I get paid now?"

"Not yet," Carver said slowly.

Damian glared at him. "Why the hell not?"

"You said one of them is immortal, correct?"

"So?"

Hill said, "That means there are only *eight* dead robbers accounted for, unless our scavengers found something in the plane...?"

"Nothing's turned up," Carver said.

"That's your problem," Damian said.

"No," Hill fired back, "it's *yours*."

"Like fuck it is."

"No ninth body, no paycheck." He let Damian stew for a moment before continuing, "The job's not over yet, Damian. You get us our man, and we'll give you your money. And Damian? Try to bring him in alive."

Damian couldn't believe it. He was floored. He shifted his dumbfounded look back and forth between Hill and Carver. Then he leaped out of his seat, lunged across the desk and grabbed Hill by the collar, spilling the bastard's coffee on the floor. Pulled him in close until he could hear Hill's heart racing in his chest, their noses mere inches apart. Jenny gripped his other arm. Carver had his pistol drawn and ready for a headshot. "When this is over," Damian hissed, "I'm gonna fucking gut you." His point made, he shoved Hill back into his chair and stormed out of the office. "Fucking pigs." A detective stood just outside the door—another one of Hill's pals. Damian shoved him aside. "Move, asshole."

"'Scuse you," the detective said without dropping the unlit cigarette hanging from his lips. The guy sported a bad eighties mullet, but other than the hairstyle, he carried himself like the suave detective version of Brosnan's Bond. Dressed similar to Hill, right down to the rolled-up sleeves, carrying his bike jacket over his shoulder with his left arm.

Jenny lingered. She looked contemptuously at the two cops. "Watch yourselves."

Then she left without giving the detective a second glance, knowing full well what *his* eyes were watching until she was out of sight.

"Detective Campbell," Carver said.

"Cap," Campbell replied as he entered the office. He gave Hill a quick nod. "Sarge."

Hill raised his mug in response.

"What's on the menu today?" Campbell asked.

The drive home was uncomfortably quiet for most of the trip. Jenny said nothing, knowing Damian would seize the slightest opportunity to explode into a tirade about his latest piss-off. She leaned against the door and stared out the window as the city passed them by.

COBALT CHRISTMAS: A COBALT ROGUE STORY

Stiff, dry, cold December. Usually the city was a warmer place, even in the coldest months of winter. Frost-glazed trees girdled with flashing Christmas lights lined the medians in the bustling streets, their long branches glittering brightly as they extended over the early morning rush hour. Iridescent lights strung all over storefronts and office buildings blinked and glittered. An endless variety of overused Christmas tunes pervaded the air with the clouds of steam that rolled up from the sewers, overlapping with the bell-jingling and exaggerated bellows of charity Santas. Their donation pots *pinged* every time someone tossed a dime or a quarter into it.

The iridescent neon blaze and glitzy decor layering the overcrowded metropolis didn't limit itself at street level; it spread out all over like a disease at work. Its shimmering cells made spiral patterns on community centre rooftops and imposing glass domes that reached up higher than half of the original Seven Wonders of the World. Like grape vines, billions of tiny lights crawled up the sides of skyscrapers and starscrapers alike—many of these buildings pierced the night's cloudy sky. The clouds that generously sprinkled flurries of snow over the city-state would be grey if it weren't for the city's powerful multi-coloured radiance burning an unnatural rainbow hue through their wispy valleys and brushstroke swirls. Fiery orange-saturated fluff twisted around the mighty steel trunks of the starscrapers that reached up higher than any naked eye could see.

The sky... stirring round and round in slow, ominous motion above a claustrophobic entanglement of freeways and daunting towers. Hovercrafts and blimps twinkled like fireflies projecting holographic screens and Christmas-themed imagery.

With the joy and cheer of the holidays filling the streets, all seemed right with the world.

The enlightened, however, knew the world was anything but right.

They reached a red light at an intersection, surrounded by Cryo City's morning commute.

"Those fucking cunts," Damian muttered.

"I know," she said. *It begins.*

"I bust my ass for three fucking hours... and they tell me I can't get paid."

"I know, honey."

"Just... just... what the *fuck*, man. What the fuck."

"We just have to find that ninth guy."

"Yeah, and how the fuck am I supposed to find him? He could be out of the fucking country by now for all I know."

"I don't know," she said calmly. "You saw his face, right? You said he looked familiar."

"Yeah. I did. But so what? I can't do anything with just a face. I can't remember where I last saw him. And I can't draw worth shit."

"So ask a sketch artist to draw it for you?"

He fired up a cigarette with a telekinetic blue flame on the tip of his thumb. He shook his hand to put it out. "I'm too fucking tired to do that right now."

"I didn't mean right this second, baby. Sleep on it. At least then you'll have a cool head when you get back to it."

He growled, waiting for the red light to turn green. "This fucking light..."

"Besides," Jenny said as she stroked her finger up and down his arm, "I do think we were in the middle of something before that phone call..."

He looked at her. Blinked. Smirked. "Were we?"

She gave him a teasing smile, letting the lust gleam in her eyes. "Pretty sure we were."

The light turned green. Damian guided the Shelby Cobra down the street.

"We gotta make a stop first, though."

"Where?"

"Convenience store."

"Convenience store?"

"I need milk."

"Thought we had a couple cartons left."

"Nope. One carton, and that's not enough for dinner tonight."

That's when Damian remembered Mrs. Gammy and their dinner arrangement for tonight. "Oh, yeah. I just remembered—"

"Mrs. Gammy wanted to have dinner with us?"

"How did you—"

"The door isn't *that* solid, hon."

Damian shrugged. "Guess not."

Chapter 006
Stick to the Plan

They stopped around the corner for milk and eggnog on the way home. Just two minutes after they stepped foot in their apartment, Damian telekinetically threw away his clothes and flopped onto the foldout bed. Jenny put their purchases in the fridge first before joining him.

The two of them lay still for a moment. Damian sighed and wrapped his arm around Jenny's waist and held her tightly against him. "I don't deserve you."

She scoffed. "That's what you think."

"I know I don't."

"Do you?"

"Yeah."

"Explain."

"That would take too long."

She chuckled and caressed his arm around her waist. "I don't care. You know I love you, flaws and all."

"I would've killed them if you weren't there."

"I know."

"I should've."

"Maybe, maybe not."

"They're gonna expose us anyway. You know that, right?"

"What's stopping us from leaving, then?"

"I like it here."

She smiled. "Really? Is that the only reason?"

"The video store down the street is pretty good."

She laughed. "Oh, honey. There are better video stores all over the world, in better places than here. Cryo City is even worse than Cloverfield."

"You don't like it here?"

"I hate it here."

"Hm." He tightened his grip around her and nuzzled his face against the back of her head lovingly. "Wish you told me sooner...

when we could've still left."

"I know you never leave a job unfinished. Couldn't help it." She sighed and rolled over to face him eye to eye. She planted a firm kiss on his lips, held for a moment or two, then parted. "I'm with you every step of the way, baby, as long as you do the same."

"What if we're being shot at by .50 caliber machine gun rounds?"

"I'll be running right beside you." She kissed his cheek.

"What if our apartment gets blown up, and we're, uh, we're outgunned?"

"I'll be watching your back." She kissed his nose.

"What if some dumbfuck is throwing handfuls of shit at us?"

"Then, baby, I'll be right behind you."

They shared a laugh together. "I love you, Damian Warkowski." She ran her fingers through his hair.

"I love you too, Jenny Knight," he replied, right before he grabbed her breasts and shook them.

She laughed and said, "That tickles!" He didn't stop. "Damian!" she shrieked, giggling, grabbing his arms.

He stopped, held her close, smiling, cherishing this moment. In the next instant, he was asleep.

She lovingly stroked his head. "Love and kisses, baby."

Downtown...

Or a rundown part of it, anyway. The residential area running a thin crescent around the southern edge of Cryo City's sprawling downtown district had few stores and even fewer people running around in the streets for fear of getting mugged or worse. Occasionally, a dark-coloured vehicle or a taxi cab would coast across its slick, slushy roads with a strange sense of caution, as if their passengers were keeping their eyes peeled for anyone crazy enough to try and rob them.

A dark figure in a long coat walked briskly down the sidewalk along a string of row houses, hands stuffed in his pockets, hood pulled over his face. A thin veil of snow drifted in from the sky. Snowflakes clung to his coat, slowly building up as his time outside lengthened.

He stole across the street and passed a Virtreality Cafe—a step up from internet cafes that were prominent in the east with virtual reality booths and the small number of androids included in its staff. The payphone was on the next corner.

A pair of leather-clad, mohawked punks dressed like they leaped out of 1980's London loitered out front, watching the figure go by before quietly deciding on their next target.

They followed him, hands gripping their switchblades in their jacket pockets.

He knew they were coming. There was no fear, only annoyance. He'd have to deal with them quickly.

He banked into the next alley.

Seeing their chance, the punks rushed after him, turned into the alley—

Nothing but trash, dumpsters, and a homeless bearded man curled up until a cardboard sheet.

"The fuck?" one of them said, brandishing his switchblade as he surveyed the narrow space. "Where'd he go?"

His partner looked up at the fire escape. Nothing there. "Dunno, man. Let's bounce."

"Fuck that. Nobody escapes Sid the Squid, motherfucker."

"Blow this, let's go."

"You scared?"

"Nah, man. The guy just looked big and then he disappeared like a ghost. I don't wanna deal with that, man."

"Pussy. You're scared."

"Am not."

"Are too."

"Am not!"

"You aren't," the figure said behind them, "but you *will* be."

The punks whirled around. Sid the Squid was the first to attack, thrust his switchblade into the figure's stomach. "Ha! Gotcha."

The figure didn't fall. Barely flinched. He looked down at the switchblade in his stomach. He grabbed Sid by the wrist and twisted his hand all the way around, breaking it.

Sid screeched in agony and collapsed on his knees.

His partner attacked next. The figure kicked him in the chest, sent him flying into a group of trash cans. Then the figure, still squeezing Sid's broken wrist, feeling the rubbery muscles and bits of bone puncturing the screaming punk's skin from inside. Quick as lightning, the figure rabbit-punched Sid in the throat, caving his Adam's apple into his windpipe.

Choking, Sid collapsed.

The second punk was next. He saw the whole thing and just about shit his pants. "Holy shit!"

The figure approached.

The second punk scrambled off the trash cans and scurried down the alley—

The figure was on him before he could get far, tripping him up, slamming him to the ground. The figure stepped on his back. The punk screamed, wriggling in panic under the figure's boot until the figure reached down and effortlessly tore his head off his shoulders.

The bum under the cardboard sheet didn't hear a damn thing— or pretended not to. Either way, the figure wasn't going to bother with him.

He tossed the second punk's head in a nearby dumpster and continued to the payphone on the corner. He slipped in a five-dollar phone credit and dialled.

Afrókrema HQ

"Sir?" Colonel James Fairman's secretary said as she peeked into his office. "You have a phone call from an outside line."

Fairman looked up from a document with 'DENIED' stamped across it in bold red lettering on his desk. He peered at her through his spectacles. "Who?"

"He wouldn't say, but he said it was important."

Fairman sighed. "Alright. Transfer him."

"Yes, sir." With a dutiful nod, his secretary disappeared behind the door, closed it.

A second later, the phone rang. Fairman answered it. "Afrókrema, this is Colonel Fairman."

"It's Drake."

"Drake? Where the hell are you?"

"Downtown."

"Downtown? You're supposed to be in Cloverfield!"

"Yeah, well, my flight was cancelled."

"Are you... are you using a payphone?"

"Yeah, but—"

"Goddamn you, Drake!"

"Relax, I have a scrambler going. Nobody's going to trace it or listen in. Relax, old man."

"Don't 'relax, old man' me, you son of a bitch. What the hell happened?"

"There was a complication."

"No shit. I heard about Kartovski. This complicates things."

"You were supposed to raid the warehouse. Why didn't you?"

"We couldn't. By the time we got there, the place was crawling with that son of a bitch Carver's men. And then there's his mercenary dog..."

"Oh, I know all about that," Drake said. "A fellow immortal with some serious skill and an infuriating amount of persistence. Calls himself Donovan."

"Calls himself? You know him?"

"If I didn't know any better, I'd say the Dead Blue ain't so dead after all."

"*What*?" Fairman asked incredulously. "You told me he died with you in Central Congoria."

"Yeah, well, he thought the same of me, too, so I guess the feeling of shock was mutual."

"Great."

"He fucked it all up."

"Word is he's still on the case."

"What case?"

"*Yours*," Fairman said. "Carver and Hill concluded that you're still alive."

"But how?"

"No body."

Donner, AKA Drake, pinched the bridge of his nose and sighed. "Damn."

"They're refusing to pay him until he finds you. That's why you have to get out."

"Not until I have that fucker's head in my hands."

"Are you retarded?" Fairman fumed. "Don't you understand? Every second you stay in Cryo City, you jeopardize the secrecy of this mission. I need you out, and I need you out *now*."

"No. He doesn't know who I am and no one else suspects a thing. As far as the majority knows, *all* the bank robbers are dead. We kill the Dead Blue; we kill Hill and Carver, and our secret is safe."

"It's not that simple," Fairman said. "Their mercenary's a tough nut to crack. A real hardcore head case. And if what you say about him is true—that he's the *real* Dead Blue—that makes this all the more dangerous. You need to proceed with the utmost caution or else he'll kill you."

"Wouldn't be the first time."

"I'm aware."

"That's war for you."

"You're not going to back out of this, are you?"

"Depends on how much you want to fight *me*, too."

Fairman didn't want that. Waging war on *another* immortal psychopath was the last thing he needed. "Very well. Kill the dog, but do *not* kill its masters. That would bring too much heat down on us."

"Why just the dog?"

"They're not supposed to have it in the first place, and it's officially dead to the world anyway. Who are they going to tell?"

"Good point, I guess."

"Do whatever you have to. Make it loud and flashy. Just remember: you're a lone criminal mastermind unaffiliated with any law enforcement—"

"Yeah, yeah, I know the plan. I'll stick to the plan. Just do me a favour."

"What's that?"

"See if you can get your hands on some FATE rounds. We're gonna need 'em."

"Very well. I'll see what I can do. Good luck to you, soldier." Fairman hung up.

Chapter 007
Dinner with the Gammys

Jenny and Damian's Place

He awoke to the sound of water running and dishes clanging together. He looked up over the back of the couch and saw Jenny with her back turned to him scrubbing dishes in the sink, wearing an apron, knee-high socks, and panties.

Damn, she looked good.

He rose up, naked, and approached her. She knew he was coming, and he knew she knew—she pretended she didn't by whistling a tune straight out of a cheesy 70's cartoon he couldn't quite place. He grabbed her and kissed her cheek. "Morning."

"Evening," she said with a chuckle, scrubbing a plate.

He reached under her apron and cupped her breasts. "Not in the mood for shirts today?"

"Nah."

"Fine by me." He planted small kisses on her neck.

"Actually, before you get too into that, can you check the clock for me? Mrs. Gammy's supposed to be here at six."

Damian pulled away from her and went over to the stove. The digital clock read 5:45. He relayed the time back to her, and she said, "Oh! Shit." She dried her hands and rushed across the apartment to the wardrobe beside the TV. She rummaged around for an outfit. When she found one, she set it on the TV and got undressed. "Hurry up and get dressed! They're gonna be here any minute."

Damian frowned. He was in the process of pouring himself a cold cup of coffee from the pot. Still naked.

She pulled on a red V-neck sweater with Christmas trees on it and scowled at him. "Did you hear me?"

"Yes." He leaned against the counter, sipping coffee, pretending to be uninterested as he watched her change.

She slipped into a green pleaded skirt. "Move your ass, boy."

"Make me," he said teasingly.

COBALT CHRISTMAS: A COBALT ROGUE STORY

She smirked. "If I had the time, I would."

He felt a chill and glanced over at the fire escape window. "Goddamn it."

"What?"

"You left the window open."

"Figured you'd be too warm," she said jokingly.

"You're wrong," he said, picking up on her amused tone.

The sinewy whine of a cat wanting attention earned Damian's dirty look. "Felix is back."

On cue, a grey Korat slinked into view and perched itself on the window sill. Felix meowed again, looking at Damian with expectant emerald eyes.

"What do you want?" Damian asked him.

"Give him some of that eggnog," Jenny suggested as she went into the bathroom. "He'll like that."

"Share some of *my* eggnog?"

"Oh, please. A little sharing never killed anyone."

"Ugh." He grunted, looked at Felix again as he telekinetically summoned a small bowl from the cupboards and a carton of eggnog from the fridge. "You better be grateful for this."

Felix meowed again.

"Yeah, yeah."

Enveloped in his dark blue aura, the items floated in front of him. The carton opened and tipped its contents into the small bowl before closing and returning to the fridge. The bowl levitated over to the window sill and landed beside Felix, who immediately started lapping it up.

"Drink it all, you little shit." Damian sipped his coffee.

Jenny emerged from the bathroom, brushing her hair. "Will you put that thing away already? Jesus."

Damian conjured up his usual casual wear—a T-shirt, jacket, jeans, and slippers; all jet black with white trimmings. "Satisfied?"

She stopped brushing and looked him up and down, unimpressed by his choice. "A little too monochromatic for Christmas, don't you think?"

Damian shrugged.

She sighed. "At least *try* to smile when Mr. and Mrs. Gammy show up."

"I'll try, but I can't promise my face muscles will cooperate."

"Uh-huh." She tugged the last knots out of her hair and returned the brush to the bathroom.

"What're they bringing?" he asked.

"What?"

"What food are they bringing over?"

"I don't know," she said. "I know as much as you do."

Old knuckles rapped against the door.

"They're here," Jenny said. She touched the edges of her mouth and made a display of pulling up a grin. "Big smile."

He made an exaggerated display of his pearly whites and rolled his eyes back.

She shook her hand at him, telling him to knock it off right before she opened the door to greet their elderly neighbours with a cheerful, "Hey!"

The couple were wearing slippers, and both of them wore clothes that reflected their age: faded, dated, and worn.

"Oh, hello, dear!" Mrs. Gammy said as she carried in a porcelain container, hands protected by stained yellow oven mitts. "I would give you a hug but I'm kind of hugging the turkey at the moment."

Jenny laughed and said, "No worries." She stepped aside and let Mr. Gammy in with his platter on which were three plastic-wrapped plates containing stuffing, mashed potatoes, and steamed vegetables. "Hello, Mr. Gammy!"

"Oh, please, call me Carl," he replied pleasantly.

Jenny approached Mrs. Gammy, whose tiny steps to the table were secretly driving her up the wall. "Here, I'll help you with that."

"Oh, no, it's quite hot..."

"It's okay; I can't get hurt by heat."

"I-I'd much rather set it down on the table here, if that's okay with you," Mrs. Gammy said as she shuffled toward the table. "I just don't want you to burn yourself, dear." She set the food down on the table, then turned around and held her arms out. "*Now* I can hug you!"

Jenny giggled and the two of them embraced. "It's nice of you to do this for us."

"Oh, it was our pleasure," Carl said as he put the platter down beside the turkey. He looked up and said, "Hello, Damian."

"Hello, Carl," he said, still gripping his cold mug.

"How have you been?"

Damian shrugged and took a sip.

Jenny pulled up a chair at the table for Mrs. Gammy. "Have a seat; I'll have the table set in just a moment."

"Thank you, dear," Mrs. Gammy said as she sat down.

As Carl sat himself down beside his wife of thirty-two years, he asked Damian, "How's the job going?"

"Uh," Damian said slowly, looking at Jenny for clues, since she obviously lied about his profession—and totally forgot to mention it to him for future reference. Or maybe she did, and he just forgot. So he said, "It's going okay."

She brought down four plates from an overhead cupboard and subtly looked at him with her 'be careful' look.

Carl said, "Gettin' tired of delivering pizzas yet?"

Damian shot a sideways scowl at his girlfriend, hiding most of it behind his mug as he took another sip. *Really? Pizza delivery?* Then he forced cold coffee down his throat and said, "Yeah, it's getting there."

"I remember when I was an errand boy. I was about your age, too."

"Yeah?"

"Yep. Only... I delivered milk."

"Dude," Damian said, "how old *are* you?"

"Damian," Jenny snapped.

Mrs. Gammy and her husband laughed. Carl said, "It's okay. I'm not offended. I know I'm old. I'm also kinda thirsty."

Jenny said, "Oh, well, we have milk, and eggnog; water, wine..."

"Eggnog sounds wonderful," Mrs. Gammy said.

"Agreed," Carl said.

As Jenny filled both their glasses with Damian's eggnog—ignoring his scowl in the process—Carl continued, "I haven't had eggnog in, oh... it must've been four years now."

"That so? That's way too long, Carl," Jenny said as she leaned over the table to pour Carl a glass, giving him a generous view of her cleavage. He couldn't help himself, pausing to stare at the tops of her breasts showing in her festive V-neck until an annoyed Mrs. Gammy gave his foot a light kick.

He jolted. "Uh."

Jenny looked up at him. "You okay?"

"Yeah, I'm fine," he said with a chuckle. "I apologize."

"No, no worries," she said as she stood up straight. She handed Damian the carton.

He noticed how bland the carton's label was—it simply said 'Eggnog.' A barcode and nutritional information, and a sparingly worded list of ingredients. No brand or expiration date to be found. *Hmm.* He peered inside the near-empty carton in dismay, then dumped the last of it in his coffee mug and drank.

Mrs. Gammy sipped her drink and almost purred. "This is divine."

"It's just eggnog," Damian said.

Jenny shot him a quick glare before smiling at their guests. "Yeah, I can tell it's been a while since you guys've had some." She started positioning plates around the table.

The turkey's intoxicating aroma couldn't be completely contained; it leaked out, filled the apartment, mixed in with the fresh smell of steamed vegetables. Damian could practically hear the recently applied layer of honey garlic barbeque sauce crackling over the turkey's crisp skin. *Damn, that smells good.*

Jenny spoke his thoughts without even realizing it: "That turkey smells delicious, Mrs. Gammy."

"I hope it tastes as good as it smells. I had to reheat it today."

"Oh, no, it smells absolutely wonderful, and I bet it'll taste even better." Jenny started placing the appropriate silverware down beside the plates. When she finished, she went into the fridge and grabbed the last carton of eggnog, opened it, and poured herself a glass.

The cat started whining again. Damian looked at it, then at the empty bowl on the window sill, and sipped his coffee. "You're not getting any more, you dumb cat."

Felix kept whining, rolling onto his back, rocking back and forth, kicking his hind legs out.

"Oh, Felix," Mrs. Gammy said, "behave."

Carl chuckled and said, "Think we might have to give you guys some adoption papers."

Jenny laughed at his joke.

Damian didn't take his eyes off Felix as his whining went up a few decibels to a frightening screech, then a drawn-out howl.

Something wasn't right. This wasn't an 'I want attention' whine.

Everyone stopped what they were doing and watched Felix writhe on the window sill.

"Felix...?" Mrs. Gammy said quietly.

Damian set his mug down on the counter and approached the cat. "What's your deal, cat?"

Felix howled again, hissed, lashing all four of his limbs out. He tumbled off the window sill and hit the floor—on his back. Couldn't even land on his feet. His emerald eyes bulging with fear and agony as his body twisted around in the corner.

"What the hell?" Damian kept his distance, but never took his eyes off the cat.

Jenny gripped her glass of eggnog with both hands, forgetting she even had it as she peered over Damian's shoulder with concern. "What's going on with him?"

"I don't know," Damian said.

Carl stood up and walked around the table, eyebrows furrowed worriedly. "Felix? What's wrong, buddy?"

Felix gurgled. A broken, high-pitched note escaped his small throat. He stood up on his legs, gagging, back rising, hair standing up.

"Just a fur ball," Damian said, no longer interested.

HACK!

"OH!" Jenny cried out, startled.

Felix vomited a blood-darkened clump of fur and screeched, right before another clump cut him off, splattered on the floor next to the first one. Felix heaved. More blood exploded from his throat, but no fur this time. He collapsed on his side, writhing weakly, stomach twisting, hind legs in the air, chin on the floor. He emptied the rest of his stomach on the floor, guts and all.

"*Blyat!*" Damian and Carl lurched away, startled by the disturbing sight. "What the *fuck*?" Damian exclaimed.

"Felix?!" Mrs. Gammy stood up. "What's happened to Felix?"

The cat was still, lying in a pool of his own blood, grey fur soaked black, pink bubbles fizzing out of his mouth and nose.

Nobody said a word for what seemed like forever. They heard nothing but the evening commute outside their window.

Then, Jenny, trembling, said slowly, "D-Damian... what... what did you give him?"

It took Damian a moment to pry his eyes away from the cat to his girlfriend. "I just gave him—"

That's when it hit him. He looked at the eggnog cartons on the counter, then at the glasses on the table. Carl's was half empty. He looked at Carl. Carl looked at him.

"What?" Carl asked.

Everyone stared at Carl, waiting for something to happen. Pure dread.

"What is it?" Carl asked nervously. He coughed. Furrowed his brow, massaged his throat. "What—"

His head snapped forward as thick red projectile vomit gushed out of his mouth and splattered on the floor. "What...?"

Jenny's breath caught in her throat. She stayed behind Damian, watching Carl in horror.

"Carl!" Mrs. Gammy screamed. She jumped to his aid, reached for him...

...then she doubled over and threw up all over the floor— crimson goop, thick and syrupy.

"Oh, my God!" Jenny gasped.

Damian looked at the glass his girlfriend was holding and smacked it out of her hands. It shattered on the floor, splattering the tainted, custard-coloured concoction across the kitchen tiles. "Did you drink any?"

Jenny looked at him, stunned.

"DID YOU HAVE ANY?!" he shouted.

"No! No! I didn't!" she yelled back.

Relieved, Damian said, "G—"

Sudden, burning, excruciating...

Damian felt it claw its way up his throat, in a hurry to spew out of his mouth, across the table. The poison. The eggnog... *the coffee. Fuck.*

"DAMIAN!" Jenny shrieked, grabbing hold of him. "No! No, no, no, no!"

Damian's legs buckled. He collapsed on his knees, despite Jenny's clumsy efforts to hold him steady. He choked, couldn't breathe. More of that shit rushed up his throat. He spat some of it out, but too early. The rest of it erupted from the back of his throat, flooding his mouth and nostrils. Dizzy... everything fading...

Carl leaned against a chair, chest heaving. He threw up again, painting the chair red. He collapsed, pulling the chair down with him. "Ugh... *uuuuuuhhhhaaaaauugghh*...!"

Mrs. Gammy convulsed on the floor, moaning in manic horror and agony, blood spraying out of her mouth, all over the chair legs under the table. Eyes rolled in the back of her head, nothing but the whites.

Damian's body contorted. Felt a dozen knifes shredding his stomach. More of it came up. He hacked on it, watched it dribble down his front.

Jenny pleaded in rapid-fire panic, gripping him tightly, sobbing. "No! No! Baby, stay with me! Fight it! Damian!"

Carl's face distorted in unimaginable pain as scarlet tears streamed down his cheeks. He trembled, moaned as the last of it came up, then he heaved. Something thicker and darker than blood crawled out of his mouth, long and stringy. It thickened as more of it poured out; dark, ugly sheen. A mixture of organs, all pulsing randomly and out of sync with each other, steaming in the cool air, fluids coagulating into a thick paste beneath the expelled heap.

Carl died lying face down in it.

Mrs. Gammy managed to stand herself back up on her knees. Her guts expelled from her stomach like a soul being exercised from a possessed victim. It slithered out of her gaping mouth and coiled up on her lap. The last of it, strands, dangled from her chin. She looked blankly at Jenny.

Jenny felt eyes on her. She looked over the tabletop at Mrs. Gammy. Too shocked to speak now.

Mrs. Gammy's lifeless eyes remained fixed on her for a moment longer, then she keeled over and hit the floor.

Damian pivoted forward. This was it. He could feel everything inside squirming up, filling his airways, squeezing through his lungs. It all came pouring out, plastering against the floor under him.

"Damian! Baby!" Jenny held him tight, watching his innards pile up in horror. Blood and sinew slid up from the back of his throat.

Damian's vision faded to nothing. He felt nothing. Saw nothing. Heard nothing.

Cold. He was *cold*. Even that was going away. Felt like he was floating. *Was* he floating? Fading into nothingness? The afterlife?

He opened his eyes and found himself standing in a field with tall grass and flowers with petals that shimmered yellow, orange, red, green, blue, purple...

He glanced up at the sky. It was black and spinning, spiralling in an eternal stir, but somehow the field was bright as day.

The Spirit Core—the in-between for the recently deceased. A realm that he'd visited quite often, given his profession.

"Oh, great," he muttered. "I fucking died again."

Chapter 008
Inconvenience Store

Jenny and Damian's Place

Jenny cradled her boyfriend's bloody corpse in her arms, sobbing uncontrollably. "Please come back... please..."

She glanced at Mr. and Mrs. Gammy's corpses. She knew she had to call it in.

She gave Damian's cheek a small kiss and set him against the fridge door. "I love you," she whispered. *Come on, Jenny,* she thought to herself, *he's died a million times and always comes back. Get a grip.*

She sniffled and went over to the phone. Dialled Sergeant Hill's direct office number.

Two rings, then: "Sergeant Donald Hill's office."

"It's Jenny."

"What do you want? Did you find our missing body?"

"Just get the fuck down here, you asshole." She hung up.

The Spirit Core

"Well, I better not keep the lady waiting too long." Damian heaved an annoyed sigh and started walking across the field. Children ran around him, playing their games and giggling without a care in the world. Carl and Mrs. Gammy were playing with Felix, who was rolling happily in the grass, pawing at their hands.

"Sorry, guys," Damian said to them.

The couple looked up at him. They didn't recognize him at first, but then: "Damian! When did you get here?"

Carl said, "It's been a while, kiddo."

"You guys died like three minutes ago," Damian said.

The couple looked at each other, then at Damian again. "Really?" Mrs. Gammy asked. "Feels like it's been years."

"No, it's been minutes," Damian said. "That's normal, though. Time doesn't work here like it does in the world of the living."

"I suppose not."

"I like it here," Carl said.

"Me, too," Mrs. Gammy concurred. "And Felix likes it, too. Don't you, Felix?"

Felix meowed. Mrs. Gammy stroked his small head. He started to purr.

Damian shrugged. "Well, if you guys like it here, I guess I can't complain. See ya."

"Where are you going?"

"I'm going back. Again."

"Okay. Have fun!" Carl said.

"Tell Jenny I said hello! I do miss her."

"Will do," Damian answered.

He left them behind and headed for the Crystal Mountains in the distance. They lived up to their name, appearing as if they were intricately carved out of clear glass.

In a matter of minutes disguised as hours, Damian reached the base of the first mountain. There, he found a staircase winding up the slope to the top, hidden away by a fluffy ceiling of grey clouds. He ascended the steps, whistling Led Zeppelin's *Stairway to Heaven* as he did so, maintaining a casual air about himself. Behind the mountainside's crystalline rocks, a huge abundance of marine life swam around; all species at peace with one another, from crayfish to sharks, whales to krakens and their octopus cousins. Jellyfish, dolphins, starfish; sea serpents long faded into myth and legend, thought to have never existed by the modern world swam within the mountainous tank in tranquility.

Damian finally reached the flat top of the mountain. A sea of clouds spun around it. The occasional flash of lightning revealed dark silhouettes of creatures that mankind could never fully comprehend shifting around inside them. The blue glow of the water through the clear floor provided dim lighting for the ritualistic mountaintop.

Three portals up ahead: a circle of fire, a blinding doorway, and in the center—Damian's kitchen. Damian could see Jenny speaking to Sergeant Hill as a CSI crew scoured the site for clues.

He approached the central portal, waiting for the gatekeeper to show up.

And she did. A figure of divine beauty rose up from the floor. A white robe covered her body like a pure silk scarf. Her silver hair shined; her grey eyes had no pupils, but despite her appearance, she wasn't blind. Her skin was fair, and her face had a pure, innocent look to it that few people possessed these days.

"Hello, Marner."

Marner looked at him and smiled. "Damian. You're back. Are you astral, or did you die again?"

"I died again."

Marner sighed. "Of course you did. You know, Jenny can't ever get over watching you die."

"I know."

"You need to be more careful."

"It wasn't my fault. Some fucker poisoned my eggnog."

"You're lucky you're immortal."

"Depends on how you look at it. I'm getting tired of walking up those stairs."

Marner giggled and stepped aside. "Go on, Damian. I'll see you again soon."

"Yeah, yeah."

"It was nice seeing you again."

"Oh, uh." He stopped just a few steps away from the kitchen portal. "When are you coming back down to the living world? Jenny wants to catch up over coffee or something."

"Hmm..." Marner pondered her answer, then said, "Ask her how the middle of January works for her. Say, the 14th?"

"I'll run it by her and then check back with you."

"Sure thing. Bye now." She smiled and waved.

He waved back, then hopped through the portal.

"Fucking Christ," Hill said as he observed the horrific scene. Hill had seen things nobody else ever wanted to see, but even *this* was a bit much for him, especially since he'd eaten just an hour ago. "You guys get that eggnog from the convenience store up the street?"

Jenny looked at him with suspicion. "How did you know?"

"Been getting reports of similar cases all over this neighbourhood in the past half-hour. Only narrowed down the search to that corner store five minutes after. We've already sent out a news bulletin." He fired up a cigarette and looked over at Damian slumped against the fridge. "What a goddamn waste."

"Fuck off," Jenny snapped.

Damian suddenly jolted awake—and alive, startling the quartet of crime scene investigators standing around him half to death. He sucked in air and immediately started choking on the strands of sinew and gore stuck in his throat. He gagged, groaned.

Jenny rushed to his side. "Baby! Baby, you're back!"

Still choking, Damian pointed at his heaped innards on the floor, then pointed at his open mouth.

"Huh?"

He wasn't in the goddamn mood for charades, so he started to shovel it all back into his mouth himself.

Jenny recoiled in disgust. "*EW*!"

He tried to say, "Help me, you idiot!" but since he was half choking, half swallowing his own expelled organs, it came out as gibberish.

Somehow, Jenny still understood, and tentatively picked up the last half of his intestines like a first-time snake handler, and started sliding it all down his throat, grimacing in disgust as she did. He kept choking, convulsing a bit, forcing it all down in strained swallows. Eventually, the two of them managed to get everything back inside of him, leaving just a puddle of blood on the floor and more of it soaking into their clothes, much to the horror and disgust of all present law enforcement—two of whom threw up in the kitchen sink.

Jenny gripped Damian's arm tighter than she meant to. "Are you gonna be okay?"

He shook his head slowly.

"Say something."

"'A little sharing never killed anyone,' you said... *RIGHT*."

Jenny stroked his bangs away from his eyes.

"W-water," Damian groaned.

Jenny got him some water in a glass.

He gulped it all down and cleared his throat. Spat some blood to the side and wiped his mouth. At least now he could breathe.

"Wow." Jenny and Damian looked at Hill, who followed up with, "That was the most disgusting thing I have ever seen."

"Agreed," one of the CSI units leaning over the sink moaned.

"Don't ever do that in my presence again," Hill said. "Please."

"I don't plan to do it again *period*," Damian snapped as he handed Jenny his empty glass.

She refilled it and gave it back, then asked Hill, "You said this is happening all over the neighbourhood?"

"It was," Hill said. "Thirteen reported fatalities have been confirmed so far." He looked at Mr. and Mrs. Gammy. "Er... *fifteen* confirmed fatalities."

Jenny looked at the bodies as a CSI unit called for a coroner on his radio.

"They're fine," Damian said reassuringly. "They're in the Core. They seem pretty content up there."

Jenny looked at him.

"Marner says hi, by the way."

"Yeah...?"

"Wants to know if mid-January is okay for drinks or something."

"Yeah... sure." She sniffled.

Damian rubbed her tears off her cheeks with a bloody thumb, leaving pink smears. "Shh."

"They were good people," Jenny said.

"I know," he said.

"They didn't deserve this."

"I know."

"W-Why did this have to happen to them?"

It didn't take Damian long to think of an answer: "Because they were our friends." He held her close, resting his chin on her head as she buried her face in his chest. He looked over at Hill and said, "You said something about a convenience store?"

"That's the apparent source. No other reports from anywhere else so far, but believe me, we're looking."

"I want to see it."

"The convenience store?"

"Yeah."

"I was afraid you'd say that."

The Convenience Store

The clerk was sitting against the tobacco shelf behind the counter with his head and torso riddled with about ten inches of lead. Detective Campbell was looking him over when Hill arrived with Damian and Jenny. Campbell flashed Jenny with a charming smile that would melt any teenage romantic's heart. Jenny responded with an icy glare. "Good evening," Campbell said. "Here for the special blowout sale?"

"Knock it off, Campbell," Hill snapped. "This ain't the time or the place..."

"Just trying to lighten up the mood." Indicating Damian and Jenny's frazzled, blood-soaked appearances, Campbell said, "You guys look like you jumped into a wood chipper."

Damian leaned over the counter at the dead clerk. "So they killed the clerk before or after they sold some of their brand?"

"*What* brand?" Campbell asked. "There's no logo on it, or even an address. Can't tell where it came from."

"You didn't answer my question."

"Before," Campbell said as he approached the chips and dip section. "That's not the clerk. Just a stand-in."

"Stand-in?"

"Yeah, I guess they decided not to leave any witnesses behind. It was kind of weird."

"Where's the real one?"

"His head's clogging the toilet in the back, but I have no idea where the rest of him is." Campbell selected a bag of corn twists and ripped the bag open, winning him a disapproving glare from Hill.

"Appetizing thought."

"Right?" Hill turned to Jenny, who lingered in the doorway and hadn't once stepped foot into the place since they'd arrived. "You alright?"

"I'm fine," she said, much more composed now than before. "I've seen worse."

"You satisfied now?" Hill asked Damian. "Isn't much more for you to see."

"Surveillance footage?"

Campbell pointed a handful of corn twists behind him. "That way."

Hill sighed, and led them into the back. Campbell followed. They passed the restroom and entered the main office where the surveillance monitor was. They rewound the footage through the whole day until Campbell told them when to stop—around the 10:03 PM mark, yesterday. Three men with indistinguishable faces came in and spoke to the clerk over the counter for a few minutes. One of the men carried a cardboard box, taped shut. After their conversation ended, the clerk led the trio into the main office. The one with the box left two minutes later, traveled down the aisles to the dairy refrigerator, set the box down on the floor. He opened the fridge and pushed a certain brand of eggnog—and only eggnog—all the way to the back of the fridge, making them spill out into the walk-in fridge behind the wall. He knelt down, ripped the tape off the box, and loaded 'fresh' cartons of eggnog from the box onto the rack. Once he finished, he left the store.

Another man came out of the back—not the clerk, but he wore the clerk's clothing now—and he went behind the counter. The third man emerged from the office, went up to the counter, spoke to the stand-in clerk briefly, and then left.

The quality was so bad that all of their faces were fuzzy and pixilated.

"Motherfuckers," Damian said.

"You're telling me," Campbell said, mouth full of corn twists. "The shit quality doesn't help us identify them much, either. Fast forward about an hour ago."

Hill did just that and returned it to its normal play speed as a masked man walked in and immediately sprayed the 'clerk' with an Uzi. He immediately left.

"Who the hell was that?" Damian asked.

"Not entirely sure," Campbell said. "Got a hunch they changed their minds about bringing in a stand-in."

"Look at that timing," Jenny said, indicating the time code on the screen. "They picked the perfect opportunity to pull this shit."

"Huh?" Damian asked.

"When was that bank robbery? Nine? Ten?"

"Lasted a few hours, I think."

"Well, I think this happened right at the end of that bank robbery, babe," Jenny said. "These guys must've seen it on TV and knew the cops would be too preoccupied with it."

Hill squinted. "Or they were in on it."

"Also a possibility." Jenny nodded. "It's just too coincidental, you know?"

"Yeah."

"You guys might be on to something there," Campbell said

thoughtfully, squinting at the monitor screen.

"See that fucking box that guy was carrying?" Damian scoffed. "No way were they capitalizing on anything." Damian thought it through—a possibility, anyway: *two teams. One takes the bank while the other takes the convenience store. Bank team makes a scene to attract the cops while these eggnoggers slip in under the radar. Once their objective for the convenience store is met— whatever it is—they take out the last witness. The how makes sense, but the why... that's a whole other story.*

"It's funny," he said aloud, "the more I think about this, the more it all looks like a planned operation. Only one problem: it doesn't make any fucking sense." He gave his girlfriend's head a playful pat. "Still. Good work, Nancy Drew."

Jenny frowned.

Campbell snickered.

"Let's not get ahead of ourselves here," Hill said as he drew a smoke from his breast pocket. "Any idiot can act on speculation. I like to think we're a little bit smarter than that."

"You might be," Damian said, "I'll take my chances."

"Just remember what we told you, Blue. Just because you work for us under the table doesn't mean we gave you a license to kill. Play it smart and play it safe."

"I'll think about it," Damian said sarcastically. "I'm gonna find that piece of shit who got away. Ask him a couple questions. See what he knows."

"Think you can get answers out of an immortal?"

"I've managed to do it before. During a certain mission in a certain third world country during a time of civil unrest, I caught a spy. He had a faster healing factor than usual, but I made that work to his disadvantage."

"What'd you use? Electric shock? Hammers?"

"Just my hands, and splinters from the wall of the hut I took him to. My point is, after five hours of what I put him through, anyone would be willing to talk. After *six* hours, they all sing like canaries."

"Why the extra hour?"

Damian shrugged. "I try to be thorough."

Hill scoffed.

"You're such an asshole," Jenny said.

"You love me anyway, though." Damian smirked.

"I ask myself why every day," she replied jokingly.

Campbell smirked as he chewed more corn twists.

Hill cleared his throat. "So, uh... we'll have your apartment cleaned in about three hours." He darkened their moods, and he knew it. "Know if they have any next of kin? Grandkids, maybe? Distant relatives?"

"I'll give your their contact information when... when the floor's all cleaned up." Jenny swallowed, fighting back another wave of tears.

"Sure thing."

Damian wrapped his arm around her and brought her close to kiss the top of her head. She appreciated the gesture, but he knew he couldn't console her right now. "I'll find out who did this, baby."

Hill said, "You mean *I* will. *You* just focus on finding that immortal. Until a connection can be more than just speculated, I suggest you steer clear of this poisoned eggnog business. Campbell and I will deal with that. Last thing the gutters in these streets need is another river of blood. You understand?"

"No," Damian said sarcastically.

Hill glared at him. "I'm warning you, Damian. Stay the fuck out of this case."

Chapter 009
Girl Goes Through Hell for Her Man

Safehouse at the Edge of Hillarm River

Damian and Jenny sat alone in the dark. Strips of red neon bled through the window blinds, casting crimson slants across the floors and walls. The windows themselves were shut.

The two of them were quiet silhouettes on the foldout couch.

"We have to kill them," Jenny said.

"I know."

"Good."

Damian paused. "Wait, you mean the bastards who poisoned—"

"Everyone. *All* of them. The people who poisoned Mr. and Mrs. Gammy. Hill and Carver, and anyone else who knows. We have to get out of this."

"I know."

"I don't want anyone else who doesn't deserve it to die."

"I know," he said again. "Can't kill Hill or Carver, yet. I suspect we can't let them die, either. Not until I get that slippery fuck."

"So what're you waiting for?"

"A lead would be nice. He's probably lying low after the heist."

"I don't care," Jenny said, standing up. "We're gonna find him and we're gonna rip his fucking head off, and then we're gonna spoon-feed it to those bastards at the station and get our fucking money."

"And *then* we can go on vacation?"

She said nothing.

"Or are you gonna keep bitching about the cost?"

She sighed. "Sure. I guess I could use one after this is all over."

"Great." He stood up and peered through the window blinds at the red lamppost standing tall at the edge of the river. Then he said,

"This mean you're helping out with this one?"

She cocked her head to the side, cracking her neck. "You bet your ass I am, sweetheart."

The garage below their safehouse tripled as a bomb shelter and an armoury. Their weapons were stored in a caged gun room to the far left. They stepped off the elevator looking more prepared for fall than winter. Damian's usual white-trimmed monochromatic outfit had an extra layer over it, while Jenny wore a brown leather jacket, unzipped to reveal a plain white shirt underneath, and jeans with ripped thighs.

"Why do you even bother with that façade?" he asked.

"What façade?"

"Dressing up like you're actually cold. Can you even *get* cold?"

She shrugged. "When I lose a lot of blood, yeah, I feel cold. But you already knew that."

"I did. But what about sub-zero conditions?"

"Dunno. Never been in sub-zero conditions. Don't think it'll do much to me, either."

They hopped into the Shelby Cobra. Damian started it up. Jenny adjusted her seat, setting it back a few notches so she could relax her feet on the dashboard.

"Feet on the floor," Damian said.

"Make me."

He glared at her. She glared back.

He wasn't in the mood to fight with her. He taxied out of his parking spot and coasted out of the underground garage and into Cryo City's evening commute. A fresh layer of white covered the roofs of sidewalk vendors and cars stuck in traffic. The snow was still falling. "Any idea where we're going? Because I don't have a clue."

"You're supposed to be smart," she teased.

"Fuck off."

"You mentioned hostages. Why don't we try asking them?"

"Where are we supposed to find them? None of them were injured, so the hospital wouldn't have them, and I don't wanna rely on the cops more than I have to. And we don't know where they live."

"*We* don't know where they live, but the cops probably found out when they took their statements."

"I just said I don't want to talk to those assholes."

"That's really too bad."

He looked at her. She had that look on her face—one of the many looks he couldn't simply say no to. "I hate you sometimes."

She smiled. "I love you."

"Yeah, right." He took out his cell phone and called Hill. Waited through the rings. Then: "It's Damian."

"What do you want?" Hill asked.

"I need the addresses of those hostages you took statements from. The ones you found in the warehouse."

"Why?"

"Ask them a few questions. See if I can get any clues leading to my boy"

"Absolutely not."

A punk on a hovercycle nicked the sideview mirror as he zoomed up between two crowded lanes a foot off the ground. Damian swore, checked the mirror. A small scratch on the rim, and a diagonal crack on the mirror. "Fucking cocksucker!"

"You hear me?" Hill asked.

"Yes, I fucking heard you. Why?"

"You're not torturing the victims of the man you're supposed to be hunting down for information about him. Are you insane? Don't answer that."

"Didn't say I was going to torture them. Just give me their phone numbers."

"No."

"I'm not gonna torture them, you shithead."

"How come I find that hard to believe?"

They moved up another block, infuriatingly slow, leaving ample opportunities for a diverse crowd of jaywalkers to navigate their way between the vehicles to the other side of the street. A cyborg accidentally scratched his prosthetic hand across the hood of a testy businessman's car in the next lane over, prompting the driver to get out and start a verbal argument with the culprit.

"Jenny's with me; she'll keep me in line."

"Will she, though?"

"Fine. Then arrange a three-way phone conversation with me,

you, and each of the victims, you untrusting faggot." Damian strained to hear Hill's responses over the sounds of car horns blaring as the businessman's argument with the cyborg got physical. He watched them tackle each other on the hood of the businessman's car with an annoyed scowl.

"We already took their statements," Hill said, and then suggested, "Why don't I just read you those?"

"They could've hidden something."

"Why would victims in a bank heist hide anything about their attackers?"

"I don't know. How can you expect me to get results if you don't cooperate?"

"*You're* the one who isn't cooperating, you blue-haired son of a bitch!"

Damian shouted, "We'll see who fucking cooperates when I find my way into your goddamn office, you fucking—"

Jenny grabbed the phone and said, "It's Jenny. Yeah, I know. Uh-huh. Uh-huh. We just need something to go on, is all. Yeah. Oh? Not even for little ol' me?"

Damian rolled his eyes and watched the businessman's brawl with the cyborg draw to a close—as the cyborg lifted his opponent up and over his head, and smashed his body into the windshield of his car. He then fled. Damian chuckled at the sight.

Traffic in his lane started moving again. Damian eased the car forward, leaving the comical sight of the unconscious businessman half-inserted through the front of his car in the rearview mirror.

Damian tuned his girlfriend out, focusing on the road. This part of town maintained a retro-futuristic 1960's vibe with its vibrant clutter of pop art imagery and neon banners recreating abstract shapes and patterns hovering over the street. Psychedelic flower holograms with big company brand logos on their petals spun chaotically above the evening rush hour between huge rectangular signs clinging to the sides of buildings over every storefront.

He drove by a diner with its nostalgic interior decor catching his eye despite the distance between them—its mirrored ceiling reflected the pink booths and black-and-white checkered floor as android waitresses served their customers. 2D cartoon characters danced gracefully and energetically in the window panes, hopping from pane to pane across the strip of windows without missing a beat.

A cyborg vendor sprouting eight prosthetic arms offered passersby a variety of fresh food like hot dogs and hamburgers. A projected pink Cadillac peeled down an invisible road above the street, running circles around the large image projector on the roof of a three-storey tenement building. On the other side, an orange-and-white striped awning supported a conveyer belt on which a three-storey-tall alien astronaut automaton straight out of a Steve Ditko comic walked, its shoulder connected to the front of the Pop Culture of a Past Lifetime Art Museum to prevent him from teetering into the street.

Jenny hung up and said, "Know of any repo agencies in the area?"

Damian looked at her. "How did you—"

"Oh, my dear Blue," she cooed, "my powers of persuasion are far, *far* greater than you could ever imagine."

"He asked for a lap dance again, didn't he?"

"I... yeah."

"And you fucking accepted?"

"First for everything, I guess."

"No, no, no, no. You're not giving that piece of shit a fucking lap dance."

"You're right, I'm not. But agreeing with his terms got me something."

"You don't... *intend* to?"

"Oh, hell, no. Ick, dude. *Ick*." She scoffed. "You think I would willingly give anyone whose name isn't 'Damian Warkowski' an up-close-and-personal lap dance?"

"In everyone else's dreams, I hope."

"Took the words right out of my mouth."

"Okay, okay. So what about these 'repo agencies' you mentioned?"

"I had Hill read out the statements to me. Apparently one of our dead bank robbers was a wannabe preacher with a gun. Talked about working for a repo company, and not just *any* repo company— one directly affiliated with a certain bank..."

"The one they were stealing from."

"Bingo."

"Okay... but aren't banks their own repo companies?"

"No, not always. I mean, some of them have collection agents. But most of the time, they hire private agencies for that. It's good business."

"How do you know anything about that?"

"You mean you don't?"

"For all I know, you're spouting bullshit."

"I worked a few side jobs here and there."

He looked at her, doubtful. "You never repossessed a car in your life."

"Obviously," she said, frowning. "I meant I took on a case you previously turned down, because you thought it was 'a pointless waste of time.' Some poor bastard had his car repossessed and wanted us to track it down. His name was Cannertunken."

"Cannertunken," Damian repeated, running the name through his memory. "Weird name. Sounds familiar."

"Back when he was totally broke and didn't have much money."

Damian shrugged. "Probably why I didn't take his case. So why did you?"

"*Because* unlike some people, I have this wonderful little thing called 'empathy.'"

Damian scoffed. "So you did a job for free. You chased some dude's taillights and gave him back his car."

"No. I traced his car back to the dealership he bought it from *just two weeks earlier*. The guy got ripped off, and nobody could prove that, and *that's* why I took the job. It pisses me off when companies shit on their customers to squeeze more cash out of them."

"Alright, fine."

"Besides, it worked to our benefit."

"How?"

Jenny smirked and folded her arms across her chest. "You know all those guns we've got hidden around the apartment and the safehouses?"

Damian looked at her. "Wait, *that's* our supplier's name?"

Smugly, she said, "Yep."

"No shit?"

"No shit. Gave me a whole wagon full of 'em when I brought his car back and still gives me a generous discount whenever I visit his gun shop."

"And you never thought to tell me about this because...?"

"I *did* tell you."

"When?"

"At least twice a month, whenever I bring something back from his shop. Dolt."

Damian frowned. "Okay, whatever. We're getting off track. What about these private agencies?"

"Just that. They're private agencies. Not much different from what we do—we wait for a call, then we do the job, and then we get paid. Only our services are a lot broader."

"'Private' as in, it's going to be a pain in the ass finding out which one the wannabe preacher originally worked for."

Jenny said quietly, "Yeah. Pretty much."

"Which means we've still got absolute fuck-all. Even if we go to every single repo agency in the city, how are we supposed to get them to know who we're looking for when we don't know his name? We don't even know what the guy looks like."

"Not... necessarily." She sounded hesitant.

"What? What do you mean?"

Hill's Office

Hill was damn-near asleep when his cell phone beeped. He jolted in his seat, startled awake by his own ringtone. He groaned and fished it out of his breast pocket and looked at the notification. When he saw Jenny's name, his heart jumped. *What does she want now?* He unlocked his phone and read Jenny's message:

>Heeeyyy can I ask u for another favor?

Hill furrowed his eyebrows and typed cautiously:

>Depends what it is...

She responded quickly:

>What's the state of those dead guys?

He wrote:

>Burned. The van exploded... y?

Her reply came almost as quickly as the first:

>Damn! We think we found a lead but we don't even have a picture to go off of. Unless... you already ID'd them?

Hill glanced at his laptop. Lucky him—someone from records

had just sent him an email with the dead thieves' backgrounds, with mug shots. All of them were convicted felons. Hill went through the attachments quickly, then responded to Jenny:

>I might...

She said:

>What do you want for them? ;)

He raised an eyebrow at the emoticon. His thoughts drifted to a place where no professional cop's thoughts should ever willingly drift to. He could picture it now: *'How about we discuss this at my place... say, over dinner?'* and her inevitable *'OMG you fucking pervert!'*

As if sensing the delay, she wrote:

>You can ask for anything.

His hands started to shake. He knew why. This didn't seem real. In fact, it seemed too good to be true.

>Are you trying to bribe an officer of the law for evidence in a current investigation?

She replied:

>No, I'm asking for an exchange that could move the investigation forward. And both of us might have something to lose if anyone else sees this conversation... of course, it all depends on what you ask for.

He struggled to type properly, having to use both hands to hold the phone steady because of all the trembling.

>What can I ask for?

She said:

>ANYTHING.

His heart jumped again.

>Oh really.

She wrote:

>Oh ya.

He decided to test the water a bit more...

>What if it's something outrageous?

She replied:

>You gonna grow some balls or what?

Annoyed, but nonetheless aroused by the curiosity and the feeling of control over this woman, he wrote:

>Fine. I want pictures.

She said:

>Ooooooh? What kind of pictures?

He wrote:

>Of you.

Immediately he received a picture file. He downloaded it and opened it. There she was, standing in a bathroom of some kind, smirking. Her jacket was unzipped and pulled back, revealing her shirt, and her chest puffed out to add emphasis to the generous size of her breasts.

"Damn," he whispered.

>Send me more.

She replied:

>LOL. Not until you hold up your end.

He immediately opened the email app on his phone, downloaded the attachments from the records department, and then sent her one. He was quick to write:

>Don't go away, doll. There're eight more.

She said:

>Guess I gotta send one for one, huh? Fair trade.

He said:

>Yeah.

She wrote:

>So what else do you want?

If Hill was dreaming, he vowed to himself he would kill any fool stupid enough to wake him.

>Lift your shirt up.

Another attachment. He quickly downloaded it. A close-up shot of her body, shirt rolled up to her collar, revealing her breasts cupped in a black sports bra. The sight nearly left him breathless. But he wasn't done. He sent her another file. Seven left.

>Take those off.

She asked:

>Take what off exactly?

Heart pounding, he wrote:

>Jacket, shirt, bra.

Another attachment. He slowly opened it and gazed upon her naked, teardrop-shaped breasts in shock. He gasped, trying to steady his breathing. His palms were sweating, he wiped them on his pants. "Jesus Christ, holy shit." He sent her another file. Six left...

They finally finished the exchange twenty minutes later.

Jenny stood naked in the bathroom, leaning over the sink. Left hand gripping the edge of the counter. Right hand holding the phone. Her whole body trembled with rage and shame.

DING!

Another message. She sighed and looked at it.

>I'm deleting this conversation but I'm keeping those pics. I suggest you do the same.

She replied:

>Sure. G2G.

He didn't respond. Good.

She sucked in air, composing herself. Then she slowly got dressed, unable to stop the shaking completely. When she was back in her clothes, she looked at her reflection in the mirror again. Anger spiked. She shattered it with her fist. "Fuck! Goddamn it! MOTHERFUCKER!" She ripped the sink out of the counter and hurled it through the toilet.

KRRAASSHH!

Porcelain exploded. Water sprayed from the countertop and the wall where the toilet bowl used to be.

Jenny stormed out of the bathroom and stomped across the dining area of the donut shop to the counter where Damian was enjoying a cup of coffee and a powdered donut. She grabbed his shoulder and yanked him off the stool. "Let's go, dipshit."

"Hey, whoa," he yelped, stumbling behind her as she dragged him to the door.

The patrons watched in silence. The cashier shouted, "Hey! You didn't pay for that!"

"Just put it on my tab," Damian yelled back. He struggled, trying to free his arm from Jenny's iron grip. "Jesus, what's your problem?"

"This isn't a bar, you asshole," the cashier replied as he hurried around the counter.

Jenny kicked the door open and dragged Damian onto the sidewalk with her. The car was parked right in front. She heaved him toward it. Damian staggered and fell onto the car's hood. "Start the fucking car."

"What happened?" Damian asked, totally confused.

"I said start the fucking car!"

The cashier burst out into the street, still yelling. "You didn't pay! You didn't—"

Jenny whirled around, drawing a pistol from the inner breast pocket of her jacket, stuck it right in the terrified cashier's face. "BACK THE FUCK OFF, YOU OBNOXIOUS, MOTHERFUCKING CUNT!"

Nearby pedestrians shrieked in terror and scattered.

"Okay! Okay!" the cashier squealed as he scrambled back into the donut shop.

Damian started the car, eager to get out of the area. "Come on!" He punched the horn. "Let's go!"

Jenny roared, "GODDAMN FUCK!" and climbed into the passenger seat.

Damian peeled off the curb, sideswiping a truck as they made their getaway down the street.

Chapter 010
Repo Madness

"What the fuck was that back there?" Damian asked as he expertly weaved through traffic.

"I don't wanna fucking talk about it," Jenny snapped. "Fucking Christ!" She banged the butt of her pistol against the dash, shouting, "Fuck! *Fuuuuuuck*!"

"Yeah, yeah, you don't wanna talk about it, but you're gonna tell me about it. And while you're telling me about it, you're gonna put that gun away before you kill yourself with it."

"You wanna know? Huh? You wanna know?"

"Yeah, I do! I want to know!"

"Fuck you. Of course you do!" She punched his shoulder. Once. Twice.

"'Don't—"

Three times.

He snarled, "Don't fucking hit me, bitch! What the fuck's up your ass?!" He parried a fourth attempt. "Fuck off!"

"Fine!" She threw her phone into his lap. "Eat it!"

Damian sighed and guided the car into an alley. Once they were at a full stop, he picked up Jenny's phone and went through the entire conversation without saying a word, all while Jenny cussed and muttered angrily under her breath, fighting back tears as she looked out the window. She never let go of the gun.

When he was finished, he sighed and dropped the phone into a vacant cup holder. "The least that piece of shit could've done is give you their personal addresses or something..."

"What?"

"Names and faces won't get us far."

"You gonna break up with me now?"

"What?"

"You happy now? You fucking got what you wanted."

"Could've done it differently. You're not your sister, and you know that."

"I don't know how the fuck she does it! I honestly fucking don't."

"Because she's a sex-crazed Looney Tune, and you aren't."

They sat in silence for a moment.

She exhaled, long and hard, then sucked in air, trying to compose herself. "Please don't break up with me."

"I'm not going to do that."

"Promise?"

"I promise I'm not gonna break up with you, Jenny."

"You're not just saying that because I'm holding a gun, are you?"

He chuckled. She did the same.

"No. No. *Govno*, Jenny. You got us something, at least. You could've gone about it differently, but it's something."

"Hill's mine."

"Hm?"

"When this is all over, and we reach the stage where we have to eliminate those bastards... you can kill as many of them as you want. I don't care." She turned her furious eyes, glistening with tears, to him. "Hill is *mine*."

He stared at her. He hated seeing her like this—too much fire, and nowhere to put it.

"Got it?"

He nodded slowly.

"Good." She tossed the gun across the dashboard. "I'm hungry. Let's get some food."

"You promise not to pull a gun on the waiter?"

She looked at him impatiently.

Damian took the gun off the dash and tossed it in the back seat. Then he shifted gears and started to back up. "Crazy bitch. You are one crazy bitch. God, I fucking love you anyway."

"I love you too," she said.

He stopped backing up and kissed her lips. Then he looked back to make sure the way back onto the street was clear. "Crazy... we're taking the drive thru just in case. I'm not taking any chances with your mood right now. *Khristos*, woman, *Khristos*."

"Okay, I get it."

They ate their food in the car near the very back of the

McRaunchie's restaurant parking lot. Most of their meal went down without either of them speaking a word. A man on the radio narrated the brutal goings-on in the fourth round of the *Zerodome Runners* holiday tournament.

"I feel raped," she said.

"Yeah."

"I... I feel like..."

"I know."

"Do you?"

"Well, no. But I can guess."

"Can you?"

He shrugged.

She finished her fries and her burger and groaned. "I can't keep eating this shit."

"It's good, though." He slurped up the last of his milkshake.

"It tastes good. That's about it." She went through the images she received from Hill, looking at each profile for any mention of cars or repossession. When she found something, she said, "Harry Roland. Aged forty-three. Worked part-time for a used car salesman named Dexter Finnegan, owner of Dexter's Used Classics on 14th and 11th. Got fired after he apparently 'repossessed' the wrong car. Pay dirt. Let's go."

Damian looked at the clock. "It's three in the morning. They're closed."

"We can still look around."

"What's the hurry? At this point, we're just gathering evidence on a dead man's associate who's probably halfway around the world."

"Might be something on his computer."

"His computer?"

"You know those machines that most businesses have these days?"

Damian scowled at her sarcastic response. "I know what a computer is, you shithead."

"Well then?"

"I'm not going to try and hack into a password-protected computer to find something we can get the owner to find for us. Computers aren't exactly my forte, you know."

"There's always a chance there *isn't* a password on it."

"Yeah, right. Maybe one percent."

"Better than zero."

Damian scowled. "Christ, you're annoying."

She smiled.

Twenty-five minutes later, they were in the Iconotto borough, a rundown area made up mostly of crumbling tenements, condemned buildings; shattered, empty lots where projects were never realized, with two-foot weeds and dull-coloured flowers filling every crack. A grassy trailer park lay a few blocks south of the dealership.

A police chopper buzzed in the sky, playing its searchlight over the borough, probably in search of Donner. Damian hadn't noticed them before, but that could simply be due to the retro-futuristic light show going on downtown. A chopper's searchlight could be easily overlooked down there.

Here, it seemed to be the only thing that moved.

Parked across the street from Dexter's Used Classics, the superhuman pair looked at the chain link fence that ran around the lot's perimeter. Cars from as far back as 1955 with hand-written price signs on their dashboards sat waiting for someone to pick them out. Beyond the parking area was an office trailer with a wraparound deck and a flag pole hitched on the roof, providing the meeting point for an overhead web of multi-colour pennant banners.

"All the lights're out," Damian said. "Big surprise."

"Now's your chance, boyo."

Damian sighed.

"Come on, it's time to make good use of that creepy shadow teleportation thing you do."

His skin tone started to darken. "Gimme a few minutes. If that computer's password-protected, don't lose your shit when I say I told you so."

"Worth a shot."

"Is it, though?"

"We've been through this already. Like, five minutes ago. And twenty minutes before that. What's with the hesitation?"

"I'm not hesitating."

"What's this, then? You'd be back by now if you weren't so hell-bent on complaining about it. Jesus."

"*Alright*, fine. I'm going." Like in the bus depot two nights before, the details of his appearance faded as his body transformed into a black, translucent phantom mass. His mouth and glowing cobalt eyes were the only prominent features on his face. He slipped under the steering wheel, beneath the dash, and in the darkness, he vanished, leaving his girlfriend alone in the car.

She shuddered. "That will never *not* be creepy."

In the office trailer, a dark figure emerged from the wall behind the computer desk. A distorted body twisted through the wall panels, dreamlike in its surreal shaping, limbs shifting in stop-motion. As more of it passed through the wall, the shadowy intruder's features reverted to something more human—or as close to 'human' as Damian Warkowski would ever be.

He approached the laptop on the desk and noted its model—something from the early 2010's, and *way* outdated. Most computers these days were holographic screens or thin folding tablets, so seeing a 2013 laptop here told him one of two things: this particular owner didn't care much for the newer stuff—and given the cars outside, that came as no surprise; or the owner wasn't very 'tech-savvy.'

He opened the laptop. Booted it up.

Password screen.

"I fucking told you so," he said when he returned to the car.

"You proud of your little accomplishment?" she asked.

"No, not really." He reclined the seat back and made himself comfortable.

"What're you doing?"

"Going to sleep. You're first watch."

"Hey, what? Why me?"

"It was your idea. Wake me when the owner shows."

She scowled. "Damian."

He ignored her.

"*Damian*," she snapped.

"What?"

"Love and kisses, baby."

He grunted in acknowledgement and fell asleep.

They're screaming again. Oh, fuck, they're screaming. All

around me. Burning... screaming... too late.

I'm too late.

Fuck. FUCK!

A gunman gets in my way. He dies faster than they do. I'm in a hurry.

They're still screaming.

Someone else tries to stop me. I break his neck.

Their helicopter is finally shot down. I hear it fall, nose slicing into an apartment building across the street. Two floors explode. A family of four will be sleeping a lot longer than they expected when they went to bed. I know this because I saw the reports.

Fuck.

A girl screams for her mommy to save her. Mommy can't talk with a support beam lying where her head used to be.

I'm coming. Just hold on.

I pass three dead cops, one dead gunman. I look up and see more from both sides. They're everywhere.

Hostages are upstairs. Screaming.

I'm in the flames, burning up. It melts my clothes into my flesh, more painful than anything else in recent memory. Hurts like a motherfucker.

The screams fade, mostly. Lisa's still screaming at the top of her lungs. I promise her I'm on my way. Not long now, Lisa.

I'm in the stairwell. Burning boards and rickety, melting frames are all that's left of the stairs. I jump. I break through the stairs and the door.

They're fucking dead. All of them. They look like wax museum exhibits on the hottest day of summer, and the A/C's broken. Flaming, shrivelling, bubbling...

Lisa's not screaming anymore.

Lisa. Where are you?

She whimpers just loud enough for me to hear her over the roar of the fire. Good girl.

I run across the room. Boot splashes through a boiling stomach and catches fire. The heat's unbearable. How the hell is she still breathing?

A flash of white blinds me the same time my eardrums suddenly rupture. Heat worse than before hits me, burns the air out of my lungs as a fiery tongue sears down my throat. My eyes explode out of their sockets. They feel like runny eggs the way they ooze down my face.

Fuck, I'm screaming! FUCK! FUCK! JESUS CHRIST!

I stumble where it's hot—and everything is hot. I can't tell if I'm sweating or melting. My skin hurts just from being near it, but now all of me is being hugged by it.

I find her. I can't see her with my sockets burned hollow, but Jesus Christ, I know it's her because the body is small and feels like something raggedy and fragile's been smashed on the floor.

Lisa.

I can feel her dying in my arms. Oh, God.

Lisa.

Daylight. Saturday, December 23rd, 2031.

Jenny shook him awake. "Hey. Hey."

Damian's eyes snapped open. He jolted forward, kicking the steering wheel with a startled gasp. Soaked in perspiration, skin squeaking on the seat. He sat naked in the driver seat, chest heaving as he breathed heavily, trembling, either from cold or fear. Wasn't sure which. Probably both. He never could keep his telekinetic clothes intact while he slept. He conjured up a thick, warm outfit just like the one he had one yesterday.

The car was dark; windows covered under a thick, grey layer of snow. Jenny had the interior light on, but the engine was off. No wonder it was so fucking cold in here.

"You were having that nightmare again."

"What nightmare?"

"The little girl. Lisa."

"How would you know?"

"I told you before that you talk in your sleep."

"You did?"

She nodded. "Especially when you're having nightmares like that one."

Damian sighed and fell back against the seat. He closed his eyes and created another telekinetic layer to wrap himself in. "Why's it so fucking cold in here?"

"I turned the car off a few hours ago. Drains the battery."

"And the light doesn't?"

"Not nearly as much as keeping the heat on. Here." Her skin

started to glow as she started to radiate heat. He could already feel it. Oh, the advantages of having a pyrokinetic girlfriend.

"I'm going back to sleep."

"Might as well stay awake," she said. "Pretty sure he's here."

Damian opened his eyes and looked around the interior, but of course, he couldn't see through the layer of snow packed over the car. "Uh." He indicated the snow.

"Yeah, yeah, keep your pants on."

Jenny reached over and touched the glass with her index finger. Channeled her heat through it. The snow broke away, slid down the door, revealing a view of the used car lot. He saw that the gate was open, and a green pickup truck that wasn't there before sat parked in front of the office portable. Everything blanketed in white, and the snow was *still* coming down. The owner was busying himself with wiping it off his merchandise with a brush and scraper.

He turned to Jenny. "When did he come in?"

"About twenty minutes ago, if that *was* his engine I heard."

"Why didn't you wake me?"

"I just did."

"No, smartass, when he first arrived."

"You weren't muttering then."

He looked at her.

"Besides, you're cute when you're asleep." After a beat, she quickly added, "When you're not having PTSD nightmares, anyway."

He sighed again. "Get your phone." He opened the door. "Let's go." His boot sank into almost a full foot of snow. The plows hadn't come through this neighborhood yet. Shocker.

Their breath plumed in front of their faces as they trudged across the street toward the lot. Snow crunched underfoot until they hit the shovelled sidewalk. The owner had already run his snow blower through the lot, apparently. Now he was brushing snow off a yellow 1963 Chrysler AP5 Valiant with his back facing them, dressed in snow pants and a flannel coat, black scarf and matching toque.

"Excuse me!" Damian called out to him.

He turned around. He scrutinized the two of them for the briefest of moments before smiling warmly. "G'morning! I'm not quite open yet, but feel free to look around."

"Actually, we wanted to talk to you."

He looked at Jenny, then back at Damian. "About what?"

"You're Dexter, right?"

"Yeah... that's my name on that there sign. What did you wanna talk about?"

Jenny showed him Harry Roland's photo on her phone.

Dexter's eyes turned cautious. "Who are you?"

"Private investigators," Damian said, and offered his hand in greeting. "Jim Donovan."

Dexter tentatively shook his hand. "Nice to meet ya..."

"Recognize him?" Damian asked, indicating the photo.

"Yeah, uh... he worked here for a while. Roland, I think? Yeah, Roland. Harry Roland?"

"Right. Yeah."

Jenny tucked her phone away in her jacket.

Dexter exhaled and said, "We can talk in my office. Coffee should be just about ready."

Damian nodded slowly. "Lead the way."

They went over to the trailer. Like a gentleman, Dexter opened the door and stepped aside, allowing them first entry before coming in behind them and shutting the door. He immediately went over to the coffee table and checked the machine. "Almost." He went around the couple behind the reception counter. The door to his office was right behind him. "So what do you guys need to know, exactly?"

"Anything and everything you've got on him," Damian said. "Addresses, employment history, why he was fired, etcetera."

"Got a warrant?"

"No."

"Then I can't help you."

"You can't, but you will."

"Excuse me?"

Damian leaned over the counter. "You heard about that bank robbery?"

"Yeah...?"

"You'd have to have been living under a rock not to."

"What about it? You implying Roland had something to do with it?"

"He most definitely *did* have something to do with it."

"How would you know?"

"He's in a police morgue because of it."

Dexter's mouth hung open momentarily as the news sunk in. "Doesn't prove anything."

"Dental records do."

"Dental records?"

"Only way he could be identified. He kinda got blown up."

"Jesus. And how do you know this? Did *you* blow him up?"

"It's complicated," Damian said, stifling a chuckle, "but fact of the matter is, Roland and seven other men are dead. One of them is still out there, and we need to find him."

"Why should I help you?"

Damian was running out of patience. He grabbed Dexter by the scarf, pulled him in real close, and poked his jawbone with the muzzle of a telekinetic energy pistol. "Because if you don't, I'm going to get *agitated*."

"Okay. Okay. Okay." Dexter whimpered, "Alright, I-I'll help you. Jesus. Holy shit."

Damian released him. He flew back against the wall, chest heaving, eyes bulging in terror. "Holy shit, Jesus Christ."

"Breathe," Damian said.

"O-okay, uh... uh... h-his records are in the office." He indicated the door to his office. "I'll be right back, okay? Please don't shoot me."

"Not if you cooperate," Damian said. "Go on."

Dexter stumbled into his office and shut the door.

"Jenny."

Jenny looked at her boyfriend, then at the pistol he offered her. "You think?" she asked.

"Oh, I know." He cocked his head to the window above the coffee station.

She sighed and stepped out of the trailer. Down the steps, looking both ways. She turned, slogged through the snow around back. She saw Dexter leaping out of the farthest window at the other end. He tucked and rolled through the snow, hopped to his feet, and started running in the opposite direction.

BKAM!

Jenny put a round through his right leg. Dexter screamed and fell on his face.

COBALT CHRISTMAS: A COBALT ROGUE STORY

*

Jenny tied him to a folding chair in his office. He didn't struggle long, given that Damian had his blackish-blue energy revolver, his signature Model 500 with a 4-inch barrel, in his face most of the time; but he didn't stop crying.

"You shot me!" Dexter cried in disbelief. "You... y-y-you shot me!"

"Technically, *she* shot you," Damian replied, cocking his head toward Jenny.

"You said—"

"I said I wouldn't shoot you if you cooperated. *If...* you *cooperated.* Trying to escape through the window before we can get information from you isn't cooperation, Dexter. That's just difficult assholery. Neither of us are in the mood for that kind of shit right now, so please, for the love of Christ, start talking, or pull up some files on your computer. *Cooperate.*"

"What do you people want with me?"

"We already told you. We want everything you've got on Roland."

"I'm not authorized to—to do that! Not unless you've got a warrant, o-or something."

"I've got something better than a fucking warrant." Damian thumbed back the hammer on his energy revolver for dramatic effect. "You think *she* hurt you? *I* will hurt you. That tunnel in your leg's gonna look like a scratch compared to what this thing will do to your face!"

"Okay! Okay! JESUS!"

"I'm running out of patience, motherfucker!"

"I'm tied to a goddamn chair! I can't..."

"Yeah?"

"I can't move. Please, I'll do what you ask!"

"*Yeah?*"

"Yes!" Dexter nodded furiously. "I will! I'll do it! Just puh-please don't kill me!"

Damian telekinetically severed the ropes around Dexter, who immediately teetered out of his chair and hit the floor.

"Get the files, fuckhead!"

Dexter scrambled around his desk and opened his laptop, breathing heavily. His snowsuit stuck to his sweat-soaked clothes as he struck the keyboard with trembling fingers. It took him a couple tries, but he eventually got the password in correctly and started going through his computer's archives. A minute later, the printer started buzzing, spitting out sheets onto the tray.

When it was done, Jenny took the small stack of papers and flipped through them. Then she gave Damian a nod of approval.

"Was that so hard?" Damian asked Dexter.

Dexter curled up on the floor, whimpering.

Damian to Jenny: "Let's go."

She followed him out of the office, apologizing to Dexter as she stepped over him.

Howdlin Dairy

Campbell recruited two men for their first stakeout. Skirting the north edge of the Varding industrial district was Howdlin Dairy, the first on Campbell's list. From the outside, the plant looked like a normal plant. Nothing out of the ordinary from far off.

Their observation point was on the gravel roof of a steelworks plant. Campbell had himself a rifle scope. Probationary Officer Conners, the most inexperienced of the three by a long shot, leaned over the railing, staring at the plant across the river with a pair of old binoculars without making a sound despite the relentless wind chill. The third cop, Officer Bart, was a cyborg with obvious eyeball implants undergoing the process of scanning the area in infrared.

Not much that Campbell could do from here. He tucked the scope in his pocket and said to the other two, "You guys keep watch. I'm going in for a closer look."

"Careful, sir." Conners' genuine concern put a smile on Campbell's face.

"Relax, kid. I've been doing this for a few years now."

Chapter 011
House Call

In the car, Damian asked her, "Where to?"

She sifted through the papers and found his address and contact information on the third page. "453 Cammer's Road. Same district, uhh... just a few blocks up ahead, I think." She leaned over and entered the address into the GPS. The digital map confirmed her hunch. "Seven blocks up the road."

They pulled up in front of an old bungalow with a fenced yard and wood showing through its scaling, faded yellow paint. The windows were netted and the screen door was wide open. A police cruiser was parked outside on the curb.

"What a shit hole." Damian stepped into the street and looked around. The other houses weren't looking much better. Rundown and abandoned, all with chain link fences and windows that were broken, boarded up, or netted. A dog barked in the distance. A cold wind whistled through the street, swinging front yard gates open and shut.

Jenny got out and took note of the cruiser. "Looks like we're in for an awkward meet-up, huh?"

"Sure, sure. We can just tell him to—"

Crack!

The couple stiffened. They exchanged looks. Definitely a gunshot. They rushed to the gate—

—and that's when the front door opened. A highway patrolman—or someone dressed like one—stepped out onto the porch. He stopped dead when he saw Damian and Jenny on the sidewalk.

Beat.

He went for his gun—

KABLAM!

Damian blasted him with a telekinetic revolver, sent him flying back into the house. The shot echoed through the neighborhood.

Another dog from a block or so away started barking.

"Jesus!" Jenny exclaimed.

"What? He was gonna shoot me."

"Christ, Damian. He saw that we were armed."

"Did he?"

"I mean... I don't know... fuck, what're we gonna do?"

"Hope he's still alive, for now."

He was still alive. Damian and Jenny could hear him moaning in pain.

"See? He's fine."

Jenny heaved an exasperated sigh and looked at the other cruiser. She exhaled sharply, relieved to find it empty. "You know better! You can't just shoot a cop first thing like that. What if he had a partner with him?"

"He didn't."

"Did you know that he didn't?"

"Obviously."

"Why don't I believe you?"

"Don't really care if you do right now." Damian kicked the gate open, crossed the yard up, up the steps, into the house...

The cop was spread-eagled on the floor with a smoking cavity in his stomach. Moaning. Barely alive—alive enough to process that he was in danger, and thus reached for his gun...

Damian entered the foyer and telekinetically sent the patrolman's pistol spinning across the floor toward the back of the house.

The cop groaned in dismay and looked at Damian. "The fuck..."

"Don't move."

"You can't shoot a fuckin' cop... crazy..."

Damian looked around. A staircase leading to the second floor on his left. In front of him, a corridor leading to the kitchen in the back. To his right, the wide entryway to the living room, inside of which sat an old lady in a rocking chair with two bullet holes in her chest.

"Why'd you shoot her?" Damian asked the cop.

The cop was busy looking at the smoking hole in his stomach in disbelief. "You fucking... shot... me..."

Damian leaned forward and pressed his foot down on his

pelvis. The toe of his boot dug into the wound, making the cop scream. "Answer my fucking question."

"Fuck! I'm a cop!"

"I don't give a shit if you *are* a cop, you dirty asshole," Damian snapped. "Answer. My. Fucking. Question. *Govnyuk.*"

"Fuck you, you goddamn freak!"

Damian added pressure on the wound.

The cop's vocals grinded in agony, right before he howled.

"Talk, goddamn you!" Damian bounced his heel off his crotch. "*TALK!*"

Jenny put a hand on her boyfriend's shoulder. "Hey. Hey. Easy."

"Oh, hello," the old lady said from her rocking chair.

Startled, Damian and Jenny looked over at her.

The old lady smiled sweetly. "Are you here to see Harry?"

Jenny slowly closed the gap between them, leaving Damian with the cop. The smell of old people mixed with some putrid odour reached her nostrils, and only intensified the closer she came. She said tentatively, "Mrs. Roland...?"

"Harry's not here right now, but I can let him know you came to see him... when he gets home."

Jenny stopped two feet in front of Mrs. Roland. She indicated the bullet wounds. "You're hurt. You need to get to the hospital."

"Hurt?" Mrs. Roland looked down at the black circles in her grey sweater. "Oh, no. No, no, no, child. Don't worry about those."

"Mrs. Roland, you've been shot."

"When?"

Jenny looked at Damian, who shrugged. She turned back to Mrs. Roland. "Can you stand?"

"I haven't stood on my own two legs in a long time, child." Mrs. Roland chuckled. "If you see Harry, can you tell him to hurry home? I really need to pee."

Jenny looked down at the dark stains on the carpet beneath Mrs. Roland's chair. That would've been what the putrid smell was. "Jesus."

"Do you know when lunch is? I'm hungry and I can't get up."

Jenny dialled 911 on her cell phone.

"What the hell are you doing?" Damian asked.

"This woman needs a goddamn ambulance."

"Looks like a lost cause to me."

Jenny turned and glared at him.

"Or not," he said. He looked at the patrolman.

The patrolman was lying still, eyes staring lifelessly at the ceiling.

"Shit," Damian said.

"What?" Jenny asked.

"Cop's dead."

Jenny shook her head slowly, her expression full of disapproval and concern. "Hello, operator? I'm on 453 Cammer's Road and I need an ambulance. An old lady's been shot and I think she might have been left by herself for a couple days before we found her. S-she doesn't seem to have eaten or anything..."

"Oh, hello," Mrs. Roland said with a cheerful twinkle in her old, tired eyes. "Are you here to see Harry?"

Jenny looked at Damian again.

Damian shook his head slowly.

"He's not here right now, but I can tell him you stopped by," Mrs. Roland said. Then, confused, she looked down at the dark crimson holes in her chest. "Oh, my... oh, dear..." She touched her wounds with a trembling, skeletal hand. "Oh..."

Jenny pressed her hands over Mrs. Roland's bullet wounds. "Don't talk. Just breathe. The ambulance is on its way."

Damian felt something... strange. Eyes on his neck. He turned around and saw a second patrolman sitting casually on the hood of the cruiser, arms folded across his chest, aviator sunglasses reflecting the mid-morning sun, cigarette burning in front of his face. Blonde. Hollow cheeks. He wasn't going for his gun or calling for backup. He wasn't doing anything. That made Damian feel something close to *nervous*.

Damian crossed the porch and down the steps, leaving Jenny inside with her futile attempts to keep Mrs. Roland conscious.

The patrolman pushed off the cruiser's hood and positioned himself behind the gate, arms still crossed.

Damian stopped in the middle of the yard. "Who the hell are you?"

"Don't recognize me?" the patrolman asked.

"All you boys in blue look the same to me," Damian replied. He scrutinized the patrolman, trying to match his features to something in his memory. Something about him *was* familiar...

"Allow me to pull a Clark Kent, then." The patrolman took off his sunglasses and gloated at Damian with mocking hazelnut eyes.

That's when it clicked. "You," Damian snarled.

Drake—or Donner, as Damian knew him. He shook his sunglasses and smirked. "Bingo."

Damian telekinetically pulled Donner off his feet, through the gate. Donner lurched across the yard and slammed into Damian's fist. Damian caught him by the collar and drew an energy blade, poised, ready to decapitate the son of a bitch.

Calmly, Donner said, "Do you really wanna do that?"

"Yes."

"Really? You wanna decapitate a police officer?"

"You're not a fucking police officer."

"They don't know that," he said, pointing over his shoulder at a couple of kids standing in the front yard of their house with their mother talking on the phone behind them. "All they see is a crazy person about to kill his second cop this morning."

Damian didn't falter.

"You wanna know what's *really* funny? I know what you're thinking. You're thinking that the guy you killed in there wasn't a cop, but here's the thing: *that* guy *was* a real cop."

"Bullshit."

"I have eyes and ears everywhere, Mr. Donovan. Or should I say... Damian Warkowski?"

Damian said nothing.

"I knew it was you. I've heard the stories. I remember what you did to my lab in the tropics. Memory's a bit fuzzy about our first meeting, but... eh. The way you were described to me... the way I imagined you... the things I always heard and saw on the radio and the TV reports. I heard you were dead, but at Kartovski's, the way you fought? All that power? There's no way it couldn't have been you. For a guy in some sorta witness protection, you're *very* conspicuous."

"Right."

"Our mutual acquaintance at the dealership made you an even easier find. We got you, boy. You've just been stung."

"Fuck you."

Donner made a bad journalistic impression as he said, "I'm

Chris Hansen with—"

Damian's blade flashed for his throat. It bit into Donner's left arm instead, while his right hand drew a pistol and put a bullet in Damian's face.

Damian felt the bullet whiz through his brain and out the back of his skull and collapsed to the ground.

Donner staggered back with the blade embedded in his arm, shooting Damian a few more times just for the satisfaction it brought him. "Huh! Fucker! Not quite *that* fast, are you?"

VMM...VMM...VMM...

The blade in his arm started to throb with its own pulse, flashing in sync. Donner looked at it, perplexed. The blade started to get hotter. His skin around the blade began to sizzle. He grimaced, straining as the heat intensified, cooked his arm from the inside out. "What the f—"

KAPOWW!

The blade ignited like a pipe bomb. A black, rapidly expanding fireball blasted Donner skyward, sprayed bits of the fence across the street, blew in the windows of Mrs. Roland's house. Inside, Jenny made a startled shout and ducked to avoid flying glass.

The mother on the other side rushed her children into their house.

Donner's flaming, twisted body twirled awkwardly in midair, pivoted through the windshield of the police cruiser. His left hand landed on an icy gutter. Black debris and pieces of red flesh speckled the snow around the yard.

Jenny scrambled to Mrs. Roland's aid. "You okay?"

Mrs. Roland's eyes were shut. Jenny checked for a pulse. Nothing.

Sirens wailed not too far off. The neighborhood echo made it impossible to determine where they were coming from. Maybe everywhere...

Damian slowly pulled back into consciousness as the tunnel in his skull closed itself up and all damaged nerves, muscles, skin, and grey matter regenerated. He could feel it all filling in the space in his head, shifting about, thickening...

He wiped his bloody face on his sleeve and stood upright, unsteady. The world was spinning and his head pounded. Hard to find his footing. Even harder to get a good sense of direction after he'd been shot in the head. Smoke filled his blurry vision. His hearing faded in and out. The approaching sirens and the confused chatter of frightened neighbours—

"Damian!" Jenny shouted from the blown-out living room window. "What the hell happened out there?"

"Our puzzle piece... fell right into our lap."

"What?"

Damian glanced at the police cruiser. Donner was still splayed across the hood and slumped over the dashboard.

Jenny hopped down the front steps. "Mrs. Roland's dead."

"Typical."

"We gotta get out of here."

"Not without that fucking *pizda* in the trunk."

"Who?"

"*Him!*" Damian pointed at Donner's body. "He's already healing." He stumbled toward the cruiser, still unable to totally balance himself. "Come on."

"Who's he?" Jenny asked.

"Our runaway paycheck."

"Oh."

They crossed the sidewalk and stepped in front of the cruiser. "Grab a leg," Damian said.

The sirens were getting louder.

"Hurry up."

They each grabbed a leg and pulled Donner out of the windshield and down the front of the cruiser. Then Donner rolled on his back, smiling, holding up two live grenades! "Surprise, motherfuckers!"

Jenny froze up.

The grenades went off with a cacophonous *KAPOW*, spraying shrapnel into—

—the telekinetic shield Damian had formed at the last possible split second.

The blast rebounded off the shield back at Donner. The front half of the cruiser came apart like wet cardboard. The fuel tank ignited, launching the trunk skyward. Fireballs rolled across the street and curled into the sky behind Damian's shield.

A stunned Jenny turned to her boyfriend, chest heaving. "Nice save..."

"It pays to think fast sometimes."

Jenny stared at the flaming wreck on the curb. She moved her arm to the side, dismissing the flames. Her pyrokinesis caused the flames to recede. The smouldering wreck had bits of Donner spread all over it. "We can't take him like this."

Damian looked at Donner's severed foot lying in the middle of the street. "No... but we can *make* him come to us. Maybe."

"How?" she asked with growing curiosity as she watched Damian pick up Donner's foot.

"There are many types of immortals in this world, my love," Damian said, "and the best way to find out which one each one is... is by stealing their severed limbs."

"You're joking... right?"

Damian smirked and waggled Donner's foot. "Who, me?"

She sighed.

The sirens indicated law enforcement was a block away, maybe less.

"We need to get outta here," she said urgently.

"Yeah, yeah."

Damian jogged to his car. Jenny scooted across the hood and climbed into the passenger seat. The two of them sped off down the street and disappeared around the first corner they reached just as a duo of police cruisers were stopping in front of the Roland household.

Varding District

Campbell had just exited Varding with Conners and Bart in his 1984 Mercedes-Benz 190E. Despite the car's age and visible wear, it was slick without being slippery—a must in the worsening road conditions. It was starting to snow again, which meant traffic would be a bitch to get through.

"Where to?" Conners asked from the passenger seat.

"Lucky for us, there aren't very many dairy farms in this part of town. Unless our perps were willing to put the extra effort into shipping these tainted products from overseas or something, it won't be long before we've struck gold." He fired up a cigarette. "Bart's got the list. What's next on the list, Bart?"

"Monterey Dairy," Bart answered behind Conners.

"Then Monterey Dairy's exactly where we're headed."

"Way out there?" Conners asked. "In the pines?"

"That's right, out in the sticks, fellas. It'll take us a couple hours to get there. I suggest you catch up on your sleep while you still can."

Chapter 012
A Foot in the Door

"Agh," a regenerated Drake groaned as he rolled off the flaming police cruiser and collided with the road sludge in a splattering heap. "Jesus, fuck."

"We got a live one over here!" Two cops rushed to his aid. They dragged him away from the burning car.

Two android paramedics approached with a stretcher and had Drake lifted onto it. They checked his vitals and inspected him for wounds, and weren't particularly astonished to find him in almost pristine health—they *were* androids, after all—with one glaring exception, which one of them announced matter-of-factly, "His left foot is missing. Has anyone seen it?"

"What?" Drake jolted upright and looked at the stump where his left foot should have been. "Those fuckers! They... they stole my foot! THEY STOLE MY FOOOOOOOOT!"

Damian and Jenny's Safe House

Damian was sitting on the arm of a recliner eating a bag of salted peanuts, watching in amusement as Donner's severed foot hopped around, trying to kick its way through the steel blast door. "It's not stopping. Look."

Jenny sighed and looked up from her phone. She watched Drake's foot's feeble attempts to escape, then said to Damian, "You sicken me sometimes, you know that?"

Damian chuckled. "Doesn't stop you from loving me though, does it?"

"Eh."

Drake's foot gave up and started hopping in circles as if it were frustrated.

Damian laughed mockingly, watching it stomp about. "Getting tired yet?"

"Damian, put it in a cage."

"Why?"

"It's giving me the creeps."

"How can something like *that* give you the creeps?"

"*Look* at it!"

"I am."

"It's fucking weird!"

"I've seen worse." Damian popped a handful of peanuts in his mouth.

"So have I, but that doesn't mean I want to watch this guy's severed foot hop around our fucking safe house like this."

Damian sighed. He telekinetically lifted the foot off the floor and hurled it into a small dog crate. Then he shut the door and locked it. The foot banged around, struggling to escape its much smaller confines.

"Satisfied?"

"No," she said.

Damian got up and kicked the crate down the stairs into the basement—separated from the garage by a concrete wall. Then he slammed the door shut and asked her, "*Now* are you satisfied?"

"Yes, dear," she said sarcastically, "I'm perfectly satisfied knowing that the severed foot of an immortal psycho killer has gone sentient and is now banging around in a flimsy Tupperware cage beneath us."

"Spoilsport," he said.

"Can't we just get rid of it? Why bring it with us?"

"To lure him out. He'll be wanting his foot back, and when he does... *BAM*! We nail the fucker and collect the reward."

"That simple, huh?"

"That simple. Who the fuck would want to hobble around town on a peg leg?"

"Somehow I doubt the success ratio of this plan."

"I don't need your pessimism right now. It's a solid plan."

"No, it isn't. We don't have very many safe houses left to retreat to should everything go against your plan. And what's stopping him from sending a task force here to get his foot for him?"

He scowled at her.

"Did you even *think* about that possibility?"

"Shut up."

"Uh-huh. That's what I thought."

Damian switched on the TV and flicked to the news channel.

After about five minutes, a report came on about the incident at the Roland household. "Two suspects in the shooting are still at large. One officer was found dead at the scene and one more was rushed to Armaliker's Hospital, where he is now recovering in stable condition."

"Perfect," Damian said. He took out his phone and called Hill.

"Hill's office."

"It's me," he said.

"What do you want?" Hill asked.

"I found the fucker."

"The missing bank robber?"

"No, Santa Claus," he answered sarcastically. "*Yes*, the bank robber, you fucking idiot. He's the so-called cop at Armaliker's."

"You honestly expect me to believe that after what you've done?"

"What'd I do?"

"You shot a fucking cop, you fucking idiot!"

"Fuck him! He was dirty."

"Ten years on the force. Wife, two kids, a perfect record. Bullshit he was dirty."

"He was working for the bank robber."

"Right, and I'm the second coming of Jesus."

Dismissing Hill's sarcasm, Damian asked, "Did you get an official statement from the guy?"

"Don't dodge the question, you little shit."

"We can talk about that sorry statistic when I get there. Did you get a statement from the other one?"

"Not yet. He was too busy screaming and yelling. Nurses had to put him under."

"He's unconscious?"

"Yeah, no thanks to you. Apparently you stole his foot?"

"I did."

"Why?"

"Because he's *that* kind of immortal."

"There are different *kinds* now?"

"Yeah, three or four: one who can sprout new parts, one who can live forever but doesn't have the rejuvenation capabilities—and can die like any other human; and one who needs the part that's been cut off in order to heal. There might be more. I don't remember."

"I'm not following..."

"Look, I'll explain when I get there. Right now, you need to trust me."

Hill scoffed.

"Yeah, yeah, before you say it, I know that's hard to do. But *trust me*, you *want*—*nyet*, you *need* to put that son of a bitch under heavy guard. You understand? He's dangerous."

"I'll humour you. But you're gonna have to come down here for questioning. Right now I've got the Captain breathing up my ass wondering why I haven't arrested you for murdering a cop! And for fuck's sake, bring that asshole's foot with you!"

"Fine." Damian hung up and looked at Jenny.

"Bad idea," she said.

"How much of that did you hear from over there?"

"All of it. It's a trap. They're gonna put us down for that cop."

"They can fucking try."

"Why didn't you just wound him? Why did you have to be so fucking quick to kill him?"

"Hey, he drew on me first."

"That's not gonna stand in a court of law, Damian!"

"Hey, now." Damian placed his hands on her cheeks and kissed her. "If I'm not back in two hours—"

She swatted his hands away and exclaimed, "What? You gonna tell me to leave? Pack my shit up and go?"

"Actually, I was going to say 'wait longer, then bail me out,' but if you really want to..."

She sighed and drew a few spikes of hair behind her ear. She couldn't help but chuckle at his joke. "You're ridiculous..."

"I've gotten myself out of worse scenarios. The proof is in the basement. They can't touch me."

"What do you think you're gonna prove to them by reattaching a guy's foot?"

"I'll prove he's an immortal. The same immortal I fought on the plane. The very same immortal who escaped..."

Damian went down into the basement and approached the cage. It was still shaking from its prisoner's struggles to break free. Damian looked through the door and squinted at what he saw.

The foot was now a leg curled up awkwardly within the small

space.

"What the fuck?" he said. He opened the door and dumped the leg on the floor. It wriggled like a fish out of water. Damian drew an energy blade and sliced through its ankle. He dropped the foot back into its cage and threw the leg into a nearby trash can. To ensure it wouldn't get free, he strapped the lid down with hooked bungee cords. When he was done, he stood there and watched the can wobble back and forth. He booted it into a corner. It stopped moving.

He scoffed and shook his head. "Fucking weird."

He went upstairs with the dog crate.

"What was that noise?" Jenny asked.

He held up the crate and chuckled. "Evil's afoot."

She scowled, annoyed by his pun. "Get outta here, you moron."

He kissed her cheek and said, "Love you."

She giggled, "Piss off!" and smacked his ass on his way to the lift—hidden behind a false wall in the narrow foyer's closet. He descended to the garage and passed the armoury on his way to the Shelby Cobra. A few parking spaces down, an old 2017 Honda Rebel 500 motorcycle sat collecting dust. Its once glossy metallic black sheen dulled by the silver layers of time and neglect. A sad sight and a damn shame. If he wasn't carrying a dog crate with him, Damian would take the bike to the hospital. "Next time, baby."

"It's a trap," His mind repeated what Jenny had said.

No shit, he thought.

Chapter 013
Foot Race

Afrókrema HQ

The minute Drake's hospitalization came up in the news, Colonel James Fairman nearly had a heart attack right there in his office. The possibility of that heart attack became more imminent when he received a call on the private line. Only two people have access to that line...

He composed himself and answered, "Colonel Fairman's office."

A man's voice said through a modulator, "Why is Drake in police custody?"

"They don't know that he's impersonating an officer yet. He's a good soldier. He'll get out of there."

"No excuses."

"Please, sir, he's an essential part of Project Catalyst. Without him, the operation is—"

"The operation is compromised if he talks. I told you when you hired him that we cannot afford any leaks."

"He's no threat to us unless we make him one."

"He had his chance. Now it's time you gave *her* a chance."

"Sir—"

"I'll hear no more excuses from you, Colonel. I have just as much riding on this as you do. Our dear Murder Queen is on standby. Handle it, quickly, or I might have to add another name to her ever-growing list."

Click!

Hung up.

"Goddamn it!" Fairman growled as he called his secretary on the phone.

"Yes, sir?" she answered.

"You're aware of Drake's hospitalization?"

"Yes, sir."

"Arrange a special visitor for him. We can't risk any of this getting out."

Location Unknown

It was a shitty motel in a shitty part of town. The motel's electric sign glared through the window blinds, laying narrow, hot pink slits over the curved back of a naked woman lying face down on the bed, snoring into the pillow. Her left hand touched the floor, gripping a pistol, index finger resting on the trigger guard.

Her cell phone rang on the bedside table. She snorted, and considered letting it go to voicemail. The flowery ringtone rang on and on, and then finally silenced as the call went to voicemail. She muttered in her half-sleep, allowing herself to fall back into the full embrace of her dreams.

Then the phone rang again.

She groaned and groped around the table's surface for it. Found it. She rolled on her side and answered, "What."

Fairman's secretary on the other end: "Armaliker's hospital. Drake. I'll send you the mug shot. If you can't get him out, you have permission to terminate on the premises. Deadline's in one hour. Three times the usual rate."

"That's nice."

"Well?"

"What?"

"Do you accept?"

She yawned and pushed herself into a crossed-legged sitting position. She pulled a mess of crimson hair from her face and said, "At three times the rate for this broke gal, you better believe I accept."

She hung up. Crawled out of bed and went into the bathroom where she discovered a restrained man in a gimp suit filling her bathtub. She looked at him and said, "Oh, yeah."

The gimp muttered something under his oxygen mask, hissing at her.

"You can go home now," she said.

Armaliker's Hospital

Damian picked a spot in the underground parking lot beneath the hospital. He got out and found himself immediately surrounded by a dozen cops in militarized combat suits armed with assault rifles, all pointed at him. Sergeant Hill emerged from behind the line with his hands buried in the pockets of his coat and a cigarette burning from the corner of his lips. "You ought to know the drill by now, Blue."

Damian didn't bother raising his hands. He shut the driver side door and slowly moved to the rear door. "I'm getting the foot."

Hill scoffed and signalled his men to hold fire.

Damian lifted the crate for Hill to see. By now, the foot had regenerated its leg up to the thigh, and was still wriggling around within its tiny prison. Damian shook the crate up and down. "Express delivery. Didn't have time to wrap a pretty bow on it. Sorry."

Hill squinted, peering into the front of the crate. He didn't look astonished or even the least bit disgusted to see Drake's leg cramped in there. "Still doesn't beat the sight of you swallowing your own guts."

Damian shrugged. "Am I still under arrest?"

"Until you can prove something, yeah. You just brought the severed foot of your latest victim to the hospital they're staying at."

"He still under?"

"Yeah."

"Your first clue, Sergeant: I stole his *foot*. There's a whole leg in here."

"For all I know, you cut off someone else's leg to further your own little agenda. Which wouldn't surprise me, honestly."

"Right. Well then, let me enlighten you." Damian unlatched the crate's door and dumped the leg on the ground. The other officers recoiled in disgust. A rookie rushed behind a support beam and threw up.

The leg stood upright and started hopping toward the elevator. Two cops jumped out of its way, watching in shock and astonishment.

Damian briskly followed it, asking Hill as he passed him, "Coming, or are you gonna sit this one out?"

Hill frowned and followed, barking orders for his men to split up: "Three of you with me, the rest—take the stairs."

The leg hopped up and down in front of the elevator panel. Damian hit the top arrow for it. The doors opened, and the leg went in. Damian, Hill, and three of his men grouped together in the elevator car.

"What floor?" Damian asked.

Hill said, "Third."

Damian hit F3, and the group stood in silence as the elevator lurched upward. Bad renditions of classic Christmas carols played on tinny speakers. Drake's disembodied leg hopped up and down in front of the doors in anticipation.

Hill glanced at the leg and said, "That thing's giving me the creeps."

"Thought it didn't beat the sight of me swallowing my own guts?" Damian asked. "Have you lost your nerve, *robkiy*?"

"Do I want to know what you just called me?"

"I don't know. Do you?"

Hill sniffed, grunted. "I said it doesn't beat that; I didn't say it wasn't fucked up in its own right."

"Seen worse," one of Hill's men said.

"What was that?" Hill snapped.

"I didn't say anything, sir."

"Uh-huh."

Ding!

The elevator opened to a busy floor. Hospital staff rushed to and fro to tend to their patients. Afternoon rush hour. That didn't stop Drake's leg from hopping into traffic.

A woman shrieked. A startled nurse swerved her wheelchair-bound patient out of the way.

The corridor had exploded into anarchy as people either scrambled away from Drake's leg or stood/sat out of its path, watching it in stunned silence.

"Goddamn it." Hill bolted out of the elevator after it. "Police business! Police business! Nothing to worry about, people. Just returning a patient's lost property. Ricky, crowd control!"

One of Hill's men took it upon himself to try and assure the startled masses in the halls that everything was fine.

Damian chuckled and followed Hill down the corridor, flanked by the other two cops.

Drake's leg kicked through the double door entrance of the emergency ward and bounded past reception, inciting more screams. Hill was in hot pursuit, shouting half-assed assurances to the mortified onlookers.

A nurse approached him, frantic. "Sir, what the hell is this?! What's going on?"

"Police officer, ma'am." He shoved her out of the way. "Step aside!"

Damian and the two cops dashed by the fallen nurse.

Drake's leg bounded down the corridor. A nurse shrieked. A doctor dropped his tray, spilling medication everywhere. A stretcher burst through one of the exits with half a dozen EMTs around it rushing a patient to the nearest operating table, squealing into the hall toward the leg. Drake's leg launched itself in the air, bounced off the patient's chest, and flipped over a startled EMT's head.

Hill threw himself flat against the wall, allowing the EMTs to pass him with their patient, then continued his pursuit. He couldn't see Drake's leg. He rushed to the next intersection in the corridors and looked both ways. To his left, the exit; to his right, a path formed by terrified staff, and Drake's leg entering a room. The path started to fill in as people gathered around the room, curious and disturbed. "Move!" Hill shouted as he pushed through the crowd. "Get out of my goddamn way!"

He shoved an elderly patient aside and stepped into Drake's room. Drake was still unconscious, still only had one foot, and his disembodied, seemingly possessed leg was standing upright at the foot of the bed.

Hill couldn't focus with all the chatter going on outside. He kicked the door shut and approached the bed. He looked at the leg, then at Drake. "What the fuck are you?"

The door burst open. Hill whirled—

—Damian was in the process of shutting the door in the faces of his police escorts. "See? I told you so."

"Look again, genius," Hill said, indicating the stump at Drake's ankle. "That entire leg can't fit onto an ankle stump."

Damian looked out the windows and saw a group of wide-eyed patients looking in. He drew all the blinds shut and then went back to the bed. He grabbed the leg, drew an energy blade, and severed the foot at the ankle. Flecks of blood streaked across the bed sheets.

"Jesus!" Hill exclaimed, recoiling.

Damian tossed the leg in a nearby trash bin and pressed the foot against Drake's ankle stump. And waited. Waited.

Waited...

"It's not doing anything," Hill said, frowning.

"Give it a minute."

"Should I cuff you now or later?"

"Give it a minute, goddamn it."

Beat.

He let go of the foot. It stuck to the ankle stump.

Astonished, Hill leaned in for a closer look. He saw the skin tissue from Drake's leg and his severed foot starting to glue together in small, thin strands. The muscle tissue slithered beneath the skin, tangling together...

"Do you believe me now?" Damian asked.

Hill straightened, still staring at the foot as Drake's regeneration abilities fastened it to the stump. "Yeah, sure. But that still doesn't absolve you for shooting that other cop."

"That cop was dirty."

"*Was* he? Or did Mr. Immortal #2 here force him into helping him? Maybe he threatened his family—"

"They killed a harmless old lady together, and you want me to feel sympathy for one of them? Are you fuckin' kidding me, Hill? Open your eyes, and *look* at the goddamned evidence." He pointed at Drake.

Hill looked at Drake, still doubtful. "You know, *I'll* be the one who'll have to let his family know he was killed in the line of duty. Corrupt or not."

"That's your problem," Damian said.

Hill glared at him.

"You have your man now," Damian said, "now pay up. We're done here."

Hill took out two pairs of handcuffs and attached Drake's hands to the rails of his hospital bed. Then he turned to Damian and said, "Come with me." He opened the door to see two of his men ushering the onlookers away until they noticed him staring at them. "Lieutenant Kwok, Lieutenant Mason, keep an eye on this scumbag for me."

The two cops looked at Damian.

Damian scowled. "Fuck are you looking at?"

Hill chuckled and cocked his head toward Drake. "The *other* scumbag."

"Oh," Kwok said.

"Yeah, you assholes," Damian replied.

"But isn't he a cop?" Mason asked.

Hill glanced over at Drake and said in disgust, "Quite the opposite."

Chapter 014
Another House Call

Early evening. The sky was a bright orange-pink clashing against a silver background.

They went driving in Hill's 1989 Chrysler Imperial down a quiet neighbourhood road Damian couldn't recognize. Bungalows decked in flickering Christmas lights shimmered behind sleety white front lawns. Inflatable Christmas figures stood tall on their rooftops, their warm smiles frozen on their plastic faces, hands caught in permanent greetings. Snowmen stood in a few yards, smiling their raisin-dotted smiles, carrot noses jutting out between button eyes.

"Where're we going?" Damian asked as he reclined in his seat and propped his feet up on the dash.

Hill said grimly, "Making a quick stop before we go to the station."

"The station? Hopefully to pay me."

"You'll get your money. I'm a man of my word."

Damian scoffed. "That's a new one."

"Mhm," Hill grunted.

"Got a smoke?"

Hill handed him a carton with a cigarette poking out. Damian took the whole pack, much to Hill's annoyance. "Hey, motherfucker."

"What?"

"I'm not giving you twelve cigarettes for free."

"Oh." Damian took two and tossed the pack in Hill's lap.

"Ass." Hill tucked the pack in his breast pocket.

Damian pocketed one and fired up the other with a blue energy flame on the tip of his thumb. When it was lit, he shook the flame out and leaned back in his seat, staring at the ceiling, inhaling its intoxicating nicotine.

"Don't get too comfortable," Hill said, "we're just about there."

"You never told me where we're going."

"It's a surprise."

"I don't like surprises. You know that."

"And you know I don't care."

Damian sat up. "You know, I could just hop out—"

"Don't even think about it."

"You gonna stop me?"

"No, but that doesn't mean I won't stop your secret from blowing up. That'd be bad for everyone."

"Especially you," Damian said.

"Right, because when the entire world comes after you, I'll totally be the only one you'll focus your attention on."

"You won't be the only one, but you'll be the first. Captain's the second."

"Mhm. We're here." Hill pulled into the driveway of a traditional bungalow house with a fenced-in yard and a swing set.

Damian sat upright. He knew exactly what Hill was doing now. "Oh, you son of a bitch..."

Hill shut off the ignition, jangled the keys, then pocketed them. "Let's go."

"Fuck I am."

"You are... coming with me. Whether you like it or not."

"That's what you think."

"What's the matter, Damian? Can't stand to face reality?"

"What reality is that?"

"Are you really afraid to face the loved ones of someone you murdered?"

"It's not very fun, if that's what you're getting at."

"Humour me for a minute."

"I don't find this funny."

"You think I do?"

"Why else would you drag my ass out here and yell, 'Surprise, motherfucker!'?"

"I didn't say 'surprise, motherfucker,' I just asked you to step out here and be a man."

"Wow," Damian said, absolutely floored. "I know you're a lot of things, Hill, but a holier-than-thou cunt wasn't one of 'em."

"I'm a hypocritical asshole just doing what I can to survive this cesspool of a city, Blue. Perhaps I've lost my way. We all have one way or another. We come to this city with our own values, our own rules. We think they're unbendable, and we're unbreakable, until we're given circumstances we can't help—circumstances that cage us and pit us against the very things we stand for. Sooner or later it forces us to decide who lives and who dies."

"You're pathetic," Damian sneered. "I can't wait for the day I get to watch you die."

Giving him the stink eye, Hill pushed open the door on his side. "Get out."

Damian kicked the passenger side door off its hinges. It slid across the sleet-covered lawn and stopped at the swing set. Damian snorted nonchalantly and looked at Hill.

Hill said, "You're fixing that before we leave here."

"Let's get this over with."

They got out and went up the stairs. They heard children's laughter inside as they crossed the deck and approached the front door. Hill knocked. A woman opened up shortly after, clutching the trims of her sweater together, draped over her shoulders like a poncho.

"Mrs. Zimmerman?" Hill said quietly.

Her eyes went wide as they darted from Hill to Damian to Hill again. They both knew she had that feeling. All new widows seemed to just *know*. "Yes?" she said tentatively. Her grip tightened on her sweater.

"I'm sorry," Hill said, "I have some terrible news..."

"No." She broke down. Her legs gave out. She collapsed on her knees, releasing a drawn-out whine that evolved into a hysterical wail. Her children stopped playing and peeked out from the living room to see what the commotion was.

Damian looked at them, then looked away. No way was he going to go through with this.

Hill knelt down and offered her a hand.

"Get away from me!" she shouted. She slapped him. "Get away!"

Damian said, "We should go."

Hill stood up straight and looked at him, scowling hatefully.

Mrs. Zimmerman's oldest child, a seven-year-old boy, shuffled to his mother's side. "Mum? Why are you crying?"

She quickly composed herself, re-assuming the role of a strong mother. She tousled her boy's hair and said, "Go play with your sister, Jimmy. Go on. It's okay."

Jimmy hesitated. He looked at Hill, then at Damian. His small eyes blinking in confusion.

"Go!" she snapped.

Jimmy obeyed, returning to the living room, glancing over his shoulder as he went.

"Sorry for your loss, ma'am." Damian tapped Hill's shoulder. "Come on."

Hill shook his head.

"There's nothing else we can do here. We're the assholes. Let's go."

"How?" Mrs. Zimmerman asked, stopping them.

Damian and Hill looked at her, then at each other.

"How did he die?" Mrs. Zimmerman asked, her eyes glistening sadly, reddened. She sniffled, wiped her eyes on her sweater.

Damian couldn't stand it. He knew she deserved an explanation. He knew he ruined another household. He knew Hill had a point, goddamn it. That bastard was right: he *couldn't* face this part of reality. It was something he actively avoided. With all the guns and explosions and fast quips and faster draws; the telekinesis, the energy radiating from his very core, ready to explode at his fingertips, at his beck and call. He could handle getting shot, or sliced, or run over, or beaten; any physical abuses known to the world, he could take. It's all fun and games until you have to answer the big questions: "How?" and its first cousin, "Why?"

He might have said something, had Hill not spoken up.

"Bravely," Hill said. "He took down a known criminal disguising himself as a cop. The city is safer because of him."

Mrs. Zimmerman started to cry again.

That's it. Damian went back to the car, only he didn't get in. He headed down the driveway instead, and then took the sidewalk. Mrs. Zimmerman's mournful cries followed him to the corner, ringing out across the neighborhood.

I wonder, he thought. *How many times someone had to answer to the families of the men I've killed.* He fired up another cigarette as he crossed the street, trudging through brown-yellow slush. *What's it matter, anyway? They died as they lived. It was their selfishness that put them down. I just finish these fights. I shouldn't have to live with their deaths.*

"Is that what you really think?"

Damian whirled. There in the park, on the other side of a short chain link fence, Lisa stood under the monkey bars in the base of a cone of flickering light shining down from a lamppost. The bangs of her snow white hair cast dark shadows over her eyes. "Lisa..."

"You're running away again."

"You're not here."

"You're running away from yourself, right?"

"Be quiet."

"No."

"Go back to the Spirit Core."

"I don't want to go back."

"You can't stay here. Leave me alone."

"Where else am I supposed to go?"

"Anywhere but here."

She drifted toward him.

"Get back," he barked.

She reached the fence, gripped the top of it with her small fingers, and looked up at him with the empty black pits her eyes had just shrank into. "What are you afraid of?"

Damian recoiled with a startled gasp. He staggered into a lamppost, staring at the girl behind the fence. "Stop it! I tried, goddamn you! I *tried*!"

"You didn't try hard enough," she replied. She didn't seem to notice that her flesh was starting to melt off her face.

Damian turned and broke into a brisk walk up the street. Lisa started wailing behind him, just like she did when she was burning to death in his arms. "Stop it. Stop it. Stop it. Stop it."

He failed to notice Hill driving up beside him until Hill called out to him. "Hey, Blue!"

"Fuck off."

"You still need to fix my door, you ass."

Damian's short fuse was getting shorter. He turned and telekinetically tore *all three* of Hill's remaining door panels off his car.

"What the fuck!" Hill shouted angrily.

Damian started walking again.

Hill parked and got out, stomped after him. "Hey! *HEY*! Jerkoff, I'm fucking talking to you!" He caught up to him, grabbed his shoulder. "Look at me, you piece of shit."

Damian turned on his heel, jabbed a finger in Hill's face, and shouted, "You touch me again and I'll break every fucking bone in your miserable goddamn body, cunt!"

"I had your ass back there. Don't give me any of this attitude shit!"

"Oh, *that* was 'having my ass,' huh?"

"That's right."

Damian scoffed and did a mock salute. "Fantastic job, Sarge!"

"Listen to me: I know you acted in self-defense. I *know* it. I do."

"What the fuck was *that*, then? Huh? You made me confront the wife of a man I killed! *And* his kids! That was fucking humiliating! That was the worst thing you could've done."

"All about you, isn't it?"

"Oh, fuck you!" Damian turned his back on Hill again. He stomped down the sidewalk, swearing in Russian.

Hill heaved a sigh and yelled after him, "Now you know how I feel, kid!"

Damian glanced over his shoulder. "What was that?"

Hill didn't want to shout it in this neighborhood. He approached Damian and said, "You have no idea how much I have to lie to cover for you when you go off the rails. We do each other a whole lot of good, Damian, and we can do a lot for this town. But it's hard, kid. It's *real* hard to cover for you sometimes. All I've ever asked of you is to practice some restraint."

"So that was some kind of penalty? Seeing you work your magic on that widow?"

"In a sense, yes. I have to do that a lot because of you."

"Go fuck yourself."

"No, no, no, no. Listen to me, goddamn you!"

"No, I'm *done* listening to you. Fuck you, asshole! The sooner this ends, the better I'll be. After this business with Drake—" Damian paused. Then he said, "Give me the rest of my money."

Hill sighed wearily.

"Right fucking now."

Hill glanced at his car, then looked back at Damian. Shrugged. "Sure, fine. Get in the car."

"No more fucking detours."

"No more detours, I promise."

"Anymore bullshit and I'll break more than your car and then your fucking face."

"I got it, I got it."

Chapter 015
Visiting Hours

The jungles of Central Congoria. He remembered walking right into it—a full-scale execution—or a village massacre, depending on how you looked at it. He saw them all lined up against the wall of their temple, blindfolded, hands bound behind their backs. Mostly men, but a few women and children deemed undesirable for one reason or another.

The mercenaries had a job to do, and he was still new when it came to this sort of thing. Should he object? Should he defend the villagers?

"Do you know why they're blindfolded, newbie?"

*He turned to the man who spoke to him—somehow, he just **knew** it was he whom the man addressed. The man sat in a folding chair with his feet propped up on a crate. He was enjoying a fine red wine from 1945. The man's jungle fatigues were tattered, dirty, and covered in dried blood and cracked patches of mud. His wide-brimmed hat protected his tanned skin from getting too much sun.*

"Why?" he asked.

*The man in the chair said, "They say your life flashes before your eyes when you know you're going to die. Sometimes the killers see it. Don't ask me how we see it. We just do. Something about the way their eyes look at you; it's something that will never, and I mean **never** leave your brain. You look a man in the eyes when you kill him, and what you see in his eyes is forever burned into your memory. There's no washing it out." He sipped his wine. "A man in our profession'd go crazy if he looked into the eyes of every man he killed. It adds up fast. All those eyes." He pointed at the villagers sobbing and slumping against the wall of their temple. "Imagine looking into their eyes, son."*

He looked at the villagers. A sad, doomed lot. Men and women alike wailed in terror, crying for mercy or shouting the names of their children. He looked away.

"Take a good, long look."

COBALT CHRISTMAS: A COBALT ROGUE STORY

He glanced back at the villagers as a collective series of shots rang out, startling him. The thunderous cracks of gunfire echoed through the jungle as the villagers collapsed against the bloodied wall of their temple.

The man in the chair smiled. "It's easier this way." He looked up at him. Fairman himself, swishing his wine glass around. "Take away their eyes, and they may as well be faceless. Blank. It's easier to forget a blank slate than a beautifully painted canvas, kiddo. You'll understand soon enough. One thing at a time." He planted both feet on the dusty ground, set his wine down on the crate. He picked up a shovel lying beside his chair, stood up, and handed it to him. "Before the smell of death sets in, I suggest you start digging. No one wants to smell that."

Armaliker's Hospital

Drake opened his eyes and found himself staring at an unfamiliar ceiling. Foam tiles. The room was dim. The blinds were all drawn. He could hear phones ringing, muffled chatter outside. Tried to move his hands. Couldn't move them, just heard a series of metallic clinking.

He looked at his hands, both cuffed to the bed. He noticed two cops, Kwok and Mason, standing guard on either side of the door. "Oh. Hey."

Neither one of them responded. They didn't even blink. *Androids,* he guessed.

No sense trying to escape just yet. He relaxed his head on the pillow and sighed.

The garbage can rattled in its corner.

Drake and the cops looked at it.

The two of them were sitting in Hill's car, now with the doors reattached, parked in an empty lot.

Hill finished his call with the Captain and said to Damian, "The money should be in your account in the next five minutes."

"Good."

"What're you gonna do with it?"

"None of your goddamn business."

"Fair enough."

They sat in silence for a time. Damian rolled down the

window and smoked a cigarette. The distant white noise of traffic filled the cold night air. More snow started to fall.

Hill said, "I need a vacation."

"*You* need a vacation? Like fuck you do. *I* need a vacation."

"Oh, yeah? And what makes *you* so special, snowflake?" Hill smirked.

"I've been at this nonstop. Can't seem to shake all the people in this world who want me dead. They're like flies. They just keep coming no matter how many of them I kill."

"Can't say I blame them. You're obnoxious."

Damian scoffed.

Hill chuckled. Then his face went serious again. "Ask you a question?"

"You might not get an answer, depending on the question."

"Why the terrorism-for-hire, kid?"

"Hm?"

"Before you washed up here after your raid on that government lab... what was going through your head when you were doing the things you did?"

"Necessity."

"'Necessity'... hm."

"Isn't that how it all starts?"

"I don't know about 'necessity.' Maybe the term you're looking for is 'liberation.'"

"Give me a break. Liberation from what? From you? You think because I'm young and arrogant and hate everything you stand for, I lash out without meaning or purpose? I'm a *super-powered terrorist-for-hire* only because I don't like the rules."

"Isn't that it, though?"

"No, you're right. I don't like the rules. But there's a lot more to it than that."

"Like what?"

"A *lot* more." They stared at each other. Damian added, "You keep probing me, you're going to get a very unpleasant story."

"Maybe I'm just curious what makes someone of your status tick."

"Unwise."

"How come you never lived a normal life?"

"What do you mean?"

"You never went to school? You never... never tried to get a job? A straight job? Make a living? Marry Jenny, have kids, get a house, a salary..."

"Fuck that capitalist slavery bullshit. I'm a free man, Hill. Even as I sit in this car with you and your bargaining chips, I'm a free bird."

"Whatever." Hill scoffed. "Whatever works for you, I guess."

"It doesn't always work out," Damian said slowly. "It's just what I've got. I make the best of it." He shrugged. "Sometimes I even make money doing it."

"What made you like this? I'm genuinely curious. Why are you so fucked up? Did your mom run out? Did daddy not pay any attention to you?"

Damian stared at him. His eyes distant and hollow; if he was pissed, Hill couldn't tell. Quietly, Damian said, "I'm gonna tell you a personal story. Share it with anyone, and I will kill you in ways you never thought a man could die."

"Humour me." Hill took a water bottle out of the cup holder between them, and started drinking.

"Let me tell you something about my family. My mother was always around, but she was never *there*. My father was a bastard. A military hard-ass. My siblings and I were at constant war with him; we were always fighting for his approval. When my siblings got it, they couldn't be convinced that he was being genuine. With me, it seemed like he couldn't even be bothered to fake it with me. That motherfucker *hated* me. He had other plans for me.

"He trained me for months. It was hell. Survival training, combat training, conditioning me to be hard and without remorse; that sort of thing. Five months after this starts, I wake up in mid-freefall after he tossed my ass out of a plane without a fucking chute. I land in some forest in the dead of winter with nothing but a note. My healing factor keeps me from freezing to death, but that doesn't mean I wasn't stuck in a ditch for half a day trying to crawl out of it. Turns out extreme cold slows down my healing factor to a considerable degree. At least, back then it did. And buddy, *every* bone in my little body was fucking broken from that fall.

"Eventually I get out of that ditch, and I find out *that* was the easy part. I walk straight into a war camp like a dumbass—some terror cell. It's mostly empty; the bulk of them are cleansing towns or some shit. Still, the few guards that're there manage to capture me. You know what I found? Kids. Just like me. Hundreds of them, taken from all the towns. Their mothers were there, too, but there were only half as many of them as there were kids, and unlike the kids, the mothers were piled up on top of each other, being burned in a locked shack."

"Jesus..."

"I'm not finished," Damian snapped. "See, these guys, these militant cunts, I guess you could say they didn't really have any preferences or lines to be drawn in the sand. Once they were done with the mothers, they started raping all the girls, and once they were done with them, they came for us boys."

Hill heaved a sigh and guzzled down the last of his water.

"I didn't get raped, mind you. I put a stake through the eye of the fucker who tried. And then I carried that stake to every tent, and I killed them all."

"All of them?"

"Every last one. An average of three per minute. Sometimes more, sometimes less. It took over an hour."

"So then what?"

"My dad wanted to see if I would survive the winter. I'm sure the camp being so close to the drop point wasn't a coincidence, but it wasn't the objective. Survival was the objective, and I had four months to go. A blizzard hit us, and hit us hard. We're in the mountains, so we can't go anywhere. We run out of food supplies in two weeks because there's so many of us. And by that point, if the extreme cold wasn't killing us off, the lingering fumes of the dead were. A month passed, and none of us left the control center. It had toilets and sinks and showers, until the pipes froze over. We found a nest of rats. That lasted us two days. Three days after that, we ran out of clean water. We pissed in buckets and took turns drinking that."

Hill's face contorted in disgust.

"Another four days, and we were too hungry to think straight." Damian couldn't help but smile, almost dementedly. "Carl was the fattest. He kept us going for two whole days. Then it was Samuel. Mike. Raymond. Nobody slept for fear of being turned into food." He glanced over at a horrified Hill. "That's when the secret butcher got to work. And since nobody slept, the butcher didn't work, so when the butcher didn't work, nobody ate, and it would be brought down to straws. You draw the short straw, you get eaten."

"You're still in one piece. Clearly you got out of it okay."

"They all saw what I did. What I *could* do. No one dared attack me for the first two months. By the third month, they were too screw-loose to know the difference between a wolf and a sheep. By then, our once two-hundred-strong numbers had shrunk to thirty. In the last month, even the worst of us knew better than to attack me, because I made a good fucking example of the ones who didn't.

"By the time the storms let up and my father returned for me, just *four* of us remained. That winter marked the first season I started killing people. The first time was *necessity*. The rest were because I fucking wanted to. Then it was back to necessity. It fluctuates, you see."

"What happened to the other three?"

Damian put out his cigarette on the dashboard, much to Hill's chagrin. "Dad made me shoot them. Execution-style, right in the forehead. Was very specific about me looking into their eyes while I did it."

Hill was at a loss for words.

Damian looked at him and smiled darkly. "I was eight."

"Fucking Christ, dude."

Damian chuckled. "My life's been like that winter ever since, Hill. Shifting dramatically between necessity and luxury. That control center is the world, and I'm sure you can guess who the kids represent."

"Sure. Alright, then."

Damian leaned back in his chair.

Hill sighed. "Remind me never to ask you anymore personal questions."

"Appreciate it."

Hill wanted to push that story out of his mind. He didn't know whether to pity or fear Damian at this point. Best way to forget a subject is to change it to something else. He cleared his throat and said, "You gonna be ready for the next job?"

"What next job?"

"We got a lead on that eggnog case. Thought you might be interested."

"I should have all the money I want right now, so why should I care anymore?"

"Figured you liked those people. The ones who died in your apartment."

The horrific scene started to replay in Damian's memory for the thousandth time. They weren't bad people. They were good to them. They deserved some kind of closure. "What's your lead?"

"The poison originates from a compound that could only be found in the jungles of Indania."

"Long way from home."

"It was accidentally discovered in a network of underground caves after authorities started to investigate a series of tourist disappearances. They suspected a person or a group of people were responsible..."

"Like *The Hills Have Eyes*?"

"Uh... sure, I guess. But people weren't responsible for those disappearances. It was a toxic fume in these caves rising from the chemicals in the caves' water, most likely due to all the runoff from factory dumping, all mixed together into something else. Killed them almost instantly. It wasn't utilized until about a year later, when their military scientists got hold of it."

"Utilized? For war?"

"Obviously. It made things like ethnic cleansing a whole lot easier. Cheaper than blasting off millions of bullets, anyway. They could put it in a village's water supply or release it in the air. It couldn't burn your skin like mustard gas, but ingesting it was a whole different story."

"So someone put that shit in a convenience store's supply of eggnog?"

"Either imported from a secret lab in Indania, or replicated right here in town. If it's the latter, we've got a big fucking problem, because that would mean the convenience store was just a test. If it's the former, it's still one hell of an issue, but at least I've got a damn good guess where it came from."

"Where?"

"Not sure yet, but if it was imported, all evidence points to the smuggler you killed. Kartovski."

Damian looked at him with a raised eyebrow. "Kartovski?"

"That's my theory."

Damian peered through the windshield, scowling. "Great."

"Too bad you killed him. He might've been useful in finding out *where* he smuggled it from."

Damian shrugged. "We've got Donner."

"And we've got an army stationed at the hospital in case someone tries to bail him out."

"And if he *still* manages to escape?"

"I've got guys tracking it back to its source anyhow."

"What guys?"

"Top guys."

"What kind of 'top guys?'"

Hill gave him a look. "Top. Guys."

Damian's heart skipped. He didn't like the way Hill looked at him, like he suspected him of something. "What's with the secrecy? We're in this together, aren't we?"

"Does this mean you accept?"

"You haven't told me what exactly I'll be accepting. You telling me to track the source?"

"No. I'm telling you to find out where the rest of it is. It's out there in the city somewhere. If there's a lab, I want to know about it before the next attack."

"What makes you think there's gonna *be* another attack?"

Hill scoffed. "It never stops at just one. There's gonna be another attack. Thirty-two deaths were linked to that convenience store. Imagine what would happen if that shit was put into a supermarket?"

Damian sighed. "There would be a lot more than thirty-two deaths..."

"You bet. So what's your answer?"

"What's the pay?"

"I'll have to talk it over with the Captain."

"Then I'll give you an answer when you do."

Hill gaped at him. "What are you, serious?"

"Dead serious."

"There are people's lives at stake here, you asshole."

"Not mine." Damian opened the door.

Hill grabbed his shoulder.

Damian looked at Hill. "How attached are you to that hand?"

"We need you, kid."

"I thought you didn't want me on the eggnog case?"

"That's before I found out it's connected to Donner."

"I told you so."

Hill grit his teeth. "Fifty grand. Like in the original deal."

"Seventy."

"*Fifty*, you greedy little asshole."

"You want me on this case, my price is seventy and no lower."

"Sixty."

"I'm getting out of this car, with or without your hand."

Hill withdrew his hand. "Seventy, then."

Damian smiled. "Seventy, on top of the original fifty-a-head deal." He relished the anger in Hill's face as he tossed his cigarette butt in the wind. "Pleasure doing business with you." He got out and shut the door. He leaned through the window and said, "I'll go talk to Donner."

"Bad idea."

"Why?"

"Not all of those cops know about our deal. If one of them recognizes you, we're finished. I only brought my boys for a reason, but now there are guys from two other precincts lending a hand."

"I'll wear a hat and sunglasses, then. Those two guys you told to keep watch on him should still be there, right?"

"Well, yeah, but that's still a dumb idea. Wait till he's moved somewhere more secure."

"By then someone will've bailed him out, legally or otherwise."

"How can you be so sure?"

"Gut feeling. These guys *never* stay in one place too long. Trust me. I've seen people weaker than Drake escape max-security compounds the noisy way before. Without me, those cops are dead. And isn't that one of the reasons you brought me along?"

Hill sighed. "I guess. I'll head over there now. Get in."

"I've got a better idea."

"What's that?"

"You have any of those trackers with you?"

Hill rummaged through the glove box and came up with a device the size of an eraser—just like the one Carver gave him during the bank job. He handed it to Damian.

Damian stuffed it in his pants pocket. "Pier 7, Hill, at eh..." he checked the digital clock in Hill's car "midnight. 12:30 tops."

Hill gave him a good, long look. A genuine blend of surprise and suspicion. "You know about the warehouse?"

Damian nodded, shooting him a snarky grin.

"How?"

"Trade secret. If I'm not there by 12:35, *then* you can start following the tracker. No earlier."

"Fine. Whatever. Am I drivin' you or what?"

Damian shook his head. "My way is faster." And, with that, Damian made a powerful leap off the ground, and never came back down. Surrounded by his own manipulated matter and a telekinetic shield, Damian flew straight for the hospital, fading into the snowy night sky.

The Safehouse

Jenny was in the shower. She didn't hear the noise Drake's leg made downstairs when it sprouted another foot for itself, and popped out of the garbage can despite the bungee cords. It rolled on the floor as its thigh started to grow a new crotch.

Jenny's cell phone played classic rock on the bathroom counter, further masking the noise.

Armaliker's Hospital

Damian entered the lobby in a black stand collar jacket and jeans. His conspicuous blue hair was concealed by a black *ushanka* with a red star on the front flap. His cobalt eyes were concealed behind a pair of mirrored wraparound sunglasses.

Totally inconspicuous.

The place was packed, swarming with cops and orderlies. He weaved his way through the crowd toward the emergency ward without anyone paying him a second glance—at first. Once he reached the entrance to the corridors beyond the waiting room, he found himself stopped by a trio of cops he didn't recognize.

"Where do you think you're going?" one of them asked.

"Got a cousin in there," he said.

"Visiting hours are over, kid. Go home."

"But—"

Another cop asked, "You wanna get arrested, punk?"

Damian didn't want to start a fight here, as much as he wanted to knock these guys out. He backed away and said, "I'll come back later."

As he left, one of the cops said, "Don't come back at all. That'd be better."

Damian went into the restroom. Didn't bother locking it, since it could only accommodate one person, and he wasn't going to be here long. He kept the light off, and faded into the darkness...

In his shadow state, he could move through walls without a hassle, but any light would keep him at bay. It was like walking into a wall. If every room around the restroom had its light on, he might have to try the basement, and if the lights were on down there, he would be shit out of luck.

After some groping around, he found a bathroom in one of the adjacent rooms. He entered, then assumed his physical form again and peeked out into the room. A burn victim slept alone in his bed, slowly recovering from the shock of bacon grease melting his left arm.

Damian crossed the room and entered the tall, narrow closet. Assumed his shadow form once again, and found himself squeezing into a locker. He remained in his shadow form for a moment longer, listening for any noise to indicate whether or not he was alone.

Nothing. Nobody here.

He solidified, checked the door. Padlocked. He scowled and punched the door open. The broken lock bounced off the locker across from him. He stepped out and looked into the locker he just exited. Regular day clothes and a bad romance novel with a man's rock-hard abs photoshopped onto the cover. Typical erotica garbage.

Damian had to break a few locks to find what he was looking for in a locker: scrubs. Blue ones, too. A white doctor's coat and a surgical mask and cap were also conveniently piled in the locker. He quickly pulled the scrubs on over his outfit.

He entered the corridor in his disguise, wondering how far he'll be able to go before someone notices something strange about him. He made his way toward Drake's room, avoiding wheelchair-bound patients and orderlies rushing about. A stretcher with a car accident victim flew by. He couldn't remember the last time he'd seen a hospital in such disarray; maybe the eggnog attack had something to do with it. He passed a nurse—

Slow down.

The nurse looked *right* at him as she went by. Her surgical mask covered her face, and she wore a cap that hid most of her hair, except for the crimson spikes sticking out of a crudely knotted bun behind her head. And her eyes... pitch black and soulless, like a night sky without stars...

She passed him.

Damian paused, and turned around to get another look.

She was gone, blended into the crowd. But he saw her, and she saw him, and both of them knew it.

He amused himself with the brief thought that maybe *she* killed Drake.

He scoffed. *Yeah, right.* He turned and rushed down the hall toward Drake's room. Just another corner.

He banked left, found himself staring down a corridor with a dozen cops stationed around Drake's room, standing three feet from each other.

One of the cops addressed Damian and asked, "Can we help you, sir?"

"Here for our amputated officer," he said.

"He's not a real cop, and a nurse was just in to check on him."

Interesting. Damian furrowed his brow. *So she **was** here for Donner.* He said aloud, "Oh, good. Wasn't sure if she got to him or not."

"She did. He's resting now. Go on your way." The cop pointed down the hall behind him. "Go on."

"I'm going, I'm going." Damian backed away slowly, stealing a glance at the door Drake was supposed to be resting behind.

He wasn't moving fast enough for the cop, who shoved him back. "Get outta here."

"Yeah, I'm off." Damian turned. First things first: he had to find that familiar dame in the scrubs and get—

KAPOOWW!

A lightning flash, then a concussive blast disintegrated the entry to Drake's room, swallowed all the guards. It tore through the corridor, throwing Damian and several unlucky patients and orderlies off their feet in a shower of hot concrete. A violent flush of smoke and the partial collapse of the roof sent debris and light fixtures crashing to the floor.

Damian felt something oozing out of his head as his fractured skull panged away.   Screams and shouts and alarms and panic muffled, almost completely drowned out by his own deafening pulse and that terrible high-pitched ringing sound that comes with the territory of being a mere fifteen feet from a large indoor explosion.

Good ol' confined-space detonations.

"Oh," Damian groaned as he lifted himself up off the floor, wracked with pain. His healing factor pushed shrapnel out of their entry wounds at an agonizingly slow rate. He ground his teeth, equal parts rage and painful grimace. "That bitch..."

He would've gone after her, too, if it weren't for the gutted hall in front of him. He needed to know what shape Drake was in. He crawled across the floor, pushing debris and dead cops aside. Shreds from his torn, bloody scrubs snagged on the sharp edges of shattered concrete and drywall until he stood up and tore them off; cap, mask, pants and all, leaving just his tattered night clothes.

Still dazed and shaken from the explosion. The walls and the floor seemed to be trading places, dancing before his eyes. Damian staggered through the wreckage and the bodies into the smoke, coughing and gagging on it. He used what remained of the wall as support.

He reached Drake's room and peered through the smoke. A few patches of fire lit the haze; the room's ceiling was gone and its walls were almost completely nonexistent. The bed was destroyed, scattered about with the rest of the equipment. Drake himself wasn't in one piece; he was splattered all over the place in patches of red and black, though his blown-apart innards, limbs, and fluids were slowly shifting toward the center of the room, magnetized by his immortal rejuvenation. Damian watched as his blood dripped down from the exposed ceiling fixtures.

His senses were getting back to normal. The ringing in his ears started to fade. His blurred vision focusing once more.

The gore in the room merged together, congealing into a disgusting mass of flesh and organs; entangling, squirming. Damian took a small object the size of a 2B eraser out of his pants pocket and flicked it into the mass, watched it disappear into its muscle tissue. The metamorphosing *thing* sprouted upward. More of its liquefied body flowed into its base as the formation itself assumed the appearance of a fetus, and grew from there.

Damian watched silently as Drake rapidly grew through the

stages of infancy, childhood, pre-adolescence, adolescence, and finally, the middle of his adulthood—all while a gaping mouth in the middle of his stomach greedily sucked the rest of his organs off the floor.

There Drake stood, naked, staring at Damian with crazed eyes and a condescending Cheshire smile. "That was one foxy nurse..."

Damian didn't skip a beat. He created an energy shotgun in his hands and blasted Drake to the back of the room. Watching his enemy crumple to the floor gave him a satisfactory smile that he couldn't hold back. "Happy birthday."

Chapter 016
Flattery

Sunday, December 24ᵗʰ, 2031

"Where the fuck're you taking me?" Drake shouted from the back of the ambulance, struggling to break free of his restraints on a stretcher. When he didn't get an answer, he roared, "HEY! Goddamn you, I know you can hear me!"

Damian smirked behind the wheel. *That's right,* he thought, *I can.*

Stealing an ambulance proved to be easier than expected. They slipped through the chaos of panicking orderlies and patients in the midst of Aria's emergency ward bombing, unnoticed even as Damian stole an ambulance from the garage and sped out onto the freeway, cherries off.

Drake was still yelling. "You think because you got me strapped down, my boys won't continue the mission?"

Damian decided to reply. "And what mission might that be?"

Drake laughed. "Like I'll tell you anything, bitch!"

"Oh, you'll tell me."

"Bullshit!"

"You'll talk, Donner. Sooner or later, they always talk."

"Stop calling me 'Donner.' My name's not fucking 'Donner.'"

"Why not? I never took the time to find out your real name."

"You can call me 'Drake.'"

"Drake? Lame. Lame and clichéd. I'm not impressed."

"You can't make me talk."

"Sure I can."

"You don't get it, shithead. I've been trained to keep my mouth shut for punks like you."

"That's what the others said, too. Everyone has a breaking point, Drake. Even immortals."

"Confident man. I like that."

"Not for long." Damian turned left at the next intersection and followed the late evening commute down a street lined with holographic Christmas decorations—towering light show figures of Santa Claus and his elves stood and danced above the lampposts, lip-syncing perfectly to familiar Christmas tunes that played on an outdoor PA system. Damian found himself momentarily distracted by the three-storey-tall Santa hologram as he drove the ambulance under his black, shiny boots.

"You're like me."

"How so?"

"Hear me out."

"Sure, why not. Got nothing better to do."

"You're a killer, like me."

"True."

"You don't deny it?"

"I accepted what I am a long time ago."

"Interesting. I was expecting the whole 'I'm not like you' bullshit routine that I usually get from guys like you."

"That's not me anymore."

"What's not you?"

"I already told you—I'm not in denial. I'm just a scumbag killer looking to make an honest living doing what I do best."

"A fellow mercenary, huh?"

"Something like that."

Drake chuckled. "We really *are* alike."

"Sure, sure." Damian stopped at a red light. A trailer with brightly coloured, animated scrawls of summer beachside imagery sped by, temporarily filling the cab with its wondrous 3D slideshow. Damian fired up a cigarette with a bluish thumb-flame, shook his hand to put it out.

"So how long you been at it?"

"At what?"

"You know... killing."

"A long time."

"A long time?"

"A *very* long time..."

"You seem pretty young."

"I'm older than I look."

"Interesting. So, you're the fucking Dead Blue?" He scoffed. "I thought someone with your reputation would be older or something."

"Because it's been around for so long?"

"How old are you?"

"None of your goddamn business."

"Okay, okay. I'll just guess... eh... twenty-seven?"

"No."

"Twenty-four?"

"No."

"Twenty—"

"That's enough. Shut up back there."

"Just making small talk."

"I hate small talk, so why don't you shut the fuck up?"

"Ain't my style."

"Change your style."

"Where's the fun in that?"

"The fun comes later."

"You never said where we're going."

"That's for me to know and you to find out."

The traffic light turned green. Damian pushed the ambulance forward, ahead of the traffic flow. For a moment, nothing was spoken between the two of them. Fleeting neon strobed the cab interior; the brief darkness in between dominated by the dim red glow from the end of his cigarette.

The light snowfall spiralled down between corporate towers and shimmering walls of glass. Red light at the next multi-lane intersection; a seven-storey holographic Christmas tree rotated above the middle, its colours shifting from red to green to red to yellow to red to blue to...

Drake started talking again: "So what're your plans for the holidays?"

"I told you to shut up," Damian snapped.

"Hey, I'm about to be painfully tortured for information I refuse to give, probably for days on end—"

"You don't have days."

"Regardless... humour me, will ya? Killer to killer."

Damian groaned. "If I knew you were gonna be this annoying, I would've kept one of your bank job associates alive instead."

"Them? They didn't know shit about shit. They were mindless goons I picked up off the street; amateurs looking to make a quick buck. Sure, a few of 'em had experience, but they didn't know anything about me aside from the job."

"Then what were you doing at the old woman's house?"

"The mother of that ex-repo guy? I was cleaning up loose ends, nothin' more." Beat. "Don't think you tricked me into talking. All I've been feeding you is useless up to this point."

"You're an idiot if that's what you really think. No information is useless."

"You gonna kill me?"

"Eventually."

"Any way I can make you change your mind?"

"No, I'm *definitely* going to kill you. Your eggnog stunt in my neighborhood killed some pleasant neighbours of mine. And nearly killed me."

"That a fact?"

"That's a cold, hard fact."

"Well, shit."

"Yup."

"But what makes you think I'm responsible for the eggnog incident?"

"I know you are."

"But how?"

"The lab, you fucking idiot. *Your* lab. The one in Central Congoria."

"The one you burned down? Gimme a break. We were making guns, bullets, and meth. Why the fuck would we be making tainted eggnog in a tropical rainforest for?"

"Don't play dumb with me." Damian added sarcastically, "I find that highly offensive."

Drake laughed. "I wouldn't dream of it."

Damian couldn't help but smirk.

12:23 AM is when they reached the warehouse on the pier. Damian coasted the ambulance right up to the loading dock and telekinetically closed the shutter doors. Hill's car was parked behind a half-glass partition in the farthest corner of the loading bay, with the owner fuming on a cigarette. Arms folded across his chest, brooding, glaring at Damian as he stepped out of the ambulance.

"You look happy to see me," Damian quipped.

Hill made a sarcastic giggle. Then he snarled, "I'm not."

"Come on, let it out."

"Do you know how many officers you killed at that hospital?"

"Who, me?"

"You caused a fucking panic! You're a maniac! You're out of control!"

"Hate to burst your bubble, pig, but I didn't blow *anything* up." Damian pointed his thumb over his shoulder at the ambulance. "His employers sent somebody. *They* blew up his room. I just happened to be there."

"Carver's losing his shit. He's beginning to regret our little deal."

"That so?"

"Frankly, so am I."

"That's too damn bad, Hill. I guess this means you won't be needing Donner... or Drake, whatever."

Hill perked right up: "You mean you got him?"

Damian nodded, smirking.

Hill took a balaclava out of his pocket and slipped it over his head. "Why the fuck didn't you say that sooner?"

Damian shrugged.

"Asshole." Hill walked behind the ambulance and threw open the doors.

There he was—Drake, strapped down on the stretcher, just about dozed off from sheer boredom, snapped awake and alert when the doors open. He looked at Hill and said, "Hi, there. What's your name?"

"We won't be doing names tonight, you bastard," Hill said. He barked at Damian to "Get this fucker out here."

Next thing Drake knew, he was chained naked to a chair next to a long table in a big room. On that table were a variety of things: tools ranging from screwdrivers, a claw hammer, tweezers, and a monkey wrench to a battery-powered drill, circular saw, and a jackhammer. A variety of kitchen utensils and cooking supplies were also present, along with spools of razor wire, a nutcracker doll, and a guillotine paper cutter. A sheet of sandpaper, a spray bottle full of vinegar, and rubber tubing were also present.

Drake looked at the table and whistled. "Department store offer fifty percent discounts on all torture items?"

"Hilarious," Hill said sarcastically. He said to Damian, "He's got your sense of humour."

"Flattery will get neither of you anywhere." Damian positioned an office chair adjacent to Drake and sat down in it. "I'm gonna cut the shit, 'Drake,' if that's even your real name."

"Honestly?" Drake said, "I've gone by so many fake names, I don't even remember what my real one is." He shrugged. "Must not've been all that great."

"Guess not," Hill said.

"Here's how it's gonna go," Damian said, "I use these things on the table here to cause you considerable pain until you tell me one little thing: who your employer is. We can do this the easy way, or we can do this the hard way... *ooorrrrr* we can do it *my* way."

"Does he have to be naked?" Hill asked, indicating Drake's spread legs. "I don't think our boy here is too shy about who sees his junk."

"He was like that when I found him," Damian said. "You got any clothes to spare?"

"No."

"Well then." Damian shrugged.

Drake asked, "What's the hard way? Torture?"

"By him," Damian answered, pointing at a scowling Hill. "He's a bit more lenient and empathetic. My way hurts a lot more."

"Intriguing."

"Not really."

"Let's see what'cha got, then, Blue."

Damian squinted. "You're serious?"

"Dead."

Hill butted in. "Wait. Hold on. 'Blue?'" He said to Drake, "You know who he is?"

Drake smiled at Hill. "He's the fucking Dead Blue, right?"

Hill backed away, hands on his head, and nervously started to pace behind Damian. "Christ. Oh, Christ..."

Damian ignored him, staring at Drake with cold, empty eyes that nonetheless betrayed a hint of amusement. "You're a fucking oddball. Most guys start spewing right away. Some guys choose the hard way, and then start spewing after one or two minutes. No one's ever chosen *my* way before."

"If you can dish it, I can take it."

Damian scoffed. "We'll see about that."

"Do your worst, man. Do it. I fucking *love* pain. Fucking *love it!*"

Damian turned to face Hill and asked, "You got it going?"

"We're rolling." Hill took an audio recorder out of his back pocket and set it down on the table.

Damian nodded with approval. "Good, good. Then let's get started." He summoned the spool of razor wire. Shrouded in black energy, the razor wire floated off the table, slowly uncoiled itself above Drake's head. It formed a spiral column around him, orbiting its prey. Then it started to move in, slithering around his feet and curling its way up, careful not to scrape the chains that bound him. The flickering light from the overhanging fluorescent tubes glinted off the small razors as they moved.

Drake trembled with anticipation, twitching when a razor's edge lightly nicked his thigh.

The razor wire snaked up and around his torso, over his shoulders, then right back down to his ankles where both ends met.

Damian showed Drake his palms. "Last chance."

"Do it, you pussy."

Damian closed his fists. The razor wire followed suit, constricting Drake's body, slicing into his naked flesh. Drake moaned in a loud fit of agony and pleasure as the razor wire slithered under his skin. Red ribbons coursed over his body and dribbled down his front, spurting in every direction. The razor wire burrowed even further under his flesh, causing him further pain, forcing him to scream out. His skin had been divided into irregular, diamond-shaped patterns shifting in the directions the razor wire went. Pieces of him peeled off and splattered on the floor. Drake's face became a nightmarish distortion of immeasurable ecstasy and unimaginable pain, twitching violently, eyes bulging under flickering eyelids.

That's when Hill turned away, lifted his mask to his hairline, and threw up.

"Weakling," Damian said to Hill, never looking away from his victim, and never blinking.

"Fuck you, you sick piece of shit," Hill snarled.

Damian ignored him. He watched Drake squirm in his chair as the razor wire continued to carve deep rivets all over his convulsing body. Skinned him alive, sprinkling his blood all over the floor around him. A droplet hit Damian's cheek and slid down to his jaw line.

Drake's healing factor sowed his skin shut as fast as the razor wire sliced it back open again. Drake made a long, drawn-out groan, sounding like a small motor droning on and on...

With a wave of his hand, Damian's telekinesis violently uprooted the razor wire from Drake's body, all at once, ripping his flesh apart once again. The wire formed a spool around Drake and fell to the floor. He didn't let Drake's wounds heal. He snatched the spray bottle off the table and spritzed his victim's lacerations with vinegar until he was soaking in vinegar.

Drake howled. Then he shouted, "YES! YES!"

Damian cackled. "You're fucked, man." He sprayed vinegar in Drake's eyes.

Drake yelped and clamped his eyes shut, slamming his feet on the floor and groaning as he felt his eyeballs burn beneath their lids. "Fucker!"

"Guilty as charged." Drake's wounds were closing up. Damian gave them one last spray with the bottle, relishing Drake's torment.

Drake, soaking in his own blood mixed with vinegar, skin healed to a deep red tone. He panted heavily. Opened his glazed eyes and looked up. "That all you got?"

Damian raised his eyebrows and smirked. He looked at a disturbed Sergeant Hill. "This is going to be fun."

"I'm not having fun."

"Come on. You're no stranger to torture. Don't be a pussy."

"*Torture*, yes. Cigarette burning, electrocution by car battery, that sort of classic shit. I don't know where you learned to do something like *this*. *This* is just fucked up."

"This is what my kind of people do to his kind of people, Sergeant—"

"Hey, don't say my rank."

"—we do the same things your kind of cop does, only we take it to the absolute *extreme*. It's no secret you're a shady guy. I've hung around the station long enough to hear a few of the rumours. Unproven rumours, of course, until a promotion-happy sergeant starts digging around."

"Not on my force, he won't."

Drake grinned. "Cops... I *hate* cops."

COBALT CHRISTMAS: A COBALT ROGUE STORY

Hill stepped beside Damian and snapped at Drake, "*We're* not too fond of *you*, either, you son of a bitch. You killed several good men during that bank job. I'm gonna make sure you're stuck here till next year. Torture, twenty-four/seven. By year's end I *might* decide if you've suffered enough to put their souls at ease."

Drake scoffed. "Oh, gimme a goddamn break, pig. I was just roastin' some pigs. Nothing wrong with that, unless you're a vegan, I guess. Or an animal rights activist."

BANG-BANG!

Hill drew his pistol and blew out both of Drake's kneecaps. Drake threw his head back and released an ear-splitting shriek. Hill growled, "Keep talking!"

Drake hissed through grit teeth, "With pleasure, piglet!"

Damian nonchalantly spritzed Drake's knees with vinegar. Drake snarled at him like an angry dog in a cage.

Fuming, Hill asked Damian, "What's next?" He scanned the table for something he thought would be a satisfactory follow-up to the razor wire method.

Damian telekinetically lifted the claw hammer and a box of rusty nails between them and their captive. "Since our guest is a little slow, we're gonna really *hammer* the message home. Make sure he gets it."

The nails rattled as the box lid popped open.

Drake gulped.

Chapter 017
Richard's Army

Monterey Dairy Farm

Campbell found a back road off HWY 37-B and took it, careful not to drive his car into any rivets or icy patches. The car dipped a few times, but for the most part, the slow ascension up the hill through the pine trees was easy enough even with the headlights off. He parked at the top of the hill and pulled his toque over his mullet. Lit himself a cigarette. Put on his gloves. Got out, feet crunching in the fresh blanket of snow. He looked over the roof of his car at the plant down below. Lots of activity down there at this hour. All the lights were on. Vehicles seemed to be patrolling the fenced-in property.

Campbell rapped his knuckles on the roof, startling awake Bart and Conners. "Wake up, boys."

The cops stirred in their seats, yawned, moaned tiredly.

"Up and at 'em. Early bird gets the worm." Campbell reached in and retrieved his rifle scope from a cup holder. He leaned on the hood of his car and peered through the scope to get a better look at the activity down below.

Ten, maybe fifteen cargo trucks were parked behind the plant, out of sight from the highway, surrounded by men in winter fatigues with rifles slung across their backs. Most of them appeared to be sentries and patrolmen walking around. A few of them had noticeable cybernetic enhancements, with bionic arms and prosthetic legs. Campbell couldn't be sure about the others. They all wore helmets that covered everything above their necks except their chins.

"Hmm." Eyes narrowing, Campbell looked around and spotted three commercial trailers with the Monterey Farms logo emblazoned on their sides; a friendly, cool-coloured contrast to the hardened war men that surrounded it. They were barely visible from their parking spaces in the loading bay, but even from Campbell's vantage point, it was obvious that they were being loaded with something. "Early bird gets the worm, indeed..."

"What's that?" Bart asked.

"Look down there," Campbell instructed. "Tell me what your eyes see."

Conners stretched in his seat, yawning. "Could go for a coffee right about now."

Bart scanned the premises overlooked by the hill they stood on with increasing concern. His eyes counted every heat signature, bringing up the tally in his right eye while his left eye continued the head count. "What the hell is the military doing in a dairy plant? Unless it *isn't...*"

"What do you think?" Campbell asked, dragging on his cigarette.

"They're wearing winter fatigues, but I don't recognize the helmets. Systems Corporation has those gas masks, so I know it isn't them."

"Systems has officially gone legit in their business practices. Or haven't you heard?"

"I don't remember them being this sloppy anyway. These guys are right out in the open."

Conners stepped out of the car with his binoculars.

"Mercenaries," Campbell said. "It's gotta be."

"A whole goddamned army's down there," Bart said. "I'm counting about a hundred and thirty, inside and out."

Conners remained silent as he watched the activity through his binoculars. "What do you think they're loading down there?"

"More of that poison, I reckon," Campbell said.

"Poison?"

"The eggnog, like the convenience store, but on a much broader scale. If it ain't in the eggnog, it's in some other dairy product. Milk. Yogurt. Cheese. Could be anything. And from the looks of things, they're planning to ship it out tonight." Campbell tossed his cigarette and hopped in the driver seat, getting out his phone. He hit up Carver's number and waited for him to answer. "Carver, it's me. I think I found something going down at the Monterey Dairy Farm on Highway 37-B."

"What do you mean?" Carver asked, sitting up in his bed at home.

"I think this is where they first mixed that poison with the eggnog, sir. I'm sure of it."

More alert now, Carver said, "Monterey Dairy?"

"Yessir.   Got a whole lot of uniforms down here, too. Mercenaries, we think. A hundred of 'em, maybe two."

"Definitely not two," Bart said.

"Oh, Bart says it's definitely not two."

"More like one-forty, one-fifty tops."

"One-forty, one-fifty maximum."

Carver ran his fingers through his thinning hair. "Jesus H. Christ."

"They're loading stuff into trucks. Commercial trailers and military transports. I've only seen crates, but I'm guessing they're not packing donations for the Salvation Army. Poison for sure, maybe guns, too. They look ready to ship out tonight. What should we do?"

"Get back to the city," Carver said urgently. "I'll have to put something together."

Lowering his voice, Campbell asked, "Gonna use Warkowski and his war buddies?"

"Hell, no. His 'war buddies' don't even know that he's still alive."

"Who, then? Afrókrema?"

"Not if I can help it. I don't like those cowboys. And the last thing we need is another media circus like after their stunt in Konnerd."

"Same.   But who else is there to call?   Our blue-haired 'employee' limits our options; otherwise I would recommend calling Systems for their skilled expertise in wiping the floors spotless with armies like this one."

"He's becoming a liability, I'll give you that. But perhaps he can still be useful to us..."

"How do we even reach him? I never did find out that part."

"That was always the way we wanted it. Made things less complicated. I'll have Hill send him their way."

"And if he refuses...?"

Carver smiled. "He can't."

"Guess I'll leave that to you and get the hell out of Dodge here. Talk soon." Campbell hung up and pulled the door shut. "C'mon, boys. We're going back."

Bart and Conners jumped back into the car as Campbell started it up. They failed to notice the merc hiding in the bushes with his rifle pointed at the car's engine block until it was too late.

The Safehouse

Jenny stepped out of the shower and started drying herself off, humming to the tune of Accept's *Balls to the Wall*. She wrapped herself in a towel and got to work on drying her hair.

Then the song abruptly ended, followed by a *DOOT-DOOT-DOOT*, indicating that her phone had a new message.

That's when she realized the TV was on. Sounded like *The Growing Family*, a bad sitcom that lasted twenty seasons too long, and is unfortunately still running strong.

Strange... she didn't remember leaving it on. Clutching the knot in the towel, Jenny opened the bathroom door and peeked out.

Drake's leg had grown a Siamese companion of sorts, joined at the crotch, of course, with the torso working its way back into existence. It sat on the couch, pretending to watch the TV.

Jenny's heart stopped for about three seconds. She couldn't stop staring at Drake's slowly regenerating lower half. Sentient legs? Is that what the world has come to? "What. The. Actual. *Fuck*."

All ten toes suddenly swerved in her direction. The torso jumped off the couch. Drake's sentient lower half approached the TV and stopped in the middle of the room, and turned to face her, cock wagging back and forth.

Jenny squinted in disgust. "What the fuck," was all she could think to say.

A standoff between Jenny and a self-aware pair of hairy legs attached to an even hairier pair of balls.

Jenny raised her hands in a confused shrug. "Just... *what the fuck*."

The legs charged straight for her!

Jenny punched her fist into the bathroom wall and yanked a pump-action shotgun through the drywall. Chambered a round. *Blasted* the crotch into a thousand bloody pieces. The divided legs toppled over and wriggled on the floor.

Jenny watched with morbid fascination. She couldn't help but laugh at the weirdness of it all. "Ha! We got guns all over the place, bitch." The legs bounced around, lost and seemingly confused.

"Aw, whatsamatter?" she asked mockingly, "Did your balls drop off?"

All the giblets from the exploded crotch formed a speckled, gory carpet on the floor... then they started to shake, and regenerate at a faster rate than before, regaining their natural forms.

In a startling matter of seconds, Jenny found herself staring at a rising group of penises—and they were all turning their pink chestburster-like heads in her direction. The two legs themselves had grown new crotches, and new companions opposite them.

Jenny dropped the shotgun, eyes bulging. Her response was a terrified "Why, God?"

They charged for her. Jenny screamed and retreated into the bathroom, slamming the door shut and locking it behind her. They banged against the door, smacking themselves against it.

"Ugh!" Jenny exclaimed in disgust. "Get the fuck outta here, you dickheads!"

They didn't stop trying to barge their way in, slapping themselves against the door's base while the two pairs of feet kicked it above them.

Jenny picked up her phone and called Damian.

BRRRRRIINNNGG!
"Oh."
THUNK!
"AAAGGHHH!"
"What was that?"
"What was what?"
BRRRRRIINNNGG!
"*That*, Damian. What was *that*?"
"My phone, I think. Unless it's yours?"
"Mine's in the car."
BRRRRRIINNNGG!
"Go answer the goddamn phone."
"Ugh... uhh... you guys think this'll make me talk?"
"Quiet, you!"
Smack!
BRRRRRIINNNGG!
"Will you answer the goddamn phone already? Jesus Christ."
"Alright, alright. Fuck."

Damian left a moaning Drake to Hill's supervision. "Shut him up."

Hill shoved a vinegar-soaked cloth into Drake's mouth and nodded with approval at the sour look Drake's face had twisted into. He slapped some duct tape over it for good measure.

Damian checked the caller ID. He lifted his phone off the table and answered it. "Hey, babe."

"Damian, you need to get your ass down here!"

Alarmed, Damian asked, "What? What's going on?"

"I'm being attacked by an army of penises!"

Damian's mouth hung open. He stared across the room. He narrowed his eyes. "Uh... you're... you're what?"

"You heard me! I'm literally being attacked by an army of fucking *dicks*! They're trying to break the door down!"

Damian snorted. Then he burst into a fit of uncontrollable laughter. His knees gave way under him. He collapsed on the floor, guffawing.

"It's not funny, goddamn it!"

Damian kept laughing.

"DAMIAN!"

"What?!"

Hill raised an eyebrow. "What the hell is so funny?"

Damian looked at Hill, his face crimson, tears in his eyes. "Jenny... Jenny..."

"What about Jenny?"

Damian couldn't get the words out. He fell on his side, tittering.

Jenny shouted into the phone, "I swear to God, I'm gonna fucking *kill* you next time I see you!"

"What is it? What's so goddamned funny?" Tired of listening, Hill walked over and took the phone from a trembling, laughing Damian. "What the hell's going on?"

"Hill? That you?"

"Yeah."

Jenny felt a twinge of hatred surge through her. "Like I'd tell *you*, you disgusting piece of shit."

"What?"

"You wouldn't believe it anyway. *I* don't believe it! Jesus... Jesus!"

"Try me."

Jenny heard a crackle in the wooden door behind her. She sighed and said, "A bunch of sentient penises are trying to get into the bathroom."

At first Hill didn't respond. His face remained blank. "A bunch of *what*?"

"PENISES, HILL!" Jenny roared. "DICKS! IT'S A LITERAL SWARM OF DICKS!"

Hill sputtered, and then *he* started to laugh.

"Oh, goddamn it!" Jenny yelled.

Hill couldn't stop laughing. It went up a few decibels; he hollered, unable to stop himself from crying tears of mirth right next to Damian on the floor.

Jenny scowled, listening to the two of them laughing into her ear as Drake's body parts continued to ram against the bathroom door. She sighed and hung up. "Men," she muttered.

The door kept rattling.

Jenny got dressed post-haste. Her pants were the last thing she put on, and by the time she got both her legs in, the door started to splinter. It cracked down the middle. "Persistent, aren't you?" she said, as she conjured up a ball of flame in her hand. She traded hands, rolling the fireball between her palms, nurturing it to the size of a beach ball. Then she hurled it at the door, blasted it to splinters. Controlled gout of fire wormed across the carpet, devouring Drake's sentient body parts. It only took a few seconds for the flames to burn them to ashes, and a minute to burn away the ashes, too. The carpet burned away with them.

She clapped her hands once, putting all the flames out. Nothing but smoke and a black, smouldering stretch of burnt floor running across the living room, past the TV.

She tentatively stepped out, cautiously looking around. Her eyes darted around the place with each measured step. Through the gaping hole with charred edges in the doorway onto the floor. The floor's charred surface crunched under her bare feet. The stink of rotten flesh pervaded her nostrils. She gagged on it, wincing.

No sign of Drake's remains.

She went to the kitchen to fix herself a drink. Anything with alcohol. She did *not* want to remember this. She took a bottle of vodka out of the liquor cabinet by the fridge and chugged half of it down like a goddamn trooper.

She glanced over the island counter into the living room. It was still filled with wispy stalks of smoke rising into the ceiling.

A pair of feet leaped into view, landed on the counter. All she saw at first was a penis wagging not too far from her face. Jenny choked back a mouthful of vodka right before Drake's lower half spin-kicked her in the face. She twirled, spraying vodka from her mouth, slamming against the sink.

The lower half bent its knees, dashed across the island toward her.

Jenny smashed the vodka bottle against its left kneecap, snapping it back in a V, spraying vodka everywhere. The lower half staggered off the counter waist first, feet flailing, tumbling across the stovetop. It kicked out, sensing its prey was near.

Jenny stood a safe distance away from its wildly flying legs, then grabbed an ankle. The other foot shot out; she grabbed that one by the ankle too. Then she dragged the wiggling lower half across the floor. She kicked the rear door open and dragged Drake's torso across the snow-covered patio, down the steps, across the backyard into the small thicket of pine trees that surrounded the safehouse in a crescent, with an eight-foot wooden perimeter fence beyond them. Hidden in the thicket were two things: a wood chipper and an old well. She kicked the wooden cover off the well and dropped Drake's legs into it. She waited a few seconds, listening to its kneecaps crack against the well's stone walls, until she heard a splash.

She pulled the cover back over the well and returned to the safehouse to get a hammer and some nails...

Chapter 018
Enter the Crimson Bitch

The Warehouse

Damian and Hill had managed to calm themselves down after a few minutes. Drake sat there in his chair, unable to move, wincing every time he twitched. His toes had all been individually nailed to the floor, and all five fingers on his right hand had been nailed to a wooden plank. Watching his torturers laughing pissed him off. "What the fuck's so funny?" he tried to say, but his mouth was full of vinegar and cloth.

Damian took a few seconds to breathe, face red.

Hill got up and clapped Drake in the jaw with a brick. "Hey, Damian! As funny as that was, we're running out of time." He turned back to Drake. The cuts on his face from the brick were closing up, so Hill hit him again. "Start talking, you prick! Who's your employer, and when's the next attack?" He ripped the tape off his face and pulled out the cloth. Tossed it.

Drake spat blood all over Hill's shirt. "Can't tell you who my employer is."

Furious, Hill raised the brick over his head. "You son of a bitch!"

"*BUT* I can tell you about the attack!" Drake sputtered.

Hill paused.

Damian got up and stood himself beside Hill. "Go on."

Hill lowered the brick to his side.

"What time is it?"

Hill glanced at his wristwatch. "Five past one."

"It's the twenty-fourth, right?"

"Yeah? So?"

Drake smiled. "Next one happens today."

Damian and Hill exchanged looks.

Damian asked, "Where?"

"Can't tell you that. You're gonna have to torture me a little more."

Damian smirked. "Get the car battery."

Hill returned with a cart containing a car battery and a couple jumper cables with clamps.

Damian turned around and saw Lisa peeking over the loading dock, her burnt little fingers clinging to the edge on either side of her melting face. "Go away," he said. "This isn't something a kid should be seeing."

Hill and Drake looked at him. "What?" Hill asked.

Drake said nothing.

Hill drew his gun. "Somebody else here? Where'd you see them?"

"Just the ghost of Christmas past, Hill. That's all." Damian turned his attention to the car battery as Hill jogged toward the loading dock to investigate.

Damian telekinetically lifted the clamps off the cart and carried them between Drake's legs.

Drake tensed, and then winced when more pain burned up from his toes.

"One more chance," Damian said.

"Don't be a pussy," Drake said.

Damian shrugged. Both clamps bit down on each of Drake's testicles, making him yelp as a low current of electricity coursed through his crotch. His legs shook, knees wobbled.

"Talk," Damian ordered.

"Fuck you!" Drake's face twisted in a psychotic grin.

Damian upped the wattage.

Drake howled into the rafters. His body quaked with enough violence to uproot his mutilated toes from the floorboards, twisted nails protruding from them. Drake's reaction only worsened as Damian raised the electricity levels high enough for Drake's pubes to catch fire. His skin started to cook and smoulder. Drake shrieked and guffawed with manic giddiness, pain and pleasure cranked to eleven, his cock pointing straight up, hard as stone.

Damian scowled. This wasn't working. Drake was getting off to this shit. He cranked it to maximum. Drake let out an ear-splitting howl. His skin lit up; black outlines of his skeleton flashing through his melting flesh before he burst into flames. The lights flickered above their heads.

Hill had had enough. He drew his revolver and blasted the car battery off the cart, severing the cables and ending the torture. The lights blinked, then came back on, back to their uninterrupted buzzing.

Damian turned to face Hill. "Lose your nerve?"

"That's enough." Hill kicked the cart away. He looked at Drake, whose skin had opened up in patches, resembling a pinkish ooze rather than flesh, revealing his sizzling insides.

Still, Drake was still very much alive, chest heaving, the twisted strands of flesh sticking to his blackened teeth somehow twisted in a macabre smile.

Hill looked at his legs and noticed a smoking white puddle on the floor by his feet. "Christ!" he exclaimed in disgust. "He fucking *came* from that?!"

"Apparently," Damian replied, staring at Drake. "You're one tough nut to crack, Drake. But I wonder... how much more of this can you take?"

Drake's skin started to heal, crawling over muscle tissue that glistened like raw meat on a flaming grill, filling in gaps that had been burned and torn open during his electric convulsions. "I... I... ugh... I... I was o-once held in a... in a torture room f-f-for eight months... I can take this."

Damian grabbed the hammer off the table.

"The attack will commence with or without me," Drake said. "You think I'm an important component to the plan?" He laughed. "You idiots think you caught yourselves a rook or a bishop? I'm nothin' but a fucking pawn. There are more where I came from."

Damian plunged the hammer's claws into Drake's right thigh. Drake choked down a garbled cry. Damian looked him in the eyes and snarled, "Enough. Start talking. Now."

"Fuck you!"

Damian pulled the claw back, tearing Drake's thigh open down to his kneecap. The hammer's claws scraped against the bone. Damian ignored Drake's screams and peeled his kneecap out of its socket.

SHOOMP!

Like taking a ball out of a suction cup. Drake's kneecap rolled across the floor. Its owner bellowed in equal parts rage and agony, "FUCK! FUCK! I'M NOT TELLING YOU A FUCKING

THING!"

Damian spritzed his gutted knee socket with vinegar.

"*KKGGGAAAAARRRRGGHH*!"

Damian hit him across the head with the spray bottle. "Shut the fuck up!"

"How does it feel, you piece of shit?" Drake roared. "How does it feel?! You think there's nothing you can't do? You *hate* it when someone proves you wrong, don't you? *Don't you*?!"

"I said, shut the fuck up!" Damian swung the hammer. Drake's jaw shattered from the impact. Blood and bone splattered Drake's lap. Gore and spit dribbled out of Drake's open mouth. He rasped, groaning, eyes rolling around in a pained daze.

"Now how's he supposed to talk with you smashing his jawbone to pieces?" Hill asked.

"Fuck off."

Hill grabbed his arm. "I need a word with you in private, kid."

"What for?"

Hill motioned for him to follow, cocking his head toward the rear half-glass-and-pine-partition office. "Come on."

Damian sighed and followed him inside.

"Get the blinds." Hill perched himself on the edge of an oak desk and switched on the lamp.

Damian telekinetically dropped all the blinds and kicked the door shut. Then he looked at Hill, who wore the expression of a disappointed father glaring at his troublesome child, arms folded across his chest. "What?" Damian asked.

"What're you doing?"

"What do you mean?"

"I mean w*hat* are you doing with Drake?"

"Information extraction."

Hill scoffed. "Right. You know what it looks like to me?"

"No, and I don't care."

"It looks like a hopeless pursuit of satisfaction."

"That your diagnosis?"

"Just my professional opinion. You're not as professional as you like to think you are."

"You'd know, right?"

"By now, yeah."

"Right."

Hill pointed at the windows. "That right there is proof enough. You're torturing a man for information you know you could get by simpler means. Where's the tracker?"

"In his body somewhere."

Hill scrunched his eyebrows. "What'd you do, make him eat it?"

"Burned a hole in his stomach. Tossed it into the hole before it healed up."

"But it *is* still inside him?"

"Yeah."

"So what the hell are we waiting for? Why're we torturing him, exactly, when there are easier methods of extraction at our disposal?"

"...Okay, you got me." Damian shrugged. "Satisfaction."

Hill scoffed. "Seriously?"

"Who knows, maybe I'll get something else out of him while I'm at it."

"Bullshit," Hill snapped. "We skinned him alive with five feet of razor wire, nailed his toes to the floorboards and then electrocuted his balls until they *literally melted* out of his sack. If he ain't talking after *that*, he ain't talking *period*!"

"Where's the faith?" Damian asked sarcastically. "Where's the trust?"

"Don't you talk to me about faith and trust. We both know there's none of either in this arrangement of ours." He muttered, "Even when you're presented with an easy way out, you insist on taking the hard road."

"Who, me?"

"Yeah. You." Hill scowled as he watched Damian put some actual effort into crossing the office and pouring himself a cup of water from the cooler. "We don't have time to waste on these idiotic games. I propose a simple 'catch and release.'"

Damian stood up and sipped his water. "Catch and release? But why?"

"Didn't you just hear what I said?"

"The trickling water was kinda loud..."

"No, it wasn't, you smug little asshole."

Damian chuckled at that.

Hill sighed and lit himself a cigarette. "We live in an era

where we are surrounded by technology that continues to evolve and invent new ways to improve our lives, or perhaps... *pretend* to. We don't care what the machines do, so long as they continue to convenience us. Take that tracker for example: every cell phone, GPS, computer, tablet, whatever—all have one just like it built into their hardware. Easy to track if they're stolen."

"And it makes the fugitive's life all the more difficult," Damian added tersely.

Hill shrugged. "You'd know."

"Yeah, I do. That's why I don't generally use them. Makes my ghostly persona even easier to maintain." He sipped more water, arrogantly cocking an eyebrow. "But you already know that, don't you?"

Hill grunted. "My point is that Drake is as good as our property. A tracking device. He can lead us right to his employers if we're smart about this." A sly smirk crossed Hill's unshaven face. "And it's got audio... easier to hold up in court."

"Don't you guys have amendment rights to worry about or something? Last I checked, I wasn't in the motherland. How do you expect any lawyer in this town to overlook incriminating evidence obtained without a warrant?"

"We'll figure something out."

"Sure, sure." Damian pondered something. Sipped his water. Then he said, "And if he kills again, who'll be to blame? You?"

"Yeah, right."

"Your idea."

"Hey, we cops have an image to protect."

"Me, then?"

"That's how it's been so far. We never mentioned you by name, of course, only that you're a mysterious assailant interfering with police business."

"Anybody come up with a nickname for me yet?"

"The boys at the precinct refer to you as the 'Shadow Cunt.'"

"Classy."

"I sure thought it was. Now finish that water. It's time to decide. Catch and release?"

"You're really adamant about letting him go."

"It's the only logical solution."

"Right. Sparing an immortal psychopath and releasing him

back into society is *totally* logical."

Ignoring Damian's sarcasm, Hill replied, "Who knows? It might actually work."

Damian finished his water and crushed the paper cup in his fist. Tossed it into a nearby bin. "Fine. Let's see what it gets us. But not until he tells us more about the impending attack."

"I don't think he will. But if there *is* an attack, then one would think he'll head over to some rendezvous point during the final stages of preparation to make sure everything is running smoothly. You know, after he decides he isn't being followed."

"Which could be never. Which is why I think we should beat it out of him now before we decide to let him go. He won't be convinced otherwise. He'll sense a trap."

"'Damned if we do, damned if we don't.' Is that what you're saying?"

"Exactly. That's *exactly* what I'm saying."

"It's worth a shot, isn't it? He might take us to their secret lab, if you're correct in your assumption that Drake is behind the eggnog incident."

"I *know* he is."

"How do you know that for sure?"

"I've dealt with him before."

"And you didn't think to tell me because...?"

Damian shrugged.

Hill frowned. "You're hiding something."

"Am not."

"You are so, and don't you fucking insult my intelligence by trying to deny it. What is it? What're you hiding?"

Damian leaned against the door and started nonchalantly whistling the main theme from *Lone Wolf McQuade*.

Fuming, Hill shouted, "Hey, asshole! Don't think you can blow me off like that!" He grabbed Damian by the shirt and shook him. "What the fuck aren't you telling me?!"

Damian stopped whistling as something caught his attention, moving in the corner of his eye. His eyes followed a single red dot flicking across the desk, then over the windows, then to the side of Hill's pulsing, red, angry head. He couldn't hear what Hill was snarling about. Too focused on the dot...

"GET DOWN!"

COBALT CHRISTMAS: A COBALT ROGUE STORY

BRACKACKACKACKACKA!

The echoing stutter of a machine gun ripped into the office. The windows exploded, showering them with glass. The slats in the blinds disintegrated and flew across the room. The lights went out. Damian and Hill hit the floor as a hundred bullets sliced over their heads and shredded the woodwork in the partitions. The water jug bounced off its cooler.

Drake twisted his head around to see what all the commotion was about, not at all concerned about the odd stray bullet flying past him here and there.

In ten seconds, it stopped. The dot pranced around the dark office, searching for prey. Both men could hear the mechanic whirring of an approaching snowmobile outside.

"Jesus, Jesus, Jesus," Hill rasped. "Should've known his friends would've tracked him here."

"Hey, Damian!" Drake shouted mockingly from his chair, "What's your hurry? Don't you want to know where we're gonna strike next?"

"Shut up," Damian snapped as he swiped bits of glass off his coat.

Footsteps on the dock. They both heard the unmistakable click of a gun being cocked.

"Christ," Hill snarled, drawing his gun. "This is the last thing we need."

Boots fell against the dock's old planks. *Thump. Thump. Thump.*

Single assailant. Not very heavy on their own; probably female. Damian knew exactly who it was.

"Time to go," he said.

"Fuck no. What about our hostage?"

"Aren't you the one who wanted to do catch and release? Well, now you can! I hope you're happy. Our hostage is gonna get rescued and you get your way in the end—which may be soon, depending on how bloodthirsty our mystery guest is feeling tonight."

Hill gave him the stink eye. "Oh, screw you."

Klak-klak!

They stiffened, listening to the heavy thumping sounds of cue balls hitting the floor. They looked toward the direction of the noise as two live grenades rolled toward them.

COBALT CHRISTMAS: A COBALT ROGUE STORY

Damian said, "Oh. *Definitely* out for blood tonight."

BKAMM!

The office partitions exploded outward, coming apart like wet cardboard. Pieces of wood bounced off Drake as the sheer force of the explosion rip slammed him to the ground. "Ow."

A shroud of smoke filled the warehouse. Damian and Hill hid within it, surrounded by Damian's telekinetic energy, unharmed.

The assailant kicked a few chewed-up planks out of the wall and stepped into the office with her light machine hanging from a shoulder strap, primed and ready. No longer wearing the nurse's scrubs from the hospital, she was now decked out in full combat fatigues under a black winter coat with a red lightning bolt on the back. Her crimson hair was still tied back in a spiky bun, this time by a faded green and yellow polka-dotted bandana, with two thick bangs hanging over her eyes. She took measured steps through the smoke, unfazed by it, gnawing on the end of a toothpick, pitch black eyes searching for a target through a pair of pink tinted aviator sunglasses.

The smoke began to clear. The remaining lights would give away Damian and Hill's position. They started to ease backward, approaching the stairs leading to the basement. The slightest pressure on the floor, however, sent out a telltale creak.

With a playful smile, she yelled, "Hello, boys!" The assailant's gun barrel swivelled in their direction, and loosed a volley of flaming lead.

Damian and Hill scattered in separate directions. Bullets stitched across the floor after Damian, blowing up knick-knacks and equipment off faraway shelves across the warehouse.

Damian returned fire with an energy pistol, tearing chunks out of the assassin's hip. She cried out, twirling to the floor, her light machine gun blasting a clumsy arc up the wall and across the ceiling above her. Light fixtures burst; the rafters started to come apart. A ceiling truss pierced the floor next to Damian, startling him.

The assassin rolled to her feet, absorbing additional shots from Hill's revolver. She turned and sprayed a hell storm at him.

Hill leaped and rolled across the floor, touching concrete, kept rolling as the assassin's bullets pounded the floor in hot pursuit. He reached the loading dock and threw himself into the bay, across the hood of the ambulance, out of her field of vision. Hill flattened himself as a few bullets skipped off the loading dock and punched holes into the ambulance's windshield.

Damian aimed for her head, fired. Flash of blue. A streak of black energy burned a tunnel through her cranium. The assassin's head snapped to the side as her shattered sunglasses flew off her face in sparkling shards. Her bandana came undone, fluttered away. She collapsed in a heap in front of Drake, who looked at her piteously and said, "Aaaww..."

With a heavy sigh, Damian lowered his gun. It dissipated like smoke in his hand.

Hill climbed off the ambulance and righted himself on his feet. "Christ," he muttered. "Who the hell was that?" he yelled over the loading dock. "One of *his* friends?"

"Mine?" Drake laughed and shook his head. "Never seen her before tonight."

"You sure about that?" Damian asked.

"Trust me, I would remember a babe like this," Drake replied. He tilted his head when he gave her corpse another look and squinted. "She looks kinda familiar..."

Suddenly her corpse *moved*—flipping on her back, the hole in her head closing up. She brandished a grenade launcher, pointed it at Damian.

Damian blood went cold. "Sh—"

KAPOW!

A 40mm grenade punched him between the ribs and blasted him wide open, propelling what was left of him through the far wall into an alley in a blaze of fire and shrapnel. Skin peeled, burned away; clothes shredded, disintegrated under a coat of fire.

"WAHOO!" Drake whooped as he watched her work.

Hill choked back a horrified gasp when he found himself looking down the barrel of her grenade launcher. He turned and bolted for the shutters. The screech of another grenade chased him to the door—

BOOM!

The ambulance blew apart in a fiery conflagration, shaking the warehouse to its foundations, hitting Hill with a gust of hot air and flying debris. The emitted force shoved him face first into the shutters with a resounding *WHAM*. He slumped to the floor. Stars and purple circles danced in his eyes as the floor he fell on spun him round and round...

The assassin blew smoke away from her grenade launcher.

Drake stared up at her buttocks, silently making note of the upside-down heart shape of her ass with lustful glee. "God!" He shouted. "What a woman!"

She turned and looked down at him. A sly, upward curl at the corner of her mouth added an unusually playful vibe to her despite the cold emptiness in her eyes. Her hair took on a rosy radiance Drake had never seen before. She seemed to be all business, but something about her almost screamed 'more play, less serious.' "They call me the 'Crimson Bitch,'" she said with a subtle layer of seductiveness he almost missed. "At your service, baby."

Chapter 019
Hitting the Showers

"Can you stand?" She'd just smashed his chair apart with a single stomp, and was in the process of breaking his chains with her bare hands. When she saw his bloody, mangled toes with nails twisting through them, she figured it would be a smart thing to ask. "Those bastards sure gave ya one helluva foot job, didn't they?"

Drake chuckled, then winced when he moved his feet and felt the nails scrape across the floor. "Ow..."

The chain links snapped. Drake was a free man, in a sense. She stooped down and retrieved her bandanna off the floor, dropped her light machine gun beside Drake and hoisted him up, draping his arm over her shoulders. "Let's go, big boy. They won't stay down forever."

As she started to drag him toward the gutted office, Drake said, "Oh, you know them?"

"One of 'em."

"Let me guess: the guy you just blew through the wall?"

"That's the one."

"Then you know that didn't kill him?"

"Objective wasn't *to* kill him."

"Then what was your objective? Who sent you?"

"Two birds with one stone: your boss sent me to pick you up."

"Then why blow up my friggin' hospital room?"

"Would you prefer I risk the whole operation duking it out with those cops? How else was I gonna get them to isolate you? Besides, it's not like I endangered your life."

Drake would have shrugged if he had the willpower. He was busy wincing from having his toes scraping across the floor as she dragged him, snagging over every crack and crevice between the floorboards. "Guess you got a point there." Drake glanced at the smouldering hole in the wall. "Why don't we finish him while we have the opportunity?"

"Right. Sure. And then when his healing factor revives him at the worst possible time, I can explain to my employer why I'll be returning to him empty-handed. *Or* I can take you back in one piece. We've got a job to do."

"Oh, yeah. That."

"Yeah, *that*." She grunted as she dragged him out onto the dock. "Move your ass. You're wasting time."

"I have *nails* in my goddamn toes. *Fuck*! Careful."

"Not my fault you don't clip your toenails, dumbass."

"You... you got a boat out here?"

"Snowmobile. Water's too frozen for a friggin' boat."

"Oh. Wait, it's cold out. I don't have any fuckin' clothes."

"I brought some in the car."

"Thought there was a snowmobile..."

"On the other side of the river, dumbass. Jesus. Just hold on a bit."

"Ugh... fuck, it's cold."

"I'm starting to wonder why Fairman wanted me to put any effort into saving you..."

Damian came to a few minutes after they made their escape. Felt like he had a brick lodged in his throat, shredding the inside of his windpipe. He coughed and gagged, tears welling in his eyes. Caked in a blanket of flames, writhing in agony as his flesh shrivelled and charred under the intense heat. A broken rasp escaped his mouth. He slammed his palms on the ground and strong telekinetic shockwaves burst from them, putting out the flames, leaving behind a black patch and a thick shroud of wispy smoke.

Nothing but pain. Dark red flesh glistened, crackling like bacon fat in a skillet. Smoke hissed off his back. His hair had been burned away, gradually sprouting as his skin healed rapidly.

Still red and burnt, Damian pushed himself up off the ground, gagging. Lungs not yet healed; windpipe still scratchy and dry. He croaked, "Ow."

"How does it feel?"

He turned and looked at little Lisa standing just outside of the wreckage.

"It hurts, doesn't it?" she asked as her voice deepened... face started to melt... eyes liquefied and dribbled down her cheeks...

"Sh-shut up!" Damian gasped.

She wiped her face on the sleeve of her sweater—literally, like a red paste, revealing a bare cheekbone and a few small teeth.

"That's... that's enough, goddamn you." Damian's healing factor had just about finished the job. He coughed up phlegm and ash, and stood up, approached the girl.

BRRRRIIIINNNGG!

He stopped as Hill's ringtone whistled from inside the warehouse.

Hill's cell went off. He followed the sound of his ringtone from a dark hole in his unconscious mind, back into the real world. His car. He forced himself to crawl over to his car. Jerked open the door. His hand reached in, trembling, fell on the phone. He dragged it toward him, answered it without checking the caller ID. "Hill."

The Captain's voice greeted him on the other end. "Morning, sunshine. Did I wake you?" Maybe it was the tinny sound coming through the speaker of his phone, but it sparked a sudden shot of pain in the back of his head that burned through his eyeballs.

"Something like that." He closed his eyes. His eyelids seemed to calm the burning sensation as long as they blanketed his retinas.

"Well, I hope you're well rested, because our boys've got a lead."

"A lead? What?"

"You're aware of our suspect's escape from the hospital?"

"Yeah. What about it?"

"Nothing; just wanted to make sure you were on top of something, at least. I'm assuming you're on the hunt for that son of a bitch. Detective Campbell had a hunch that our poisoned eggnog wasn't poisoned from the start, so he went snooping around every dairy plant in and around the city. His suspicions seem to have paid off: he found something at the Monterey Dairy Farm in the pines south of Highway 37-B. Haven't heard from him since, but he should be back in town in a few hours."

"Okay." Hill grunted as he sat himself in the passenger seat. The ambulance continued to burn quietly in front of the loading dock. He was thankful that his car was still in one piece.

"I need you to send Damian down there."

"Why?"

"Campbell reported an army of alleged mercenaries were

down there preparing a shipment for tonight. Over a hundred of them."

Hill sighed and massaged the back of his head. "The kid's with me at the moment. We're chasing Drake."

"He's probably heading there as we speak, Hill."

"And if he isn't?"

"Drake isn't top priority. Stopping that shipment is."

"It's gonna be a pain in the ass to get the kid to focus on something else right now."

"Just do your job. It's your ass if that shipment makes it into town."

"Alright, alright. I'm on it." Hill hung up. "Fucking asshole."

HWY 37-B

"Boss man never told me where that shit was kept till tonight," Drake's saviour said from behind the wheel of a 1984 Audi 5000.

Drake winced as he pulled the last nail out of his pinky toe. His entire body had just about healed by now, but his skin was tinged red with dried blood. He was now dressed in a pair of track pants and a grey hoodie. "The whole operation's been kept under wraps for months now. Couldn't risk any leaks. There's no stopping us now, and you, Ms. Murder Queen, you've been with us almost from the start, apparently. How come I've never seen you before?"

She shrugged. "Same reason newspaper delivery boys rarely run into each other when they're doing their routes, I guess. We just never had the opportunity." She shrugged. "Shame."

"I'll say," Drake said, giving her body another look. "You're pretty damn fine."

"Why, thank you," she said. She put a toothpick in her mouth.

"I can't shake the feeling I know you from somewhere else."

She looked at him. "Where else do you think you've seen me?"

"Dunno. I can't place it."

She switched on the radio and tuned to an advertisement announcing another re-release of John Carpenter's *They Live*. "How're your feet?"

"Just about healed."

"You able to walk?"

"Don't see why not."

"Good. We're almost there."

They passed under a holographic traffic sign crowned with red and green tinsel that blinked in and out of existence, and thirty more just like it. Android versions of Santa's elves in neon-trimmed green-and-white suits held up big shimmering signs for drivers, reading: 'Drive safe! Eyes on the road!'

"There it is," Aria said as the first perimeter lights of the Monterey Dairy Farm peeked up over the snowy horizon. "Home sweet home."

"Temporarily."

"Hm?"

"Didn't Fairman tell you?"

She shook her head. "Said to take you there and await further instructions."

"Damn. Even after all this, that stingy prick's still keeping you out of the loop."

"Yep," she grunted. "Tells me to assist in making Operation Catalyst a resounding success, but keeps almost everything I need to know a secret till the last minute. Talk about annoying."

"What's your name?"

"I have a good dozen, man." She guided the car into the gate and stopped at the booth. She rolled down her window for the guard, who flashed his light into the car, studying their faces with implanted computer eyes that instantly linked their faces to an internal data bank implanted in his brain.

"You're clear. I'll open the gate," the guard said. "Welcome back, Ms. Murder Queen, Mr. Drake."

She rolled up the window as the guard returned to his booth and opened the gate.

"I meant *your* name," Drake said. "Your *real* name."

She made a small, coy smile. "Why're you so curious?"

"I just can't shake the feeling I know you from somewhere. Maybe from a past date or somethin'."

She chuckled. "Ooh, someone's sure of himself."

"Come on, tell me your name."

"You first, big boy."

Two dozen mercs in winter camouflage made a path for the car as it crawled across the bustling parking lot. Most of the spaces were occupied by armoured vans and snowmobiles. They went around back, stopping briefly to let a forklift pass through. She drove by the commercial trailers in the loading bay and picked the very last parking space available next to a row of cargo trucks.

"You got a coat?" Drake asked. "I didn't find one in the bundle of clothes you brought me."

"Just mine. Sorry"

"Snowmobiling on that river gave me some nasty frostbite. I'm *still* shivering."

"You'll live." She got out and shut the door.

Drake scoffed. "Ice cold bitch." He got out and followed her inside the plant. A few mercs saluted to the two of them before continuing with their own tasks. Drake stopped at the entrance and watched her get a progress report from a supervisor in the loading bay before she went to the women's locker room. Drake went over to the supervisor and said, "Morning, Mall."

The supervisor, Mall, turned, adjusted his thick-rimmed glasses, and said, "Morning, Drake. Heard they caught you. Christ, I would believe it. You look like hell."

"Thanks. I feel like hell. Didn't tell 'em shit. Our 'Murder Queen' got me out anyhow."

"Naturally."

"Hey, you got a spare coat lying around anywhere? I'm freezing."

"Uh, yeah, the workers should have some spares in one of the locker rooms. Midnight shift's all working."

"No one's curious?"

"They're too busy milking cows and processing whatever comes out of 'em." Mall chuckled.

"Perfect. Everything in place?"

"Just about ready to go," Mall said as he watched a forklift push a crate into the back of one of the trailers. "We'll be outta here before any of the night workers go on break and potentially see anything that would arouse their suspicion. Wouldn't want that."

"No," Drake said.

"Lunch break starts in one hour. I'd give us about forty minutes."

"Fair enough."

Which reminds me: we caught a few spies from the hill.

They're locked in the shower room for the time being."

"Spies? Workers?"

Mall shook his balding head. "Cops."

"Shitting fuck. That means they could be on us any minute. Why wasn't Fairman told?"

"He was. By Frank."

"And what'd he tell Frank?"

"I don't know. Ask Frank."

"Well where is he?"

"Showers. Hasn't let those pigs out of his sight."

"Good work, Mall. I'll talk to you later."

"Sure thing. See you at the reservoir."

"That's your department, not mine. Loose lips sink ships, my friend. Loose lips sink ships."

Mall made a show of 'zipping' his lips shut and smiled.

Drake went over to the two corridors leading to the locker rooms. Considered the men's for a moment, and then went to the women's. A narrow corridor with two doors like a decontamination zone, only in this case, it was to keep the heat from escaping the main areas of the plant, given how open the loading bay was. He zigzagged through a winding, cinderblock corridor until finally he reached the locker room. Mostly empty, with the restroom and the shower room on the other side, but he knew she was still in here. That fiery-haired vixen fascinated him, and he wouldn't mind seeing that ass out of those pants.

He stalked the aisles, looking for her. Found her in the last row with her top off, her naked back facing him as she tossed her shirt on a bench. He leaned against the nearest locker and smiled, watching her.

She didn't have to turn around to know he was there. "It's not very polite to spy on a lady when she's changing."

Sensing the flirty tone in her voice, Drake replied, "Who said I was polite?"

She glanced over her shoulder at him, a teasing glimmer in her eyes as she slipped her arms through another shirt, this one black. She pulled it on, fluffed her hair out from under the collar.

"I never got your name."

"I never gave it." She turned around to face him, revealing a corny Christmas tree etched into the front of her shirt.

"That's an ugly shirt."

"Thanks," she said. "My dead mother gave it to me."

"I'm sorry," he said unapologetically. "You just look terrible in that shirt."

She smiled. A lady with a sense of humour. Drake was really starting to like her. "Don't worry your pretty little eyes," she said, "it's only temporary till I hit the showers."

"Oh, I wouldn't use those showers if I were you," he said with exaggerated concern. "There are spies lurking."

She laughed. "Not exactly 'lurking.' I can hear Frank's punches landing all the way out here."

"Semantics."

"*Tomayto, tomahto*," she said.

"I bet you've got a pretty name. Real sexy."

"You're very persistent."

"I'm just curious."

"What makes you so curious? I'm sure you've met plenty of sexy women who can more than hold her own with grenade launchers and handguns."

"Most of them can't get up after taking a head shot," Drake said.

"Haven't you heard? Ladies can be immortal, too. Not as many of us, but a good number. You men think you can hog all the fun."

"I'd prefer a woman with a gun over a man, actually."

"Oh, yeah?" She grabbed her shirt off the bench and stuffed it in a duffel bag. "And why's that?"

"Just my preference. Reminds me of those old noir movies. The beautiful woman with a gun. The *femme fatale*."

Smiling, she said, "I'm not so easily charmed, Drakey-boy. I sense a question burning behind this charming display of yours."

Very observant, he thought. *Then again, all the best women— and the worst—are.* He folded his arms across his chest. "Now that you mention it, yeah, I guess I do have one."

"If it's about my name, you're going to have to try harder than that."

"No, no." He chuckled. "Back at the warehouse, you said you knew our mutual blue-haired friend back there."

She scoffed. "Damian Warkowski."

"Oh, you *do* know him."

"I already said I did. I ain't hiding anything from you, Drake."

"Except your name."

"Right. Except my name."

"Why's that?"

She smirked. "I feel like we're going in circles."

"I hadn't met you before tonight."

"I'm sure Fairman's mentioned me once or twice."

"He has, he has."

"Well, I hope he told you I like to keep things interesting." She slung her bag over her shoulder. "And this conversation is, unfortunately, starting to bore me."

"Where're you going?"

"I'm gonna see if Frank has something more interesting to talk about." She left the aisle and started up the other side of the locker room toward the shower room. Drake followed her from the opposite end.

"I'm comin' with you."

"Planning on scrubbing my back for me?"

"Don't mind if I do."

She chuckled. "Don't count on it just yet."

Frank, with the backup of his two Asian cronies, Jim and Kim, was working over the three cops like it was another day at the gym. Bart was strung up by his neck in one of the other stalls, piano wire noose cutting deep enough to drain the blood from his jugular all over his front.

In a different stall: the rookie, Conners, was whimpering under a torrent of freezing water in a ball cradling the elbow stump his right arm used to be attached to.

Campbell took the full brunt of Frank's wrath, beaten to a pulp and then some. His face was a grotesque, swollen mishmash of black and purple flesh; the shape of his nose had been warped by Frank's merciless abuse. His left arm had been mangled, and both of his kneecaps were shot out.

Frank examined his bloody knuckles. "Looks like I got carried away."

Kim offered Frank a hand towel.

"Oh, thank you." Frank took it and wiped his hands,

permanently staining it red. He looked at the half-conscious Campbell sitting upright in the farthest corner of his respective stall with mild amusement. "Never seen a regular human stay awake this long after I beat 'em senseless. You still got some sense in ya, don't ya?"

Campbell murmured a spiteful, "Fuck you."

Frank laughed. "You're somethin' else."

"Let the kid go," Campbell rasped. He coughed, choked on his own blood. He spat it into his lap and groaned. "He's just... just a rookie."

"Rookie who knows too much," Frank said. "Tell ya what: tell us who tipped you off about this place, and I'll let the boy go. I'll even give ya a quick an' easy death as an extra bonus."

"I told you... after the eggnog incident I had... had a hunch... I staked out a bunch o' dairy farms... this one was on the list."

"Bullshit," Frank said. "Our informant told us you guys were lookin' for a drug lab completely unrelated to dairy. Now, he's a very reliable source. Matter of fact, it's all his operation. So I hope you'll forgive me if I don't believe the story you're telling me. Somebody tipped you off. Who?"

"Nobody. Fuck you."

"You're a funny guy, Detective Campbell. Stubborn as a fuckin' mule. About as tough as one's hide, too. Jesus. You look like a chicken nugget before they bread it."

Campbell forced a laugh. Then he said, "Cunt."

Frank's smile vanished. "I don't like that word."

"Most cunts don't like the word 'cunt.'" Campbell sneered at him, an achievement given how swelled up his face was. "It's an ugly word; a savage... *disgusting* word. You... you're a savage, disgusting man, F-Frank. It suits you."

"You shouldn't say things like that. Bad for your health. Bad for certain people around you, too."

"You already killed Bart. Who am I kidding? You're gonna kill the rest of us, too. Why don't you get it over with?"

The Murder Queen entered. "What's up, boys?"

Frank and his two cronies whirled to face her. Jim and Kim aimed suppressed pistols at her. Frank asked, "Who the fuck're you?"

Unfazed, she said, "I'm the Murder Queen. Duh."

"Oh," Frank said. His cronies lowered their pistols.

"Tell me one thing," Campbell said.

Frank looked at him, annoyed. "What now?"

"How did you bribe an entire factory of workers to churn out your brand of shit?"

Frank chuckled. "*I* didn't do shit. And it wasn't the entire factory. You don't need an entire factory, not even for an operation like this. All we needed were about two dozen or so guys in the right positions. Didn't even need to strike all the chords on the guitar; just the ones that could make the right sound." He nodded, grinning from ear to ear. "Yeah." He said to the Murder Queen, "We made some minor adjustments. Hope you don't mind."

Alarmed, she asked, "What 'adjustments?'"

"Relax, the plan's still going exactly as it should. We just added some flash."

"You know the score. Don't alter the plan in any way, shape, or form," she said quickly.

"Relax, lady. We know what we're doin'."

"And what *are* you doing, exactly?"

Frank shrugged. "Just threw some fireworks into the mix."

"You're gonna piss off the Boss."

"The 'Boss,' whoever he is, ain't *our* boss. He's *your* boss. He's Fairman's boss, and Fairman's our boss. We don't answer to no one else. Oh." Frank looked at Campbell and the shocked expression on his face. "Fuck's sake." He took Jim's suppressed pistol and popped a round through Campbell's forehead. He shot his jolting corpse a couple more times for good measure, then watched Campbell slump lifelessly on the floor of the stall, blood flowing down the drain. Then he turned and emptied his pistol into Conners. "Me and my big, fat mouth," he said unapologetically as he handed the pistol back to its owner. He looked at the Murder Queen and shrugged. "Oops."

She sighed, looking at the three dead cops. "This complicates things further."

"Nah. We're leaving the plant soon anyway."

She twirled her finger at the stalls, indicating the fresh patches of blood and grey matter on the walls. "Gonna do a quick clean-up, or...?"

"Relax, lady. We'll be long gone by the time this is noticed by anyone important."

Drake lingered in the entryway, silent for a time until he decided to comment on this strange new side to the Murder Queen. "I didn't peg you for such a hard-ass, lady. Or maybe you just don't like to see cops get hurt..."

"I'm just concerned about the brashness of you and your men, Drake. Wouldn't want to spoil the holiday special before it's even wrapped," she said to him.

"Oh, not to worry, my dear," Drake said as he slinked across the wall around her, stepping between her and Frank. "It's going smooth as silk. Your reaction has made me... curious, though. What do you care if a couple of cops are murdered?"

"I already told you," she said calmly.

"I find it odd that Fairman seems to be making an effort to keep you out of the loop... why do you think that is?"

She didn't have to look around to notice Jim positioning himself behind her should the need to restrain her—or worse—arise. She stayed cool, internally and externally. She wasn't afraid of these men. She was far too invulnerable for that. "Same reason he hasn't told *you* his motivations behind Operation Catalyst, or who the 'Boss' is, or what *he* wants. That's how businesses generally operate. The cogs don't need to know everything. Their only requirement is to keep on turning. I'm just an enforcer. You're the muscle. End of story."

Drake nodded slowly, his amusement wiping away any doubt in his features. "Good. I like that." He said to Frank, "That's mighty efficient of our employer, isn't it?"

Frank nodded.

"Or *employers*, whatever." Drake shrugged. He asked Frank, "So what's the deal? Should we get a move-on?"

Frank said, "They insisted they found this place by pure luck. Given 'ow things turned out for 'em, I'd argue misfortune rather than luck. This guy here with no kneecaps said he made a list and staked out a couple other dairy farms before this one, but I wouldn't trust it."

"No big deal," Drake said coolly, "we were just leaving. Soon as I hit the showers."

"About that," Frank said, looking him up and down, "What the fuck happened to you?"

"Got eviscerated by razor wire and my balls were turned into smouldering mush by a car battery. How's your day going?"

"Christ. You alright?"

"I'll heal."

"Right. Healing factor."

"Oh, but I won't forget this, that's for damn sure. Now leave, please."

Frank and his two cronies exchanged looks. "What for?"

Drake frowned. "Well unless you want to watch me shower, I suggest you fuck off. I'm covered in blood. Leave one of your knives here." He glanced at the Murder Queen, gave her a sly wink. "You can stay."

She smirked. "Maybe next time."

Drake stood alone in a vacant shower stall next to the one Conners' body occupied; naked, washing the blood off his skin under a torrent of hot water. When he was clean, he grabbed a serrated combat knife off the soap holder, took a deep breath, and then pulled it into his stomach. His muscles contorted as he strained, dragging the handle from his left hip to his right, grinding his teeth, shuddering in pleasurable agony as his organs started to slip out in a scarlet torrent of gore, piling up between his feet. Something else fell out—the tracker.

He took the knife out and dropped it on the floor. Waited till his stomach healed before he stooped down and picked up the tracker. He washed the blood off the gleaming, silver little nugget and smiled. "Clever fucker, aren't you."

Chapter 020
The Gift that Keeps on Giving

The Safehouse

Jenny grimaced under a half-face respirator as she ran the shop-vac over the scorched floor where the carpet used to be. All the windows were open and an ionizer was running in the corner. She knew there was no point in trying to get the smell out, but she also knew they only had one other safehouse out of the six they'd acquired when they first moved into Cryo City. It was a lost cause and she knew it.

"Ugh!" She turned off the shop-vac and threw the hose on the floor. "Shit! Fuck this." She went into the bedroom, crossed it to the screen door, and stepped out onto the deck overlooking the peninsula's shoreline and the river beyond. She took off the respirator and set it on the railing.

The city and all its glitzy patterns; flashing holograms hovering over its streets. The hiss of the early morning commute would fool a stranger into thinking it was anything but a crime-ridden hellhole.

But Jenny knew better than that. Even the cool breeze that swept through her hair brought a stale, almost toxic odour with it, tempting her to put the respirator back on. The dead cold of the winter's night hardly affected her; like most pyrokinetic superhumans, she was immune to the effects the season had on most living beings, like dry skin or frostbite. She could stand barefoot on this deck all night long if she had that kind of time.

She leaned on the railing and looked down at the small rocky slope leading to the thin bar of concrete lining the river. She sighed and took out her phone. Hit Damian's speed dial and let it ring.

Two rings, then he answered. "What's up?"

"When are you getting back?"

"I don't know. Might be a while. Why? Did the army of dicks attack you again?" A snicker came through the phone like static.

Scowling, Jenny said, "Our immortal friend's body parts grew a whole bottom half, Damian. I shot him with a shotgun. That just made things worse."

"What'd you do?"

"Burned them. Burned them all. The safehouse smells like shit now. Where are you? I'll help you out."

"We're way out on the outskirts, babe. No sense in coming to us."

"What're you doing way out there?"

"Tracking Drake."

"Drake?"

"That immortal piece of shit. Just another name he goes by."

"I see. Well, I'm not staying here. I can't get the smell out."

"That's the second safehouse you've burned, woman." There was a joking tone in his voice.

She couldn't help but smile. "Yeah. Oh well. Sue me."

"Where're you going to go at this hour? It's three in the morning." He yawned. "Fuck, I'm tired."

"Same. Haven't been able to sleep here. Not with the smell of burnt sausage filling the fuckin' place."

"Go to a hotel or something."

"What about the guns?"

"The place isn't a total lost cause, yet. Don't worry about them for now. Just get some sleep. Pack a few things, whatever."

"Fine. Call me later, okay?"

"Will do."

"Damian?"

"What?"

"Be safe, okay?"

"Yeah, yeah."

"I love you."

"Love you too."

She hung up and went back inside. Gathered a few things; a toothbrush, hairbrush, toothpaste, her own shampoo/conditioner and body wash; her wallet, a pair of pistols from the bedside drawer, still tucked in their shoulder holsters, which she strapped on and concealed under her brown leather jacket. She took the keys to the bike, grabbed a large backpack, slipped two cans of Broweiser beer into it, and headed down into the garage via the secret lift. She stepped into the caged armoury and packed a few pistols and an MP5K submachine gun off the racks, with their respective clips. She approached the 2017 Honda Rebel 500, finally, after what seemed like an eternity since she'd last ridden it. She swiped the tarp off, pulled the modular helmet on. She started it up, enjoyed the rumbling sensation as it roared to life. She gave it a loving pat on the handlebars. "Been too long, baby."

Two men were staking the place out in a blue armoured van on the other side of a frozen-over flood control channel. The channel was the only thing between the curb they were parked on and the fenced-in crescent of pine trees surrounding the safehouse.

One of them slept in the back while the other kept watch behind the wheel. The driver was beginning to doze when suddenly he saw something he thought he'd never see: Jenny speeding out of a hidden entrance in the channel and skidding across its icy surface with expert control and smoothness. In seconds, she was gone, vanished under the bridge connecting the side road to the peninsula, with the roar of the motorcycle's engine fading with her.

"Get up," the driver said. "Hey! Get up."

The man in the back rolled over in his sleeping bag and groaned. "What?" He mumbled.

"The girl left."

"What?"

"The girl. She just left."

The man sat upright in his sleeping bag. It was Drake—or a man bearing an uncanny resemblance to Drake. "How much time do you think we have?"

"I don't know. Heard her complain about the smell. Don't think she'll be back anytime soon."

"Time's a-wasting," the second man said as he slipped into a coat and put on a toque and mitts. "Drive around."

"You're sure?"

"Yes, idiot, I'm sure."

"Alright. Fine." The driver brought the van around, across the bridge and around the corner once it reached the safehouse's street. A summer cottage neighbourhood—doubtful anyone of consequence would notice anything. They parked right in the driveway, put on night vision visors. The Drake lookalike grabbed an ax. They both got out, headed around the garage to the back, trudging through a fresh foot of snow. They stumbled over a sudden dip in the ground. "Shit," the driver muttered. "Goddamn snow."

"Quiet," the Drake lookalike hissed.

They reached the back patio and spotted the well. They crossed the backyard. The Drake lookalike tapped the ax head against the wooden well cover and said, "Wonder how much he's grown since she threw him in here."

He hacked away at the well cover until it was a gaping hole with jagged, splintery edges. The nails Jenny had used still held the ends of the wooden planks in place.

The two of them peaked into the well.

Another Drake, looking frightened and shivering violently, waste deep in water, looked up at them with bulging eyes. Teeth chattering, hugging himself, barely any colour left in his skin.

The driver said, "It puts the lotion on its skin or else it gets the hose again."

"Aww," Drake #2 said. "You poor, poor thing. Wonder how much of your intelligence has developed by this point. Hey! Can you talk yet?"

"C-c-c-c-c-c-co...cold..."

"Well, that's something, I guess. Can you get him out?"

"With what? My enhanced senses can't dig a guy out of a well."

"Good point. Maybe the fuckers have something useful in the house." Drake #2 went over to the house and kicked the screen door. The strengthened glass spiderwebbed, didn't break. "Hm." Drake #2 kicked it a few more times, throwing everything he had into the screen until finally, it gave in, folding inward out of its frame and sliding across the floor like a wobbly magic carpet.

Drake #2 stepped inside and sniffed the sour stench of burnt flesh and mould. "Ugh. I smell awful when I'm overcooked. He whistled a little ditty he made up as he searched the place for anything that could be used to pull his clone up from the well. He tossed the place, gagging on the stench in the living room where it was strongest, and eventually went into the bedroom. He jerked the sheets off the bed and tied the ends together to make a crude rope. He spooled it, carried it outside with the excess portions of the sheets dragging behind him. He reached the well. Tossed one end down it and said, "Climb up."

Drake #3 looked at the rope, almost frozen stiff, hands tucked under his armpits.

"Grab the rope, you fucking retard," Drake #2 snapped.

Drake #3 grabbed the rope, and held on tight as Drake #2 and his driver hoisted him up into the snow. Drake #3 shivered on his knees, his jaws clapping uncontrollably.

Drake #2 and his driver wordlessly lifted him to his feet. The driver walked over to the wood chipper and started it up.

Startled by the sudden growling of the motor, Drake #3 looked up, eyes bulging in terror. He was too cold and numb to fight back as Drake #2 dragged him toward it. "N-n-n-no! *NO!*"

The whirling blades drew closer. Drake #3 screamed as the driver grabbed his other arm. Another scream was abruptly cut short by the wood chipper's whine as the intruders fed Drake #3 to it headfirst. Flailing legs went in one end, and a violent spray of red shot out the other, blasting the pine trees in red mist and saturating the snow scarlet.

Once they managed to push Drake #3's feet into the wood chipper, Drake #2 and his driver stepped around the rumbling machine to observe their handiwork. There wasn't a single portion of the snow or the trees that wasn't covered in Drake #3's blood. A few bits of bone littered the ground here and there.

And then the sea of gore started to shift around in the snow, writhing unnaturally. The little pieces started to grow flesh and bone around them. The tiny specks of flesh in the crimson flood began to metamorphose into bigger things... things independent of themselves.

As the portions of Drake #3 sprouted from his remains, Drake #2 smiled with sadistic glee. "I truly am the gift that keeps on giving..."

The Warehouse

Now Hill had a new problem: Damian was lying on the floor, staring blankly up at the ceiling, refusing to move. "Get up," Hill ordered.

"Take a hike."

Hill kicked him. "Get up, you lazy asshole."

"No."

"There are lives at stake here."

"Yeah. Mine."

"Get the fuck up."

"Fuck you."

"What's your deal?"

"I'm tired."

"Too bad, princess! What, you want a cushion or something?"

"That'd be nice."

"Get the hell up."

"In a few minutes."

"We don't *have* a few minutes."

"I do."

Hill scoffed. "You're a real piece of work, you know that?"

"Yes, I do. Am I proud of that? Yes. Yes, I am."

"Cowardly, too."

Damian scowled. "What was that?"

"You heard me. You're scared, aren't you?"

"Nope."

"A hundred-twenty to nab *this* guy alone, on top of the fifty grand for the other guys, and you're refusing to get up. You're obviously scared."

"Fifty grand a *head*, don't forget. And I'm not scared. I'm resting my head."

"Bullshit."

"Hey! I just got blasted through a wall by a grenade-launching psycho-cunt. Cut me some slack."

"I did. An hour and a half ago. It's time to move out now and earn that whopping paycheck you're extorting from us."

Damian sighed and sat up. "Christ."

"Yeah, yeah, yeah. I'm not having fun either. Smoke?" Hill offered him a cigarette. Damian took it and fired it up with a blue flame appearing on the tip of his thumb. "That's a neat little trick," Hill said.

"Drake's a powerful enemy, Hill."

"I get that."

"No, I don't think you do. I killed him. I *killed* him."

"When?"

"A year ago. Central Congoria. I ripped his fucking head off. The lab burned down. Everything was lost in the flames, or so I thought, because suddenly, almost two years later, the eggnog incident happens and this motherfucker robs a goddamned bank."

"So essentially, this is your fault. Should've known."

"Go fuck yourself, Hill."

"Let's get moving, kid. That bitch didn't blow up my car. If we hurry, we'll get to Monterey in an hour."

In the car, they were silent for a time. Nobody touched the radio because of Damian's headache, which was pounding for an extraordinarily long time despite his healing factor. Hill made sure the car was nice and toasty. They didn't even need their coats. The snow was coming down hard, flying into the windshield, looking more like warp space from an episode of *Star Trek* than a dark, snowy highway.

"Hey, kid," Hill said.

"What do you want?"

"How do you think this is gonna go down?" Hill asked. "Honestly."

Damian didn't take his eyes off the road. "What do you mean?"

"Well... there's a good possibility we'll lose. If we lose, what do you think will happen?"

"Drake's a cunt. He'll make sure our loss won't be pretty."

"But you'll survive. His poison can't even kill you."

"It did, though."

"It did?"

"I was dead for a few minutes. Not really sure how long, exactly."

"Really?"

"Really."

"Huh. Didn't know that."

"You were there."

"I saw you lying there. I didn't think you were *dead*. You were swallowing your guts a minute after I showed up—which again, was *really* gross. I just might go vegan after that shit."

Damian chortled. "More for me."

Silence. Hill pondered something that had been nagging the back of his mind for a few days now. He broke the stillness: "What is this to you?"

"What do you mean?"

"Vengeance? A matter of pride? Some kind of... code of honour, or something?" Hill scoffed. "Code of honour. Right."

Damian looked at him.

"Did you like those people? The elderly couple who used to live next door to you guys. Did you like them?"

"They were okay."

"That's not what I asked."

Damian sighed. "I didn't mind them. I didn't know them very well. I'm out a lot. Jenny knew them better than I would have ever had the time to. You know?"

Hill nodded.

"It's a matter of honour, I guess. Believe it or not."

"Really?"

"Yeah. And I'm finishing what I started. Then I'm going on vacation."

"Finishing *what*, exactly?"

"Drake," Damian said spitefully. "I'm gonna make damn sure he *stays* dead this time."

"How do you plan on doing that if you couldn't the first time?"

"What do you mean by that? You saying I'm incapable?"

"Not right now. All I'm saying is, how do you know you'll kill him for good this time, if killing him the way you'd normally kill an immortal didn't seem to work? Not that I know how to kill one... never been presented with the opportunity. But you talk about them like there's a method—and your method didn't work. So. How will you know he'll stay dead?"

He had a point and Damian knew it, and hated to admit it, so he didn't: "I'll know."

"But how?"

"Shut the fuck up and drive, you faggot."

Silence. The two of them didn't speak for few seconds. Didn't make a sound—until Hill chortled and said, "Whatever."

Chapter 021
The Naughty Latte

Monterey Farms

Ironically, Hill parked in the exact same place that Campbell had; the top of the pine dune overlooking the factory's fenced perimeter. Campbell's car wasn't there.

Damian got out and looked at the disturbed snow. "We're not the first ones up here."

Hill stepped into the snow and scanned the area, finding footprints and small trenches in the snow where something dragged over the ledge. He went around and looked down the steep slope. Far below, he could see the path where the car had tumbled, and finally, partially hidden in the trees at the bottom, Campbell's upturned car, right turn signal beeping. Hill's heart sank. "Campbell!" He leaped off the ledge and half-dashed, half-rolled down the slope, skidding on his feet and snatching a low-hanging branch to stop his descent once he'd reached the car. He crouched, looked through the broken windows. The door chime *dinged* continuously, as the driver side door was twisted ajar and the rear passenger side door on the other side was missing.

No bodies inside.

Damian telekinetically lifted Hill back up the slope, letting him hit the odd rock here and there, before finally setting him down beside him. "Nothing?"

"They're gone."

"Yeah, they're gone," Damian said. "If they aren't down there, it's safe to say they're dead."

"Don't be so goddamn cynical. They might've—"

"Don't bother. They're dead. Drake got them."

Hill crumpled to his knees and groaned. "Goddamn it... Campbell..."

Damian didn't have the patience for this. "You can stay right here and mourn your boyfriend while I go down there and check it out. That place is too quiet. And yet..."

COBALT CHRISTMAS: A COBALT ROGUE STORY

Damian rummaged through Hill's coat pocket, meeting no protest from Hill, and took out the tracker, which indicated that their prey *was* inside the factory. "Hm," Damian said. He had a feeling something wasn't right. A strange, creeping chill between his shoulder blades. Additional stress, as indicated by the sudden urge to shit. It quickly passed.

Damian dropped the tracker in front of Hill and said, "I'll be back." And, with that, he leaped into the sky in a black, swirling column of energy, soared over the needle spires of the pines and a back road leading... somewhere. He passed over the fence, swooped toward the roof, landed without a sound on top of an air conditioning unit. He dashed across the roof like a dark blue phantom to the ledge overlooking the rear lot. He leaned over the side, looking down at the column of light streaming out of the loading bay. Shutters hadn't been dropped. His suspicions were heightened.

Cautiously, he went over the side—halfway, waist-deep in the shadows on the side of the building above the entryway, drifting toward the top of the frame. He dived out of the wall, flipped and turned, hovered in a thin blue aura inside the loading bay.

Not a soul in sight. Not a creature was stirring, not even a mouse. The trucks were gone, too.

Staying in the rafters, Damian perched himself on a steel beam, listening to the industrial hum vibrating through the factory. *Weird... maybe he found the tracker.*

From his perch, he spotted something he never wanted to ever see again: a big, grey rectangular box about three feet tall, five feet long, and three feet wide. A digital console was on the side of it with a timer display. On top of it was a tablet folded in a triangle, screen facing forward, and in front of it, a small China... teacup?

A fucking A/N bomb was Damian's first guess as he dropped to a crouch from the rafters. Two hundred tonnes of ammonium nitrate packed inside a container with a small remote-controlled charge on the lock. A favourite for insane radicals and gung-ho terror cells on the black market. Damian himself had used one once—he'd be lying if he said he didn't enjoy the result.

But now he was standing in front of one under the control of a man whose whereabouts were officially unknown. *Great.* He cautiously approached the box. Carefully lifted the teacup off of it and looked into it. Just a harmless latte with the words 'FUCK

YOU' skillfully written on the surface in cursive with steamed milk. *Cute.*

The tablet screen lit up. Damian looked up and saw Drake smiling ear-to-ear at him. "I knew you'd find this place eventually," Drake said.

Damian scowled at him, eyes burning with hatred.

"Don't look so glum. You should be grateful. Even after you and your cop friend tortured me mercilessly, I was still gracious enough to have left you an early Christmas present."

"The bomb?"

"The latte!" Drake laughed.

"Go fuck yourself, Drake."

"Oh, I wouldn't drop that latte, either, if I were you." The image flickered as he adjusted the position of the screen. "I laced it with a little something. Heh. Nothing like a little nitroglycerin to kick-start your senses early in the morning."

Damian's blood ran cold. He looked at the teacup in his hands, and suddenly, getting his hands to stop shaking just got a whole lot harder, and a lot more dangerous.

Drake chuckled. "And I wouldn't use my telekinesis to move the bomb or the teacup, either. That box is on a thin pressure-sensitive plate, and there's no fuckin' way you'll ever be able to pull an Indiana Jones out of your ass and replace it with something else in the nick of time. Not just because it only takes an eighth of a second to set off the pressure plate, but also because there's nothing within a mile of you that weighs two hundred tonnes for you to replace it with. Also, you're trapped in an invisible laser box that was activated by motion sensors picking up your approach. If you step out of that perimeter, you're Christmas past, and so are the, oh, four hundred and thirty-two workers currently working the night shift in that plant. Even if *you* somehow managed to survive the blast, you'd have the deaths of over four hundred workers on your conscience. You're fucked, kid. You're *fucked*! That latte's gonna kill you good, boy!"

"What makes you think any of this can kill me?"

"Excuse me—two hundred tonnes of compressed ammonium nitrate detonating when you're just a foot away from it *won't* kill you?" Drake scoffed. "Please. The force of the blast alone would just about *incinerate* you. There won't *be* enough left of you to heal."

Damian snarled, "You've thought of everything, haven't you?"

"Maybe."

"And when this is all over, how do you plan on escaping after doing... whatever it is you're about to do?"

"Who said anything about escaping? Maybe this is where it'll all end for me."

"Bullshit. That's not how you want this to go."

"No, that's how *you* want this to go, isn't it?"

"I'm talking to a genius," Damian said sarcastically. "How much are you getting paid for this stunt, Drake?"

"Enough."

"Oh, really?"

"Yeah, I think so. Especially now that you're here. Goddamn, this was just another operation, but then *you*, of all people, back from the dead and everything, came along and... and I just *had* to stay in town! There was no fuckin' way I was going to skip out on the opportunity to finish you off. I owe you for Central Congoria. That raid you pulled on our lab *really* set us back. My boss hates your guts."

"Oh yeah, your boss." Damian squinted. "What was his name again?"

"Nice try."

"Damn it."

Drake scoffed. "Even if you found out, it wouldn't matter. You can't hold that latte forever. Sooner or later, you gotta disintegrate."

"Over my dead body."

"Oh, you mean the little itty-bitty pile of ashes you're gonna be soon?"

"If I'm gonna die anyway, why not tell me the plan? At least let me know what I failed to stop."

"Uh, no."

"Why not?!"

"Because I've seen every *James Bond* movie ever made, that's why."

"So what? Did you lose your balls on that warehouse floor?"

Drake scowled. "My balls regenerated just fine, thank you."

"Oooh, getting defensive, are we?"

"No."

"*Dā.*"

"No."

"*Dā!*"

"*No*, I'm not."

"Fucking faggot."

"Says the guy holding a teacup to prolong his doom!"

"Oh, yeah?" Damian waved his free hand around. He took five steps back, five steps forward. "No motion sensor? I knew it! I *knew*! I bet this isn't even laced with nitroglycerin."

Drake's frown darkened.

Damian held his hand out and poured a drop onto the floor. It hit the concrete, sizzled, then depressed, burning a small hole into the concrete. "Acid," Damian said. He turned around to face Drake. "You think you're *so* clever."

"I *am* clever."

"You sound like an ugly child trying to remember his pep talks with his over-bearing mom that he's beautiful during his first day at school despite everyone telling him he looks fucking hideous. What do they call that? Oh yeah. Deluded."

"Wow, you're an asshole."

"And *you're* going down, bitch!"

"No, you."

"*Nyet.* Now I'm going to disarm your little toy." Damian started to trickle the acid on the lock and watched the metal rapidly corrode. As the acid ate away at the lock and the receiver, Drake started to snicker. Damian asked, "What's so funny?"

"I wasn't lying about the pressure-sensitive plate."

It took Damian a second. He looked at the acid and how it was making the box just a little bit lighter. Then he said, "Fuck."

From his spot, Hill couldn't see a damn thing. He figured he'd just wait in the car, smoking a cigarette, mourning Campbell. Then—

KASSSHHRRRRRRRRRAAAAAAAAAAKKKKK!

An ear-splitting roar ripped the sky apart as a blinding burst of light filled the car and blinded Hill, making him scream in terror. A shockwave slammed into the car's passenger side, flipped it off the ground, smashed it against a pine tree.

COBALT CHRISTMAS: A COBALT ROGUE STORY

Down below, a huge red fireball rose up high above the trees, spreading outward, devouring everything—instantaneously melting the snow, exploding every vehicle in the parking lot as it tossed them across the highway like toys; incinerating the trees, uprooting the fences and road signs. Everything from the roads to the rocks peeled off the surface of the earth and wilted away, fading into nothingness in the harsh flames. The slope absorbed the flames, its surface blackening as the violent waves sent blazing rocks tumbling upward from the sheer force.

The fireball stretched into the clouds and curled at the top, blossoming into a flickering mushroom cloud. The brilliant light faded as it became a column of black smoke. Any trace of the factory had been replaced by a gigantic crater in the earth. The trees and the portion of the highway up to a half-mile of the blast were nowhere to seen. Just scorched blackness emitting smoke into the night amidst a low, menacing rumble.

Hill groaned in his overturned car. Ears ringing. Vision blurred and blocked by purple dots, head feeling like it was about to burst. Curled upside down on his shoulders, seatbelt stubbornly pinning him against his seat. He groaned, drew a knife from a sheath under his right pant leg, and severed his seatbelt. He collapsed in a heap and crawled out of his car onto the warm ground. He got up, staggered against his car. Looked behind him and up at the monolithic mushroom cloud that seemed to loom over him. "Jesus... Jesus Christ... Oh, Jesus."

Damian. What the hell happened to Damian?

Hill stumbled around his car and reached the edge. He dropped to his knees, looked at ground zero and its glowing crater in awe and terror. "God..."

Six kilometres out along a back road, Drake's truck led the motorcade of armoured vans, cargo trucks, and tankers flanked by snowmobiles. The commercial transports had left a bit earlier, taking the highway to the city. Nobody would suspect them just yet, and they would never survive these back roads through the pines— far too bumpy, with too many sharp turns and dips.

Drake listened to the thunderous roar of the explosion and giggled. "No milky latte for you!"

Frank grinned behind the wheel. In the back, the Murder

Queen was biting the end of a toothpick with a sour look on her face.

Drake closed the tablet and tossed it out the window. Then he rolled up his window and looked at the Murder Queen in the rearview mirror. "Why so glum, babe?"

"That was bound to get somebody's attention. Keep it up and they'll issue a state of emergency. That's gonna make our job harder."

"Always looking at the negative side of life, eh? I'd hoped you'd be a little more optimistic about this. You gotta look at it differently. With Damian Warkowski dead and gone, there's very little that can get in our way."

"What makes you think you killed him?"

"Lady, he was standing two feet away from two hundred fucking tonnes of ammonium nitrate. If he ain't completely *dust* after that, then there truly *is* a God, and *we're* not the ones that holy prick is smiling on. Besides," he added as he set his seat back a couple notches and placed his feet on the dash, "our job is *literally* to force a state of emergency, and then some. I'd say we were over-qualified for this job."

"You can say that again," Frank said.

The two men laughed in front of her. The Murder Queen's brow furrowed in anger.

Chapter 022
Burnout

Monterey Farms

5:32 AM. Emergency responders finally arrived to quell the raging fires. Paramedics and chemical experts arrived on the scene as police cordoned off the highway and redirected traffic.

Hill sat on the back of a fire truck, wrapped in a blanket, breathing through an oxygen mask. He was surrounded by two firemen and a chemical expert looking for any signs of radiation or infection. He was still dazed, being bombarded with questions. He felt out of breath; only able to answer in short sentences.

"Christ, I don't know," Hill said. "All I knew was that the place... produced milk and then it just... exploded."

"Do you feel woozy?" the chemical expert asked. "Did you notice any strange odours in the smoke?"

"Yes and no."

"What do you mean 'yes and no'?"

"The explosion flipped my car. I'm still dizzy. My ears are still ringing. It was loud..."

"Any strange colours?"

"Not that I could tell."

"You didn't see anything that would warrant a chemical search?"

"You're gonna look anyway. Why keep asking me these fucking questions?"

"Just want to make sure there's no immediate threat, sir."

Hill felt himself start to drown in all the noise. So many voices... the sirens, the blaring horns, the rumble of the flames on either side of the obliterated highway, the whirring helicopters in the air.

"Keep that fire from spreading!" a firefighter shouted, pointing at the slope Hill had parked on top of.

"Haven't ruled out the possibility that we're dealing with a chemical fire..."

"Might be at least three cops in there somewhere..."

"Doubt we'll find 'em."

"Anybody got an official tally on the worker casualties?"

"My men are still in the first wing—I *think* it's the first wing... no signs of—"

"Hey! I think I see something!"

"Someone's... *walking* in that!"

"Jesus Christ Almighty."

"We got a survivor!"

Hill looked up. He jumped off the fire truck bumper and went around; saw a large crowd gathering at the edge of the safety barrier, clamouring to see a figure in the orange smoke. Hill lost his blanket, kept his breathing apparatus as he started shoving his way through the crowd. "Move! *Move*, goddamn it! Move!" He reached the barrier and saw, sure enough, a black skeletal figure lumbering toward them. Ghastly, inhuman, silhouetted by the flames behind it. But Hill knew exactly who it was. It couldn't be anyone else.

"Get him out of there!" Carver barked. Hill started to move in the direction of his voice.

"It's too hot! Fire's too strong," the fire chief yelled. "Nothing we can do!"

The spectral figure staggered out of the flames. A burning phantom, almost demonic in his appearance as his healing factor struggled to keep up with the flames. He reached the Plexiglas barrier and pressed a bloody, burning hand against it. The crowd of frightened cops and firemen started to pull back. The blazing man climbed over the barrier and plummeted to the ground, inciting a few screams from the crowd as it landed in a crumpled heap.

"Christ, *now* will someone help him?!" Carver roared.

Two fireman rushed through the crowd with buckets of water and dumped them on the figure, putting out the flames, a cloud of smoke rising from his skin.

Sssssssssssssss!

Another fireman threw a thick blanket over the survivor. Everyone watched in awe as his severe burns healed, his skin reverted back to its normal peach colour. His cobalt blue hair started to sprout from his head. That's when Hill intervened, saying, "Come on, let's take you to an ambulance." He draped one of Damian's arms over his shoulder and carried him away from the crowd, though many curious onlookers followed.

Sitting in the back of an ambulance with the blanket pulled over his face like a hood, Damian's eyes remained distant as an astonished paramedic checked him out. "Not a friggin' scratch!"

Hill was standing outside, watching until he noticed a few curious firemen and cops approaching from both sides. He climbed into the ambulance and shut the doors. "Alright, doc. Is he okay?"

"Can't say about any internal damage, but he looks okay. Pupils respond to the light. The inside of his mouth looks fine. I don't get it. He should be dead. *More* than dead."

"Yeah, he *should* be," Hill joked. "Give us a minute?"

The paramedic nodded and jumped outside. He was gracious enough to shut the door behind him, leaving the two of them alone in the ambulance.

Hill stooped in front of Damian and studied the thousand-yard stare in his eyes. "Hey. Can you hear me, kid?"

No response.

Hill gave his cheek a light slap. "Hey! You alright?"

"What do you think?" Damian rasped.

"Okay, good. You can talk."

"I'm not retarded. Fuck."

"You just survived an explosion."

"I'm fucking aware."

"Do you know what was in it?"

"Ammo—" Damian coughed.

"Ammo...?"

"Ammonium nitrate."

Hill furrowed his brow. "How much?"

"Two hundred tonnes, maybe."

"Did any of the workers get out?"

Damian shook his head slowly. "Never knew what hit them."

"How did *you* get out?"

"Put up a shield before I... could be completely... completely disintegrated..."

"Here, here." Hill gave him his oxygen. Damian took it and took steady breaths through the mask. "He knew we were coming..."

Damian nodded. "Found the tracker. Planted it on the bomb."

"Are you sure it was ammonium nitrate? Maybe it was a

chemical bomb?"

"Relax, dipshit. There's nothing in that smoke that could... kill a guy except the smoke itself... trust me... I've used one before."

"Not gonna ask about that."

"Good."

The door swung open. Damian and Hill turned to see Captain Carver climbing into the box with them, fuming. He slammed the door shut behind him. "Do you stupid sons of bitches have *any* idea what you've done?"

Damian had a snappy response ready, but Hill cut him off with a quick hand gesture right in his face. Annoyed, Damian nonetheless said nothing, instead breathing through the apparatus.

Carver said, "You blew up a multi-million dollar factory. You *killed* three hundred workers, and you fuckers have nothing to show for it, do you?"

Hill was about to protest when Damian started to say something, only to break into a violent coughing fit. The two cops waited until Damian got himself under control. Carver asked him, "Something you wanna say, freak?"

Damian cleared his throat and said, "*Four* hundred workers."

Carver was reaching boiling point when Hill stepped in, "Captain, I know we fucked up—"

"You're goddamn right you fucked up. Where's Drake? Where are they going to strike next? Hell, have you possibly heard from Campbell? He was supposed to call me an hour ago."

"Campbell's dead," Damian said bluntly.

Carver gaped at him. "What?"

"Drake bragged about it right before he sparked the bomb." The last thing Damian needed was for Carver to know that *he* accidentally set off the bomb. He was already pissed off.

Carver heaved a sigh and leaned against the wall, giving himself a moment to process the loss. His voice was significantly lower, almost a burning whisper. "Before I do something I'll regret, I'm going to send you both home. Is your car in working order?"

"Not really," Hill said.

Carver sighed. "You guys are such a fucking thorn in my side... I'll have Fritz drive you home. You're both off the case."

"Suspended, sir?" Hill asked.

"I'm thinking about. Take the day off in the meantime."

"Hey, wait one goddamn minute," Damian said. "What about my pay?"

"You'll get paid for services rendered. Don't you worry. You'll get what's comin' to you."

Damian scoffed at the implication. "So will you."

Hill wasn't about to argue with the Captain. "Come on, kid. We're outta here." He walked by his boss and kicked the ambulance door open. Damian followed wrapped in the blanket, stealing one last icy glare Carver's way before stepping down from the ambulance.

The road home in Fritz's patrol car was quiet and strangely peaceful. Fritz had lo-fi music playing softly on the radio. Damian and Hill sat behind the divider, staring out their respective windows for a time. Something was eating away at Hill.

"Hey, kid."

"Stop calling me that," Damian snapped.

"Fine. How about 'Blue'?"

"Whatever."

Hill chuckled, trying to be friendly. "You know, it's funny. I used to have a great reputation. Then I met you."

Damian didn't make a sound.

Hill cleared his throat. "So I guess this'll be the last time I'll be seeing you for a while, huh?"

"What makes you think so?"

"Carver's pissed. He might just about fire us both."

"I wish I was that lucky."

"Hey, at least you get paid."

"Meh."

Hill looked out the window.

"I'm pissed off."

"Okay."

"I hate getting burned alive."

"I guess anyone would."

Lisa said from the passenger seat beside Fritz, "It hurts, doesn't it?"

"Shut up, Lisa."

"Who?" Hill asked.

Fritz looked at Damian in the rearview mirror.

Damian shook his head. "You know Drake's gonna win if we leave this alone, right?"

"What choice do we have? Captain wants us gone."

"Fuck the Captain."

Fritz said, "I wouldn't go against the Captain if I were you."

"Shut the fuck up and drive, shithead."

Fritz scoffed and pulled over to the curb in front of Hill's house. "We're already here." He got out and opened Hill's door like a chauffeur. Hill and Damian climbed out into the cold morning air. "Heed my advice, freak," Fritz said.

"Blow it out your ass," Damian snarled.

Fritz shook his head, got back into his car, and drove off down the street.

Damian looked around, clutching his blanket, still naked under it. It was a nice enough neighbourhood; bungalows lined the quiet streets, guarded by large trees that ranged from maple to pine. A snowman loitered on every other front yard.

Hill's house had a front porch with dry vines running up the posts and across the roof like veins. Old-fashioned brick house with a picture window in front. Hill reached the door and turned to look at Damian. "Want a coffee?"

"What makes you think I want your hospitality?"

"Aren't you cold? You're barefoot in fresh snow."

Damian looked down at the snow squishing between his toes. His powers... they were in recession again. Shit.

"Come on inside, you idiot," Hill said as he unlocked the door and opened it.

Damian sighed, embarrassed by the shameful position he'd found himself in. He scaled the steps and stomped inside past Hill. The place was surprisingly clean for a bachelor's house. Framed pictures adorned the fireplace mantle. An eighty-inch widescreen TV hung from the wall next to a corridor beside the kitchen. The kitchen itself was pretty standard, surrounded by a partition wall that doubled as a bar counter. A small dining area adjacent to the front door, with a screen door leading to a snow-covered patio on the other side. A few framed movie posters hung on the walls.

Hill chuckled and shut the door. Locked it. "I'm guessing that explosion destroyed your phone, too."

"I was a quarter-conscious burning skeleton before my shield went up. *Way* too close."

"He almost got you?"

"Goddamn right he did. That's twice now he's almost succeeded in killing me these past couple days."

"I have some spare clothes in my room. They might fit you."

"Better than this blanket." Damian dropped onto the couch and sighed, back facing Hill.

"Make yourself at home," Hill said. He kicked his boots off, slipped out of his coat and hung it on the hook, and then went between the living room and the kitchen into the corridor that led to the bathroom, closet, and the bedroom. He called out from the bedroom, "You want to call your girlfriend? My landline still works."

"She's asleep. Nobody wakes her up. Trust me."

"I'll take your word for it. Hey, do you know what size you are?"

"Large, I guess."

"Don't have too many large shirts..."

"Probably because you're a fat fuck."

"Don't make me regret welcoming you into my home, Damian."

Damian reached for the remote, which was on the coffee table. Silently ordered it to move. It didn't. Telekinesis wasn't working. He grunted as he leaned forward and snatched the remote off the table. He turned on the TV and started flipping through channels. Found nothing interesting on.

Hill returned with a pair of army fatigue pants and a bad Hawaiian shirt—puke green with brilliantly coloured aloha flowers all over it. He held up the clothes for Damian to see.

Damian stared at the shirt, not sure whether or not he should be taking this seriously. "What... is *that*?"

"It's an aloha shirt."

"I know *what* it is, you shit. What the hell do you think you're doing with it?"

"Letting you wear it." Hill couldn't stop himself from grinning.

"I hate you."

Hill laughed.

"I hate you so much."

Hill tossed the clothes his way. "Not much else for you to wear in this house. Nothing I don't want, anyway."

Damian caught the clothes and scowled.

Hill went into the kitchen. "You can use my shower while you wait for that coffee, too."

"Why would I want to do that?"

"Because you smell like cow shit that's been cooked on brimstone, that's why."

Damian grunted and stood up off the couch with the clothes. "Got a spare shaving kit?"

"Second drawer."

Damian entered the bathroom and locked the door.

Hill sat down on a stool behind the counter and opened up the photos on his phone. He scrolled through the folders and noticed two folders—one had a woman in it, smiling brightly. The other had the pictures Jenny had sent him the other day. He squinted. By some cruel turn, the two folders just *happened* to be right next to each other.

He felt a wave of disgust hit him where it hurt. The failures, the things he's done. He opened the folder next to Jenny's, the one with the smiling woman. A brunette dressed in a white shirt and tight jeans, sitting on a rock by the lake. His heart pounded; every beat against his chest a spirit-smashing pang.

He tried to scroll through the folder and instead hit the back button on the touch screen. "Shit," he muttered. He saw Jenny again. He pressed down on Jenny's folder and immediately deleted it.

After his shower, Damian wiped steam off the mirror and took a good, long look at himself. He looked like hell. Couldn't remember the last time he'd slept. The dark circles under his eyes were nothing new to him, but something about his face, at least to him, looked lifeless. Maybe it was the recession.

He ran his hand across his chin, feeling the stubble, the growing beard. It felt prickly and uncomfortable. He shaved it and got dressed in the clothes Hill provided for him, noting the lack of underwear and socks. Luckily the pants weren't tight-fitting.

He stepped out in a cloud of steam and headed for the kitchen, smelling a fresh pot of coffee in the air. He found Hill slumped over the bar staring at his phone. Sensing something was off, Damian said, "Coffee's ready."

Hill looked up suddenly, as if snapped out of a trance. "What?"

Damian pointed at the black coffee pot.

"Oh. Here, let me get that." Hill stood up and went around tending to their drinks as Damian took a seat on the stool beside Hill's.

Filling their mugs with coffee, Hill glanced over his shoulder at him. "You look better without the beard." Turned back to their mugs. "More professional."

Damian didn't say anything.

"You take cream? Sugar?"

"Lots of both."

"Lots of both, huh. Didn't peg you to have much of a sweet tooth."

"Making up for lost time."

"Didn't you eat sweets when you were a kid? Maybe you went trick-r-treating?"

"I was too busy fighting my father's wars. I didn't have the time nor the privilege to be a kid like the other kids."

"Why'd he do it?"

"Haven't you heard enough of my war stories?"

"They intrigue me despite how fucked up they are."

"Maybe you're just rooting for information."

"Not today." Hill finished preparing their mugs, and brought Damian's over to him with a teaspoon in it. "I'm not a nosy cop today. I'm just Donald Hill, a lonely bachelor with nothing but time to kill."

"'Lonely—'?" Damian looked at him, arched an eyebrow. "You're not a queer, are you?"

"You know, for a kid born in the 2010s, you sure are anything *but* progressive. And no, I'm not gay."

Damian stirred his coffee.

"Ask you something?"

"You've asked me plenty already."

"Why haven't your clothes regenerated?"

Damian sighed and leaned back on the stool. He glared at Hill.

"It's called a recession."

"What does the decline of the economy have to do with your powers?"

"No, idiot. It's a telekinetic recession. It used to be called something else but then everybody started making menstruation jokes out of it, so I started calling it a recession."

"Okay..."

"Every month, depending on how often I use my powers, my body starts to slow down. I can't use my powers. It's more-or-less a self-preserving mechanism to keep my body from 'overheating,' I guess. If I use my powers too much, especially during the recession, my body might not be able to take it. It might get overwhelmed, and that's when the shit will really hit the fan."

"What happens then?"

"Well, I only tried it once." He sipped his coffee. "It didn't end well. Ever watch *Akira*?"

"*Akira*? No."

"1988."

"That's a long time ago, even for me, kid."

"Okay, well, forget it, then. But that's pretty much what happened."

"Okay, so what you're saying is that you're basically useless now."

"Not at all. I still have most of my strength. That's what those old wars were for. So I'd be prepared and more than ready to win against any odds even *without* the majority of my powers. That's why I have actual guns stashed all over the place."

"With permits?"

"Oh, *sure*, sure." Damian smirked.

"I'll take that as a 'no.'" Hill shook his head and sipped his coffee. "So what're we going to do about Drake?"

"You still want to take them down?"

"Of course."

"But your Captain..."

"You said it yourself, kid. 'Fuck the Captain.'"

Damian said, "We don't even know where they went. My contact hasn't gotten back to me. Or maybe they did, I don't know... my phone's gone."

"Your contact?" Hill's eyes lit up. "You have someone inside

Drake's organization?!"

"Yeah," Damian said.

"Who?"

"I can't tell you that. Can't risk any leaks."

"But it's *me*."

"Right. A cop. A crooked one."

"I'm not *that* crooked."

"Yes, you are."

"Fine. Okay. Putting that aside. So your phone's lost in the explosion. How do we get your contact to call us?"

Damian shrugged. "I only gave them two numbers."

"Two numbers, good. What is it, a spare cell phone? A pager?"

"A *pager*? In this day and age?"

"Some people still use them..."

"It's another phone."

"Where's the other phone?"

"In my car."

"Where's your car?"

Damian paused, trying to remember. "Where *is* my car...?"

They retraced their steps. Hill was the fastest. He jumped and yelled, "The hospital! Right? The hospital. You drove that ambulance out of the hospital."

"Right, yeah. The hospital. It's probably still there."

"It's a twenty-minute walk from here."

"Too long. Too tired. Going to sleep."

"We don't have time for sleep. The next attack is gonna happen today."

"No, it's going to happen *tonight*. It's only 7 AM. Let's sleep while we still can and get back to it when we wake up." Damian finished his coffee and headed for the couch.

"Meanwhile, your contact will be with the enemy, possibly arriving in their next target location in an hour, if that, and then they'll try to call your phone, but you won't answer, so we'll miss our opportunity to nab them."

"It has voicemail, you moron." Damian fell on the couch and fell right to sleep.

"Damian."

No answer.

"Hey!"

Still nothing. Hill sighed. "Fine. But only till noon." He yawned. "Guess I could use some myself..."

Chapter 023
Proposition

Campturn District

10:52 AM.

In the far southern area of Cryo City, the snow was at its lightest, melting away under the sun. The black community that populated the district's streets enjoyed the warm change in the midst of a harsh winter. Even the gangsters that ruled their own self-designated areas were relaxing, enjoying themselves on their front porches and in their backyards.

In a fenced-in basketball court surrounded on three sides by homes with gardens and tall oak fences, a group of hoods were playing each other on the court; not so much keeping score, just shooting hoops and stealing the ball from whoever had it. Even in this day and age, a modernized boom box-style CD player blasted hip hop music from the court's edge.

There weren't too many cars in the street. The mid-morning commute was calm and steady. That is, until an armoured van started to back up toward the court; bounced over the curb, crossed the sidewalk, and knocked the fence flat.

The hoods jumped away, chattering in confusion as the van knocked the basketball net right out of the ground.

"What the fuck?"

"Hell is this?"

"Somebody got damn drunk or somethin'."

"Bet that's a white boy behind the wheel..."

The van stopped in the middle of the court. The front doors opened—Jim hopped out of the passenger side while Frank emerged from the driver's seat. He approached the group of hoods, taking note of a few firearms being discreetly drawn from under waistbands. He smiled warmly and said, "Gentlemen, there's no need for violence here."

"Who the fuck're you?" a tall, muscular man in a jersey and shorts stepped forward, looming over Frank. "What'cha think you're doin', bargin' in here like you own the damn place?"

"Got a proposition for you boys."

"Oh, really? Who are you?"

"I'm Santa Claus. This is my elf," Frank said, indicating Jim. "It doesn't matter *who* I am... what matters is what I can give you... and what you have to do to earn what I have to give you."

"What makes you think I *want* whatever it is you got to give me?"

"Because... what's your name?"

"They call me Djimon Ice."

"Because, Mr. Ice—mind if I call you 'Mr. Ice'?"

Ice shrugged.

"What I've got for ya is power. A special kinda power." Frank cocked his head toward Jim, who immediately threw open the back doors to the van, revealing four crates bristling with assault rifles and rockets. Munitions cases were crammed in the back seat.

The crowd of hoods shared a collective gasp. The more paranoid ones started looking around, trying to figure out if this was a setup or the real deal; looking for anyone who shouldn't be there, watching them. The coast was clear, as far as they knew.

"*Fire*power," Frank said with a mischievous grin.

Djimon narrowed his eyes, shifting suspicious glances from Jim to Frank. "Who are you?"

"I told you, that's not important," Frank said. "All of this is yours if you do one thing for us. Think about it. You won't just have control of the park up to the convenience store on 45th... all of Campturn will be your turf. They got little machine pistols, sawn-offs, and knives, maybe a grenade or two... you? You'll have *rockets*. Mortars. RPGs. Assault rifles. Submachine guns. All military-grade and completely untraceable. Nobody will be able to touch you, and the world is yours. You won't have to be cramped up in that one-bedroom apartment with your wife and kids."

Djimon's eyes darted from the arsenal to Frank, alarmed.

Frank kept on grinning. "Or that little slice of white bread you keep on the side. Didn't you have a kid with that one, too?"

Djimon snarled, "What did you do with them?"

"Nothin', nothin'. Keep your lead in your guns, boys. S'alright. We ain't gonna harm anybody's special someone unless we gotta. Just extra leverage."

"How do we know you're telling the truth?"

Frank cleared his throat. Pointed at Djimon. "You live in the apartment complex on 34th Street South." He pointed at a scrawny hood standing on Djimon's left. "CJ Smith, twenty-four, got a pregnant girlfriend waiting for you in the same building. I believe there's a Michael Mund'har hiding back there somewhere..."

"Enough," Djimon said.

Frank looked at him expectantly.

Djimon looked at his crew. His boys exchanged looks with him. They'd grown up together. They could communicate just by eye contact and physical gestures. Everything seemed to be unanimous. Djimon sighed, and turned to Frank again. He asked, slowly, "What do you want us to do?"

Manharttigan Mall

11:30 AM.

The Manharttigan Mall was the largest mall in Cryo City, dominating the downtown area with a vast, wraparound parking lot surrounding forty acres of neo-postmodern towers bristling from a cross-shaped structure; an intricate blend of steel, marble, and glass. Its four wings stretched out in different directions lined with glass-plated domes tipped by blinking spires. The central structure was a thirty-acre dome designed to resemble a giant disco ball, crowned by ten observation towers. The dome's highest point reached 6,500 feet off the ground. The perfectly symmetrical design was ruined by the rear loading dock and storage area—a concrete block seemingly wedged in between the east and south wings.

Inside, the place was packed with shoppers rushing to get last-minute gifts for close family and not-so-close relatives. Little neon cartoons danced across the surfaces of glass block dividers that lined the strips and additional parapets surrounding all the walkways. Potted palm trees stood beside every pillar, wrapped in tinsel. Animated holograms of glamorous women dressed according to the latest trends pranced above kiosks and independent stalls. Electric strips of peach and teal lined the mint-coloured walls.

Under the central dome, an artificially enhanced Christmas tree stood tall, its star shining brightly. The gigantic tree was adorned with thousands of Christmas baubles, four kilometres of sparkling tinsel, hundreds of packaged toys donated from a dozen store chains;

and around the middle, a belt made of digital Christmas countdown clocks counting down the days, hours, minutes, and seconds till Christmas Day. Eight-foot-tall nutcrackers stood guard around the base of the tree. Facing the north wing was Santa's chair on an appropriately colourful North Pole backdrop, with stairs lined with candy cane poles leading straight to it. The hired Santa Claus had a long line of children patiently waiting their turn to sit on his lap.

Outside, a caravan led by the commercial trailers with three cargo trucks trailing behind arrived at the gate. Drake leaned out the driver's window of the leading cab, looked at the guard in the booth. The guard fixed him a quick look, nodded, opened the gate. Drake smiled and drove into the lot. The trailers and cargo trucks were pushed up against the loading docks, ready to be unloaded.

The Murder Queen climbed out of Drake's cab and watched as a foot soldier closed the shutters by remote, leaving only the cold, steel-blue saturation from the fluorescent lights hanging above them.

"What do you think?" Drake asked her.

"How the hell did you manage to get this much clearance from security? Or did you just take over the whole damn mall?"

"Cut a deal with big man billionaire Manharttigan. Wasn't too hard. The insurance'll pay more than it took to build this place."

The Murder Queen said nothing else.

Drake and the Murder Queen went to the security room and found themselves surrounded on three sides by video walls; hundreds of screens showed them just about every interior area of the mall outside of the employees-only sector. Drake went over to the phone, turning on a remote scrambler as he hit 9 to go to the outside line. He dialed a number and waited.

"Fairman's office," Fairman said as he dismissed his secretary. "Is it all going as planned?"

"Smooth as silk," Drake said. "Got the Murder Queen here with me."

"Good. You'll need an extra set of eyes and ears for this. What about the Dead Blue?"

"Taken care of."

"Are you sure?"

"Kid's less than ashes. I made sure of that at the dairy farm."

"You better be damn sure, Drake. I don't want a repeat of what happened in Central Congoria."

"It's all good, Colonel. I kinda doubt even *he* could survive the explosion from the distance he was in."

"Has Frank gotten back to you yet?"

"Yeah, about half an hour ago. He's got the gangs locked and loaded. When they show up, we'll send the guards who're none-the-wiser in first. Ought to tie up a few loose ends that way."

"Good. This is good. Keep it up, Drake. After tomorrow, Afrókrema will be basking in its former glory."

"Yessir. Over and out." Drake hung up. Waited another second before he switched off the scrambler.

"There a ladies room around here somewhere?" the Murder Queen asked.

Drake smiled at her. "Down the center hall, take a left, then a right."

"Thanks."

He watched her leave. As soon as the door was shut behind her, Drake turned to one of his men and said, "Keep an eye on her."

She left the control room and waited for a foot soldier to pass her as he pushed a crate full of rockets on a dolly down the corridor. She went straight down the corridor, following Drake's directions, passing security guards and workers on her way to the restroom. She sensed a tail. *Really? Don't trust little ol' me?* She smirked as she turned the last corner and entered the women's restroom. Her tail was definitely a man, and a lousy one by the looks of him. If he tried anything—doubtful, but she wouldn't put it past one of these guys—she could easily take him down.

She went into a stall and locked it. Sat down. Listened. She couldn't hear anything except for a voice on the intercom, distant, muffled by the concrete walls and the ventilation system. She looked up at the vent above her stall and started to climb.

As an automated forklift buzzed out of the waste management sector, a vent in the ceiling opened up. The Murder Queen peeked out of the vent and looked around. Most of the waste management sector was a raised platform just wide enough for the forklifts to get through. Beside the platform sat a thirty-yard self-contained compactor with a rear-loading doghouse. On the other side of the platform on a higher elevation was an office encased in glass. Between them was a ramp leading to the rear exit, currently shuttered.

Coast clear.

She swooped down out of the vent and landed in a crouch with cat-like agility and jogged up the stairs and across the catwalk to the office. She snatched the portable phone and took it with her underneath the desk, hidden from view. She activated her own scrambler, hit 9 to get to the outside line, and then dialled a number.

"We're sorry. The number you're trying to reach is not available at this time..."

Cocking an eyebrow, she started to wonder if he really *did* die in that explosion. She tried a different number. This one rang out a few times. Damian's voice said, *"Leave a message."*

Beeeeeeeep.

"Damian," she said, "it's me. They're gonna hit the Manharttigan Mall. It's all being set up now. A whole army of 'em. I think they're gonna hit tonight. They also mentioned Campturn and a reservoir, if that means anything to you. Get your ass down here, if you're still alive." She hung up and debated whether or not she should try Jenny's phone. *Well, lives **are** at stake. Some help's better than none.* She called Jenny.

West Hillington Hotel

Judas Priest's *Heavy Metal* exploded from Jenny's cell phone on the nightstand. She moaned, stirring under the soft sheets, rolling under the thick duvet. The music filled the room. She reached out from under the duvet and answered it. "Hello?"

"Heyyyy, Sis! What's up?"

Jenny sat upright, surprised. "Aria? Haven't heard from you in a while."

"What're you doin'?"

"At a hotel... why?"

"What're you doin' at a hotel? You and Damian split up?"

"What? No. No, it's... it's a *long* story, but I just had to get out of the safehouse for a while. It was gross."

"I see, I see."

"What've you been up to?"

"Undercover work."

"Oh."

"Yeah, listen... uh, so, you know the Manharttigan Mall?"

"What about it?"

"It's gonna be attacked tonight."

Jenny's eyes opened wide. "...What?"

"Yeah, it's gonna be attacked, so I kinda need backup."

"Attacked by what?"

"What else? An army of psychotics. Hasn't Damian been filling you in?"

"I haven't seen Damian since yesterday evening."

Aria figured she would take the light approach. "Okay, well, he's not answering his phone."

"That's weird. I spoke to him around three last night. He was answering then."

"He ain't now. Doesn't matter. He'll find out soon enough, I'm sure. But I need help."

"Yeah? What do you need?"

"Backup. I don't think I can stop what's coming. Not by myself. Uh... the waste management sector seems like the easiest point of entry. Meet me here around 5:30, alright? I think it's in the south area..."

"I'll see what I can do. I'll need to get some guns, first."

"Take your time. Just don't take too—whoops. Gotta go."

Click!

Jenny looked at her phone, perplexed. Then she hopped out of bed, got dressed, grabbed her bag, and ran into the bathroom.

The Waste Management Sector

Footsteps on the catwalk. Aria hung up the phone just as the waste management supervisor walked in. He stopped in the doorway, staring at her.

She was still under the desk, only now she had a lustful smirk on her face and her hand down the front of her pants. "Can't a girl get some privacy around here?"

"What the hell do you think you're doin'?"

"I *was* havin' phone sex, till you walked in."

"Get out. I'm calling Drake." He took out his cell phone. Big mistake. She lunged out from under the desk, pinned him against the cabinets, arm pressing against his throat. She grabbed his head and twisted sharply, snapping his neck. He went limp. She released him, watched him slide to the floor.

"Ah, shit." She searched the cabinets and found a box of blue extra-large garbage bags. She spent the next two minutes stuffing him into one. Sealed him in with a tight knot. She peeked through the window enclosure at the platform below. Clear. She slung the bag over her shoulder and hoped it was strong enough to hold the corpse long enough for her to get across.

She sprinted across the catwalk and down the steps. Crossed the platform to the doghouse, where she dropped the bag. It was starting to tear. She glanced over her shoulder at the indoor entrance as an automated forklift flew by. Nobody noticed her yet. She turned back and threw open the doors. Lifted the supervisor and dropped him down the chute into the compactor. She closed the doors and hit the power button on the control panel. The compactor roared to life, slowly crushing the supervisor and the heap of trash she'd thrown him into. Glass broke. Bones snapped. Debris rustled. Arteries burst. She had to keep her thumb down on the button for the damn thing to do its entire job. Kept stealing nervous glances at that entryway. Two foot soldiers walked by but they were too preoccupied with their conversation to make good use of their peripheral vision.

Finally, the compactor finished the job. Aria bolted for the ramp until she was directly under the vent. A harpoon gun *sprouted* out of her hand like a flower blooming in fast forward. She gripped it, fired a harpoon with a cable into the vent and started to pull herself up. She was in there and out of sight right before a worker entered the room pushing a dolly with garbage bins on it toward the compactor. She stuck around just a little longer, watching from her vantage point as the oblivious worker dumped the garbage bins into the chute and crushed them with the compactor. None the wiser. She smiled and made her way back toward the restroom.

Chapter 024
Not-So-Safehouse

11:35 AM.

Jenny checked out of the hotel shortly after she got the phone call, stopping briefly at a coffee shop to get a quick bite to eat and a cup of coffee. She tried to call Damian, but she got the same thing Aria got. She tried twice, frowning. Then she tried calling the car phone. No answer there, either. "Where the hell *are* you?" she whispered, pocketing her cell. She figured she'd return to the safehouse to get a few more guns, and then try to come up with a plan on how to approach this shopping mall situation before nightfall.

She rode the Honda Rebel back to the safehouse—

—and stopped on the corner when she spotted a van in the driveway. *What the hell?*

She popped the kickstand and stepped off the bike. She drew her MP5K from her backpack and cocked it as she slowly moved up the ice-slicked sidewalk, listening to the wood chipper's gurgling roar. She heard shouting and talking behind the fence. Couldn't see anything. She reached the end of the fence and peeked around it, down the side of the house, her submachine gun close to her chest. From this point, she couldn't see much of the backyard. She couldn't even see the well. She saw patches of blood in the snow, but that was it. The voices were coming from directly behind the house.

She glanced at the van, looking for anyone in the front. No one. She moved to the side of the van and made for the garage. Started to ease her way along the side of the house, inching toward the backyard, submachine gun ready to fire. She slid across the wall, listening to the wood chipper's grinding. Someone screamed in agony as a few onlookers laughed and told the sufferer to suck it up. She reached the end and hesitated. Peeked out.

The backyard had become a grisly slaughter ground. The snow had long since melted from all the body heat and blood breaking it away as the night and day wore on, staining the grass crimson and creating pools in the middle of the yard while the rest of it streamed into the flood control channel. Hundreds of severed hands and feet and arms and legs were scattered about; the arms and legs were stacked like firewood under the trees while the hands and feet scurried around in aimless circles. A score of Drake copies filled the backyard, wearing Damian's clothes they'd stolen from the safehouse; they encouraged a naked, sobbing, blood-coated Drake #3 to continue hacking up another copy with an ax. Two other copies shoved a fellow clone headfirst into the wood chipper, laughing as a fresh spray of blood and gore hit the trees.

Jenny's eyes bulged. Her blood went cold. She thought her heart might've stopped beating for a few seconds too long. Her mouth went slack. She wanted to run. She didn't want to shoot them, or burn up the whole backyard until it was a pit of ash. She'd seen some shit, but nothing like *this*.

Kachik!

She jumped at the sound.

"Don't move, bitch," Drake #2 snarled behind her, aiming an M16 with an underhand grenade launcher at the back of her head. "One false move and I'll turn your head into a beehive."

She was frozen stiff.

"Drop it. Slowly."

She held the MP5K out for him to see and then dropped it in the snow. She could feel the muzzle of Drake #2's assault rifle grazing through her hair. She dunked her head, reached back, yanked the barrel over her shoulder. Drake fired a shot as he stumbled toward her. She drove her heel into his stomach hard enough to burst it and snap his spine. Sent him reeling with his guts trailing after him.

The other Drakes reacted to the gunshot. They whirled, but too late.

Jenny took the assault rifle in her hands and hosed them all down, splattering them from the waist down and shredding the sentient limbs around them. She knew it wouldn't stop them—but it *would* slow the bastards down.

POW!

A bullet ripped through the wall an inch from her head, scattering brick dust in her face. Another echoing *POP* resounded from indoors. She flinched, ducked as another bullet exploded out where her head just was. She rubbed her eyes and squinted. Panic started to take hold; the last thing she needed was to be blind in the middle of an enemy camp. She fired blind, ears rewarded by a few more yelps and groans. *POW*—more brick fragments exploded off the wall. The jagged portion in the center of all the holes crumbled away.

Fuckers beat me to the armoury, Jenny thought. She blinked again. A speck was still lodged in her right eye; felt like a rusty tack. With her good eye, she aimed the underhand launcher at the gaping hole in the wall and shot a grenade into it.

KABOOM!

The entire rear wall of the garage disintegrated in a concussive spray of debris that knocked the recovering clones back on their asses. The shutter doors on the other side were violently dislodged and flapping over the driveway as the garage's contents sailed flaming over the driveway and into the van's grille.

Jenny blasted the wood chipper out of commission. Then the rifle clicked dry. A shotgun blast burned a hole through the fence behind her. Jenny dropped the rifle in favour of her MP5K and bolted for the sidewalk. Drake #2 sat up and went for a gun tucked in the back of his waistband. Jenny karate-chopped him through the neck, sent his head spinning through the air.

More gunfire barked from the backyard. Bullets chewed up the fence in hot pursuit of her as she leaped over a pile of snow onto the sidewalk, dropped to a crouch, swivelled around with her submachine gun raised. Four of them were coming around the corner, clothed and armed to the teeth. She riddled them with bullets. Drake #24's shotgun disintegrated the corner of the fence before he collapsed, writhing in agony.

Jenny bolted down the sidewalk, racing to her motorcycle. To burn this many of them at once with her pyrokinesis would be exhausting. She couldn't afford to be exhausted in her getaway.

She mounted the Rebel and whipped out her phone, keeping an eye on the van two houses down. She accessed her contacts list. Scrolled through a long list of names. The bottom one was highlighted in red: *DETONATE.* She tapped it and hit dial—

Pop!

A bullet whistled over her head. She returned fire, slamming

Drake #45 against the side of the van. She looked at her phone, desperate. *Calling...*

"Hurry up! Fuck!" She tucked her submachine gun under her arm to start up the bike. More gunfire crackled from the front yard. Two Drakes, five, eight, twelve Drakes emerged from behind the fence and the van; bloody, armed, and pissed. Drake #2's driver joined them as they poured into the street. Jenny drew her submachine gun and razed them to the ground. Most of them shouted and swore. The driver violently convulsed against the van as Jenny's bullets ripped through his chest. He slid down, bulging eyes staring blankly at the sky.

The others were starting to get up, threatening and insulting her.

She reloaded her gun. Noticed a black Sedan with tinted windows parked in a driveway across the street. Something about it...

Looked at her phone. The answering machine finally picked up. She spoke into it. "Jenny Knight."

An AOL voice responded, "Voice code confirmed."

She smiled and said, "Merry Christmas, fuckers."

The Armoury

With over two dozen gun racks, four lockers containing armoured battle suits, and twenty cabinets full of ammunition packs and explosives, it's no wonder that, despite the Drake copies' ransacking of the armoury, they failed to notice the cell phone bombs strategically placed in every corner of the room behind the shelves. Five clones lingered in the armoury when they heard the phones ring. By the time they found one of the phones wired to a pound block and a half of C4, it was already too late. The phones went to voicemail.

The five of them shared a collective, "Oh, fuck."

BAKWWHHOOOOMM!

The safehouse roof leaped a hundred feet in the air. The walls exploded outward, shooting out across the street as an earth-shattering roar shook the neighbourhood. A shockwave blew out every window within a two-block radius; almost toppled Jenny off the bike—instead she used the momentum to turn the bike around and speed off down the road, riding it to the next corner. Dozens of

COBALT CHRISTMAS: A COBALT ROGUE STORY

Drake clones near the house sailed screaming away from the blast. The van sprang out of the driveway and flipped engine over taillight onto the road, crushing a pair of Drake copies under its roof. The power lines wobbled and hissed.

A secondary explosion decimated the front lawn. Patches of soil and grass shot upward and showered the street and the van's underside. Flaming debris caked the bodies writhing in the street and the overturned van.

Drake #54 moaned as he cradled his mangled left arm, covered in soot and blood. He looked up the street and listened to the sound of Jenny's motorcycle engine fading off. The van's fuel tank erupted behind him, belching a much smaller fireball into the smoggy clouds curling above them. Drake #54 looked at the burning wreck, then at the fiery pit where the safehouse used to be. He turned again, back to the street. "Foxy bitch!"

Chapter 025
Load Up!

12:21 PM.
Armaliker's Hospital—Underground Parking

Damian and Hill found the Shelby Cobra exactly where Damian had left it. The car lit up once they shut the doors. Hill liked the looks of this. "Whoa."

"You like?" Damian asked as he started up the engine.

"It's very... blue."

"Don't touch anything." Damian opened a small compartment between their seats, revealing an old-fashioned car phone with a newly installed touch-screen voicemail device attached. Damian put the receiver to his ear and opened his voicemail box. Only one message. He hit play.

Aria's voice came through: "Damian, it's me. They're gonna hit the Manharttigan Mall. It's all being set up now. A whole army of 'em. I think they're gonna hit tonight. They also mentioned Campturn and a reservoir, if that means anything to you. Get your ass down here, if you're still alive."

An AOL voice announced, "End of message."

He hung up. "Of course!"

"What?" Hill asked.

Damian looked at him. "The mall."

"Which mall? There's *four* of them in this district alone."

"Downtown. *The* shopping mall, Hill."

"Manharttigan?"

"My contact's there now. I don't think their cover's been blown just yet."

"Jesus Christ. Tomorrow's Christmas... it's gonna be packed with shoppers looking for last-minute gifts..."

"Yup," Damian growled. "Just the way that motherfucker likes it." Damian floored the gas and peeled out of the parking lot into the street, cutting off a honking Beetle.

"Christ, watch where you're driving!"

"We don't have much time."

"The mall's *behind* us, kid."

"We're not going to the mall just yet. We need guns, Hill. *Lots* of guns."

"Did your contact say anything else?"

"Something about Campturn. Oh, and a reservoir, but no details on either one."

"I don't have a clue about Campturn... but a reservoir...? I think I have an idea."

"Yeah, that one couldn't be more obvious," Damian said as he swerved into the center lane, clipping a pickup truck. The driver swore at him, but Damian could hardly be bothered to listen. "They're gonna poison the city's water supply."

"You're right," Hill said breathlessly. "We're gonna need a lot of guns..."

"I suggest you start calling a friend at the precinct."

"Why?"

"Reservoir's isolated from the rest of the city, right?"

"Yeah."

"Sooooo... three ways they can transport the poison: by air, across one of the bridges, or on the ice."

"It's a little warm to take that risk on ice today."

"Helicopter's the best way to go, but then again, they'd need a *lot* of that poison to really do the job."

"Not really. About twenty or thirty gallons ought to do."

"Oh, yeah, you're an expert on that stuff now," Damian said sarcastically. "Get on the phone and get me a fucking chopper."

"Sure, gimme a second while I pull that miracle outta my ass."

"We're gonna hit them from the air."

"In the unlikely event we actually *get* a chopper, how do you propose we shoot 'em out of the air?"

"We won't be shooting them *out* of the air; we'll be shooting them *from* the air. Betting there's too much of it to transport via air mail without someone noticing. Soooo... they'll be standing on the ground. But *we* won't be."

The Safehouse

They could see the smoke from a kilometre away, but even when they drove up to the police cordon to see the entire property up in flames, Damian *still* couldn't believe it. Police and firefighters fought the smouldering pit where the safehouse once stood. They worked around the smoking van wreck. Only a few posts and some scattered brick stacks from the garage remained standing on the actual property; the rest of the house was spread across the street, all over the neighbours' lawns and on the roof of the house next door.

The Drake clones were long gone by this point.

"*Yob*! That's a lot more than just the carpet," Damian muttered. "The fuck..."

"You had a safehouse here?" Hill asked.

"*Had* a safehouse here," Damian said, watching the thick pillar of smoke rise.

"Let's get out of here before somebody spots us."

Damian did a U-turn and drove around the corner, heading for the bridge.

"Now what?" Hill asked.

"Got a guy. You can't do anything to him, though."

"Why would I?"

"Because you're a cop."

"I can be reasonable."

"Can you?"

"Look, I'll make an exception."

They crossed the bridge over the flood control channel.

Hill said, "What's your guy?"

"Secret government arms supplier. Runs a chain of weapons depots all over the country. Mainly specializes in helping out undercover agents and covert ops when they're in a tight fix. Doesn't supply to hoods or petty crooks or Paul Kersey wannabes. Hell, hoods don't even know that he *has* guns stashed away."

"Oh, man. A government-sanctioned arms dealer selling weapons to terrorists like you?"

"Does that *really* surprise you?"

Hill didn't have a response for that.

"Anyway, I keep forgetting his name..."

Rollerball Pawn

"Cannertunken!" Jenny called out as she entered the pawn shop. A door chime rang out as the door swung shut behind her. The place was open, but nobody was here. No one stood behind the cash wrap with a display case front showcasing statuettes from ancient exotic countries located at the other end of the shop adjacent to the door. The walls were stocked with all kinds of junk, and racks in the middle were filled with videotapes, DVDs, high-definition DVDs, CDs, cassette tapes, and so on.

"Cannertunken!" Jenny shouted.

A voice replied from the back room behind the counter, "Who is that?"

"It's me, Jenny."

"Oh! Jenny! It's been a while; I couldn't quite recognize your voice... I'll be out in just one moment."

"Take your time." She started sifting through a selection of DVDs when Cannertunken came out to greet her.

He was short, about four feet; bald with a black spade adorning his skullcap. His burly arms were covered in tangled tattoos of skulls, roses, and thorns. He came out from behind the counter, arms outstretched. "Heeeyyyy!"

"C'mere, little guy!" Jenny hugged him fondly. "How've you been keeping up?"

"Been doing okay, love. How goes it on your end?"

"Not so good."

"Oh."

"Which brings up why I'm here..."

"Aw, you didn't come here just because you missed me?" He grinned.

She chuckled. "You're a big ol' bonus, Tunk."

"Glad to hear it. What can I get for ya?"

"Guns," she said. "Lots of guns."

"How many?"

"As many as I can carry."

He whistled. "Sounds like an emergency."

"A major one. If I were you, I'd stay away from the Manharttigan Mall. It might be a hot zone."

"A hot zone?"

"Terror attack; maybe a bombing, maybe a mass shooting. I'm not entirely sure *what* will happen, but I know that something *will* happen, and it's gonna be bad."

"Now that you mention it, a dairy farm went up in smoke last night. It's all over the news."

"A dairy farm, huh? Poisoned eggnog, a dairy farm bombing... can't be a coincidence."

"Should I call someone?"

"Yeah, do that. In the meantime, I'm gonna need some firepower. What've you got?"

"Depends on what you're lookin' for. Follow me."

She slinked around the counter behind him and followed him through a narrow walkway. He stepped aside, allowed her entry. He shut the door behind them and hit the lights—

Fwoosh!

—revealing a gun room that, while stocked to the ceiling, was the total opposite of Jenny and Damian's armouries. Theirs were organized, with shelves and racks and crates all neatly lined up and categorized; like Sears in its heyday. *This* was disorganized—everything was on the floor or in chaotic piles and scattered about... *also* like Sears—on its last legs.

Jenny was used to the mess by this point. She stooped down and picked up an MP5 submachine gun. She looked around at the multitude of guns carpeting the floor and saw a few crates and blue bins pushed against the walls. "Ammo?"

"Crates. I'm not *that* messy."

"Could've fooled me," she joked half-heartedly as she peered into all the bins and crates until she found clips that matched her current weapon of choice. "Cart, please."

Cannertunken pulled a small cart from the nearest corner of the room and pushed it her way.

She took it and spun it around, caught it by the handlebar. "Thanks."

"You got a truck or something parked around back?"

"Nope."

"How're you gonna get it all out without anybody noticing?"

"I know a guy who knows a guy who could bring a van around."

"Oh." The colour started to drain from his face. "You haven't been telling people about this place, have you?"

"Just my boyfriend. Don't worry, he wouldn't tell anyone."

"Good, good..."

"Hell, he doesn't even remember your name." She could see the nervousness on his face plain as day. "Relax, dude. Your secret's safe with us." She picked up an Ithaca 37 and dropped it in the cart. She rummaged through a bin and tossed two boxes of shells beside it. The floor was so cluttered she couldn't move the cart any further than three feet from the door. She left it at the edge of the sea of guns to see what she could find.

She had the cart filled in ten minutes with pistols, submachine guns, assault rifles, grenade launchers, a light machine gun, and a fancy compact flamethrower with a pistol grip; and enough ammo and explosives to take on every gang in the Campturn District with a severely unfair advantage.

They heard the door chime and looked up at a wall-mounted surveillance monitor hanging above the door. Damian and Hill walked in and were looking around.

Jenny gasped happily and skipped out of the gun room. She leaned over the counter and said, "Hello, sweetie!" She saw his shirt and raised an eyebrow.

Damian looked surprised to see her. "Oh." Then he adopted a charming smile and said, "Why, hello there, pretty lady." He approached the counter and leaned against it.

"Hello, handsome," she said, tracing her index finger down his cheek to the tip of his chin. "I kinda miss the beard. Not that you need it to turn me on."

"Don't suppose you have a few... armaments... that I could purchase?"

"That depends on what you're going to use them for," she said teasingly.

"Got some squirrels in my chimney. They won't shut up."

"Infestation, eh? They have regular traps for that..."

"They're too smart for traps."

"How smart?" She suppressed a giggle.

"When I tell them to shut up, they say, '*You* shut up!'"

Jenny laughed and gave him a loving peck on the cheek. "Where were you?"

"Oh, you know," he replied, "torturing a guy for information and getting blown to smithereens."

"You wouldn't have had something to do with that dairy farm explosion, would you?"

"I was *in it* if that's what you mean."

"Oh, damn." She started looking him over, searching for

anything out of the ordinary. "You okay?"

"Healing factor saved my ass. It almost disintegrated me, though."

"Speaking of disintegration," she said, squinting at his aloha shirt in disgust. "*What* are you wearing?"

"It's an aloha shirt."

"It's hideous."

"That's what I said. It's cozy, though."

"You should stick to your usual monochromatic wardrobe, honey, because you clearly have no idea how coloured clothing works."

"Thanks, babe. I'll do that." He added dryly, "Did you know that carpets aren't flammable?"

"Whoa, now. You can stop right there," she said. "It really *was* just the carpet."

"Right, to destroy the, uh, 'army of penises' that were attacking you."

Jenny said, "I shit you not, man: Drake's body parts regenerate, a-and they act like they have minds of their own or something! Don't even think of passing this off as some kind of crazy talk, either."

"I don't. I've seen it."

"You have?"

"Yeah, Hill and I followed a severed foot through the hospital right back to its owner."

"You better not be making that up."

"Now why would I do that?"

Cannertunken came out and greeted Damian with a friendly, "Hello, there!"

Damian replied, "Heeeeeyyyyyy..." He hesitated.

Jenny said, "Cannertunken."

"Cannertunken!" Damian exclaimed. "Nice to see you again."

"The feeling is mutual, my friend," Cannertunken said, offering his hand.

Damian shook it.

Cannertunken leaned over the counter and whispered to the two of them, "So, uh..." he cocked his head toward Hill as he browsed some old DVDs "...who is he?"

"It's a cop," Damian said bluntly.

Jenny sighed.

"Don't look so surprised," he said to her, "you knew he was here."

"I was ignoring his presence, actually."

Cannertunken sighed, running his hand over his bald head. "Oh, man..."

"Relax, he's on our side," Damian said.

"Since *when*?" Jenny asked.

"I don't know. But he's afraid of me. He won't bust you, man." He leaned in closer and whispered, "I told him you supply arms to undercover feds. He thinks you're government." He snickered.

Jenny gave his face a good slap. "I do not approve."

"Neither do I," Cannertunken said. "Please, get him out of here."

Jenny added, "Or I will kill you both instead of just him."

Damian frowned, rubbing the spot where she slapped him. "Was that necessary?"

"Yes," she said. "And mildly satisfying."

"You get satisfaction out of hitting me?"

"Why not? You get satisfaction out of hitting *me*."

Damian scoffed. "When you *want* me to hit you!"

"You spank like a girl."

"I'll keep that in mind for next time—"

"Uh," Cannertunken said.

Damian and Jenny looked at him. "What?" they asked in unison.

"That cop's making me nervous..."

Damian yelled, "Hill!"

Hill peeked up over the DVD racks. "What?"

"Stop pretending we don't exist and get your dumb ass over here."

As Hill shuffled over, the three of them started bickering in hushed tones. By the time Hill reached them, Damian had turned back around, smiling like there wasn't an issue. "Hill, buddy. Let me ask you something."

Hill's nervous eyes did their best to avoid contact with Jenny's. He could tell she was extremely displeased with his presence. He could almost *feel* the daggers shooting from her eyes.

"What is it?"

"Everything you're about to see is top secret. Classified. Normally you wouldn't even know about it, but due to... *special* circumstances, we're making an exception."

"*You* are," Jenny snapped, folding her arms across her chest, glaring at the two of them.

Cannertunken stared at Hill with suspicion.

Damian continued, "If you tell *anyone* about this... if you even *hint* at its existence, you just might wake up one morning with a black ops ghost slicing your foreskin open with your own toenails. Do you want that?"

Just *thinking* about it made Hill's toes curl. "No," he said. "No, I don't."

"Good boy."

They had to hitch a small utility trailer to the back of the Shelby Cobra for all the ordnance they bought, which they packed into crates before loading on the curb. The neighbourhood was quiet and damn-near empty anyway, but no one wanted to take any risks with it.

Damian was giddy with excitement. He couldn't wait to use half of these things. "Hoooboy, those motherfuckers are in for a surprise!"

"Patience, baby Blue," Jenny said. She was more than accustomed to Damian's near-manic anticipation before a showdown. She reached in her jacket pocket and handed Cannertunken a key. "Here. Take my bike as collateral for now."

"Thanks, love. We really need to get coffee sometime."

Jenny chuckled. "Might make my sociopathic sweetheart jealous."

"But I'm gay," Cannertunken protested.

"Yeah, that doesn't make things better. He's kind of a homophobe." She leaned closer and whispered, "He doesn't even know you're gay."

"Oh..."

She gave him a friendly peck on the forehead. "Thanks, love. Catch ya later."

Cannertunken smiled. "Good luck!"

Jenny waved goodbye as she went over to the car. She

climbed in the back and found herself caught in the middle of another one of Damian and Hill's arguments.

"I'm telling you *exactly* what they told me," Hill said, "they're not gonna back us up, but they *will* clear the bridges and have a look."

"That's not good enough," Damian snarled. "Call them again!"

"What the fuck is that gonna do?!"

"Tell them I'm here."

"That'll make it even worse."

"No, it won't."

"Yes, it will."

"*Nyet, suka*, it won't."

"*Yes*, it will!"

Frowning, Jenny asked, "What's this all about?"

Damian said, "He's telling me the fucking cops aren't sending reinforcements our way. That includes a chopper!"

"What do you need a chopper for? If they're in a mall, shouldn't we sneak in on foot?"

Hill said, in a more even tone, "The mall's only part of the issue. We suspect they might try to put the same shit that was in that eggnog into the reservoir."

Jenny's heart skipped. She leaned back in her seat and said a small, "Oh."

Damian snapped, "And *this* useless shithead can't even get us a fucking chopper!"

"We're *suspended*, Damian. All they can do is look into it. But if that convoy blends in, then we're either wrong, or fucked."

"*Cyka blyat!*"

"Don't you dare use your Russki fucking swear words at me, you miserable little blue-haired son of a bitch!"

"Don't fucking insult my hair!"

"Are you twelve?"

"Cunt!"

"Guess that answers *that* question!"

Jenny groaned, exasperated, and got out of the car. She went back into the shop. Cannertunken reacted to the door chime and looked up from behind the counter. "Oh, you're back. That was fast..."

"I hate to do this, but I need to ask another favour of you."

"What's up?"

"Do you, by any chance, happen to know a pilot? More specifically, a helicopter pilot?"

"I do, actually. But it's a chopper pilot."

"Uh." Jenny narrowed her eyes, shaking her head as she asked, "What's the difference?"

"One's a helicopter, one's a chopper."

"...Okay." She didn't feel like starting an inane argument of her own. "Would you be able to reach him?"

"I think I can," he said, smiling as he brought out his phone and hit speed dial three. He waited through a couple rings, then finally, someone answered, and he replied, "Paul, my love. Listen, I got a couple friends here... yeah, no, they're not tourists, they're long-time customers. It's kind of an emergency. Life and death. Yes, really. Sure to be lotsa guns and explosions and stuff. Knowing these guys, a raid of some kind. Uh-huh. Uh-huh. For me? Aw, thank you! When and where? Yeah, I know the place. Okay. Okay! Thank you, honey. I'll talk to you soon. Mwah!" He hung up and looked at Jenny. "He just needs to get it out of storage. He doesn't usually fly it in the winter."

"Okay, so when and where?"

"He should be circling Murnham Public School in about an hour. Throw up a flare in the soccer field so he knows it's you. Here." He handed her a flare gun. "It's one of those revolver types. Holds six flares." He chuckled. "I doubt you'll need all six, though."

"Thanks, Tunk. You're the best." She rushed toward the door.

"Just remember that when you buy me my Christmas present!" Cannertunken yelled after her. When she left, he sighed happily and leaned on the counter. "What a sweetheart."

Jenny hopped back into the car to find them still bickering. She slapped her hands over their mouths and gripped their chins with fingers that could crush their jawbones into dust if she really wanted to. "Okay, boys," she said. "I got us a chopper. You can shut up now." She released them and folded her arms across her chest, looking at the dumb expressions on their faces as they stared at her. "What?"

"Where did you get a chopper?" Damian asked.

"Cannertunken's got friends in high places," she said.

Damian and Hill exchanged looks. Hill asked him, "You happy now?"

Damian turned in his seat and started up the car. "Yes. Yes, I am. Where to, doll?"

"Murnham Public."

Chapter 026
Mail Call

11:47 AM.
Damian and Jenny's Safehouse

It continued to burn, belching huge clouds of smoke into the sky as Drake and his copies started to recover from their wounds. A couple of them gathered the severed arms and legs off the ground and tossed them into a wheelbarrow. The hands crawled about like frightened spiders while the feet hopped around without purpose.

Drake #64 moaned as he stretched his back. His spine crackled. "Ugh... goddamn." He looked at the burning van. "Shit." Sirens wailed in the distance. He listened to them as they drew closer, louder. "Oh, for fuck's sake." He turned to the others and barked, "We gotta go! Let's get a move on!"

Drake #23 protested. "We don't have a ride, you idiot."

"We'll hitch one, then."

Drake #51 said, "Guess we'll just have to make do."

Drake #3 was curled up on the ground, sobbing pathetically. His constant torment since his 'birth' had broken him. A few other Drakes stood over him, wondering what to do. "I've never seen myself like this before," Drake #11 said.

"What should we do with him?" Drake #6 asked.

Drake #9 picked up the ax and approached Drake #3. "Simple. We take him out of his misery."

Drake #3 looked up at the ax and shrieked in terror as it came down on his neck. The blade sliced through his throat and chipped the upper part of his spine. He gurgled as blood filled his lungs. Eyes wide as saucers as he choked. Drake #9 coldly raised the ax again and cleaved Drake #3's head clean off.

Spak!

Drake #9 rested the bloody ax on his shoulder and kicked the head toward the decommissioned wood chipper. "Pop goes the weasel."

The other Drakes laughed.

"Alright," Drake #51 said, "let's go, let's go. Take only what you can carry. Burn the rest. Cops'll be here any minute."

Drake #11 and #6 picked up Drake #3's corpse by the limbs and tossed it into the safehouse inferno. The others scrambled to pick up as many limbs and firearms as possible before racing down the slope toward the flood control channel. The wheelbarrow was full; Drake #12 was having a fun time bouncing it down the hill. The rest of them lingered only to throw whatever limbs they couldn't carry into the fire before making their hasty retreat.

12:21 PM.

Drake #10 strolled down the sidewalk in a hoodie, strapped to a backpack containing a few of his sentient limbs, humming along to the tune of *Frosty the Snowman* playing on public PA speakers. He passed a charity Santa and pushed a businessman rushing to work out of his way, prompting the businessman to cuss him out before continuing on his way, all while Drake #10 pocketed the businessman's wallet with a smirk on his face. He continued walking for another block. Checked his watch. *Almost.*

He stopped in front of the 28th Precinct station and looked up its salted marble steps to the bulletproof glass doors. Then he glanced across the street at a department store just as a package delivery truck parked in front of it. He looked at his watch again. *Right on time.*

He blended in with the early afternoon pedestrian commute, crossed the street, eyes barely departing from the truck. The courier brought a package inside the department store. Now was the perfect time. He headed down the sidewalk and casually slipped into the back of the truck, and waited.

The courier returned a minute later. The minute he leaned into his truck, Drake #10 had his backpack unzipped. Two sentient hands leaped out, fingers extended, and then closed around the startled courier's throat. Drake #10 pulled him into the back with him and watched him struggle to pry the sentient hands from around his neck, choking, trying to gasp. Then he slowly went still. Life faded from his eyes. Drake #10 started to undress...

28th Precinct Station

Drake #10 entered the lobby in his newly acquired courier's

uniform with a parcel. He went up to the desk sergeant and plopped the parcel down on the sergeant's paperwork. "Package delivery."

The annoyed sergeant looked at the package. He put it to his ear and shook it. "What is it?"

"I don't know. I'm just the delivery boy." Drake #10 showed him a touch screen with a delivery form template on it. "Sign here, please."

The sergeant scribbled his initials. "Get outta here."

Drake #10 saluted and strolled out, leaving the desk sergeant to examine the parcel. A passing female officer stopped when she saw the parcel in the sergeant's hands and asked, "Hey, Mike. Somebody send you something good?"

"Not for me, Lois," Mike said as he looked over the name and address. "Take this up to the Captain, will ya?" He handed it to her.

She took it and said, "Sure thing. Not like I have anything better to do." She went two floors up to Carver's office and knocked on the frosted glass door. No answer. She sighed and pushed the package through the mail slot. It fell into a basket in Carver's dark office. And then it started to move...

12:43 PM.

As he drove down the road, Drake #10 spotted Drake #21 in the street and tossed a package wrapped in Christmas paper with a pretty red bow at him. He caught it in stride and kept on walking. Three blocks later, Drake #10 spotted Drake #29. "Mail call!" He tossed another package similar to the first at him. Drake #29 caught it and waved before ducking into a thrift store. Drake #10 drove up the next boulevard and turned left. He saw the hospital. An idea lit up in his head. He smiled and pulled over in the parking lot. He whistled *Frosty the Snowman* again now that it was stuck in his head as he gathered three more Christmas packages from his backpack and carried them across the lot to the emergency ward. The automatic doors allowed him entry. The place was packed. The waiting room full beyond capacity. A few people stood by reception. He asked them politely, "Excuse me, are any of you in line?"

"No, go ahead."

"No."

"Nah, I'm just waiting."

He nodded and took the packages to reception. The lady behind the counter flashed him a tired smile. He tipped the bill of his cap in greeting. "Afternoon! I'm making a donation on behalf of my company, ma'am."

"Just over there." She pointed at the gaudily decorated Christmas tree standing majestically in the far corner of the waiting room. A multitude of gift-wrapped donations surrounded its base.

"Thank you. Merry Christmas." Drake #10 went over to the tree and stacked his 'donations' under the tree. He smiled at a little girl breathing through a nebulizer next to her mother. And then he left.

Hill's House

1:11 PM.

Drake #10 stuffed a parcel into Hill's mailbox and raised the flag. Whistling the theme for *Rudolph the Red-Nosed Reindeer* now, he returned to the truck and started heading for the rendezvous point.

2:45 PM.

A warehouse on Pier 5. Drake #10 was the last to arrive, still in his mail courier uniform. He pulled into the warehouse and found himself surrounded by all sixty-two of his clones, all busying themselves with unloading the weapons and sentient limbs they'd managed to save from the safehouse incident. He hopped out of the truck and grabbed himself an AK-47 from a crate. "Gonna be a fun, fun night tonight!"

Sixty-two Drake clones and several dozen limbs in the process of generating their own bodies were preparing for war tonight. In the farthest, darkest section of the warehouse, something sat alone on a throne made of old pulp novels and pizza boxes. A man whose body was made of pure steel with a black oxide coating; containing the latest in computer hardware and a select few human organs to keep him alive. A distorted holographic image of Drake's head with the eyes eerily cut out was projected over a chrome skull mounted on a mechanical neck, giving him an otherworldly blue-purple glow. The thing's actual eyeballs were bulging from the skull's sockets, protected by a clear Plexiglas-coating that kept the skull and all contained within it hydrated. Its life support system could be heard pumping away inside its chest. The scientific abomination's voice was a modulated version of Drake's: "Just a little more patience, my fellow immortal."

"Yeah, yeah, I gotcha."

Chapter 027
Flying over the Hills

3:28 PM.

Murnham Public School

They parked the Shelby Cobra behind the school to avoid attracting any attention from the street. They put a tarp over the utility trailer and waited in the car. Jenny radiated heat from her body to keep the car warm without having to leave the engine running.

Damian sat quietly behind the wheel with a black trench coat Jenny had insisted on buying him earlier. "I still don't think this was necessary."

"It's the middle of winter, Damian," she said. "You can't go around in a T-shirt, especially one as ugly as that one."

"It's starting to grow on me."

"Uh-huh."

"Glad you like the shirt," Hill said.

"Shut up, Hill," Jenny snapped.

Hill shrugged. Rolled down the window and fired up a cigarette.

"You worry too much," Damian said. "It's warm out."

"It won't be warm when we're in the chopper."

"Speaking of which, when the fuck is it showing up? It's been an hour by now, hasn't it?"

"Another ten minutes or so."

Damian groaned impatiently. "*Svoloch.*"

"Yeah, yeah. Just a little longer."

"If it even shows up."

"Uh, guys?" Hill said. "Do we even know where we're going when the chopper actually shows up?"

"I might," Damian said as he picked up the car phone receiver. He accessed his voicemail box again and gave Aria's recording another listen. Then he hung up and asked Hill, "How many routes from Campturn to the reservoir do you think there are?"

Hill shrugged. He accessed a map app on his phone and started searching. After about a minute, he said, "Just one."

Damian waved his hands in the air and said, "*That's* just the way I like it! It's simple. It's neat. It simply can't be beat."

"It's *too* simple," Hill said.

"Now you're just second-guessing everything."

"Drake's been one step ahead of us so far. Why shouldn't I? This seems too simple. Too convenient. It smells like a trap."

"That how he *wants* it to smell, Hill. Trust me. You think he made it look simple for the sake of simplicity?" He shook his head. "No. Not Drake. He made it look simple *because* it looks simple. He wants us to second-guess it."

"But he knows you, doesn't he?" Hill asked.

"What're you getting at?"

"If he knows you, won't he know that you'll know that? What makes you think he *didn't* already take your assumption into account? What if, in theory, your deduction that he made it look simple for the sake of *not* throwing you off instead of the 'desired effect' to throw you off was the whole point all along? What if *that's* where he's throwing you off?"

"You're not making any sense at all."

"I'll simplify it: what if he *knew* you would know that, under normal circumstances, this super-convenient route to the reservoir would look like it's not the route to the reservoir because of how convenient it is, when in actuality it *is* the route to the reservoir, but really isn't?"

"You fucking call that 'simplifying'? Jesus Christ."

Hill breathed an exasperated sigh and said, "It's what I call a double-red herring, even though that's probably not the most accurate term to use for something like this."

"Oooohhhhhh. Like misdirection toward the *right* direction that *isn't* actually the right direction—or at least, made to *look* like it isn't the right direction while really being the right direction all along?"

"Uh... sure."

"You were talking in circles."

Jenny said, "My brain is going in circles after hearing you two talk about it. Jesus, fuck."

Damian felt satisfied. Hill enjoyed his smoke.

Jenny asked, "So, um... *where* exactly are we going?"

Damian and Hill exchanged looks. "Oh, yeah," Damian said, frowning. Before Hill could have his say, Damian said, "The bridge. It's the most logical option."

"Or is it?"

"Don't start that shit again, Hill. I swear to fuck. Our only clue is that bridge. If there's nothing on it, *then* we can rack our brains. Till then..."

Something flapping in the distance caught their attention. It went up a few decibels once they noticed it.

"The chopper!" Jenny exclaimed as she got out of the car with the flare gun. She fired a blue shot into the sky.

"About damn time," Damian said. He reached into the glove box and took out a pair of fingerless biking gloves and aviator sunglasses. Stepped out into the snow and stuffed his hands in his pockets. Craned his neck and scanned the cloudy blue sky for the approaching chopper. It surfaced above the trees, flying nap-o'-the-earth from the south.

Damian and Hill went around back. Damian popped the trunk overflowing with guns of almost every handheld calibre, with a few M79 grenade launchers laid on top of the pile. They each stocked up on pistols, stuffing them in their waistbands and inner breast pockets. Damian took a grenade launcher and a bandolier for himself, then grabbed the compact flamethrower currently stored in a flame-retardant sack. His shoulders now strapped, and his waistband full, he didn't have many places left to keep a weapon besides his feet. He strapped a thigh holster around his right leg and sheathed a combat knife into it. Tucked a couple grenades into his coat pockets. Good to go.

Hill strapped an Uzi submachine gun over his right shoulder and an M79 for himself, with a bandolier loaded with 40mm grenades going over his left shoulder. Hill fished around and eventually found a couple spare clips for his Uzi, stuffed them into a hidden pocket inside of his coat. He exchanged looks with Damian. They both let their grenade launchers rest against their shoulders. Two peas in a pod.

Hill spat out his cigarette. "Ready?"

"Obviously." Damian shut the trunk.

A Bell UH-1 Iroquois gunship with an elaborately stylized

tiger paint job descended onto the soccer field. Rotor wash swept up a cyclonic rush of snow that transformed the once still air into a cold flurry. Damian shivered from the chill as the trio approached the chopper. To Damian's delight, it came complete with wing-mounted M134 miniguns and dual rocket pods, and a door-mounted M60 machine gun. "Hell, yes!" He hopped onto the chopper, grinning from ear to ear. "*Now* it's beginning to feel a lot like Christmas."

The pilot turned his head in their direction and shouted over the loud droning of the rotors. "Ya'll ready to lift off?"

Hill's eyes went wide as saucers when he saw the rocket pods and climbed around the M60. "Jesus. How the hell did he get this thing past customs?"

Damian strapped himself into a seat beside Jenny and gave her an affectionate kiss on the cheek. "Trade secret."

"Uh-huh." Hill strapped himself in.

The pilot shouted, "Put your helmets on so that I don't have to yell at ya."

They each found a flight helmet hanging above their heads and promptly put them on. Damian was surprised to discover that the helmet didn't render his sunglasses an uncomfortable annoyance.

"Testing," the pilot said into the mic, transferred to their headsets smoothly.

"Good here," Jenny said.

"Good."

"Good."

"Great," the pilot said. "Name's Paul. Heard you and Tunk were good friends."

"Hi, Paul!" Jenny replied cheerfully. "I'm Jenny. The blue-haired hunk on my right is my boyfriend Damian. The douche who doesn't shave is Hill."

"Howdy," Paul said. The helicopter started to rise. They stiffened as the gunship lifted off the ground. Felt a lot like being in an elevator when it suddenly lurches between floors. "Where're we going? I ain't a mind reader."

"Fossforn River. Campturn Bridge," Damian said. "Those rocket pods loaded?"

"Like my rich uncle!"

"Fucking beautiful!" Damian exclaimed.

"We gonna need 'em?" Paul asked.

"If we find what we're looking for."

"Bad guys? Tunk didn't tell me much."

"*Real* bad guys."

"How bad?"

"They're gonna poison the city's water supply."

"Oh, yeah, I guess that's why they're taking the bridge... yep. I'd say that's pretty bad."

Hill watched anxiously as the schoolyard shrank under him. He looked away and took a deep breath. "Hooooboy."

Damian asked him, "Nervous?"

"Ask you a question?"

"You're always asking me questions."

The gunship dipped forward and headed southbound. Hill felt his heart lurch around in his ribcage and forced a lump of fear down his throat. "Ever... ever feel like you're in over your head during major cases like this one?"

"I'm used to the pressure and odds by now."

"Really?"

"Yeah, I deal with one of these overblown clusterfucks at least once a month."

Jenny added emphasis on Damian's statement: "At *least* once... sometimes twice."

"Jesus Christ."

"It's usually much worse than this, though," Damian said.

"How can it be much worse than this?" Hill asked. He tightly gripped his restraints as the gunship dipped forward again. His knuckles turned white. He clenched his teeth and moaned, "Jeeeeeeezuzzz..."

"Normally it's just me an' her up against a whole army. And I don't mean like, mercs and shit. I mean *full-on armies*. Revolutionaries sometimes, or terrorist training camps, or mutant laboratories, super-powered cartels, or aliens... there was one time, we uh, we raided a ninja training camp."

Jenny said, "I don't ever want to raid another ninja training camp *ever* again."

"Neither do I, love," Damian replied gravely. "Neither do I."

Hill knew there was a story behind that, and he didn't want to know. He said instead, "Aliens?"

"Yeah, aliens," Damian said.

Jenny interjected, "We're not totally sure, though. I didn't see any actual aliens and Blue was tripping on hallucinogenic adrenaline drugs half the time."

"I'm telling you, *those* things were real. I punched one."

"Okay, honey."

Hill said slowly, "I see..."

Paul said, "You guys're interesting, I'll give ya that." He chuckled to himself. "Aha, aliens..."

Talking to them was distracting Hill from the terrifying heights and the biting cold, at least a little. "So, uh... all that for money, huh?"

"Principals, sometimes, are a factor," Damian said.

"Principals?" Hill scoffed. "You?"

Damian and Jenny scowled at him. "Yeah," Jenny replied, "something *you* don't have."

"I have principals. I wouldn't have the job I have if I didn't. And who're you to judge? You're mercenaries. Terrorists-for-hire."

"Oh, we're not judging," Jenny said, "we're just tellin' it like it is."

"Hell, we've done jobs for free before," Damian said.

Now Hill was *really* doubtful. "Right..."

Damian figured he ought to elaborate: "When I see warlords and dictators massacre people who don't stand a chance, I get a little pissed, alright? Often, if those civilians know I'm there, they'll offer me everything they have to take on the people who threaten them. Sometimes I pity them enough to do the killing for free—but only in the case where I still get satisfaction out of watching those pussies die.

"Maybe, maybe not... you'd be amazed how many of these 'armies' can't put up a fight when someone with experience takes them head-on. I like to take things slow at first. I like to interrupt their shooting gallery and turn it into a war zone—that's my only warning to them. They never take the hint. That's something I can always count on. And let me tell you, Hill: there's nothing more satisfying than watching those cowardly little shits squirm under the pressure I put them under."

"And what if the civilians *don't* know you're there?"

"They find out eventually. They might not always be educated—matter of fact, most of the time, they aren't. But they're not stupid. Those people know when they've got a guardian angel on their side. I've always stepped in, Hill. Always. Especially if I don't like what I'm seeing."

"Don't tell me what you were doing in Central Congoria was because of some humanitarian cause," Hill said, trying to suppress his laughter.

"It wasn't. I'd just finished up a diamond heist with a few other mercs in the northeastern part of Congoria. I didn't see what was going on in the central region until they shot down my plane and stole my cut of the diamonds. I never did get those back..."

"So... what happened?"

Damian could still hear the screams of the villagers as they tried to escape the razing of their home. A small army of mercs tore through, pillaging every hut before burning it, raping every girl and woman they were attracted to, and gunning down all the men and boys. He remembered being rooted to his hiding spot, genuinely disturbed, stricken by what he was seeing. It reminded him of the destruction of his own village over a decade earlier...

He intervened, but too late—the last of the villagers had been killed in front of a firing squad while Colonel Fairman watched comfortably in a folding chair with a bottle of wine from a safe distance. He was too late to stop Drake from taking Fairman's order to kill the sole survivor in the firing squad's wake: a little girl, no more than four. Drake had approached her, held a pistol to her head.

Damian had certainly intervened, killing every merc who got in his way—but too many of them did. Too many bodies to cleave through with an energy blade or tear apart with an energy gun or rip into pieces with a telekinetic blast before he could get to the girl.

Drake seemed to hesitate when he looked into the girl's eyes. He started to lower his gun.

Fairman barked at him again.

Drake shot her.

Damian had one weak spot—right between the shoulder blades. The girl's body seemed to fall in slow motion. He couldn't pry his eyes away. A big mistake when you're surrounded by angry mercs. They cut him down. One of them blasted his weak spot. It seemed like the girl still hadn't hit the ground yet when he went down. He was out long enough for them to escape with the assumption that he'd been killed by that gunshot.

Their biggest mistake was that they didn't finish him off. It wasn't an execution like they believed—it was an act of war. Damian tracked them to their lab and burned the whole fucking evil place to the ground. He killed anyone he could find. He killed *everyone*, including Drake, or so it seemed. Fairman was already long gone.

It took Damian a long time to think of a suitable answer to Hill's question, but he settled on, "I saw Drake execute a little girl. Watched his boys slaughter an entire village, and found about several others they'd wiped out with that poison."

Jenny gripped his arm, hoping her touch could console him a little.

"So I did what I do best."

Hill thought, *Guess your best wasn't good enough.* He actually felt guilty for thinking that.

"Imagine my disappointment when I found out Drake was behind the bank job."

"Yeah," Hill said. "Strange coincidence that both of you wound up here."

"*Da.* It is."

No one spoke for a while. Hill fought against the urge to look out at the city passing below them, and his chin was getting numb and frostbitten from the harsh wind. On Damian's side, he watched the city's early afternoon commute function like it always did. It all looked so small and insignificant from up here. The skyscrapers could never reach them. The starscrapers were a different story; Paul had to manoeuvre around those structural wonders that reached into the clouds with seemingly no end in sight. One could see entire isolated districts populated with hundreds of colonists and tourists on every floor of every starscraper if one were to carefully look through the steel-rimmed, strengthened plate glass windows. They eventually left the monolithic towers behind them.

The city's complicated network of roads and railways and bridges converged into singular smaller roads that all joined together on the highway as it stretched out over the frozen, icy plains of the Fossforn River.

Paul banked further east, tipping the gunship, veering over a dozen concrete bridges that provided safe passage across the river. He spotted a highway sign on an entry ramp indicating Campturn

Bridge. "We're here. What am I lookin' for?"

Damian got out of his seat and manned the M60. "Keep us level. Don't stop our crossing until I spot something." He scanned the steady traffic for anything suspicious. Every motorcade he'd ever ambushed had either black vehicles driving single-file, or cargo trucks and military jeeps—bottom line: they stood out in any kind of traffic like a sore thumb.

No exception here. He spotted the convoy up ahead—two tankers in front, with three pickup trucks trailing behind them with bed covers hiding the weapon mounts; two more tankers in the middle, two cargo trucks behind them, and two jeeps in the rear. Damian's eyes went all the way back and spotted two more pickup trucks falling behind in case there was an ambush. "Move ahead!" he barked at Paul. "Faster!"

"I'm on it, I'm on it." The gunship lurched forward, picking up speed.

Damian peered further ahead of the tankers, because he had a gut feeling there was no way they would let some of the cargo take the lead in a heavily guarded convoy.

His hunch proved correct: an armoured personnel carrier with a twin Browning machine gun mount maintained a thirty-yard gap between it and the first tanker. "I spotted them. Bring us down a bit, Paul. And see if you can get that APC in the lead with a rocket."

"Won't let ya down! Hoowee! Haven't been this damn excited since Thanksgiving!" The gunship drifted downward without losing pace. Smooth descent. The gunship started to turn toward the bridge as Paul tried to get a lock on the APC.

Damian racked the bolt on the machine gun and said to Hill and Jenny, "Get ready."

They got out of their seats. Hill unshouldered the M79 and shoved a grenade into it. Snapped it shut. He looked at the road, distressed. "Goddamn it."

"What?"

Hill pointed at the civilian vehicles driving in sync with the convoy. They surrounded the target. Keeping them out of the crossfire would be impossible. "I told them to clear the road an hour ago!"

"Yeah, well, shouldn't surprise you that they fucking didn't," Damian said.

COBALT CHRISTMAS: A COBALT ROGUE STORY

Jenny positioned herself on the other side of Damian, gripping a fireball in her hand. She gave Damian a tentative look.

Damian aimed the M60 at one of the tankers, eyes narrowing to concentrating, narrow slits. "On the count of three. One... two..."

Chapter 028
The Tiger Strikes!

Campturn Bridge

Frank, Jim, and Kim led the convoy in the APC, wearing Santa hats, listening joylessly to holiday jingles. Its interior was bright red, with no other source of light except the dim holographic video screens giving them visuals of the road in front of them, behind them, and on either side of them.

Frank grabbed a CB radio and asked for an update.

"This is Tango 3. Rear looks good."

"This is Tango 2. Tankers three and four are clear."

"This is Tango 1. Tankers one and two are clear, but uhhh... there's a gunship aiming at you."

Frank and his boys exchanged looks. Frank replied, "*What was that, Tango 1?*"

KAPLOWMM!

Two rockets slammed into the APC's wheels and exploded, sent it cart-wheeling off the lane and into the pedestrian barrier.

Tankers one and two burned rubber as their drivers slammed on the brakes. The pickup trucks slewed into the next lane to avoid their fenders. The bed covers flipped off, revealing cybernetic machine gunners that were instantly vaporized by Damian's machine gun.

Damian peppered the pickups a bit longer. He noticed the tankers starting to move. "Get them, Hill!"

"Shit." Hill aimed his M79 at the tankers. Looked around for any civilians.

Noticing the hesitation, Damian roared, "Shoot, goddamn it!"

Hill fired. The grenade screamed across the sky, diving toward the tankers. Tanker one picked up speed. The grenade plummeted between the pickups and the second tanker.

BOOM!

Eruption! The pickups capsized. The tanker's cab disintegrated; its cargo burst open a second later, spraying gouts of flaming poison everywhere, engulfing everything. The explosion shook the bridge and caused an instant pile-up on the other side of the median.

Paul felt the heat from the cockpit and pulled the gunship back.

The heat burned the front tanker's rear tires out from under it. The tanker careened through the barrier, across the pedestrian walkway, and smashed through the rail. It flipped forward, dropping two hundred feet toward the river's frozen surface. Collided. The tanker flattened the cab and concussively blew apart. Fireballs swirled across the ice and reached for the gunship hovering far out of its reach.

The sudden violence on the highway caused a traffic jam. Civilian cars screeched to a unanimous stop, not without a dozen or so fender-benders. Panicked civilians scrambled in either direction down the bridge, stampeding away from the chaos. Staying out of harm's way.

The convoy broke apart as the last pickup truck and the cargo trucks raced to defend the tankers in a confused frenzy, slewing between the gunship and the cargo. The jeeps came up from the rear; their machine gunners started shooting back.

Damian ducked to avoid bullets whistling over his head and returned fire with the M60. Jenny hurled a fireball at one of the jeeps and blew it up. Hill took out the last pickup, launching its blazing front half into the sky. The machine gunner in the bed shrieked as the pickup flipped on top of him. Fuel tank ignited, scattering its pieces across the lanes and spraying the tankers with shrapnel.

The tankers started to move toward the flaming roadblock where the first tankers went up. The drivers had nowhere else to go.

One more jeep. Damian shredded the cab with the M60 and worked his way to the machine gunner in the back, sent that fucker's skullcap spinning skyways.

Frank's soldiers poured out of the cargo trucks and spread out across the bridge, taking cover where they could, shooting at the gunship with their assault rifles as the tankers went on ahead.

A shooting gallery. Damian started hosing them down.

Hill drew his Uzi and sprayed the local lane, taking out five or six of them.

Hearing metal scream from all the bullets hitting his gunship,

Paul said, "Hold on!" and turned the gunship. It swung toward the convoy and dropped, leveling itself out with the bridge, rising slightly to stay above the road. The wing-mounted miniguns roared, sent a thousand bullets stitching across the express lane, reducing a dozen soldiers to red mist.

The upturned APC's underbelly was covered in a sheet of flame, belching smoke as it lay embedded in the pedestrian walkway's destroyed barrier.

Frank kicked the door open, releasing more smoke that had filled the interior, and rolled out coughing and hacking. His clothes were burned, his hair singed, his skin tinted black from soot and dark crimson with the mixture of blood from all the fresh cuts he'd sustained. Jim crawled out after him, coughing just as much. He stole a glance back inside the APC to see his twin's twisted form splayed out, missing an arm and half his face.

Frank groaned, head spinning. He reached for his gun and fell over. Couldn't stand up straight. "Fuck." He lay there, listening to the gunship's miniguns mowing down his men. "Cocksuckers."

Jim pulled an AK-47 out of the APC and aimed it at Paul. His vision was all over the place. Rage did his thinking for him. He chanced the shot. Fired a three-round burst at the cockpit.

Paul flinched as bullets raked across the windscreen. "Whoa!"

Jim didn't stop shooting. He sprayed the chopper from cockpit to tail.

Paul ducked, jerked on the joystick. Jenny and Hill grabbed hold of a handlebar on their respective sides of the door to keep from falling out. Damian fell over the machine gun mount—only thing that stopped him from flying out of the aircraft.

Paul turned the gunship toward Jim's fire.

"Stop, you idiot!" Frank snarled. "Gonna get us killed."

Jim didn't listen. He let out a bloodcurdling war cry, assault rifle spraying the approaching gunship.

The windscreen spiderwebbed. Bullets whizzed through the cockpit and punched holes in the headrest of Paul's chair. Lucky he kept his head down. Paul launched another pair of rockets.

Jim didn't acknowledge the rockets that hurtled straight for him, but Frank did, and Frank bolted for the pedestrian walkway on the other side of the bridge as the rockets descended.

COBALT CHRISTMAS: A COBALT ROGUE STORY

KAPOW!

The rockets hit. Frank dived over the barrier. A flash, a concussive burst of fire shattered the APC and scattered what remained of it in all directions. Flames spread across the lanes. Frank curled up behind the barrier, shielding himself as a wave of fire rushed over the walkway. The heat alone burned through the sleeves of his raised arms.

Mercenaries were coming out of their hiding places. Damian saw them instantly and fell back behind the M60. Hill reloaded his Uzi. Jenny raised her MP5K. The three of them carpet-bombed the highway with a flurry of hot lead; perforating the last of the mercs and igniting the fuel tanks to the cargo trucks and the last jeep. The mercs died in a blaze of glory.

Frank peeked out from behind the barrier and saw the tankers stop on the other side of the patch of flaming poison under a highway sign with a holographic cola ad projection playing over it. He raced down the walkway toward them.

The gunship rotated above Frank's head.

A few surviving mercs jumping out from behind the pedestrian walkway opposite Frank and started blasting their machine guns at the gunship. Three or four of them, about ten paces away from the tankers.

Good. A distraction. Frank needed to find a good vantage point, and he knew just where to go. He darted down the lane and then hopped over the barrier into the local lane. He crossed the street. Ducked when he heard Damian's machine gun rip across the barrier on the other side.

Frank approached the tankers. The driver in the lead started to get out. "Sir, we're finished!"

Frank drew a pistol and snarled, "Get the fuck back in there! I'll deal with those fuckin' cunts!"

The driver scrambled back behind the wheel. Frank ran around the tanker and hopped the barrier. He reached the highway sign pole and scaled the rungs up to the platform. He ran along the sign to the end and peeked out around it, hidden within the candy-coloured electric mirage of the endless cola ad as an attractive woman's large head smiled and drank straight from the can. Paul was in his sights. He holstered his pistol and drew his revolver. Shook his head and blinked, trying to get the fuzziness out of his vision. He took aim at Paul. Fired.

POW!

The .357 round blew through the windscreen and ripped into Paul's shoulder. Paul howled, jolting in his seat. The gunship banked hard left. If Hill and Jenny hadn't been holding on to something, they would've flown out. Damian *did* fly out, losing grip of his machine gun and rolling across the floor and out the bay's open door on the other side. "Oh, shiiiiiiit!"

Jenny screamed, "DAMIAN!" *Oh God, oh God!* She leaped across the gunship as Paul struggled to regain control of the gunship. Another portion of the windscreen sprayed the empty co-pilot's seat.

Jenny fell on her hands and knees, looked over the side at the icy plains below. "Damian!"

Damian swung into her view, dangling upside down from the skid. "What?! Jesus!"

Jenny burst out laughing, unable to stop the tears from streaming down her face. "Damian, you're alive!"

"And fucking terrified!" he yelled, craning his neck to look down at the river's surface spinning under him. "*Yob!*"

"I thought I lost you! You gonna be okay?"

"Is that a trick question? I'm dangling upside down on the bottom of a tail-spinning helicopter! *NO*, I don't think I'll be okay!"

A .357 slug tore across the side and burned into the wall above Jenny's head in a burst of sparks. She shouted, "WHOA!" She looked at the holographic woman as she continued with that winning smile, raising her cola can as a toast to its success. Within the woman's shimmering head, Jenny spotted Frank on the highway sign. "Son of a bitch!"

Frank fired again. The wing-mounted minigun in front of Jenny blew apart, spilling its components into the wind. It spurted fire and smoke.

The gunship spun around the road sign. Paul tugged on the joystick, grinding his teeth in pain and terror. Tensing his muscles hurt like hell, and he needed every single one to retake control of this aircraft. "Shit... shit...!" The gunship careened over the highway; its side came adjacent to the road sign.

Damian found himself hanging face to face with the woman, and Frank standing behind her sea-green eyes... thirty-yard gap between them... and that's when Frank finally got a good look at him. Frank's eyes went wide. All colour drained from his face. "Impossible!"

Jenny took control of the M60. Aimed at Frank.

Damian drew two pistols from his waistband and pointed them at Frank. "*Improbable*, baby!" He unloaded both guns at Frank while Jenny loosed a blazing stream of lead from above, blasting their target and the hologram projectors behind him, engulfing a shrieking Frank in a series of electic explosions. Sparks shot out from all around him as ten thousand volts coursed through the platform and boiled Frank from the inside out. The woman's face flickered and for a split second, appeared distended in pain before it vanished. Sparks showered Frank's flailing form as Damian's bullets nailed him to the road sign.

Damian had stopped shooting him, but the electricity was running its course. Engulfed in flames, Frank pivoted off the platform and slammed on top of the tanker below, twitching furiously.

"Go!" Damian shouted, dropping the pistols, shrugging off the grenade launcher. "Paul, go!"

The gunship banked away from the tankers. Smoke from the burning APC whipped around in the gunship's rotor wash as it made its retreat.

Legs still locked around the skid, Damian shoved a grenade into his M79. Aimed at the tanker. Fired. The grenade traced an arc toward the tanker. Landed on Frank's chest, pounding in his ribcage—

Both tankers exploded at once. A sonic *BOOOMM* shook the air. Everything went up—the two hundred or so pedestrian cars left abandoned on the bridges, the road sign, and every little piece of Frank were tossed toward heaven. A raging firestorm ripped the bridge in half and instantly melted a massive crater in the icy surface below it. Every car on the adjacent bridge filled the air like burning meteors, shooting across the sky. Some chased after the retreating gunship. The gunship lurched violently as the shockwave swiped at its tail. Hill and Jenny held on tight as the gunship continued to shake them around. Paul struggled to maintain control of the damn thing with every alarm blaring in his ears and alert light blinking in his eyes.

Damian screamed, had to shield himself from the heat and the blinding light, feeling it burn through the sleeves of his coat. A flaming Honda flew past him. A blazing pickup dived for the gunship's right wing and nicked it on its way down. Damian looked down and watched the cars explode against the ice. A giant fragment from the road sign spun through the air like a throwing knife, sliced through shooting-star vehicles like scissors through string. Damian looked at the bridge again, watching a behemoth mushroom cloud curl into the sky from the fresh, blazing gap in the bridges.

The gunship was in the clear. Damian howled in excitement. "WOOOOOOOOO! WHAT A FUCKING RUUUUUSH! THAT'S HOW YOU DO IT! YEAH! YEEEAAAH!"

Inside the chopper, Hill sat exhausted in his seat, chest heaving. Jenny sat across from him, leaning against the back of the co-pilot's shredded seat. Absolutely drained. One leg dangling out the door. "Let's not ever do that again," she said breathlessly.

"Agreed," Hill gasped.

"Guys, did you see that?" Damian shouted from below. "Did you fucking see that? HAHAHA! *BOOM*!" He laughed maniacally. "Now *those* are Christmas lights!" His laughter slowly subsided as he felt more of his blood rush to his head. "Is... is anybody gonna help me up? Anybody?"

Jenny and Hill exchanged looks. They shook their fists at each other. Both made scissors.

Rock, paper, scissors. Two ties. Three ties. Hill made scissors against Jenny's rock. "Best two outta three," he said.

"Fine," she said. And they continued playing.

"Guys?" Damian said. "Hello?"

Chapter 029
Drake's Misfortune

Manharttigan Mall

4:57 PM.

The bridge attack was all over the news, albeit changed for the public. Instead of a gunship attack, it was reported as a terrorist bombing, possibly linked to the dairy farm explosion early in the morning. Drake knew better than that. Stewing in the control room, Drake muted the news broadcast and looked around the room. He looked at Aria, who sat backwards in an office chair, slumped over the back of it, spinning round and round...

Drake approached her. She ignored him until he stopped the chair from spinning with his foot. "You."

"Me," she said. "What's the problem?"

"Frank's dead."

"I saw. Tragic."

"You don't look too upset about it."

"We're hired guns, Drake. Expendable. One would think you'd understand that by now."

"Who did you tip off?"

She raised an eyebrow. Totally calm. "Excuse me?"

In a surge of anger, Drake flipped her food tray off the table and roared, "WHO DID YOU TIP OFF, BITCH?!"

She looked at her food on the floor. Annoyed. "That was five dollars."

"Answer me!"

"I didn't tip off anyone."

Drake glared at her, digging into her black eyes, looking for a clue. She didn't back down from him. He stood up straight and said, "You wanna play games, little girl? Fine." He took out his cell phone and hit speed-dial 4. Waited, then: "Bring me the girls." Hung up. Spent another beat glaring at Aria before he raised his voice for the whole control room to hear. "You see that? That is called 'failure.' We cannot afford failure. Failure is not our friend."

He started to pace the circular room, his hair glowing amid the backdrop of a thousand screens on the TV wall. "Somebody alerted the authorities. Somebody's been informing them of our plans since the bank job, or perhaps even earlier than that. Somebody even got the fucking Dead Blue involved. Now... could this all be coincidence? Perhaps!" He locked eyes with Aria's. "*Then* somebody warned them about our plans to poison the reservoir! You can see the result on that screen over there."

Aria turned as the door opened. Two armed mercs shoved a woman and a small child into the control room. The child had long black hair and still wore her winter hat and mittens. A spitting image of her mother. She was terrified. The mother was purposely kept separate from her daughter, dragged screaming and sobbing toward Drake, who drew a gun. "Ah," he said, "Ice's side bitch and his bastard daughter. Good choice, good choice! Even if he finds out about these two, he's still got a wife at home to worry about."

Oh, no, Aria thought. Her fingers tightened on the chair.

"We can go about this one of two ways," Drake said, grabbing a fistful of the woman's hair and yanking her head against the muzzle of his gun. She shrieked and pleaded. He kicked her. "Shut the fuck up." He said to everyone else, "The best way to flush out traitors is to hit 'em where it hurts. They fight to protect the innocent. Let's see how they feel when the innocent dies because of them." He thumbed back the hammer.

Aria's heart pounded. She could feel everyone's eyes on her. Could she save her? Her cover was already blown, wasn't it? But they couldn't *prove* it, could they? Not unless she could spin it. Or maybe she should just sit tight and let the mother die. One life for hundreds more. Could she do that to a little girl? Aria looked at the little girl and instantly regretted it. The girl sobbed, reaching for her mother, restrained by the stone-faced merc.

"When I count to three," Drake began, "and no one stands up, little Molly Todd won't be able to unwrap her Christmas presents from mommy without bursting into tears, because all she'll be able to see will be the mental image of mommy's face with her brains oozing out of the smouldering hole in her fucking face. One."

"MOMMY!" Molly screamed.

The mother blubbered, knees giving out until Drake violently hoisted her back up by her hair. "Two."

"Enough," Aria barked.

Drake smiled. "We have a traitor among us."

"On the contrary," Aria replied. "You disappoint me, Drake."

"What's that?"

"Are you really so pathetic that you have to shift blame after the slightest failure?"

Drake's face contorted in anger.

"The fact of the matter is that you failed not because of a supposed 'leak,' but because of your own incompetence. You've seen it firsthand. Frank had a big mouth. He liked to talk. That's why he had to kill those cops at the farm. That's probably how he died on that bridge."

"Like fuck it is," Drake spat. "You just don't want me to blow this bitch away."

"That's also true."

"Scared for the little girl's well-being?"

"Not particularly. I've been around. Some things in life are outta line."

"We're gonna slaughter an entire mall in what's to be the world's bloodiest fundraiser, and you're trying to tell me the murder of one girl's mother is 'outta line'?" He scoffed. "Don't make me laugh, bitch. You're weak. You were the weak link the moment Fairman tossed you into our ranks."

"Except I knew how to keep my mouth shut."

"There's one flaw in your theory, though."

"What's that?"

"Frank only mentioned the reservoir once."

"That you know of."

"And you know the funny thing?" he said, ignoring her comment. "Funny thing is, there were only three people in that truck when he said it. You were there. I was there, and I sure as hell didn't compromise him. And the third person was Frank, who's now dead. How many suspects does that leave us with? I wonder..."

Aria stood up. Every mercenary in the room pointed a gun at her.

"You talk a good game, doll," Drake said, "but you lost this round." Without blinking, he burned a tunnel through the mother's head. Everyone jumped at the shot. "Whoops!"

Aria flinched, stared at the corpse in shock as Drake shook the mother's head like a cruel puppeteer before finally dropping her to the floor. Molly started screaming.

Drake snapped his fingers and pointed at Aria and Molly. "Take 'em both out like the trash they are."

Aria turned her glare toward an approaching merc, stopped him dead in his tracks. Another one behind her grabbed her arm. She whirled; flipped him through a table and drew a bead on Molly's restrainer with a pistol in the same fluid motion. "You move, you die."

Drake laughed, applauding her skill. "God*damn*, you're hot! You know, if you weren't a traitor, I'd be more than happy to put that big mouth to good use."

"I'm not a rat," Aria said.

"Sure, sure. Any way to prove that?"

"I've been involved in Operation Catalyst from the start. I've invested too much of my time and effort to be labelled a fucking traitor by an outsider like you. For all I know, *you're* the rat."

"Fuck you. I know you're bullshitting. The more I think about it, the more it makes sense. Maybe that's why you've been protecting Damian Warkowski up till the part where I vaporized his freak ass. You didn't kill him at the warehouse when you had the chance, and you got all pissy when I blew him up. I'm not stupid, bitch. I know a rat when I see one, and *you* are *definitely* a rat."

"Call Fairman."

Drake scoffed, taken aback. "I'm sorry, *what*?"

"Go ahead and call Fairman, if you're so sure, you son of a bitch."

"Fuck do I need to call Fairman for? I got you."

"You ain't got shit. Call Fairman."

"Wrong. *Wrong*! I've got everything except your finger on the phone. I've got all I need."

"Then what've you got to lose? Are you hesitating in front of your men? Look, boys—a sign of weakness in your 'fearless leader.'"

Drake looked at his men and scowled. They were all looking at him. Drake snorted, suppressing a laugh. He reached over to the office phone and turned on the scrambler. He turned on the speaker and dialled Fairman's private line. Fairman picked up on the second ring. "Status report?"

"Good evening to you, too, Colonel," Drake said sarcastically.

"I'm not in the mood for your sarcasm, Drake."

"Been watching the news?"

"Correct. I'm extremely disappointed in you, Drake. You said you'd handle it. You said there wouldn't be any problems."

"It's a minor setback at best. Not like we killed our chemists or anything. We'll make more; we'll hit the reservoir another day."

"I need *panic*, Drake. Full-scale, citywide panic!"

"Which is why I came up with a plan B. It's my treat. But that's not why I'm calling you."

"Then why *are* you calling me?"

"I believe our little Murder Queen is a traitor to the cause," Drake said spitefully.

"That's preposterous. She's one of our best and most trusted operatives."

"What the fuck am I, then?"

"Obviously you are, too, which makes this situation all the more confusing."

"Let me elaborate, then."

"Please do..."

Drake recited every little thing he deemed suspicious of Aria's character, from the warehouse incident to the convoy ambush, to her reaction to his ultimatum. "And this bitch has the nerve to try and question *my* loyalty. Fucking. Wow. *Wow!*"

"These are... serious allegations, to be sure. Is she there now?"

"Yeah, you're on speaker."

"Ms. Murder Queen?"

"Yessir," Aria spoke up.

"What's your side?"

"My side isn't much different, other than the fact that I find Drake's brash and careless behaviour disturbing. He takes too many risks. May be what cost us the convoy."

"The fuck it is!" Drake snapped

"Drake, be quiet!" Fairman barked. "She has a point there."

"Taking her side, Colonel?"

"I haven't taken a side yet."

"Why the hell not? It should be obvious at this point."

"These are serious allegations you're making, Drake. I would tread carefully—the both of you."

"With all due respect, sir," Aria said, "I've been trying to maintain some semblance of control in this operation. Drake's a cowboy."

"Fuck off!" he shouted.

"Kiss my ass! I don't have to sit here and listen to this shit," she shouted back. "I'm shocked that your gung-ho routine hasn't compromised us sooner than this. And you have the balls to try and pin the blame on me for your failure." She let Drake stew a moment before continuing, "What the fuck were you expecting? The city's on high alert thanks to your stunt at the farm, and then you send a convoy with tankers toward the reservoir *in plain sight of anyone* with a cell phone! Oh, and then there's the little cocaine lab you've got downstairs. Real smart. Not. You really are a dumb son of a bitch if you honestly expected things to keep on chugging along all smooth-like after those Monterey fireworks."

"Shut the fuck up!"

"ENOUGH!" Fairman yelled. "Sweet Christmas. You're acting like children."

Drake said, "She started it."

Aria scoffed.

"I'm ending it. Put aside your differences tonight. It's time to shine."

"What, that's it?" Drake asked, incredulous. "Just gonna let the traitor go?"

Fairman replied, "Even *if* the Murder Queen is a traitor—which I highly doubt—there's no stopping what's coming. The Campturn gang will be here shortly. Are your men in place?"

"Yes... they're in position."

"Good. Wait for my signal to proceed."

Aria gave Drake a smug look. Drake's frown darkened.

"Miss Murder Queen," Fairman said.

"Yessir."

"I will be speaking to the Boss about this. I just wanted you to know that."

"Of course, sir. No issues here. He knows me better than anyone."

"Good to hear. Fairman out."

Click!

*

Fairman's Office—Afrókrema HQ

Fairman was outside of his office. He hung up and heaved a sigh. Said to his secretary, "No more calls for the next hour."

"Yessir," she said with a dutiful nod.

Fairman stepped back into his office and walked around Captain Carver sitting in a chair adjacent to his desk. As he shut the door, he said, "My apologies for the interruption, Captain."

"It's quite alright."

Fairman sat behind his desk and netted his fingers together. Leaned forward. "Let's continue where we left off..."

Manharttigan Mall—Control Room

The merc that held Molly asked, "What should we do about this one?"

Aria and Drake turned to face him. Drake said to Aria, "Get rid of her. We've got a cool compactor you can throw her and her mom into. They'll be closer than ever."

"Charming," she said.

Drake smirked. "I'll send a few guys to escort you there."

"Testing my loyalty, are you?"

"Better safe than sorry."

"It's too bad you didn't think that far ahead when you brought Frank on board." She felt great satisfaction in watching Drake's smirk vanish. "Oops," she said. "Too soon?"

Chapter 030
Infiltration

Manharttigan Mall

5:17 PM.

The southeastern area gate. The guard saw a set of headlights approaching and slinked into his booth. He checked the security monitor, then checked his schedule. No new arrivals for today. He reached for his radio—

POP!

A silenced shot blew his brains through the window pane, painting the rest of it black and red. Damian grabbed his shoulders and dragged him into the bushes. Returned to the booth and waved at the oncoming headlights.

"We're in," Jenny said from behind the wheel of the Shelby Cobra. She glanced over at Hill in the passenger seat. "Get those reinforcements yet?"

"Carver's gonna try to evacuate the place in the next half-hour."

"There's gonna be a lot of dead bodies in that mall by the time that happens."

"It's a delicate situation, Jenny. If we try to evacuate now, there'll be a panic, and there's the chance that Drake and his men will prematurely start the attack. Hell, they're probably planning on blowing us all up."

Jenny turned off the car's headlights as Damian opened the gate. "We're gonna try to avoid a panic, Hill. Trust me on that."

"How?"

"Damian said he's got a contact in there."

"Wouldn't tell me who."

"I wouldn't, either."

Hill frowned. "You gonna at least tell me how you plan on evacuating everybody without tipping off Drake?"

"Our contact will let us know."

"Seems like a bit of a stretch."

"Don't I know it," she said.

Damian walked parallel to the car as it coasted into the lot and moved toward the waste management section. The shutter doors were closed.

Waste Management Sector

Aria had to carry Molly to get her where they needed to go. She wouldn't walk. She wouldn't stop crying. One of the four mercs escorting them to the site dragged the girl's mother across the floor. Aria kept Molly's face against her chest, letting her sob into her shirt, doing her best to comfort the child and keep her from seeing the corpse as much as possible.

When they finally reached the compactor, the burliest of the four mercs tossed the mother in first and shut the doors. He pressed his thumb on the power button. They all listened to the compactor's walls crush everything in it. Glass breaking. Paper rustling. Bones snapping. Organs rupturing.

Aria's hold on Molly tightened. Her eyes darted from one side to the other. They had her surrounded. Assault rifles handy, but not aimed at her. They were just as suspicious as Drake.

Rightfully so.

Faster than light, Aria drew a silenced pistol and nailed the burliest merc to the control panel. The remaining three raised their weapons. She whirled, disintegrated the left eye of the merc on her left. The last two started to squeeze their fingers on the triggers—

POP-POP!

Her gun zigzagged between them. One face-planted on the concrete floor without a skullcap. The other crumpled to his knees, groaning, looking at the bloody hole in the crotch of his pants. Aria pressed the silencer against his forehead and drilled one last bullet into his head.

She looked over at the entryway as an automated forklift went by. Lucky the lab was out of view. Most of the workers were either too preoccupied with their work or busy trying to find the supervisor.

Molly whimpered. "Shh, shh," Aria said softly, discarding the gun to stroke her hair. "Nobody's gonna hurt you, sweetie." She glanced at her wristwatch. 5:25. Now or never. She turned and headed down the ramp toward the shutters.

*

Jenny parked the Shelby Cobra on the other side and got out. Hill stepped out and quietly shut the door. Damian approached them and looked at the shutters, then asked Jenny, "You sure?"

Jenny nodded.

Hill was getting annoyed. He went around the car and asked, "We're in this together, right?"

"We're paranoid fucks, Hill," Damian said.

"Yeah, tell me something I don't know. You said your man on the inside was gonna be here, right? Where the hell is he?"

The shutters creaked as they suddenly went up, startling Hill. The door only went up about a third of the way, probably to avoid attention from any workers who could be lingering nearby.

Hill drew his pistol and looked at Damian and Jenny, who were being just as cautious.

Aria stepped into view with Molly still clinging to her chest.

Hill sprang into action, snarling, "Hands up! Put the kid down and put your hands above your head."

Aria raised an eyebrow. She looked at Damian and Jenny, smiling. "You didn't tell 'im?"

Confused, Hill never took his gun off Aria, but he looked at the pair nonetheless. "Tell me... what?"

Damian stated, "I never said I had a *man* on the inside, idiot."

Hill exclaimed, "*What*? But... but she tried to..."

"It's called an act, Sergeant," Aria said. "Couldn't exactly blow my cover with Drake sitting right there, could I?"

Hill stuttered, at a loss for words.

Aria glanced at Jenny and smiled. "Hey, Sis."

"Hey," Jenny said.

"Hold on a second," Hill said, shifting his increasingly confused look from Jenny to Aria to Jenny again. "'Sis'?! You two are sisters?"

"Yeah," Jenny said.

Aria said, "You're very slow, aren't you, Sergeant?"

Hill kept his gun trained on Aria. "*You* tried to kill us yesterday. Excuse me if I'm a little on the edge... *and* confused."

Damian said, "Put the gun down. You're embarrassing me."

Hill tentatively lowered his pistol and glared at Damian. "You motherfucker."

"Hm?" Damian looked at him.

"This whole fucking time, you were playing us like fools. Me, Carver, the whole goddamn department. You were fucking with us the whole time."

"'Playing' implies I had to *pretend* you were fools," Damian replied.

Hill slugged him.

"Ow," Damian said, annoyed.

Hill waited for a counter-attack. He could see anger simmering in Damian's eyes, but Damian's lack of a follow-up reaction confused him. "You're not gonna hit me back?"

"If I did, you probably wouldn't have a head."

"Probably not."

"If you die, I don't get paid, either."

Hill shrugged. "Probably not..."

"So I guess I'll keep you alive for a while longer."

"Lucky me."

"Yeah. Lucky you."

Jenny looked at Molly with concern. Aria read her expression and said, "She's been through a lot."

"How much is 'a lot'?" Jenny asked.

"Too much. Take her somewhere safe."

"Where?" Jenny scoffed. "We have *one* safehouse that's still intact, and it's way out across town."

"The station," Hill suggested.

"Uh-uh," Jenny said. "I don't trust cops."

"Whatever."

"Well, Sis," Aria said, "you could head to that safehouse and stay there. Keep her company."

"You're blue-balling me?" Jenny asked incredulously. "*Right* at the final showdown?!"

"Yep," Aria said.

"The hell you are!"

Damian looked at the kid, then at Jenny. "I think she's cold."

"Fuck off, Damian."

"Hey, one of us has to sit this out for this kid's safety," he said.

Everyone looked at Damian with mild surprise; Hill, more so. Damian looked at them all and asked, "What the fuck is with the shock on your faces? I'm not *that* cold. Unlike her. She looks like she's freezing." He approached Molly and asked, "Hey, what's your name, kid?"

Molly cowered away from him, digging her face into Aria's bosom. He backed off. "Fine, fine."

Aria stroked her hair and said softly, "It's okay, honey. You're among friends here. Jenny, your jacket."

Jenny slipped out of her jacket and tossed it into Aria's outstretched hand. Aria gently set Molly on her feet and draped the jacket over her shoulders. Molly, shivering, nestled herself in it. Jenny sighed and took the girl's hand. "Alright, alright. I'll take her."

Molly yanked her hand away and shied toward Aria again.

Damian laughed and said, "I think she likes you."

"But I can't go," Aria said. "I have to take you guys to the control room. That's where Drake is."

"I've read the schematics," Damian said. "I know where it is."

Hill squinted at Damian. "When did you have time to read any schematics on this place?"

"That's classified."

"Oho, *really*?"

"We don't have time for any further arguments," Aria said impatiently. "Somebody has to take this kid to a safe place so we can go to war."

"Just throw her in the car," Hill said. "It's got heat. It's bulletproof, right?" He looked at Damian. "Right?"

"Well... yeah, it is," Damian answered.

"So why don't we just put her in there and lock the doors?"

"She can open the doors even if we lock them, dumbass."

"Tell her to stay. It's the safest place for her right now. Probably."

"What kid do you know actually *does* what they're told?" Damian asked.

"Good point..."

Molly started to cry. Aria patted her head. "Aw, don't cry, kiddo."

Molly squeaked, "No one wants me. I'm sorry."

Damian and Jenny exchanged pitying looks. Then Damian said to Hill, "Unhitch the trailer." As Hill went around the car, Damian knelt down and looked at Molly at face level. "It's not that nobody wants you, kid. It's just that you're in the way."

"Damian," Jenny snapped.

Damian ignored her and asked, "What's your name, kid?"

"Molly." She sniffled.

"How old are you, Molly?"

"Ten and a half."

"Ten and a half," he said, nodding. "Well, Molly, we're stuck between a rock and a hard place. Somebody has to take you to safety, but nobody wants to leave. So that leaves us with only one option. See, when I was your age, I was already sweeping up war zones with a flamethrower."

"Seriously, Damian?" Aria said. "You're gonna go there?"

Damian gave Molly one of his winning smiles. "Ever use a gun before?"

"Jesus Christ," Jenny said as she stepped between Damian and Molly. "I'll take her." She stuck her finger in Aria's face. "You owe me big time for this." She turned her forefinger in Damian's direction. "And *you* are a terrible influence and should stay as far away from her as possible."

"What?" Damian said. "I started using guns her age and I turned out just fine."

Jenny scoffed, shook her head as she led Molly to the car. Hill had just finished unhitching the trailer and was returning to the others. "You volunteered?"

"Damian didn't give me much of a choice," Jenny snarled.

Hill didn't want to know. He went to join the others.

Jenny set Molly down on the passenger seat and strapped her in. "You warm?"

Molly shook her head.

"I can fix that. Arms and legs in."

Molly tucked her knees together. Jenny shut the door and went around to the driver side, cussing out Damian as she went. Molly couldn't hear what she said. Jenny hopped in beside her and turned on the heat. Molly looked at the tube top Jenny was wearing with confusion. "How aren't you cold...?"

"Huh?" Jenny looked at her top as if she just noticed it. "Oh. Uh. I don't get cold."

"You don't?"

"Nope."

"Why?"

Jenny looked at her tentatively. Then she said, "Promise you won't freak out?"

Molly nodded slowly.

Jenny held up her hand. A small ball of flame appeared above her palm, filling the car's interior with its warm glow. Molly stared at the flame in wonder. Jenny put it out and said, "I'm too hot to get cold."

Molly stared at her, mystified. "Wow..."

Jenny smiled and started the car.

As Jenny peeled out of the parking lot, Aria dragged the trailer beside the waste management sector's doorway, out of sight. "Hopefully no one sees your payload. What's *in* these crates, anyway?"

"Toys," Damian said. "A whole lot of toys. Big, loud ones."

Aria chuckled. "My favourite kind."

Hill kept stealing nervous glances into the waste management area, hoping no one would notice them lingering around. "What's the safest way in?"

"The vents," Aria said. "I can try to take control of the main hub while you guys thin out the herd from the shadows."

"Sounds solid to me," Damian said.

"I don't like it. Feels too simple, and it's been almost anything *but* simple here," Hill said.

"If it isn't, you can say 'I told you so,'" Damian said.

"I'll keep that in mind."

Chapter 031
Inside the Hornet's Nest

Manharttigan Mall

5:36 PM.

Damian and Hill crawled through the vents, trying to keep their guns from clanging against the walls. The cold, stale stench of mould pervaded the ventilation system. They breathed sparingly because of it.

Found a grate. Damian looked down into it and saw a corridor. Five mercs in winter fatigues walked obliviously under the vent. He kept moving, careful not to put any weight on the grate. He sent a whispered command to Hill: "Go left."

"Okay," Hill replied, and went left.

Damian moved forward.

A merc was sitting on the toilet in the last restroom stall, staring at an old back-to-back issue of *Lovers and their Fetishes*, staring at a two-page spread of a naked woman lounging on an ivory loveseat. He whistled. Then his skullcap erupted, splattered on the walls around him. He slumped back against the toilet, dropped the magazine.

Damian climbed down from the open vent, biting down on a silenced pistol. He touched down in front of the dead merc and looked at him, then at the brain-spattered two-page spread. "Sorry, honey. Daddy's got work to do." He unlocked the stall and stepped out. Checked the other stalls—all empty. He slinked over to the door and opened it a crack. Two mercs were coming his way. Damian hopped over to the nearest stall. The restroom door opened. He locked the stall.

"And then I said, 'Hey, baby. I could eat a peach for hours!'" The two companions shared a laugh as they moved over to the urinals.

"I tell ya, if you said that to my old lady, she'd slap the shit out of you."

"Ah, your old lady's dry as a desert."

"Hey, now. Talk like that won't get you invited to Christmas dinner."

Damian quietly pulled the latch out and stepped into the open, pistol in hand.

"Hell, I'll be there if your sister's there. She's got an ass like an all-you-can eat buffet!"

"How 'bout an orgy?"

Damian whistled.

Both men whirled with their dicks hanging out, stunned. "What the—"

POP-POP!

Damian dropped them instantly and scoffed at their appendages hanging out of their zippers. "How embarrassing."

Hill initially headed north since his separation from Damian. He crawled through the vents, stifling a sneeze from all the dust every now and then. He heard clamouring up ahead—autonomous, rhythmic noises, like a factory. He followed the noises and eventually reached a grate. He peered through. Eyes bulged in surprise at what he discovered.

A pharmaceutical assembly line sprawling across the room; grinding, sifting, and bottling a seemingly endless supply of cocaine in glass vials, tended by a multitude of workers dressed in 'kiss the cook' aprons and half-face respirators. Guards with either shotguns or Uzi submachine guns patrolled the overhead catwalks, eyeing the workers like hawks. The air was white with coke dust. Cardboard boxes full of empty vials lined the wall under Hill. Against the farthest wall was a portable warehouse building that served as safe storage for drums full of what Hill assumed was kerosene. Steel tables lined the outside walls of the portable, where workers diluted fresh product with flour. Boxes full of the final packaged product were loaded onto skids, which were then picked up by the auto-forklifts and carried off somewhere behind the portable—possibly another loading zone.

Jesus goddamn Christ, Hill thought. He backed away, deciding to go in a different direction.

He eventually found himself hiding above the lounge filled with mercs enjoying some time off. Some of them played video games. One slept on the couch. Two others decorated a small Christmas tree on the pool table. Another merc sat comfortably on a lawn chair covered in shrink wrap with a Santa hat on his head, strumming an acoustic guitar. Four others played poker in another corner, smoking cigarettes and drinking whiskey, only talking when they felt it necessary.

One of the mercs adorning the small Christmas tree asked the others, "What're your plans for the holidays?"

"Fucking some bitches and eating Chinese while I watch the *Death Runners* game," the acoustic player said.

"Nice. What about you guys?"

The two gamers replied in unison: "Meh."

"Kenny?" the decorator asked his fellow decorator.

Kenny shrugged. "Maybe I'll celebrate it with the dogs."

"You have dogs?"

"Robot dogs. Ain't real."

"Anything real?"

"What's the point? Anything real dies when I touch it."

"Sad..."

Frowning, Hill shook his head and moved on, eventually finding himself above the loading bay. He peered through the grate, watched as Drake's men unloaded a small tank with a nutcracker mounted on top of it from the back of a commercial trailer. The nutcracker tank seemed to be almost... sentient. The cannon followed the nutcracker's eye movements; its arms raised and lowered its bayonet-fitted rifle repeatedly. Six cyborgs followed it in formation, bionic arms gripping futuristic rifles Hill had never seen before. The cyborgs lacked skin, showing muscle tissue and lidless eyeballs that bulged from their sockets, encased in clear glass shells with feeding and breathing tubes plugging their mouths and nostrils. Their battle suits gleamed in the frosty blue light cast down from fluorescent bulbs.

"Stand to attention!" a mercenary captain barked.

The cyborgs obeyed, lining up.

Hill whispered to himself, "What the fuck have you gotten yourself into, Don?"

Damian went back to the door and peeked into the corridor. Nothing but distant chatter on the PA. He leaned out slightly, looking left, then right. Coast was clear. He stepped out and jogged toward the end of the corridor. Looked out. Two coming up on the right, none on the left. Damian leaped out and cut them down. They crumpled on the floor.

A *third* walked out from around the corner. Stopped dead when he saw the two corpses. Raised his assault rifle at Damian—

POP!

Damian drilled a hole in his face, sent him staggering against the far wall. Someone out of Damian's field of vision shouted an alarm. "Goddamn it," Damian hissed under his breath. He glanced over his shoulder, checking the corridor behind him. Shadows danced on the wall at the very end, accompanied by rapid footsteps. Flanking him.

Two mercs sprang out in front of their fallen comrade, assault rifles poised.

Damian whirled. Blew them both away. They fell, shooting into the ceiling. The sudden crackle of gunfire rang through the corridors.

"Son of a bitch!" Damian snarled as he put two extra shots into each of them. "Worth it." He ejected the magazine in favour of a new one, glancing up the corridor as the shadows grew more prominent on the walls. He stood over a corpse. Stomped on the butt of a rifle lying across the corpse's chest, flipping it up into his hands.

Half a dozen mercs rounded the corner, blasting at Damian. Bullets skipped off the cinderblock walls and stitched across the concrete floor. Cool and collected, Damian turned and sprayed them, cutting down four of them. The last two took cover behind the support beams. Damian's bullets raked across the beams, shooting sparks into the air. He ran dry. Ducked around the corner for cover. The wall absorbed the duo's return fire as Damian tossed the rifle and reloaded his pistol. Waited for a break in their fire, then responded with a three-round beat. Hit steel beams and nothing more. He ducked back around again as more enemy fire tore chunks off the corner.

Down the corridor on his left, Damian heard metal groan. He turned to see the double doors to the loading bay fly open, revealing the faceless cyborgs, futuristic rifles aimed right at him.

"Shit," he said.

COBALT CHRISTMAS: A COBALT ROGUE STORY

KAKRAANNNGG!

A bolt of light shot out of the lead cyborg's rifle, streaking across the corridor. Damian ducked his head. It passed over him, burning across the wall. *"Suka syn!"*

The other cyborgs followed suit, shooting energy beams across the corridor. Damian sprang across the gap, diving through the air in an arc, pistol firing. His bullets bounced harmlessly off titanium breastplates. He tucked and rolled past the trio of mercs as the laser beams sliced them to sizzling pieces, singing Damian's heels.

The pair of mercs down the hall started shooting again. Damian kept his head down, bolting for cover as hot lead chased him. He fired his pistol in blind retaliation as he ran.

The cyborgs came around between him and the mercs. Metal screamed as their bullets bounced off the cyborgs' broad backs. The mercs stopped firing, astonished by what they were seeing. "Fuck are *those*?"

Damian fired two rounds at the lead cyborg's glass case. The bullets glanced off, cracking the surface. Faint, but noticeable. Not good enough. "Goddamn, fucking cyborgs," Damian groaned.

They raised their pulse rifles. Their targeting systems locked on.

Damian dived between two steel beams as they unleashed a deadly light show that seared across the floor and sheared the edges off the beams. Damian looked at a smouldering piece of steel as it clattered on the floor, edges red-hot. "Christ." He dug his hand into his satchel and pulled out the compact flamethrower. Fired it up. "Let's see what this baby's got."

Another flash. Damian leaped out from behind the steel beam as it instantly melted into a molten puddle. He rolled across the floor, rising in a crouch. The cyborgs readjusted their aim, but too late—Damian squeezed the trigger. A stream of flaming napalm hit them, enveloping them in flames. Damian gaped at the raging fire as it filled the corridor. "Fucking sweet!"

The fire alarm blared. The sprinklers activated. The carpet of fire sizzled, but wouldn't let up. The cyborgs, however, started to advance, unfazed.

Damian made a run for the opposite direction and beelined into the next left turn, dodging pulse rifle fire—

—and found himself cut off by twenty angry mercenaries, all

poised to shoot. "Freeze, motherfucker!"

Damian hesitated. Then he replied, *"Burn,* motherfuckers!" Hosed them all down with flaming napalm, filling the corridor with a wall of raging fireballs and a choir of anguished screams. Damian watched the mercs writhe in the dancing flames, piling on each other, blackened and deformed.

Now Damian had to find another way out. He looked down the opposite end of the corridor beyond the cyborgs' occupied territory. Another set of mercs burst through the doors. "There he is!"

"Kill the son of a bitch!"

Too far for the napalm. Damian threw the compact flamethrower's strap over his shoulder and drew a second pistol. Their assault rifles stuttered, popping in his ears as they sent bullets stitching across the floor toward him. Damian sprang off the floor, shooting both pistols at them, taking cover behind another beam as he downed a merc—four left. They fanned out in a crescent, blocking off the corridor.

The thunderous *CLOMP-CLOMP-CLOMP-CLOMP* of the cyborgs' heavy boots approached. Another second or two and he'd be trapped. He contemplated using the grenade launcher.

Instead he settled for the grenades in his pockets. Took two out, one in each hand. Thumbs flicked the pins off. The spoons flew away. Damian hurled the grenades straight at the mercs, then ducked behind his support beam.

The mercs started singing his song.

"GRENADE!"

"Oh, shit!"

"Take—"

KABOOM!

A deafening roar shook the corridors. Damian held his hands over his ears as a wave of debris rushed past him.

CLOMP-CLOMP-CLOMP-CLOMP!

Damian looked out, squinting through the smoke and drizzle. Saw a shape in the haze on the floor... a hand clinging to an AK-47. He snatched it up, pried the fingers off and tossed the severed hand into the burning napalm. Checked the magazine. Half capacity. Not bad.

A merc approached from the southern corridor, stepping in the cyborgs' way. Held up his hand. "Hold up! Hold up. I got this."

The cyborgs halted.

The merc drew a grenade from his utility belt. "Hey, shithead!" He pulled the pin. "Hope your mouth is as big as your balls, cuz you're gonna be swallowing this whole!" He hurled the grenade into the smoke.

It clacked straight toward Damian like a pool ball. Damian looked at it. Heart skipped. He swung the butt stock of his rifle across it, sent it flying back at its owner. "Fore!"

BAM!

Another wave of hot debris roared through the corridor. Shrapnel and gore sprayed the cyborgs' titanium battle suits. They exchanged looks, then continued their advance—

Damian lunged out of the smoke, assault rifle blazing in his hands, bullets pounding their heads. He bolted across the aisle, dodging pulse lasers drawing lines through the smoke and the sprinklers' downpour. He felt one burn a line across his right thigh. He gnashed his teeth as the pain seared through his leg. Two more streaked through his coat, ignited the fabric. He felt the heat on his back, the flames licking at the nape on his neck. He leaped, slammed his foot into the door, burst into the lounge.

A flaming, angry intruder confronting eight mercs who were just trying to enjoy their time off. The poker players exchanged looks. The gamers lost before they could reach their new high score. Damian raised his assault rifle. "Don't fucking move." He slipped out of his burning coat, maintaining a grip on the AK the whole time. The rest of the grenades in it were starting to burn up.

KLOMP-KLOMP-KLOMP behind the doors.

Kenny went for his gun.

BRAKABRAK!

Damian plastered him against the wall, toppling the mini Christmas tree. The guy beside him leaped out of his chair. "Oh, my God! You killed—"

Damian shot him dead. Hurled his flaming coat at the poker players, who tried to scramble, but too late: the grenades inside the coat blew them and the table apart. Poker chips showered the rampaging intruder as he sprayed the rifle in an arc, riddling the guy who was sleeping on the couch, cutting the gamers in half and destroying the TV behind them. The sprinklers inside the lounge went off.

KLOMP-KLOMP-KLOMP!

The lounge doors blew off their hinges. The cyborgs barged into a room full of corpses and nothing more.

Damian made his escape in the vents.

Aria entered the control room and immediately started counting heads: five mercs, a dozen security operators working the monitors, and Drake, who turned on his heel to face her.

"Funny coincidence," Drake said, listening to the alarm. The sprinklers hadn't gone off inside the control room, but the corridors were a different story. Aria was drenched to the bone. "I send you with an escort party, and you come back by yourself with alarms going off left and right. Explosions, gunfire... my cyborgs are hard at work dealing with a rodent infestation. I wonder who?" He smiled coyly, if only for a moment. "I knew you were a fucking traitor."

Aria stood wordlessly in the entrance, hands at her sides. Two machine pistols *sprouted* from her palms, slinking into her hands.

Drake squinted at the odd sight. "That's something I *never* saw before. But I *have* heard of it... you're the Crimson Bitch! The one and only Aria Knight."

"Wouldja look at that," she said. "I never even had to tell you my name after all."

"I'm a genius," he said.

"Yeah, you're a fuckin' super sleuth," she replied sarcastically. "The jig's up, Drake. This is as far as it goes."

"Is it?"

"Your water tainting plot's all but vaporized. Your crew's history. Fairman's fingerprints're all over this clusterfuck. He's done. You're done. This operation's been compromised."

"You think that scares me? You think I'm scared? The operation isn't done till I say it's done, soldier." Drake brandished a pistol and shot one of the operators in the face, flipping him out of his chair. The other operators yelped and whimpered in fear. "Doesn't matter who dies at this point. Pretty soon we'll *all* be dead. It's a free-for-all, baby! I got this place packed up to its eyeballs in explosives! Even if you get the shoppers out, they'll never get out of range fast enough." Drake hollered with laughter and shot another operator in the arm. The operator shrieked in agony until Drake finished him off with two more shots. The other operators started to rush to the opposite side of the room. "Where're you going?" Drake asked them, cutting two more of them down.

Aria blasted Drake against the video wall. His mercs opened up on her. She absorbed their bullets, staggering back into the hallway. Returned fire, machine pistols blazing. A merc's skullcap bounced off the ceiling. Another one's eyes disintegrated in his skull. Screen panels blew out of the video wall. Operators huddled under the console boards screamed as mercenary bodies tumbled over them. Three left.

Drake recovered. Found his elbow embedded in a TV screen and jerked it out, wincing as the jagged pieces stuck to the TV frame cut his skin. He sighed and shot at Aria.

Aria didn't bother trying to duck. A bullet pierced through her shoulder. She took it in stride. Riddled another merc, sent him spinning to the floor. Two left, hiding behind the control console. Aria underhand-tossed a grenade behind the console, blasting it apart, scattering the mercs in all directions.

Drake shielded himself with his arms from the wave of shrapnel. He lowered his arms and found himself staring directly down the barrel of Aria's machine pistol. "Christ."

Aria put two in his face, slamming the back of his head against the video wall, spiderwebbing the TV screen behind him. Another shot hollowed out his head. He collapsed into her arms, and she dragged him out of the control room and into the hall. He started to recover. She slammed him to the floor. "Where are the bombs?"

"Like... I'd tell you," he moaned.

She blew a tunnel between his ears and waited impatiently for his head to heal. Once his face reformed, she said, "I'll ask you again: where the fuck are the explosives?"

"Gonna have to find 'em yourself, bitch. Oi, my head..."

"Oh, baby," she said with a sinister chuckle, "it's only gonna get worse for you."

KLOMP-KLOMP-KLOMP-KLOMP!

Aria looked over her shoulder, peered through the sprinklers' hail at silver patterns shimming in the flickering lights. The patterns evolved; becoming breastplates, arms, legs. The cyborgs approached. Aria opened fire. Her bullets raked across the cyborgs' chests, totally ineffective. "Shit."

They raised their pulse rifles and fired beams of light her way.

She leaped up, raised Drake in their path of fire. Plasma tore through them both, slicing a circle out of Drake's torso and taking his right arm off; Aria lost four fingers on the hand she held Drake with as another plasma stream cleaved through her thigh. Both of them screamed. "AERGH!"

Drake drove his heel into her stomach, sent her sprawling against the wall. He dived for the control room. "Take her down, boys!"

The cyborgs bore down on her, pulse rifles charging up.

Aria threw her hand up. An anti-tank rifle materialized from her arm. She raised the rifle singlehandedly, blasted through one of the cyborgs' heads—sent the pieces scattering. The recoil hardly mattered to someone as superhumanly strong as she was. Her leg that had sustained a clean laser cut had luckily never separated; the wound was healing nicely.

Flash of laser fire. The spot Aria occupied was burned out of existence in a split second. Aria herself was in the air, landed on the shoulders of the cyborg she'd just beheaded. Leaped again to another cyborg's shoulders. The other cyborgs fired at her. She flipped back, sliding down the cyborg's back, the laser beams followed, slicing her cyborg shield right down the middle. She hopped around as her cover's limbs hit the floor, caught her rifle between another cyborg's legs. Pulled hard enough to twist its feet out from under it. It hit the ground.

Her fingers had grown back. Two beams flashed between her legs and worked their way up. She jumped, pivoted forward, lasers twisting through the air after her. She landed on the fallen cyborg and rolled off, let the laser beams melt the cyborg's titanium and ignite its battery. Its chest cavity belched a neon red fireball.

Aria skated across the puddles forming on the floor, blinking through the sprinklers' hail, going for another cyborg's legs. Only three left—

KLONK!

A titanium foot caught the side of her head. Lights danced before her eyes as her body spiralled through the air and *smashed* through a concrete wall, blowing out the other side into the loading bay. A group of mercs shouted with surprise as her body shattered a crate full of submachine guns, spilling the weapons across the dock. Her anti-tank rifle skidded over the edge of the loading dock.

The fifteen mercs occupying the loading bay looked at her, then at each other. "Ain't she one of us?"

"Fuck's going on?"

"Don't ask me."

Drake's voice rang out on the PA system. "Attention all personnel: our dear Murder Queen is a traitor to the cause and must be killed at all costs. Come on, boys. Snap to it!"

Aria groaned. Everything hurt. Ears rang. Eyes weren't focusing; stars glittered and danced, filling her vision. Her head spun. The floor was the ceiling, or seemed like it. Couldn't get herself up. Wasn't healing fast enough.

"Well, you heard the man," one of the mercs said. "Let's kill ourselves a Murder Queen.

BRRRAAAPP!

Uzi fire rained down from above, peppering the mercs with lead. Donald Hill fired upon them from atop the ventilation duct in the rafters, crouched under the pipes. Most of the mercs scrambled for cover beneath him. A few others ran for the dock—Hill made sure they never made it.

Bullets shot up through the duct a mere inch from his foot. Hill flinched, staggered toward the wall as the mercs' bullets made a beeline through the vents toward him. "Jesus Christ!"

Aria's head felt light, but her arm was fine and her vision was coming back. She saw the six mercs shooting up into the ceiling, trying to draw a bead on Hill. She looked up at Hill, then picked up an Uzi and started spraying. Three dropped instantly. The others looked at her, and took aim. One of them blew out her kneecap. Aria howled in agony and rage as she collapsed on her hands. Her shoulder took another bullet. Her Uzi tore flesh from a merc's thigh, making him scream and fall to a crouch.

Hill quickly reloaded. He dropped off the duct, latched himself onto the side of it, hanging by his fingers. Now he could see the bastards, and spat bullets all over them. Dust and blood exploded as they collapsed to the floor. Hill ejected the magazine and traded it for a new one, then left it hanging from the shoulder strap. "You alright?"

Aria heaved, waiting impatiently for her burning leg to heal.

Almost nothing hurt more than a kneecapping. "Ow..."

"You alright?" Hill asked again.

"I'm fine. Gimme a goddamn minute." She slammed her fist on the floor, cracking it. "FUCK!"

KLOMP-KLOMP-KLOMP-KLOMP!

The last three cyborgs appeared in the entryway and started down the ramp toward Aria. Hill looked at them. "Christ." Opened fire and watched his bullets bounce off them. He got their attention. They looked up at him. Their pulse rifles followed suit. "Oh, shit!" Hill said.

KAKRAAAANNG!

Laser beams erupted from their rifles, leaping straight for Hill, who jumped off the side of the duct into space, reaching for the catwalk down below. The ceiling exploded in a plethora of sparks behind him; the duct, pipes, and a portion of a support beam came crashing down.

Hill caught hold of the catwalk railing and vaulted over it. Fell in a crouch as another laser beam seared through the catwalk, splitting it in half. Hill's heart lurched as his share of the catwalk suddenly dipped toward the loading bay below. "WHOA!" Fingers locked in the catwalk's grated floor, feet swinging wildly above a twenty-foot drop.

The cyborgs took aim—

KAPOOWW!

The middle cyborg's head blew apart. The other two turned back to Aria, who maintained a squatting position, aiming her anti-tank rifle at them. They fired. Neon yellow streaked past her. She blasted another head off, sent it spinning over the ramp. She got the drop on the last one.

Then she noticed something much, much worse: the nutcracker tank emerging from the doorway, starting down the ramp. "What the hell—"

KAKRAAAANNG!

A laser beam shot across the dock. Aria pitched out of its path and lost a foot to the beam. Screaming, she tumbled toward an empty commercial trailer.

The nutcracker tank took aim. Its cannon roared, launching a HESH round above Aria into the trailer, decimating the cab on the other end.

COBALT CHRISTMAS: A COBALT ROGUE STORY

BOOM!

Aria squinted as a blinding flash-fire rushed through the trailer toward her. She rolled again to dodge the flames, throwing herself off the dock. Another laser beam followed, carved a chunk out of the dock.

Hill grunted as he pulled himself up the catwalk. It dangled from the slightest movement, creaking, threatening to give way and drop him on the concrete. He hooked his fingers in the grating and heaved himself up.

Aria picked herself up off the concrete floor, ignoring the flames emitted from the trailer beside her. She spat blood on the floor and wiped the rest of it off her chin. Started to growl as her body trembled with rage.

Drake crept out of the control room with an assault rifle taken off a fallen merc. He glanced both ways down the corridor, smiling when he saw the hole in the wall. He saw a flash in the doorway at the end of the hall. The whole place rumbled from the explosion. "Yeah, crack those nuts!" He went in the opposite direction, jogging through the sprinklers' rain.

BKAM-BKAM!

His kneecaps cratered. Drake screamed and pitched forward, splitting his face open on the concrete floor. "AUGH!" He pushed himself on his backside and sprayed the corridor with the AK. Nothing in the smoke and rainy haze. Drake looked at his bloodied legs hanging together by crimson muscle strands as splintered bones slowly came back together. He heard a magazine slide into place. Heard his mystery assailant rack the slide. "Warkowski!" he hollered, angrily throwing his empty clip aside. "I'm assuming that's you, Warkowski." He shoved a new clip into his AK. "Why don't you come on out? Finish me. Settle this man to man."

No response. Nothing but the distant rumble of explosions from the loading bay, and the white noise hiss of the sprinklers.

"I gotta hand it to ya, kid," Drake continued, "I was sure I got you at the farm. Even *I'm* pretty fucking shocked you're alive. I'm genuinely impressed."

"I get that a lot," Damian replied from down the corridor.

Drake's eyes darted back and forth, searching for a sign. His knees healed, he stood up, AK poised and ready. "I know you do. I know *exactly* what you mean."

"Yeah, I'll bet you do."

Drake wiped water from his eyes. Shook it out of his hair. "It was raining that night, too." He laughed. "Central Congoria. Jesus fucking Christ. That was somethin' else, wasn't it?" He looked at each support beam in turn as he cautiously treaded down the corridor.

"There's something else this night has in common with that one."

"Oh, yeah?" Drake looked in the direction of Damian's voice. Moved toward it. "And what's that?"

"You're going to die tonight. Again."

"Lightning doesn't always strike the same spot twice, kid."

"It doesn't need to." Damian rose up behind him. Pressed his pistol against the back of Drake's head, causing him to freeze. "It only needs to strike true."

Drake chuckled. "You got me."

"Or do I?"

"Or *do* you? Pulling that trigger would only give me a temporary headache."

"It'll still hurt."

"True." Drake looked over his shoulder at Damian. "But you wanna do a lot more than that, right?" He turned around, AK muzzle scraping the floor. Unafraid. Then he looked down and burst into an uncontrollable giggle.

"What the fuck is so funny?"

"That fucking shirt!" Drake said. "What *is* that?"

Damian sighed. "It's an aloha shirt."

"It's hideous!"

"Yeah, yeah." Damian put a round through his forehead. "You can shut the fuck up now." He drew his combat knife. Twelve inches of serrated steel glistened under the sprinklers, singing their own tune as droplets of water pelted the flat of the blade.

BOOM!

The loading platform erupted, filling the air with flying rubble, toppling the burning trailer on its side. Aria soared through the air like an eagle, pounced on the last cyborg, balancing on its forearms. She jammed the muzzle of her anti-tank rifle against its head case and decimated it, the head, and the battery behind its breastplate with a single shot. Nothing left but exploding components trapped inside its titanium shell.

The tank adjusted its aim at the headless cyborg. The cannon roared.

Aria sailed clear as the platform concussively blew apart under her feet. Fireballs devoured the cyborg's body under her feet, flinging it like a ragdoll. She landed gracefully at a safe distance. Aimed her rifle. Fired.

The nutcracker's head blew apart. The body spasmed on its rotating turret base. The cannon turned toward her.

Aria made a mad dash straight for it. She could see straight up the barrel. The inside flashed. Out came another round. Aria dropped low. The round whistled over her head, grazing her hair. A rush of hot air hit her face. She blinked.

BOOM!

The ground erupted behind her. She leaped, propelled by the explosion, arcing up and over the cannon, landing on the turret, which started to spin, trying to shake her off. She squatted, prying her fingers under the nutcracker's boot. Tore the headless soldier off the turret and sent it crashing to the ground. The tank lurched forward, leaping off the ramp and slamming down on the floor, rocking violently. She tore the lid off the turret and looked at the cyborg inside. This one was just a head encased in glass similar to its companions, mounted instead on a life support system and a computer tower fastened to the cockpit floor with wiry mechanical extensions on all the controls.

Its bulging red eyeballs rolled up, its lifeless pupils staring at her as she opened her palm above the cockpit. A dozen grenades spilled out of her hand and bounced around the cyborg tank operator. "Die," she growled, and jumped off just a second before the entire tank blew apart in a cacophonous explosion.

Damian grabbed a fistful of Drake's hair and moved the knife closer to the immortal's neck. The blade's serrated teeth bit into Drake's flesh. Crimson beads formed on the blade before the sprinkler water washed it away.

Drake flinched. Started to struggle. Damian sawed through to the bone. Blood dribbled out, trickling off the blade, running down

Drake's shirt as the immortal convulsed from the pain. The blade scraped against his upper spinal column. Drake gurgled.

"DAMIAN!"

Startled, Damian stopped and looked over his shoulder to see Aria and Hill standing in the hall, looking worse for wear. "What? I'm busy."

"You can't kill him yet."

"Are you fucking kidding me? Why the fuck shouldn't I kill him?"

"He's got the place wired."

"So what?"

Hill said, "Split up. Half of us can find the bombs and disarm them while the other half evacuates the people."

Drake coughed and rasped, "I wouldn't... do that... if I were... you..."

Damian jerked his head back. "What was that?"

Drake forced a smug grin. "I got... s-spotters out there. If they... sense an evac...uation... boom." He gave Damian a wheezy cackle, which Damian cut off by twisting his blade through his windpipe.

"Fucking cocksucker." Damian pulled the blade out. "Where are they?"

"Loose lips... sink ships." Drake laughed.

"*Pizda*!" Damian fumed. He slammed his heel into Drake's spine and stomped his face into the concrete. Kept stomping, pulverizing him into the floor, swearing in Russian until the top half of Drake's head was reduced to pink and red mush. The magnetic force of his healing factor prevented pieces of his brain from washing down any floor drains.

Hill looked at the mushy pile of Drake's brains as it began to expand in the pools of water on the floor. His face contorted in disgust. "Christ."

"So we have some spotters to take care of," Damian said. He pointed at Hill. "You, get Carver to bring a fucking army down here."

"It's not that simple. I've already told them about a possible attack. I don't know what the hell Carver's doing."

"Then find out." Damian turned to face Drake again.

Drake's head had reformed, good as new. He smiled.

"What?"

Damian asked him, "You gonna talk?"

"Hell no."

"Didn't think so." Damian kicked him in the face. He turned back to Hill. "This concludes our deal. Now all the bank robbers are accounted for. You even got a live one, though I strongly suggest you kill him. Book him. Then pay me. Make sure this faggot doesn't get out of your sight for a second."

"What're you two gonna do?"

"We'll be weeding out the spotters and hopefully finding the bombs."

"Oh, the glorious job, eh?"

"Got a problem with that? You got your man. I've kept my end of the bargain. Now we're gonna finish this."

"You'll get your money when this situation's resolved. Just don't blow us up in the process."

"No promises."

"Hey, Damian?" Hill said.

Damian looked at him. "What?"

Hill said, "I told you so."

Damian scowled.

Chapter 032
Hand of Fate

Sundae Family Diner

6:46 PM.

Jenny and Molly sat facing each other in a vinyl booth. The 50s' style diner was fairly pleasing to the eye, but its mirrored floor tiles added a surreal, dream-like quality to its interior. Unusual for a simple eatery.

Jenny was halfway through her burger. Molly hadn't touched her burger and fries. She sat staring distantly at her plate. Jenny sympathized. "You're not hungry?"

Molly shook her head slowly.

"It's really good."

"I don't want it."

"Okay. You don't have to eat it if you don't feel up to it," Jenny said gently.

Elvis Presley sang *That's All Right* on the diner's PA system, almost quiet enough to go unnoticed. An android waitress, so close to resembling a beautiful teenager, but not quite catching the realism, served a newly arrived couple a few booths down.

Molly asked, "Was he going to give me a gun?"

"Who? Damian?"

"I don't know..."

Jenny sighed. "He's..." she paused, struggling to find a delicate word. "Uh... hm... *unique*, I guess."

"Unique?"

"Yeah, unique could work. He lacks delicacy."

"Why?"

Jenny shrugged. "He's just different, is all."

"How's he different?"

"It's complicated..."

Molly looked at her plate again. "Is he like you?"

"What do you mean?"

"Can he make fire with his hands too?"

"Oh. No, no. Well, sort of... that's complicated, too. He can do a lot of things."

"Is he a good guy?"

Jenny hesitated. "He's not... a *bad* guy." She muttered under her breath, "Although he's not a *good* guy, either..."

"Why did he want to give me a gun?"

Jenny wasn't sure how to answer. Molly wouldn't understand the truth, but at the same time, Jenny didn't want to gloss over it with lies. "I think... he figured you'd wanna do something about it. That's his way of looking out for you. Only way he knows how, I guess."

"I don't think I'll ever want to touch a gun. I've seen what they can do."

Jenny wanted to give her a hug. "I'm sorry, kiddo..."

"Even before tonight, I've seen what they can do."

Jenny's eyebrows scrunched together. "What d'you mean?"

"My daddy used one all the time."

"He did?"

"Yeah. A lot."

"What, like, target practice?"

"On people."

"Jesus. Who was your daddy?"

"Ice."

"Ice?"

Molly nodded.

Jenny set her half-eaten burger down on the plate. She chose her next words carefully. "What were you doing at that mall?"

"That man wanted to use me as lev... lev... level-age?"

"Leverage?"

Molly said, "Yeah. Leverage."

"I don't understand...?"

"Huh?"

"You were leverage? Leverage for what?"

"They said to 'storm the mall.' What did they mean?"

The vinyl squeaked as Jenny leaned back against the seat, pondering this new information. She looked at Molly and found the girl's distant green eyes piercing into her with a kind of eerie lifelessness that Jenny found uncomfortably familiar. A long time ago, her own reflection wasn't much different from Molly. "What happened?"

Molly didn't say anything. Her expression grew shyer. She stared at the table.

"It's okay," Jenny said softly. "You can tell me."

"They broke into the house and put us in a van. I tried to fight them, but they tied me up and hit me and said that if I gave them more trouble they would kill my mom." Tears welled up in her eyes. Molly started to cry. "They killed my mommy..."

Jenny reached across the table and touched her hand. "Shh-shh-shh, it's okay, honey. You're not alone."

Molly kept on sobbing.

"I know how hard it is, kiddo."

Molly sniffled and wiped her eyes on her sleeve.

Jenny didn't know what else to say. She held Molly's hand and didn't let go.

"Why did she have to die?"

"Senseless cruelty, kiddo. Some people just don't have compassion."

"My daddy told me it's not supposed to hurt after the first few times..."

"Why would he say that?"

"He said it's weak."

"No, sweetie. No, it's not weak. It's the exact opposite of weak."

"Then why do people tease me when I cry?"

"You know what I think it is?"

"What?"

"Jealousy. They don't have it in them. It takes strength and courage to, to show your emotions like that. It shows them that you have compassion... that you have a heart."

"Does it stop hurting?"

Jenny exhaled slowly. "No. It never stops hurting. It never goes away."

Molly whined as the tears started to flow again.

"Hey. Hey. That's not what matters. There'll always be pain, sweetheart. What matters is what you do with it."

"Do you feel pain?"

"Of course I do. Everybody feels pain."

"What do you do with it?"

"I let it motivate me. I don't let it bring me down. That's the last thing I want it to do, so I don't let it." Her grip on Molly's hand tightened affectionately. "Trust me... it only gets harder from here. If my mother taught me anything valuable, it's to make your biggest weakness your greatest strength."

"How?"

Jenny pointed at Molly's chest. "With your heart, of course." She chuckled. "I know. Cheesy. My mom was kind of old-fashioned that way."

Molly managed a small smile. "I like it..."

Jenny smiled back.

"Can we go back?"

"To the mall? Why would you wanna do that?"

"My daddy's going back. I heard that man say so."

"I can't take you back there. It's too dangerous for you."

"No, it's not. You said I should make my biggest weakness my greatest strength."

"I didn't mean that you should walk into a war zone. That's not strength, that's suicide."

"But my daddy's gonna be there."

"'Storming the mall,' right? Honey, if he's doing what I think he's doing, it might be best if I keep you as far away from that mall as humanly possible."

"But I don't wanna be away from my daddy! You can't keep me away from him. He's my dad!"

"Okay, okay, simmer down." Jenny noticed the scarce patrons in the diner giving them looks and did her best to ignore them. She heaved a sigh. "What kind of irresponsible person would I be to take you back there?"

"Then *you* save him. Save my daddy. He's gonna die." Molly started to cry again. "He's gonna die..."

An android waitress approached their table. "Is everything okay here?"

"We're fine," Jenny said. "We were just leaving."

"Okay. I'll be right back with your bill."

"Thank you."

The android stalked behind the counter, leaving Jenny with a sobbing little girl in the booth. Jenny contemplated on what to do. Taking her to the safehouse would be the most logical choice, obviously. But she couldn't stand to allow her to lose two parents in one night...

"Okay," she said firmly, "on one condition."

Molly's expression lit up.

"You stay in the bulletproof car."

Molly's eyes overflowed with tears of joy. She smiled hopefully. "Okay!"

"Promise."

"I promise!"

Jenny held out her pinky finger. "Pinky promise."

Molly twisted her pinky finger around Jenny's and squeezed. "Pinky promise!"

28th Precinct Station

Carver stepped into the lobby and strode past the desk sergeant. "Evening, Mike."

"Evening, Captain. You got a package waiting for you in your office."

"What? Package?"

The desk sergeant shrugged, indifferent. "Lois dropped it in your basket."

Carver made a look and slowly went to the elevator. He checked the messages on his phone. Two from Hill. He sighed and listened to the voicemail.

When he reached his office, he was about ready to send as many units to the mall as possible. He unlocked the door and went inside. Checked the basket. Picked up the package... it was open. "What the hell?"

He went back downstairs with the opened package and dropped it onto Mike's desk. "What kinda sick joke is this, Sergeant?"

Mike inspected the package, perplexed. "No idea, Captain. I didn't open it. Neither did Lois. I mean, I don't *think* she did. No idea why she would..."

"Where is she? You know what? Never mind. We've got bigger problems."

"What's up, Cap?"

"Got a tip that the next attack might be at the Manharttigan Mall."

"Christ. That's what we need," Mike said sarcastically. "I'll help put the word out."

"Gotta do this quietly. I need an army of plainclothes cops inside. A helicopter in the air, but just to observe and report." Carver squinted and went over to the coffee machine. Took out his phone and dialled a new number. Fairman answered. "You're up."

"On it," Fairman said.

When Jenny and Molly returned to the sidewalk, Jenny looked up the street. The precinct station was *right* on the corner. A thought crossed her mind to just drop Molly off there. Perhaps if she trusted Carver's men, she might have. She wouldn't have been able to look at herself in the mirror for a while if she had; the betrayal would have eaten her alive. Molly would never understand. Jenny wouldn't have, at that age. Molly was only ten. At least her father was still alive, for now. There was still time...

Jenny sighed and opened the passenger side door. "Hop in."

Molly did as she was told. Strapped herself in and kept her hands on her lap and her feet under the dash.

"Good girl." Jenny shut the door and went around the front, stealing another glance up the street, this time at the department store on the corner opposite the precinct station. The interior started flashing. *Huh,* she thought. Touched the door handle—

KRAKABOOOMM!

Blowout sale! The front of the department store exploded, spraying glass, metal and merchandise across the street, toppling cars stuck in traffic into the next lane on top of other cars. Jenny slapped her hands over her ears, startled by the deafening roar. She whirled around to observe the destruction. Car alarms blared. People screamed. A flaming charity Santa fell from the sky, crashed through the roof of a car parked directly in front of the precinct station, flinging the parking ticket on the windshield up in the air. A flurry of blackened paper and debris rained down on the street.

The front windows of the precinct blew inward. A blast of hot air ripped the half-glass partitions apart and lifted every cop standing thirty feet from the entrance across the room. The desk sergeant went flying. Carver and the coffee station were tossed through a partition. A dozen other cops hit the floor as exploding light fixtures and pieces of the ceiling came crashing down.

Jenny stared at the gutted department store in shock. "Jesus," she gasped. Then she threw open the door and ducked her head into the car to see Molly sitting in her seat, petrified. "You okay?"

Molly didn't answer. Her eyes wide, fixed on the flames rising from inside the store.

"Molly!" Molly jolted. Looked at Jenny. "You okay?" Jenny asked.

Molly gave her a quick nod.

"Okay... okay." Jenny got into the car and slammed the door shut. Leaned against the steering wheel, breathing hard.

The station was filled with smoke and confused cops, some of whom were already trying to assess the damage. A few of them rushed out into the street to help wherever they could. Someone shouted, "We need a medic over here!"

"Jesus Christ!"

"Anybody seriously hurt?"

"Just Jess here. He'll live, though."

"Fuck, I wish I was dead. Got a goddamn stick in my shoulder!"

Carver coughed, choking on dust. He pushed a wood panel from a splintered partition off and snarled into the radio. "Where... where the fuck is my goddamn chopper?! Shit! Those sons of bitches!" He picked himself up off the floor. A rookie cop rushed over to help him, grabbing one arm. "I'm good, son, I'm good." He dusted himself off and said to the rookie, "You ever do damage control before?"

"Nosir."

"You're about to. Get on out there." He coughed. "See what you can do to help."

"Yessir!" The rookie sprinted out of the station.

"We gotta get outta here," Jenny said as she started the car up. The cops were taking control, closing the area off and helping civilians. Two ambulances were already on the scene. Jenny backed out of her parking space. Street was packed. She turned the car into the sidewalk and rode the edge of the curb to the next intersection. From there, she turned onto Jalopy Avenue, bounded over the median, and hit the throttle. She was going back to the mall.

COBALT CHRISTMAS: A COBALT ROGUE STORY

*

Ten minutes later, Carver was on the station helipad flanked by two officers. The helicopter was ready to take off. Carver stomped toward it with his designated snipers carrying their rifles.

"You alright, sir?"

"Just fuckin' peachy," Carver snapped.

The helicopter pilot watched the Captain approach. He saw something else in the window. A reflection, peach-coloured, blurry. He turned around as one of Drake's hands pounced, fingers wrapping around his face, strong enough to crack the helmet visor. The pilot shrieked. The co-pilot whirled in his seat and shouted in surprise as the pilot jerked on the stick in his struggle with the sentient hand. The helicopter lifted off, much to the surprise of the trio on the helipad.

"Where the hell's he going?" Sniper #1 asked, incredulous.

Carver watched the helicopter spin awkwardly just a few inches off the ground. It only took him a second. "Something ain't right. Get back. Get back!" He retreated toward the fenced catwalk leading back to the rooftop.

The co-pilot grabbed hold of the hand and pulled, but Drake's hand wouldn't budge.

"Get it off!" the pilot squealed in sheer panic. "Get it off me!"

"I'm trying! Oh, fuck!"

The helicopter's tail rotors scraped across the ground. The helicopter's alarms blared inside. The cockpit's lighting went red. Drake's fingers broke through the visor and squeezed around the pilot's face, pushing visor shards in his eyes. The pilot's shrieks intensified. He kicked the joystick. The helicopter whirled, teetered toward the helipad. Dived almost straight into the pavement. Rotors touched the helipad and snapped off, flying in all directions. Carver and Sniper #2 dropped to the catwalk as a rotor blade whistled through the fence. Sniper #1 turned around just before the rotor blade sheared his head clean off. The helipad exploded in a brilliant fireball that lit up the city skyline like a giant emergency flare.

BOOM!

A sheet of flame covered the helipad. The fence around the catwalk was halved by the rotor blade. Carver and Sniper #2 looked up from the floor, chests heaving, sweat pouring down their faces.

Carver turned over and sat up. Stared into the flames.

Exhausted. Terrified. At a loss for words.

Sniper #2 looked at Sniper #1's headless body and rubbed his own neck nervously. "Oh, man." He said to Carver, "What now, Captain?"

The Captain's eyes didn't leave the flames. "What now?" Beat. He turned his furious gaze toward Sniper #2. A tidal wave of fury raging in his eyes. "Now we go to war."

Chapter 033
Spotting the Spotters

Manharttigan Mall

7:03 PM.

Damian integrated himself into the crowd of shoppers on the second floor with relative ease. He had to ditch the bandoliers and the grenade launcher, but he kept his shirt buttoned to keep it from revealing the six pistols he kept tucked in his waistband; his sheathed combat knife stayed under his pant leg and the flame-retardant satchel containing the compact flamethrower stayed on his shoulder. His colourful aloha shirt and blue hair matted down from the sprinklers earned him a few looks from common shoppers, but he was too busy searching through stores and vendors to care.

He exited a clothing store, ignoring someone's comment about him picking the right place to finally toss that shirt. *Enough about the fucking shirt.* He looked up at the walkways. Up at the domed skylights. The place was a nostalgic 80's art-deco nightmare. He didn't need to be an interior decorator to know that something was seriously off-putting about this place's retro designs. Too many potted palms. Too much glass block. Too much fucking *green*.

Too many people, too. Way too many.

He still stuck out. Fine. Maybe the spotters would notice him. He would know if he were being followed. He could lead them to a quiet place and scratch them off the list.

That was another problem. How long *was* that list?

He slipped into a Virtreality arcade—arcades were making a comeback with the inclusion of virtual reality simulators. People could slap a helmet on and screw around in their ideal fantasy worlds for hours in a secure booth if they had the cash. Navigating his way through the dimly lit, neon-red-and-blue-and-green world of gaming, all Damian could see were more booths, more lines, more teens and adults fighting over game credits and spare change. He passed a *Virtual Pac Man* simulator booth and heard the occupant chanting "WAKKA-WAKKA-WAKKA-WAKKA!"

Damian shook his head. Nothing but brain-dead kids in here. He went back out into the open. Into the next store. Electronics. Felt like he'd stepped into another time with all the retro CRT TVs from the late 1990's to the early 2000's lining the shelves. Some of them were TV/VCR combos. He'd only seen them in old magazines and movies. He walked up to one and inspected it. It was bulky, awkward looking; nothing like the thin flat screens or holographic projections he was used to seeing. He poked the VCR flap inward and watched it snap back into place once he'd taken his finger out.

A tall, scrawny clerk approached him. "Hey, there," he said, flashing him a friendly smile.

Damian looked him up and down. Nope. Definitely not a spotter. He turned to leave.

"Hey, hold on."

Damian sighed. "What do you want?"

"I uh, couldn't help but notice you looking interested in that television set over there," the clerk said, sticking his hands in his pockets.

"I was just looking."

"That's alright. That's how it starts, you know. That's how the interest builds. The seed is planted. First you're just looking, a-a-a-and then you're obsessed with collecting 'em and building your own wall. Imagine: a *stack* of these things dominating your wall. An armada of classically designed television sets is all you can see."

"Meh."

The clerk stepped between Damian and the only way out of the store. "Listen, listen, listen. You seem like an open guy."

Damian scoffed. "In what world?"

"This one, of course. Look around you. We got arcades again. We got classic CRT TVs. Hell, lookit that shirt. That is... that is... wow. Moving on. The nineties are coming back i-in a big way, my friend. I'm tellin' ya, the past is the future here. Old design, new look. People who grew up in the nineties would be pushing fifty. Maybe forty, depending on... on... years and stuff. They're nostalgic. They long for the old look. They're tired of futuristic sleekness."

"I was born in 2010," Damian said. "I don't think I fit your demographic."

"Maybe so, maybe so. *But* you seem *interested* in the older stuff. You don't have to be old to appreciate the old. Am I right or am I right?" He didn't wait for Damian to answer. He went motoring on. "See, with the introduction of plasma widescreens, people started demanding their TVs to be bigger. But not big like CRT big; big like wider, taller, but *thinner*. Men like their TVs like they like their women. Not all of them, but a lot of them. But here's the problem, and I'm gonna be straight with you because you seem like a tough guy, you can handle a little harsh truth. I'm looking at you and I'm thinkin' 'Yeah, this guy can take it as well as dish it.' Well, let me tell you the problem with the demand for thinner TVs, my friend."

Damian folded his arms across his chest and exhaled through his nostrils. As the clerk went on talking, he glanced out at the passing crowds of shoppers, searching for spotters.

"See, the problem is, they had to be durable, right? They couldn't shatter in the moving truck if the family wanted to pick up everything and go. They needed strength and reliability, but they also needed a home theatre system. Something that could take up an entire wall without taking up half the room, you know what I mean? Thinner TVs. Higher quality. 3K. 4K. 5K. Yellow-ray. Double-HD. Triple-HD. But see, see, the TVs got so thin, that... that... here's the kicker: some guy took one of those ultra-thin TVs and started, uh, slashing people's throats with it. *SCHWING*! One swipe and they were—they were geysers. So now we've cycled back to these big CRT TVs because they're not thin enough to slash throats; only now the quality isn't like it was in the nineties, all fuzzy and faded; now it's 4K quality on a CRT TV. And the sound is better, too. My friend, you buy one of these TVs and you're not just putting more money towards the older, superior fashion of TVs and less money towards the flat, lifeless, ultra-thin screens of the future... you're also saving a life. Eh? Buy a CRT TV, save a life."

Damian couldn't help himself. He had to laugh.

The clerk laughed with him. "Ah? Funny, huh?"

"What's your name?"

"Clark." Clark offered his hand.

Damian didn't take it. "You've convinced me, Clark. I kinda like you. If you survive this, remind me to buy a TV off you."

Clark's smile disappeared. "Survive what?"

Damian smiled, patted his shoulder, and then headed out of the store.

Clark followed him to the video wall storefront. "Survive *what*?!"

The Control Room

The sprinklers were turned off. Hill sat on a chair by the main entrance with his Uzi, smoking a cigarette, keeping an eye on the corridors for any more of Drake's men. Drake dangled off the floor, cuffed to a pipe that ran across the ceiling so that his hands were in Hill's line of sight at all times.

"You think you've won?" Drake said.

"Shut up over there."

Drake chuckled sinisterly. "On the contrary. You've lost."

"I said, be quiet."

"Why even bother trying to book me? Why not just kill me?"

"Because I'm still a cop."

"Yeah, until I tell 'em what you did to me in that warehouse."

"Your word against mine."

"There'll still be an investigation. I know where the warehouse is"

"They can investigate all they want. The warehouse can be cleaned up, and you don't have any wounds to prove we did what we did. You'll look like another terrorist asshole seeking a lighter sentence or even freedom on grounds of cries of brutality or the like. When we find the bombs and kill the rest of your guys, you'll be so deep in shit you wouldn't be able to breathe even if you had a fucking snorkel shoved up your ass. Only way you could possibly apply for a lower sentence—and that's *if* the courts decide to count it considering all your other crimes—is if you confess who your employer is. Maybe then, you'll at least avoid the death penalty and spend the rest of your life in a maximum security prison. Either way, shithead, you're never gonna be free again." Hill blew smoke. "You can cry now, if you want to."

"Why don't you just ask Aria? She's been an undercover this whole time."

"Oh, don't worry. I'll be debriefing her soon enough."

"While you're at it, why don't you ask Damian who the 'Boss' is?"

Hill's hard eyes flicked in Drake's direction.

"Didn't you think it strange that Damian somehow seemed to be on top of things the whole time? Didn't it strike you as odd that he was prepared for anything? Hell, that explosion should've disintegrated him. He was *ready* for it."

"Or he just acted fast."

"But how can you know for sure?"

"I can't," Hill answered matter-of-factly.

"Exactly. You can't. My employer was fooled by this 'Boss' person, and Aria has direct ties to them. She also has direct ties to Damian. Coincidence?"

Hill's expression darkened. He spat his cigarette and grit his teeth. "Shut the fuck up."

Drake snickered. "You dumbass cop. They were playing you like a harp."

Hill got up. Went over to Drake. He cracked the side of his Uzi across the immortal's jaw, breaking it. Hill returned to his spot by the doorway. "Prick."

Aria stuck to the main floor of the shopping mall, leaving the second level to Damian. She went around crowds and kiosks selling jewellery and tourist information. Tried on a pair of sunglasses at a sunglasses kiosk, inconspicuously scanning the area. She spotted a shady individual sitting on a bench against a glass block partition, an earpiece in his ear. She approached him without returning her Ray-Ban sunglasses to the rack. The salesman didn't notice anything. She sat down on the bench beside the man in black and said, "Hey, hon."

The man gave her a look. "Excuse me?"

"Status report."

"What?"

She pulled her sunglasses to the tip of her nose and gave him a sly wink. "You heard me."

"You're weird." He got up and left. Said into his earpiece, "Nah, sweetheart, just some bimbo. No, that's not what I meant..."

Aria leaned back on the bench, casually propping her elbows up. She looked around. Saw two men looking at her from behind a window pane in a clothing store and pretended she hadn't noticed them. She bit down on the end of a toothpick. Got up. Made a casual beeline toward the clothes store, pretending to be distracted by a sparkling pool of water bordered by thick glass block slabs, with a waterfall coming down from the second floor. She entered the clothes store. She browsed the shirts, blouses, V-necks. Moved on to dresses. Selected a scarlet red sleeveless mini club dress and asked a clerk for a dressing room key. The clerk led her to the dressing room. Aria caught a glimpse of the two men hanging around the men's jeans area pretending to inspect price tags.

In the dressing room stall, Aria only had to wait a short time before she heard another door open in the stall next to her. A man thanked the clerk and shut the door.

A minute later, she heard the stall on the other side open up. The other man said something about his wife complaining about the holes in his jeans, making the clerk laugh before he shut the door.

Aria leaned against the wall, having left the dress hanging on a hook. Listened for the rustle of clothing being removed. All she heard was the quiet scraping of metal on metal as they rolled silencers onto their pistols. Heard the slight *clicks* of their guns being cocked. She figured she'd play dumb. "Status report?"

No answer.

"Those bombs still safe?"

"Bombs? We only have one now thanks to the freak in Monterey."

"Good to know."

Hitman #1 pointed his gun at the wall. Suddenly a spearhead shot out and pierced through his face and out the back of his head, nailing him to the other side of the stall.

Having heard the noise, Hitman #2 fired a round through the wall. Heard a mirror go *k-chink!*

Aria promptly responded with a dozen shots from a silenced pistol, riddling him with bullets, slamming him against the wall. With that out of the way, she tried on the dress and checked herself out in the cracked mirror, front and back. "Hm," she grunted. "Not bad."

She left the dressing room in the outfit she wore since Monterey—the black pants, the black shirt with the ugly Christmas tree on it. She took the dress to the counter. "I'll take it. It's nice." She looked at a rack of Santa hats. Took one off and dropped it on the dress for the cashier to scan.

"Good choice," the cashier said, flashing Aria a friendly smile.

"Find everything you were looking for tonight?"

"Not yet," Aria said.

Damian was being followed. He didn't know when they started following him, but he knew it didn't take him long to notice. He could see their reflections in the storefront windows of a toy store; wall-to-storefront-ceiling window panes gave them away. Or maybe it was the dark suits and sunglasses the four of them all wore. They were probably carrying Uzis or something. He knew their chests couldn't be as big as they were, not with those scrawny heads of theirs. They kept glancing over their shoulders, too. Paranoid fucks.

Damian passed a group of kids surrounding a holographic projection of Santa Claus holding two tall, sexy women in skimpy elf costumes by their curvy waists, laughing heartily like he always did. *Not exactly the best representation,* Damian thought.

A restroom up ahead. Damian ducked into it. Made sure the place was empty. Marble floor, walls, countertop, white tiled ceiling, wooden stalls and urinal dividers. Mostly greys and browns. Finally, something that wasn't puke green.

Damian went into a corner stall and locked it just as the four guys entered the restroom, all looking at the stall. One of them went into the stall next to his. Another went to the urinal to take a piss. The other two went to the counter and looked at their reflections in the mirror.

Damian started making low whispering noises. "*Pss-pss-pss-pss-pssssst-pssst-psssss-sss-sss...*"

The assassin in the neighbouring stall pressed his ear against the divider, sunglasses scraping against the wall. Damian could see his feet under the divider. A telltale sign that these guys were amateurs.

Following the sound, Damian made an educated guess. Drew his knife. Plunged the blade through the wall. Heard a grunt. The would-be assassin's shoe squeaked on the floor as his body convulsed against the divider. Oh, yeah. Score.

The other three reacted to the noise, but too late. Damian came out with two silenced pistols blowing two of them away, splintering the mirror beside them, kicking up chunks from the counter. As they collapsed, the guy at the urinal spun around, pissing in an arc, hands in the air.

Damian sighed. Twice in one night. "Jesus, dude." Then both of his pistols gutted the last would-be assassin and shattered the urinal behind him. Damian returned to his stall. Pulled his bloody knife out of the divider. His first victim slid the floor in a heap. Damian wiped blood off the blade with a wad of paper towel. He was sure to take the out-of-order sign out of the maintenance closet near the entrance, and propped it up as he departed.

From the edge of the food court on the other side of the waterfall opposite the clothes store, Aria caught sight of another spotter—maybe. She couldn't be sure. He wore a white winter fatigue jacket unzipped to reveal a plain black shirt. He looked rugged enough to have seen some rough days in the field. Had a shallow, jagged scar running across his cheek. He was leaning forward over the railing of the second floor, observing the steady flow of shoppers below. Fifty/fifty chance it was or wasn't.

She ate another French fry from a paper plate, watching him carefully.

Then she felt something prod her shoulder. Slowly, she turned her head to see a security guard standing behind her, Dillinger sticking out of the palm of his prosthetic hand. Another guard approached her from the left. Stopped just a few feet away. The man behind her whispered, "Come with us quietly."

"What if I don't?" she asked.

"See that family next to Marco over there?"

Aria looked over at the other guard, who snuck a sinister glance toward a family of five; a mother and father with their three young children enjoying a meal by a Christmas tree prop.

"If you don't, little Sally, Jill, and Michael will be celebrating Christmas in an orphanage."

"Fair enough," Aria said with a low growl in her voice.

Damian went into the bookstore and started casually browsing the aisles, but not for books—anyone who looked like they could work for Drake. Nothing but gentle-looking bookworms here. There were only five people in here, anyway. Damian was amazed that the place was still running despite the rise of the electronic book market over a decade earlier.

As soon as he left the bookstore, he found himself confronted by half a dozen security guards. "Can I help you with something?" he asked.

"You need to come with us," one of them said.

"Oh, yeah?"

"We have your girl."

"What girl?"

"Don't play dumb with us, kid. Maybe you'll live longer if you play it straight from here on out."

Damian scoffed. "You assholes run out of teenage girls to frisk inappropriately or something? Piss off."

A guard snuck up behind him. Clubbed him over the head with his baton. *CRACK!*

Chapter 034
"I Need You to Disappear"

Manharttigan Mall—Control Room

7:25 PM.

Hill couldn't find them on the video wall. Damian and Aria were off the grid, which meant they had to be in a staff area or a restroom. He wordlessly scanned the monitors for a sign and caught sight of the six security guards dragging Damian through a staff-only door beside the pet shop. "Shit," he hissed under his breath.

Drake laughed with his freshly healed jaw back in place. "OOOHHH, wouldja look at that!"

An irritated Hill put his Uzi down on the control console. Went over to the nearest corpse and ripped the merc's jacket off. He balled the sleeve and shoved it in Drake's mouth, then tied the rest of the jacket around his head to keep him from spitting it out.

Hill sat back down, retaking his Uzi. "Maybe now you'll keep your fucking mouth shut." He looked at the video wall again. Hope was beginning to fade. *Come on, Carver... where the hell are you?*

7:37 PM.

Next thing Damian knew, his skull was pounding, his eyes burned, and he was being dragged down a dark hallway with cement flooring. Air was cold and damp. They were underground. Couldn't move his arms. Legs were asleep. He moaned as he craned his neck, sent pain shooting up to his brain. "Ugh..."

"Morning, sunshine," Aria said beside him with her hands cuffed behind her back. Four security guards flanked her. Six others walked behind them. Three more in front.

He looked at her woozily. "They got you too?"

"Yep."

"What the hell's wrong with you?"

"Me?"

"You're supposed to be unobtainable. Lost your touch."

"You're one to talk."

The guards that were dragging Damian stopped and dropped him to the floor. "Oof!"

One of the guards snarled, "If you're awake now, we can stop dragging you." He kicked Damian lightly. "Get up."

Damian laid face down on the cold floor, groaning.

"Do it or I will put a bullet all the way up your fucking anus."

Damian pushed himself up. He straightened his back. Rotated his head, making his neck crackle. "Ugh, *Khristos*."

"Move it."

"I'm going, cunt."

"Don't call me that. It's mean and uncalled for."

Damian scoffed and looked at Aria, who shrugged one shoulder.

They went up a flight of stairs and entered another sector that resembled a prison rather than a private security area, with white painted cinderblock walls and half-glass partitions running all the way down the hall. Each partition window was bordered by flashing red and green Christmas lights, and revealed an office with a guard sitting comfortable behind a desk.

They reached the end of the hall. Double doors made of steel flanked by two more guards, who each opened a door to allow entry to the approaching group. On the other side of the doors was a conference room with folding tables set up in a U shape and two chairs situated inside the U, facing the bottom table where an open laptop was placed.

The guards forced Damian and Aria to sit down in the chairs. Cuffed their hands around the backs of their seats. Damian was starting to doze again until a guard slapped him across the face. "No sleeping!"

Fifteen of the sixteen guards that brought them in fanned out, positioning themselves all around the room. The sixteenth went around the U formation, typed something on the laptop. Then he turned the laptop around so that the screen faced Damian and Aria.

Video call. Fairman's face scowled at the two of them. "Good evening."

Damian and Aria exchanged looks.

"Aria," Fairman said, "I'm disappointed. I liked you. It's a shame what Drake suspected turned out to be true."

"Not really," she said.

"This puts a damper on my mood."

"It ain't gonna improve anytime soon," she said.

Tired of her comebacks, Fairman turned his attention toward Damian. "And you, Mr. Dead Blue. You really are a persistent pain in my ass. I've killed you so many times that I've lost count. And yet, here you are, right in the middle of my operation."

"I get that a lot," Damian said.

"So how did you do it? How did you turn our Murder Queen against us?"

"Isn't it obvious? I'm a charming motherfucker, motherfucker."

Fairman scoffed. "Quite."

"Your employer was unwise to choose you for Operation Catalyst," Damian said. "Your immortal boyfriend complicated things."

"Perhaps... or perhaps not. It's already been established. After everything plays out tonight, my men will swoop in and save the day. Afrókrema will once again get funding from the state, and we'll be able to resume all operations like nothing ever happened."

"You're not talking about enforcing the law as some elite police force though, are you?" Damian's voice went low, menacing. "This is all to back up your operations in the tropics."

"You wouldn't believe how close I was before you came along, you little shit. I could have been a goddamned king. Do you know how rich the soil is in Central Congoria? Do you realize how much oil there is? It's an untapped resource, ripe for the picking."

"Yeah, yeah, yeah," Damian said. "I've heard this speech before. The villagers were in the way. The poison was the ultimate weapon. You control the water, you control the country. If the water's killing the people and the villages are getting burned, all their neighbours will clue in and move out, leaving the land unoccupied and free for you to start digging up your precious fucking oil. On top of that, you'll monopolize the clean water and force the villagers to maintain your coca fields practically for free, in exchange for untainted nourishment. I know the score."

Fairman leaned back in his chair, nodding slowly. "Yeah... pretty much. The people won't see it now, but they will eventually. I'll be a hero for the country. But not *their* country, of course. They had their chance. It's time for *our* country to move forward. We deserve that oil, that cocaine—and the fortune it will all bring, and the weapons that fortune will buy, to win the next war before it even begins. Five years from now, the people will thank me."

"Fucking spare me. It's not about the country. It's about money. It's *always* about money."

"My boy, if you weren't so naive, I would offer you a place in my ranks alongside all the other superhumans at my disposal. Superhumans like Drake. Or those cyborgs."

"On the contrary," Damian said, "My eyes are *wide* open."

"I was sure someone like you would understand my reasoning."

"I understand it perfectly."

"Then what's the problem?"

"I don't approve of your methods."

Fairman laughed. "*You* don't approve of *my* methods?! Hypocrisy at its most front-and-center. Tell me, Damian Warkowski: what makes you so different from me?"

"I don't kill kids."

Fairman blinked.

"You have the deaths of two little girls to answer for, on top of everything else."

Fairman's forehead wrinkles became far more prominent as he furrowed his brows. "The Konnerd incident. An unfortunate setback."

"That, and back. Further back. When you had Drake kill that little girl. Execution style. You had him look in her eyes first. And then the warehouse, when you failed to save the hostages."

"So did you," Fairman snapped back.

Damian shook with anger. "At least I *tried*. And because of your lack of a spine, a little girl burned to death in my fucking arms!" Damian raised his voice to a feral shout, "And for *that*, Colonel, I... *will... fucking... GUT* you!"

Fairman looked shaken at first. Then his smug expression returned. "No, son. I'm afraid that's not what's going to happen. I need you to disappear. And you *will* disappear. You think I didn't notice that your powers were temporarily drained by that explosion? You have no powers. No guns. No... fancy flamethrower thing. All you can do now is..."

Damian's fury made him red in the face. Aria scooted a few

inches away from him.

Fairman finally decided on a word: "Vanish."

"No," Damian breathed hotly. "Not yet."

Suddenly he shot up to his feet, handcuffs snapping apart. He spun in a blur, two energy pistols blasting. Deafening staccato of booming cannons. A violent flurry of blue and black energy shooting across the room in a shockwave that turned most of the guards into big black stains on the walls. Aria had to duck to avoid it.

One guard, telekinetically summoned from his post, flew toward Damian in a frontwards V, limbs trailing behind him. Damian punched his fist through his guts. He squeezed the shrieking guard's spinal column until it burst into dust in his hand. Damian shoved his other arm in. Ripped the fucker in half, splattering his insides as both halves went flying in either direction across the room. A wild blood spray made puddles on the floor and a dark, dripping patch on the ceiling. Damian's ugly aloha shirt was even uglier now, soaked in gore. The bloody patch above Damian's head saturated the light from the fluorescent panel, casting a dark crimson aura on Damian's demonic form. Chest heaving. Cobalt eyes burning with rage. Sinewy red ribbons descending from the ceiling around him.

Damian aimed his energy pistol at Fairman's shocked face. "You first."

BOOM!

The laptop exploded in a thousand tiny pieces.

Aria effortlessly broke her cuffs and stood up, massaging her wrists. She looked around the room. It looked like it'd been turned inside out, as did the guards. "I could've saved you the trouble."

"No need." Damian headed for the exit. Then an overwhelming wave of fatigue weighed him down. Quivering legs crumpled under him. He fell.

Aria caught him. "Easy now." She felt him panting heavily in her arms. "Recession?"

"Recession," he croaked.

"You gotta take it easy. No more powers, you got me?"

"I'll try..."

"Need a minute?"

"Had a minute. They took my guns."

"You know that won't be a problem with me around." She sat

him down in a chair. "Easy, big guy."

"Could use some of that Spiral Suicide shit right about now."

"We've been down that road, Damian, and trust me, you could not." She pulled a handkerchief out of her hand and folded it, dabbed beads of sweat off his forehead. She heard shouting outside. Glanced at the exit. "We're gonna have to move shortly. Can you still walk?"

Damian inhaled deeply, exhaled. He could feel his strength returning. Just a minor punishing surge of weakness for using his powers during recession. A few more could start to take a nasty toll. "Better. I can still *kill*."

"Then get up."

Damian pushed himself out of his chair.

She handed him a combat shotgun. He took it. "You're the best sister-in-law a bastard could ever ask for."

She chuckled. "You ain't marrying my sister just yet, boy."

"We'll see about that."

The Loading Bay

A white van pulled up outside, just a few feet away from the smouldering trailer wrecks. A squad of armed commandos leaped out of the back and rushed single-file into the building.

The Control Room

Hill glanced at the video wall again. Noticed the commandos and said, "Shit." He checked his current clip. Half empty. He checked his coat. Only one spare mag. Just pistols and a couple grenades after that. "Double shit."

Drake still managed a slew of mocking noises despite being gagged by his dead henchman's sweater until Hill kicked him in the stomach.

Afrókrema HQ

Fairman was still leaning back in his chair, staring at his blank computer screen. Still processing the sudden burst of violence he'd just witnessed. He got over it quickly, and when he did, he picked up his SAT phone and said, "Commence operation."

Chapter 035
Shopping Frenzy

Warehouse on Pier 5

The army of Drakes were all locked and loaded. The cyborg thing with Drake's head projected on its chromed skull instructed the army of Drakes—now suited up in Afrókrema battle suits with the standard-issued FN P90 submachine guns—to board a hovercraft docked on the water. They filed up the ramps into the ship like trained marines off to war.

The cyborg Drake went over to a black Sedan and seated himself in the back. The driver, an android that strongly resembled a crash dummy with fish eyes slapped on it, flicked its eyes in the rearview mirror. "Where to, boss?"

"Manharttigan Mall. Let's sit back and watch the show."

Manharttigan Mall—Control Room

8:02 PM.

Hill checked all of his pockets. Found a pair of grenades, some pistols and a few spare clips; one for the Uzi. That was it. A small arsenal for a death squad. He crouched by the doorway, listening to the pitter-patter of boots hammering concrete down the corridor, getting louder, escalating from light patter to heavy hail. He pulled a grenade from his pocket. Yanked the pin. Twirled the spoon off. Tossed the grenade over his shoulder, down the corridor.

A wave of shouts in terror and alarm.

BOOM!

The corridor shook. Clouds of smoke rose as the shrapnel settled. Hill made a run for it, Uzi spraying, pistol barking at the intruding commandos as he made a backwards jog down the corridor. He tripped over a cyborg's corpse. Staggered a few feet before righting himself. Nerves were shot. Uzi ran dry. Pistol fired its last. The deafening reports of the enemy's rifles sent him in a desperate leap for cover behind a steel beam. Their bullets walked a dozen interlocking waterspout parades through the blood-tinged sprinkler flood from earlier and glanced off the steel beam's edges.

The team members filled the control room. Two members of the remaining eight-man group went to work cutting Drake down from the ceiling and untying him. Once they removed the jacket from around his head, a commando asked him, "You okay, sir?"

"Just peachy." Drake ripped an M16 out of a commando's arms. "Gimme that gun." He stormed out into the corridor, shoved a commando out of his way. He looked at the destroyed cyborgs littering the floor and moaned in dismay. "Aw, man... these guys were expensive." He looked up and yelled down the hall, "Hey, Sergeant!" He fired a five-round beat at the support beam.

Hill flinched, cowering against the wall, trying to get as far away from the edge of the beam as possible.

"Sergeant!" Drake shouted. "I owe ya, Sergeant! I owe ya big time!"

"Kiss my ass, Drake," Hill snarled.

"Shoulda killed me, Hill. Shoulda killed me. Now I'm gonna kill everybody." He headed back into the control room. Said to the four commandos outside, "When you kill him, bring me his head."

Drake shut the doors and went over to the control panel. He snapped his fingers at a black commando. "You got what I asked for?"

"Yessir." The commando reached into the breast pocket of his coat and pulled out a CD with permanent marker scribbled on a strip of masking tape on the case: *'XXXMAS TUNES, BABY!'*

"Perfect!" Drake exclaimed, snatching it out of the commando's hand. He dropped the disc into the audio control console and scrolled through a list of songs. "Let's get ready to rock and roll!" He pressed his finger on a title.

Mackey's Market

Within a two-storey hypermarket on the west side of the Manharttigan Mall, a charity Santa stood by his donation pot near the checkout area, ringing his bell and laughing like Santa should, greeting customers as they came and went with his jolly "Merry Christmas!" cheers.

Andy Williams started singing *It's the Most Wonderful Time of the Year* on the PA system, louder than most shoppers were used to. Regardless, they didn't think much of it.

COBALT CHRISTMAS: A COBALT ROGUE STORY

The automatic doors opened, letting through a group of men with duffel bags in their hands and rollerblades on their feet. They looked like stereotypes one would find prowling the 1980's Bronx in some cheap late-night exploitation film. They wore studded leather jackets and ripped jeans—guys from another world judging by their heavily outdated apparel. One of them had a ghetto blaster with heavy metal booming from its speakers resting firmly on his shoulder, which earned him more than a few annoyed glances from shoppers.

Laughing and hollering like rowdy children on a school playground, they flanked the checkout counters with their duffel bags. One of them rollerbladed between the row of counters and the strip of windows facing the parking lot and bumped into a woman carrying her groceries—all while inconspicuously dropping a live grenade into her bag. She stumbled; he nearly fell, knocking over a projector base with a shimmering holographic Jack Frost on it in the process, but managed to regain his balance and said, "Jeez... sorry, lady."

"Watch where you're going next time," the woman hissed after him as he rollerbladed away. Then she heaved an exasperated sigh and clacked toward the exit in her high heels.

KABOOM!

The grenade exploded, tearing the woman in half and hurling her flaming remains through the storefront in a fireball. The shoppers surrounding her went flying to the ground, shrapnel ripping through them.

Screams filled the checkout area as the other rollerbladers took firearms and masks out of their duffel bags. Even the charity Santa drew a sawed-off shotgun from his big red sack and fired buckshot into the ceiling. The other men put on their masks and started lighting up the place. They sprayed the front of the store with lead, chopping down cashiers and customers.

"Kiss the tile, losers!"

A rollerblader in a goalie mask wheeled his way to the rear office. The shift manager melted behind his desk; his pudgy fingers were so sweat-slicked the telephone receiver slipped out of his hand like a wet bar of soap.

"Callin' the fucking cops, fat man?" Goalie asked. He cocked his magnum and pointed it at the manager.

"N-no," the manager wheezed, throwing his hands in the air. "Don't shoot! Please—"

BANGBANGBANGBANG!

Four rounds to the manager's gut abruptly silenced his pleas.

"A lotta, lotta, lotta love!"

Goalie turned and saw the janitor dancing with his back facing him, completely oblivious to the goings-on behind him thanks to the big pair of orange headphones over his ears. He twirled his mop back and forth across the floor, singing: "DOO-DOO-DOO! ROCK N' ROLL, BABY! YEAH!"

Goalie cocked his head to the side at the odd sight. Then he fired a single shot between the janitor's shoulder blades. The janitor immediately fell on his face. When his second victim hit the floor, Goalie chuckled and said into the intercom, "We're gonna need a clean-up on aisle six!"

A group of gangsters and mercs entered the main entrance of every wing in the shopping mall and went to town, shooting down the first line of shoppers, sending the rest of them into a panicking frenzy. The attackers mostly kept their bloodlust in check after the first wave. They advanced after the fleeing masses, firing shots at the ceiling, herding hundreds of innocents into the center of the complex—Santa's village. Anyone unlucky enough to be caught in a store was either shoved out to join the others or shot dead. The cathedral-high halls of the shopping mall rang with a disturbing chorus of screams as the innocents stampeded to Santa's village, clamouring over each other, trampling those too slow and clumsy to keep up, shoving each other through glass panes, over tables, into walls, down the multi-parallel escalators...

A plainclothes cop hid in an information kiosk and drew a bead on the approaching firing squad. He shot one in the chest, dropped him like a stone before the others blew the entire kiosk away, cop and all.

Another plainclothes cop was smart enough to take advantage of the chaos and duck into an employee access door.

Security Basement—Conference Room

A trio of guards burst into the room with assault rifles. They froze in place when they saw the remains of their companions spread all over the floor and shredded walls. "Jesus Christ," one of them gasped.

Damian and Aria flanked the doorway, looking at the guards from behind. They levelled their pistols and gunned them down, inciting more yelling and shooting from the hall. Bullets *pinged* against the steel doors, slamming them shut.

"I think the neighbours are angry," Damian said.

"Shut it. Oh, I almost forgot." She retrieved her bag from a nearby corpse and pulled out a Santa hat and plopped it on Damian's head.

"The fuck?"

"Show some Christmas spirit," she said.

Damian scowled. Blew the hat's ball out of his face. "No," he said stubbornly.

The two of them slid up against the doors, pushed them into the hall just far enough to make a narrow crack in the middle. Damian peered through the opening to see a dozen guards, six crouched, six others standing behind them, all aiming M16 assault rifles at the conference room.

"Come out!" One of the guards barked. "Lay down your guns and keep your hands where we can see them!"

Damian asked Aria, "You see where my flamethrower pistol thing went?"

She made a new compact flamethrower and handed it to him.

"I'll never get over how weird that power is," he said, taking it.

"It's come in *handy*, though, hasn't it?" she asked, smiling.

"Leave the cheesy puns to me, woman." He ignited the compact's flame. Used it to light a cigarette. Sucked in the nicotine fumes. "Ready?"

"Lead the way, 'Boss.'"

Damian called out through the crack in the doors, "We're coming out! Don't shoot! We are unarmed!"

"Do it slowly!" One of the guards replied.

Damian and Aria didn't come out, but a jet of fire from the flamethrower did, filling the hall, engulfing the guards. They screamed and flailed around for a few precious seconds before falling dead in a blanket of fire.

The fire alarm blared. The lights blinked red and white. The ceiling sprinklers spritzed the floor.

COBALT CHRISTMAS: A COBALT ROGUE STORY

Damian and Aria kicked the doors into the corridor, guns ready. The guards acted predictably, leaping out of their offices with their guns blazing. Damian and Aria split up, taking either side, blasting through guards, sent them sprawling to the floor, through the partition windows, or into the flames.

A score of them swarmed into the hall like fleeing cockroaches, assault rifles roaring, bullets whizzing all over the place. The walls cratered. Pieces of the ceiling fluttered down. Damian dived through a partition window right before a shotgun could blast his legs out from under him. He rolled over a shelf in a shower of glass, landed in a squat on the floor, keeping his head low as the shelf and the partition window frame splintered. He waited for a break in the gunfire.

Aria took whatever shots they managed to land on her with a wince and swift retaliation, mowing down security personnel with her machine gun. She dropped seven in the blink of an eye, still gnawing on the end of her toothpick.

Damian sprang up from behind the partition. Aimed. Shotgun bucked in his hands. A guard's face disintegrated in a dark red mist. Damian rolled out of the office into the center of the corridor alongside Aria, who advanced. He cut down another guard as an officer behind his latest victim dived back into his office. For a moment, the corridor was clear of any living personnel; the floor was littered with bodies. They heard shouting from the offices up ahead, including one right beside Aria as she passed a partition window—

POW! POW!

The window crystallized as Aria walked past it. Two rounds whistled past both sides of her head. She backtracked to the door, kicked it down to see a guard crouched behind his desk. He squeezed off another shot from his .38 and hit her in the stomach. Aria grunted, healing factor already pushing the bullet out. Then she raised her machine gun and disintegrated the desk and the screaming guard behind it, pasted him against the far wall. She looked at the fresh hole in the stomach of her shirt, which was surrounded by at least a dozen other holes. "It was ugly anyway," she said.

Damian peeked into every window on his way up the corridor wall, Shotgun ready, compact flamethrower dangling against his side from a shoulder strap. First window: clear. Second: clear. Third: clear. Fourth—a flash, *bang, KSSSH* as the window exploded an inch from his face. Damian leaped back, dodging a flurry of glass that knocked the border of Christmas lights loose. Damian squatted under the window sill as another shotgun blast sounded from inside the office. He bolted upright and blew apart the top of the desk. The guard hid behind his chair. Damian burned a hole through it,

The guard pumped his shotgun and aimed it through the hole, right at Damian. "DIE!"

Damian retreated behind the door as the Christmas lights exploded.

Two more guards appeared up ahead. One fired at Aria. The other at Damian, who ducked his head as a stream of bullets raked across the door. Shotgun bucked in his hands. Red-hot pellets punched the guard's ribcage, knocking him flat. Aria blasted the other one.

They neared the stairs. Another pair of guards rolled out across the gap in their office chairs, assault rifles rattling. Damian and Aria ducked and rolled forward, came up in a crouch, fired, hitting them, flinging one over the back of his chair while the other crumpled forward, leaving his chair upright.

Shouting from the bottom of the stairs. Damian and Aria approached cautiously. More shooting from the left. Aria turned and disintegrated the partition under a hail of bullets—

A guard leaped out of his office from the right, baton swinging at a distracted Damian's head. Damian heard his feet pounding the floor. Turned. Heart skipped. Raised the shotgun. The guard kicked it out of his hands and cracked him over the head with the baton. White-hot flash in his eyes as Damian's brain exploded in agony—then came the rage. Rush of adrenaline. Damian went ballistic, parrying a second baton blow with his left arm and cracking two of the guard's ribs with his right fist. He kicked the guard's left kneecap and dropped him into an empty office chair. "FUCKER!" Damian snarled as he beat the guard with his own nightstick. Then he grabbed him, started pushing the chair toward the stairs. The stunned guard lashed out awkwardly, legs swinging.

Damian said, "Keep your arms and legs tucked in at all times." He punched the guard across the jaw. Ditched the nightstick and grabbed the armrest, and *heaved* the guard off the top of the stairs. Limbs up in the air as the guard soared backwards over the steps in his chair, came down, hit the middle of the staircase and toppled head over wheels all the way down to the bottom, accompanied by the *cracks* of the chair legs breaking off and the *snaps* of the guard's limbs twisting further out of shape every time he hit a step. He landed in a broken heap at the bottom. The chair landed on top of him.

Aria finished off the two guards that had barricaded themselves in the last office on the left and joined Damian. She observed him as he panted furiously, trembling. "You good?"

"Yeah." He peered over the top of the stairs—

BRRRAAAPPP!

Red-hot fusillade from the bottom. Twenty guards had gathered, blasting away at every red or blue hair that entered their sights. The top three steps crumbled.

Damian and Aria backed off as the group's attack started to rip the ceiling apart above their heads. "Now what? Grenade 'em?" Aria asked. "I got grenades."

Damian shrugged off the compact flamethrower. "I've got something better."

Aria scoffed. "You gonna try and spray 'em from up here?"

"I'm a goddamned miracle worker. I'm going to make it rain." He hurled the compact flamethrower into space, watched it clear the stairs, flying just below the pipes in the rafters. He drew a pistol as it started to fall. Aimed, following it down, down, down...

Squeezed the trigger.

BAM!

The bullet whistled across the gap and punched through the compact's tank, igniting it. The room lit up brilliantly as a napalm phoenix spread its wings above the guards and descended upon them, engulfed them. Their screams only lasted a few seconds.

Aria looked over the stairs, admiring Damian's handiwork. "Nice work, genius. Now tell me... how the hell do you plan on getting outta here now that the only exit is blocked by thirty feet of flaming napalm?"

Damian looked at the fiery carpet down below. Then he looked at Aria. "Shut up."

"Aha," she said, "that's what I thought."

The sprinklers came on, sprinkling the raging flames down below in a futile effort to put it out.

"Harpoon," she said.

"What?" he asked, watching as a harpoon gun sprouted from her arm.

She took it and aimed at the ceiling. Fired a hook at the end of a cable into the tangled canopy of rusting pipes. A telltale *clack* sounded. Aria jerked the cable taut. "Hold on."

"Whoa. Whoa. Whoa." Damian showed his palms. "We're not swinging on that."

"*I* am. And so are you."

"Eh. Not really feeling it."

"Chicken?"

"No, there's flaming napalm down there."

"Oh, come on. You're already dressed for the heat," she said, indicating his shirt. "Quit bein' a chicken."

"I'm not being a chicken."

Aria started clucking like a chicken.

"Stop that," Damian said impatiently.

Aria kept on clucking, getting louder. "Chicken!"

"Fuck off. I'm not a chicken."

"Chicken!"

"Do you know how sticky napalm is? Do you know how fucking painful it is?"

"Chick-chick-chick-chick..."

"Shut the fuck up! Look, if I was immortal, that'd be a somewhat different story."

"Chick-chick—it's called a healing factor, which you still have."

"Slowed to a crawl."

"Chick-*CHICKEN*!"

"Gimme that goddamn rope." Damian snatched the cable.

"No worries, squirt. I won't drop ya." She wrapped her arms around him and grabbed the cable, pressing her bosom against the back of his head. Her right leg curved over his thigh and pressed up into his crotch, pulling the rest of his body against hers. She stole an opportunity to teasingly rub her calf between his legs.

"I've heard that before," he muttered, gripping the cable. His palms were already sweating. He looked into the flames. The wall of smoke billowing up from it, hiding the exit from their view.

"On the count of five," she said, feeling him breathe nervously. "I gotcha."

He grunted.

"One. Two." Then she pushed them off the stairs. Damian's heart leaped up in his throat as they swooped down into the smoke. Clamped their eyes shut. Held their breaths as they passed through the smoke cloud. Hot air could have ripped the air right out of their lungs. They started to ascend. Aria opened her eyes, saw a clearing untouched by napalm leading right into the exit hallway. She kicked off the cable, pulling a yelping Damian into the air with her. Soared over the edge of the napalm pool, touched down on hot concrete and stumbled away from the flames. Damian hit the floor as Aria stood up and brushed ashes off herself.

"*SUKA BLYAT*!" Damian shouted, jumping up to his feet. He whirled, furious. "What the fuck, woman!"

"What?" she asked nonchalantly.

"You said five! 'On the count of five.' That's what you said!"

"It was better this way."

"*Better*?! No. *No*. No, it wasn't. It fucking wasn't!"

"If I counted all the way up to five, you woulda lost your nerve and then we'd *never* leave."

"I don't 'lose my nerve.' I was trying to think of a better plan."

"Uh-huh." She headed for the tunnel, playfully tracing her index finger along his jaw line as she went by him. "C'mon. Mall ain't gonna save itself."

"You know the way out?" He followed her into the tunnel. An intersection was coming up.

"Ain't the first time I've been dragged down here by security."

"What? When was the other time?"

"Oh, I was hitting on one of the loser guards to possibly get information on a target and he was trying to impress me with a tour. It was really boring. I didn't care about his job, his cats, or the sports car he couldn't afford. All I cared about was finding a quiet, private space to fuck 'im an' move on."

"Oh. Oh, I see. That's mighty convenient."

"Wish I could've said the same about the closet we eventually settled on. Or the package." She sighed.

"Limp?"

"Like a three-legged dog."

Damian laughed.

"Yeah, I thought you'd find that amusing, you sick fuck." They stopped at the intersection. Aria looked all four ways, then went left. "This way."

"You sure? These halls are the architectural equivalent of the Asian population. It all looks the same."

"You really gotta get over those prejudices of yours. It's the twenty-first century, man. Get with the times."

"No, you."

Chapter 036
Shooting in a Winter Wonderland

8:21 PM.

Hill raced toward the waste management sector in fight-and-flight mode, turning every so often to deliver a three-round beat from his Uzi at his pursuers. Boots slapping through shallow waters, Hill zigzagged down the corridor. A response from a running commando pounded a steel beam just a foot away from him. "Shit," he hissed. He whirled again, sprayed the Uzi at the shadows that chased him. Ran dry. "SHIT!" He tossed his weapon and made a mad dash for the end of the hall. Reached an intersection. "This is place is a goddamn maze!" he gasped, trying to decide which option would suit him best. Stopped just before an automated forklift could run him down as it carried its load over to the docking area. He watched it motor down the corridor he'd just exited from and got an idea...

The two commandos stopped abruptly and parted off to either side to let the automated forklift through. They barely paid it a second glance.

Big mistake. Hill was sitting on the back of it, arm wrapped around the fuel tank, pistol ready. One of the commandos sensed something and turned—

POW-POW!

Hill delivered two shots through his face.

Startled, the other commando spun on his heel. Hill capped him three times across the chest. With a rasp, the commando hit the floor.

Hill pushed himself off the forklift and left it to its duties as he rummaged through the corpses' pockets, retrieving four clips, two more pistols, and an assault rifle from his most recent kill. He tucked away the pistols in favour of the M16, which he quickly inspected.

Someone shouted down the corridor from the direction he was heading to. An intersection at the end of the hall. Footsteps coming from the hall on the left. A steel door directly in front of him. He sprinted to the end of the hall and peeked around the corner to see two security guards running toward him. Hill inhaled sharply, hopped into view and blasted the guards. They collapsed, down for the count. Hill glanced around and backed into the steel door, groping around for the handle as his eyes peered down all three corridors. Push bar, which he shoved forward. He went through the doorway and slammed it shut.

Now he was on a catwalk overlooking another wider hall. A concrete wall on the other side partially hid a lab from his view. He could see white dust floating from the entrance, along with two pairs of steel-toed boots and a stack of cardboard boxes lined up against the wall behind them. He recognized this part of the building from his recon in the vents. Nothing too significant turned up aside from the full-blown cocaine lab on the other side of that wall.

This is gonna be tricky, he thought, sliding against the wall as he descended the stairs, eyes fixed on the lab entrance, watching the workers go about their work on the assembly line, oblivious to his presence for now. He could hear a couple guards moving around on the catwalks above the entrance, their shadows prancing across the floor. He touched down at the bottom of the steps and shifted out of the workers' peripheral, behind the wall. He glanced up the corridor at the entrance to the waste management sector. In the opposite direction, behind the stairs, was a ramp leading down into the basement. A trio of security guards dashed past the base of the ramp, their boots thundering down the corridor. They were in a hurry to get somewhere. Hill didn't care so long as no one noticed him. Then he heard gunshots echoing from underground, crackling up the ramp and through the halls on his floor.

The guards in the lab started shouting. Suddenly that's when Hill started to care. "Aw, Christ."

A merc dashed out of the entryway Hill had just passed, pistol drawn. He looked down the ramp, then up the corridor. Did a double take when he saw Hill, who didn't hesitate to riddle him with a five-round burst, propelling the merc back into the lab. Glass vials shattered as the boxes crumpled under his body.

More yelling. Terrific.

Hill broke into a desperate race for the waste management sector. He heard metal creak loudly behind him. Turned to see a pair of mercs at the top of the stairs. He blasted them, then whirled back around, continuing his run for the sector as his latest victims tumbled down the stairs in bloody heaps.

In the tunnels below, Damian and Aria had just cut down a gun-toting quartet in a corridor intersection up ahead. They criss-crossed, switching sides. Advanced against their respective walls opposite each other.

"Like dog shit," Damian said.

"Because they smell?" Aria asked.

"No."

A trio of security guards came around, pistols firing wildly. Damian and Aria blew them away in an instant. They joined their companions in the center of the intersection.

Damian continued, "Because they're everywhere."

They reached the corners of the intersection and peeked around. The left was clear. Damian's right wasn't—two more guards opened fire. He reeled his head in, flinching as bullets pecked paint off the wall just an inch from his face. "*Yob!*"

Aria leaned out with her M60 and cut them in half.

"Thanks," he said.

She winked at him.

"Which way out?"

Aria scanned each direction, then cocked her head toward the turn beside her. "This way."

"You're sure?"

"Oh, yeah. Done this a hundred times."

"No, you haven't."

"Come on." She rounded the corner and sprinted down the corridor.

Sighing, Damian quickly checked his pistols each in turn, then followed her. He caught up with her and said, "How can you be so sure?"

"Hey now, where's the faith? Where's the trust? I never forget the escape route from a confusing labyrinth of tunnels that all look the same."

Damian scowled. The ball of his Santa hat kept bouncing in his face. "That inspires confidence..."

"Attaboy."

They heard gunfire up ahead and traded glances. They reached another corner with no other way but right. They took it.

Ran right into a cluster of no less than ten mercs gathered at the base of an upward ramp.

"Shit," Damian said. The mercs' heads all twisted in their direction, bloodthirsty glints streaking across their crimson visors. Damian flashed them a friendly smile. "Uh... *dobryj vyechyer?*"

One of the mercs pointed at the intruders and shouted, "KILL!"

The corridor exploded with gunfire. Damian and Aria dived behind the wall as a torrent of bullets ripped across the floor past them and up the wall at the end of the corridor.

They sat up against the wall around the corner. Aria asked, unimpressed, "'Good evening'? Really?"

"Get off my fucking back."

One of the mercs could be heard saying, "Prince an' I are goin' up top! Nobody else leaves until those two are dead! Understand?"

Damian set his pistols down on the floor and drew a pair of grenades. "Smoke them out."

Aria put down her M60 between her legs. A grenade grew into each of her hands. "Sure, why not."

Their thumbs yanked the pins off and they let the spoons fly in perfect sync. They'd done this a hundred times. They counted to two and then hurled the grenades up the corridor.

The mercs all froze, watching the grenades bounce toward them in open-mouthed terror.

BOOM!

A concussive rush of flaming shrapnel ripped them all the shreds and blasted two of them through the ceiling tiles. The explosion rolled up the ramp and raked at the backs of the two ascending mercs, throwing them to the floor.

Sergeant Hill whirled, startled by the blast. Smoke billowed up from the basement entrance. A bloodied merc rose into his sights, waving his assault rifle around as he struggled to look through his cracked visor. Hill shot him, sent him sprawling down the ramp. M16 clicked empty in Hill's hands. "Shit," he muttered, tossing the clip.

The second merc emerged from the smoke, baring his teeth at Hill, who started to panic, fumbling for a spare clip in his pocket. The merc squeezed the trigger.

BKAM!

Hill jumped. The merc's chest puffed out, spraying blood into the air. Two more shots sounded and the merc fell forward and split his face on the concrete floor, revealing Damian standing at the top of the ramp with a smoking pistol, looking smugly in Hill's direction.

Hill stared at him, stunned.

"Who's king of the hill?" Damian asked, grinning.

"That's not funny, Damian." Hill breathed a sigh of relief. He couldn't help but laugh. "That's not funny at all."

Aria stepped out of the smoke beside Damian and looked at Hill. "Oh, you're alive."

"Yeah," Hill said. "I'm managing, somehow."

"They all cooped up in there?" she asked, indicating the lab.

"Yeah, they're packed in there good an' tight."

Damian slid across the wall to the edge of the entryway. Peeked inside.

POW-POW!

He retreated as chunks of brick blew off the corner. "They're all huddled in the center. Even the workers have guns."

"Catwalks," Hill said, "what about the catwalks?"

"Gimme a second." Damian quickly leaned out and back in again, blinking as a shotgun blast tore a chunk out of the wall. "Two with Uzis. One of them definitely has a shotgun."

"That all?" Aria asked.

"All that I could see." Damian looked at Hill. "I'm gonna try it your way." He yelled into the lab, "Hey there, coke fiends! This is the police! Put your guns on the floor and your hands in the air, and we promise we'll only break your legs!"

Came the response: "Fuck you, freak!"

Annoyed, Damian said, "Okay, that's it. Fuck this. I'm getting Ol' Painless." He shifted his weight from foot to foot, counted to three in his head, then dived across the gap. Gunfire rang out. Bullets ripped through the doorway and hit nothing but concrete. Damian made a break for the waste management sector.

Hill looked at Aria, then turned to the fleeing Damian and yelled, "Where the fuck are you going?!"

"Stall them!" Damian said. He turned around and added, "Your way sucks!"

He kept on running.

Hill asked Aria, "What the hell is 'Ol' Painless'?"

In the lab, a guard on the catwalk radioed Drake: "Drake."

In the control room, Drake didn't hear him. He was too busy watching the chaotic montage of terror on the video wall. His men were doing a beautiful job of herding the hostages into the center of the mall. Santa's village was packed, overflowing with terrified shoppers to the point where the food court had to be used for extra storage. Armed mercs and recruited street gangsters held the perimeter. No one would be escaping, and any who tried were given a swift end.

"Fucking wonderful." Drake grinned sadistically. His teeth gleamed in the bluish hue from the television screens.

Static coughed from the CB radio. "Drake!"

Drake turned as a commando handed the radio over. He took it and said, "What?"

"They got the lab pinned."

"What d'ya mean? Warkowski?"

"The freak, the bitch, and the cop."

"The terrible trio." Drake chuckled. "What do you mean, they got you pinned? Did they burn down the lab?"

"They might."

"What the fuck am I paying you assholes for? Stop 'em!" He switched to a different channel. "Any security personnel left? If there are, I suggest you run over to the lab. Our rats are trying to hold the blizzard at bay." He switched to yet another channel: "Attention all commandos—get down to the lab. Save the food. Exterminate the pests. We want happy customers, or I'll be *very* unhappy. Snap to it!" He slammed the radio on the desk and heaved a sigh. He turned to the commando that had provided him with his music. "Did Fairman give you that gun I asked for?"

The commando smiled and drew a .44 magnum from his vest. Blue steel. A real beauty.

"Fucking beautiful," Drake said, taking it and beholding its shine.

"Fairman offers his apologies."

"What do you mean?"

"He wanted me to tell you that what you see is what you get.

Due to our slashed budget, he could only afford so many on such short notice. Six FATE rounds are already chambered."

Drake checked the cylinder, smiled, and jerked his hand, swung it back into place. "Fair enough. Six chances to finally kill that son of a bitch for good. Or so I heard."

"I fought in the war, sir," the commando said. "Trust me. They work on super-powered freaks and all monsters. You'll cut through anything."

"Anything?"

"Back when FATE metal was more available, we tested them out. They're not like the laser beams those cyborgs had. They're a lot more powerful than that. I think it's the residue on the metal. One bullet can tunnel through thirty yards of solid titanium like it was paper. They'll cancel his healing factor and, if you deliver a kill shot, that'll be the end of Damian Warkowski as we know it."

"Ah, a veteran." Drake was pleased. "How many'd you kill?"

"Two just like him. Wish I got more."

"Me too. What's your name, soldier?"

"Kettle."

"Is that your real name?"

"Don't remember my real name. Just remember 'Kettle.' I'm stuck with it."

"Why?"

Kettle shrugged. "Cuz I'm black."

Waste Management Sector

Damian trotted down the ramp toward the raised shutters and ran out into the cold. Light snow fluttered down from the night sky. He looked to his left. The trailer was still there against the wall. He ran over to it and pulled the tarp off, revealing crates. He lifted the lid off one of them and brandished an RPG-7 out, strung it over his shoulder on a strap. He took a satchel full of rockets out of the crate and slung them over his other shoulder; let it hang at the waist. Then he went to the side of the trailer, lifted another lid, and peered inside. Smiled at the weapon, beholding its beauty. "Hello, gorgeous."

The Drug Lab

Aria and Hill flanked the entryway of the lab. Inside, a few workers with Micro-Uzis scurried behind the halted assembly line, squatting under cover of the machine as they made their way toward the entryway. The other guards and workers on the ground kicked over tables and hid behind them in the center of the room. The guards on the roof of the portable building readied their machine gun mounts on the railing.

Up above, behind the door, a group of commandos gathered.

In the underground tunnel, two scores of security personnel armed with AKMs flocked to the bottom of the ramp, joining together, signalling each other that the enemy was directly above.

Aria whispered, "They're trying to sneak up on us."

Hill looked at her in alarm. "*What?*"

"I can hear them. They're trying to tiptoe, but it's tough to muffle the footsteps of an entire group. Maybe about thirty down that ramp. And I can hear more pushing against the door up those stairs. And here in the lab, a couple workers. I say we storm the lab. Best chance we got."

"Are you serious?"

"At least we'll have a machine to hide behind in there. Nothing out here for you to hide behind. I mean, I'll be okay. I got a healing factor. But you? Well..."

"Alright, alright, I get your point."

"Here." She tossed him a grenade. "Toss that down the ramp once I'm in the lab. Also, cover your ears and close your eyes."

"Why?" She held up a flash-bang grenade for him to see. "Oh," he said.

She activated the flash-bang and tossed it into the lab. Covered her ears and looked away. Hill did the same.

BAM!

A brilliant white flash filled the interior. Workers groaned and shouted in confusion. Someone opened fire on the entryway, unknowingly shooting the stack of boxes and the corpses that lay on them. That's when Aria made her move, M60 roaring to life, blasting through a row of vials and riddling the stunned workers on the other side. Their blood saturated clouds of white dust shooting up from the assembly line. More gunfire from above. Bullets raked across the wall above Aria's head. She raised her M60 and sent one of the overhead guards flipping backwards off his catwalk on the other side of the room and crashing through a different assembly line.

COBALT CHRISTMAS: A COBALT ROGUE STORY

*

Hill yanked the pin and tossed the grenade down the ramp. "Enjoy your Christmas dinner, motherfuckers!" He was rewarded with a cacophony of shrieks right before the grenade's violent blast cut them off. A plume of fresh smoke rose up from the tunnel. Hill coughed as he approached the top and looked down, observing the carnage. Most of them writhed in agony on the floor. Several were trying to find their guns and get back up. Hill rained hell upon them with the M16, swinging it back and forth, riddling the thick carpet of white uniform shirts and black pants until his gun went empty. As he reloaded, he could still hear a few coughs and groans. "Yeah?" he roared. A weak plea for mercy floated up from the bottom of the ramp. "You fuckers like that?" He opened up on them again. "Huh?! Huh?"

Aria held the M60 with one hand, tearing through the operation as she calmly followed the assembly line, blinking through the white dust as it started to cling to her body. Bullets sliced through a shelf full of cardboard boxes and whizzed by her. She hit the shelf with a merciless barrage, tearing it down from the ground up, cutting down anyone unlucky enough to be standing behind it.

Feet on the catwalk. Aria looked up to see a guard blinded by the flash staggering toward the stairs using the railing for support. She hoisted the M60 upward and pumped a heavy load of hot lead through the grated floor. The guard's legs exploded into swinging strands of blood and sinew. The owner of those legs shrieked in agony and collapsed on his front, convulsing above his assailant, who delivered a quick bullet stream through the floor to finish him off.

Hill slowly descended the ramp, stepping carefully over bodies and debris. The corridor was packed with them. Forty men, maybe more. Most of them were assuredly dead. A few of them still moved until Hill delivered quick close-range shots to their heads.

A guard at the very bottom moaned as he sat upright, clutching his shredded left arm. "Ugh... ah..."

Hill approached him, M16 level with the man's face.

The guard showed him the bloodied palm of his one good hand. "Please."

"Fuck you." Hill's M16 cut a dotted line across the guard's chest, slammed him against the wall.

The door at the top of the stairs banged open. Even with the deafening ruckus Aria was orchestrating in the lab, Hill could tell the difference right away. Commandos poured down the stairs and split into three groups at the bottom; one group flanked the lab entryway, one other started down the ramp, and the rest jogged down the corridor toward the waste management sector, where the other entry to the lab could eventually be found once they took a left turn at the very end of the hall.

Hill went around the corner, waited until their feet became visible before shooting five pairs legs out from under their screaming owners. They toppled forward on top of the blanket of dead security personnel. Hill blew them away.

The other commandos took the hint and stayed near the top of the ramp.

The crude machine gun nest on top of the portable kept Aria pinned behind the assembly line. Spouts of white powder and broken glass filled the air. Tiny pecks of concrete leaped from the floor as countless bullets pounded around Aria's crouched form.

A cocky worker hopped over the assembly line, MAC-10 spraying in Aria's direction. Two bullets raked across her thigh. She gnashed her teeth and paid him back with the M60, tearing his chest wide open and slamming his body against the stairs leading up to the roof of the portable.

Two commandos leaned into the entryway and fired at Aria's back, disintegrating her legs.

Aria screamed as she felt her muscle tissue tear away from bone. She fell on her shoulder, out in the open—easy pickings for the machine gun nest above. They didn't waste the opportunity, unleashing a merciless fusillade of blazing lead on her. She writhed, shrieking in unbearable pain as her insides burned away, her bones chipping and shattering as hundreds of bullets hammered her into the concrete floor. Her body was on fire for mere seconds before her brain exploded out the back of her head. Then she couldn't feel anything—not until her healing factor kicked in.

Outside, more commandos were coming down the stairs...

*

COBALT CHRISTMAS: A COBALT ROGUE STORY

BOOM!

The towers of boxes in the waste management sector suddenly blew apart; a wall of fireballs raged along the far side of the platform. The seven commandos running toward the waste management sector skidded to a stop by the sudden explosion, feeling the heat all the way out there. The shutter door above the entrance rattled as a hot gust of air slammed into it. Black smoke filled the rafters as white dust came down.

A figure moved in front of the inferno, walking through a fluttering snowstorm of cocaine toward the entrance. A dark shadow concealed his features from them, but the commandos had a damn good idea...

Damian Warkowski stood heroically in front of the flames with a burning cigarette hanging from the edge of an arrogant, sadistic smile. His cobalt eyes glinted brilliantly. His colourful Hawaiian shirt clashed against the backdrop of orange flames. The narcotic snowfall danced around him. The ball of the Santa hat was still dangling against his face, but he didn't care. He was too happy. After all, he now had a goddamned belt-fed minigun with a chainsaw grip in his hands pointed right at them.

The commandos stared at his weapon in disbelief.

Damian's smile evolved into a shit-eating grin. "Aloha, baby." He squeezed the trigger. The barrels started to turn—then with a deafening chainsaw roar they sprayed lead that instantly reduced all seven commandos into a red paste. Damian kept it going, let the stream charge down the corridor and up the stairs, obliterating every man on the steps and in the doorway in a furious explosion of blood and gore. He didn't stop there, lowering the barrel to take out every man standing at the top of the ramp and in front of the lab's entryway in mere seconds. He stopped firing only long enough to lug the metal beast toward the entryway down the corridor on his right. He heard shouting, people asking what that strange noise was. The ammo belt rattled across the floor as it trailed behind him.

He stepped into the doorway to provide them with an answer to their questions. A couple of guards standing behind their table barricade turned to face him, eyes wide as saucers. One of them yelled, "Jesus Christ!"

Damian replied, "Guess again!" He let it rip with a droning, metallic howl, strafing the broad side of the portable building, igniting two dozen barrels of kerosene all at once.

KABOOM!

The whole building went up in a concussive explosion that shook the entire sector and took out the lights. The machine gun nest was launched into the rafters and pulverized against the ceiling as gouts of fire ripped across the lab, hurling several gunmen through the air. Damian's minigun shredded through the tables and disintegrated everyone trying to hide behind them. The shelves came down and assembly lines blew apart as Damian laid down a withering curtain of lead. A sweltering hailstorm of gore and snow and flaming debris filled the lab as Damian, howling with maniacal glee, leveled everything in sight and stirred up what was left on the floor in violent splashes until the ammo belt finally ran out.

Hill slowly ascended the ramp in a bewildered daze, looking at the shredded commandos that littered the hall outside of the lab. He looked at the stairs. Not a single step remained intact; the frame was coated in a wet layer of blood as the few pieces left of the backup party either dangled from the edges of the steps or were piled up underneath. Even the steel door was warped from the onslaught and hung on a single hinge. "What the fuck... was *that*?"

He heard Damian laughing in the lab and went to check it out. The sight of the lab in total ruin stopped him dead. He looked across the room at Damian as he arched his head back and shouted, "WHEEEWWWW!" He continued his psychotic laughter as he dropped the minigun to the floor. Hill scanned the lab again. Not a single thing was left untouched by Damian's attack. The walls were cratered and everything else had been torn far beyond recognition.

"Jesus fucking Christ!" Hill gasped. He waved dust away from his face, coughing. "What the fuck did you do?!" He pointed at the minigun. "What the fuck is that?! What the fuck is... is... *THIS*?!"

Aria was almost completely healed, lying in a pool of her own blood, which her body was slowly absorbing like a sponge. "Ughhh..."

Hill jumped to her aid, helping her up. "You alright?"

"Yeah, just... in a lotta pain. It'll pass." She blinked and took in her surroundings. "What the hell happened here?"

"Damian happened," Hill said.

"Oh. Of course he did. 'Ol' Painless.'"

"You mean that friggin' *cannon* is called 'Ol' Painless'?"

"That's what he calls it." She coughed. The dust was filling her lungs, making her dizzy. "Let's get outta this smoke. Hey, Damian! We're going. Better move your ass before you get high on this shit."

"I'm already high," Damian replied, "High on *adrenaline*! YEEEEAAAHHH!"

"He's rarely like this when I'm with him," Hill said.

"Trust me, he's gotten worse over the years," she said. She said to Damian, "You're gettin' a little too excited about death there, dude."

"They had it coming." Damian spat into the blazing sea of mechanical debris and human gore before him. "Fucking assholes."

"We're gonna go kill Drake, Damian," Aria said as she stumbled toward the exit. "With or without you."

Damian drew a pistol and turned on his heel, his face suddenly dark and devoid of any joy or cheer. "Let's kill that son of a bitch." He shot Hill a hostile glance. "*My* way."

Chapter 037
Invitation to Obliteration

Control Room

8:57 PM.

Drake felt the floor vibrate under his feet as a low rumble echoed through the halls. He knew exactly what had happened. Still, he felt the need to confirm it. He picked up the radio. "Turk."

Static.

"Turk, come in."

Damian's voice replied, "Turk can't come to the phone right now. Please leave a message at the beep. *Beeeeeeep!*"

Drake trembled with rage. *He is so goddamn irritating...*

"That was a nice drug operation you had down here, Drake," Damian went on. "I enjoyed blowing my load all over her face."

"Enjoy it while it lasts, freak. You won't be around much longer."

"I've heard it all before. Blah-blah-blah. Do me a favour and make this interesting for me, Drake. Do something no one I've faced in the past has ever done before"

"What, surrender?"

"Seen it. Start barking and snarling over the radio like a rabid dog."

"Why would I ever do that?"

"Because when I get there, I'm gonna put you down like the mangy bitch that you are. Get in character. Assume thy role." Damian dropped the radio on the floor and crushed it under his boot.

SCHRACK!

Dead. Drake couldn't even hear static. His grip tightened on the radio, muscles flexing. Then a surge of rage. He hurled the radio across the room, straight through a TV screen. "COCKSUCKER!"

He looked at Kettle and said, "Drug lab's gone. It's time to make our final stand."

"Here?"

Drake shook his head.

"Where, then?"

Drake pointed at the monitors—the ones showing Santa's village from several different angles. "It's cooler that way."

"Oh."

Mackey's Market

The hypermarket parking lot looked like a Christmas party in Hell. Police and Emergency Services' cherry-tops strobed the area with red and blue light, irregularly synchronizing with amber flashers on warning and roadblock signs, all adding colour to the blinking holiday decorations that embroidered the store windows. Media camera flashes added a personal touch to the lighting pattern and random searchlights strafed the front of the market. Bystanders and reporters fought with police to get through to a top story or a loved one trapped inside. Police cruisers and tactical squads filled the lot, having formed a barricade in front of the store, squatting behind it with their firearms ready. Most news reporters remained outside of the cordoned area, though some managed to sneak into the cluster of police vehicles for a closer look with their cameramen.

The storefront windows had since been completely blown out. Bodies of shoppers and police officers were scattered between the barricade and the hypermarket, with an injured woman shrieking in agony and terror as she writhed on the concrete behind an overturned shopping cart among the bodies.

An unknown number of masked assailants stood in clear view inside the store, hooting maniacally as they fired a wide variety of automatic weapons at the police. An endless hail of bullets pelted the barricade, and some passed through and hit the cops.

"Deck the halls with bowels of shoppers!" the one in the pig mask sang, shooting his AK-47 into the fray. "FALA-LALA-LAAAA-LALA-LALA!"

As the assailants in the windows cheerfully sprayed the parking lot defenders, a few others terrorized the hostages they managed to secure, some even rollerblading from aisle to aisle, waving their guns overhead, thrusting their masks in their hostages' faces and screaming at them.

"WOO!" Goalie smashed the grip of his magnum against each cash register until it opened. He then proceeded to dump the money into a burlap sack. "Fuck yeah! I love this job! How we doin', Mr. Pork?"

One of the gangsters at the windows turned his smiling pig mask in Goalie's direction, blindly shooting his assault rifle into the lot. "Goddamn pigs ain't making this easy, Mr. Lake! Hiding behind their cars like a bunch o' pussies!"

The gangster beside Mr. Pork suddenly crumpled to the floor, clutching his shattered right elbow, screaming in agony. "Ah, goddamn motherfuckers shot me! FUCK! *FUCK*!"

"Ah, quit bein' such a bitch," Mr. Pink said as he turned back to the lot. He reloaded his assault rifle, aimed carefully, and put a round through an officer's face as soon as it came into view. Mr. Pink cheered wildly at his success and added, "That's why we give you drugs, man! We got plenty more in the back o' this mall!"

"I ain't takin' no fucking drugs!"

"That's your loss."

"No it ain't!"

Beyond the parking lot, Jenny was tooling the car in an alleyway just a few doors up the road from the mall, watching the carnage unfold at the hypermarket in dismay until the car was all the way in the niche and she couldn't see it anymore. "Shit," she muttered, "it's already starting." She parked the car behind a dumpster, then turned to face Molly. "You're sure your dad's in there?"

Molly nodded. "His name's Ice."

"'Ice'? What kinda name is that?"

Molly shrugged.

"Does he have another name or something?"

"Djimon."

Jenny blinked. Something about that name sounded familiar. She repeated it in her head: *Djimon Ice. Djimon Ice...*

Campturn.

A missing puzzle piece just crash-landed in her lap. "Ooooooohhhhhh!" She looked at Molly. "Oh, shit. Your dad's the leader of the Campturn gangs?"

"Most of them."

Jenny leaned back in her chair. *So **that's** what they were doing there. They took Molly and her mom to get Ice to cooperate. Now it* *makes sense.*

"Okay... stay in the car. I'll do what I can, okay?"

"I wanna go with you."

"Uh-huh. Outta the question."

"I wasn't asking, though."

"You're. Not. Going. Inside. Period. *Double* period. Exclamation mark times two. Understand?"

"You can't make me stay here."

Jenny heaved a sigh. "You got a lot of nerve, Molly. I'm trying to keep you safe while I save your gangster dad from getting killed by the police or my psycho trigger-happy boyfriend." Molly didn't look like she was about to budge. "If I pay you twenty bucks, will you stay in the car no matter what?"

"Make it a hundred."

Jenny's jaw dropped. "You serious right now?"

Molly nodded, her face an imitation of an 'I mean business' frown.

Jenny glared at her. "But you're ten."

"So are kids in third world countries, but they don't have any money either."

"Exactly! Ten-year-olds don't have any business carrying a hundred fucking dollars in their pockets."

"No, it's because nobody will give them any money."

"It's a bit more complicated than that."

"How?"

Jenny groaned. "You're not in a third world country, kid. You're here in this shit hole that is still somehow part of the developed world. Fifty."

"A hundred."

"Forty."

"One. Hundred."

"Seventy."

"Hundred."

"Ugh! Fine!" Jenny went through her wallet and flicked a hundred dollar bill into her lap.

Molly took it and immediately held it up to the light.

"Seriously?" Jenny asked.

"What? Just making sure it's real."

"Oh, it's real," Jenny said impatiently. "Let me tell you

something, Molly. We now have a contract. You stay in this car until I get back and the money's all yours to do with as you please. But if you *don't* stay in this car... if you step one foot onto the sidewalk, I'll take it away from you and you'll never see another dollar from me ever again."

"If you take it, I'll get it back."

"Well, that would be stealing now, wouldn't it?"

"But—"

"Stop arguing with me."

"Why would—"

"Molly." Jenny looked at her, eyes burning with suppressed rage. "Do you like that coat you're wearing?"

"Yes...?"

"Do you know what it's made of?"

"No...?"

"Neither do I. But for your sake, you'd better find out fast, because God help me, you'll end up like those children in poverty that you love to talk about so much. Except you'll be living in my basement, sewing coats just like yours for five cents a day with a third of a cup of water and a stale slice of bread to provide you with just enough nourishment to keep on making me coats for me to get rich off of. And when you finally break down in the deep, dark pit of despair in the darkest, filthiest corner of my basement covered in layers of your own piss and shit, you'll begin to wonder 'Why? Why didn't I listen to Jenny when I took that hundred dollars from her?' as you slowly fade into the endless blackness of unconsciousness and finally drift away from even that so that you can savour the luxury of the sweet, *sweeeeeet* release of... *death*."

Molly stared at her, mortified.

"*Or*," Jenny added with a friendly smile, "you can stay right there in that seat. Deal?"

Molly nodded until her head was a blur.

"Good girl. See ya soon." Jenny got out and locked the doors. Immediately her expression darkened, horrified at herself. "Oh, God, I'm a fucking monster."

She glanced over at the mall across the street. There on the curb, she noticed a black Sedan... the same one she saw at the safehouse. She was sure of it. The windows were tinted so she couldn't make out a damn thing, but this couldn't be a coincidence...

COBALT CHRISTMAS: A COBALT ROGUE STORY

*

The Control Room

9:13 PM.

Damian, Aria, and Hill burst through the doors, guns drawn—

—only to find it empty.

"What the hell?" Hill exclaimed, looking around. "Another trap?"

Damian spotted something and crossed the room to the control panel, where he found a written note nailed to the panel with his own combat knife. "No," he said, tearing the note out from the blade. "An invitation."

"What's that?" Aria asked.

"It says 'Come alone to Santa's village.' Oh, and then there's just a list of a bunch of dumb insults for the rest of the page." Damian turned to face the video wall, scanning the screens for Santa's village. He found them—and Drake, sitting in Santa's chair with a little girl on his lap. Damian's blood went cold. "Oh, fuck."

"What?" Hill asked.

"He's right where all the hostages seem to be. Looks like they uh... gathered them all in the center." Damian noticed the hypermarket footage and pointed at the screens. "Oh, except in that grocery store over there."

Hill looked at the sections of the video wall Damian was indicating. "The Mackey's Market. Jesus Christ, they turned it into a goddamn war zone!"

"Well, Sergeant," Damian said, turning to face Hill, "looks like you've got a job to do."

"What?"

"The market. Aren't you supposed to be protecting the innocent or some shit?"

"Of course."

"They've got the hostages boxed in the center. If you guys could seize control of the store, you could work your way down to the center and maybe, just *maybe*, we could clear a path for those civilians to get out."

"Damian," Aria said. "There's a bomb here. Another one just like the one in Monterey. If you go down there, there's a good chance you're not gonna come out."

Damian shrugged. "So I'll go out with a bang."

"But we don't even know where it is, or when it'll blow!"

"Then we'd better get our asses in gear."

"What about Jenny?"

"What *about* Jenny? She knew the risks when we got together. Every morning that comes, there's a damn good chance I won't live long enough to go back to bed."

Hill and Aria exchanged looks. Hill asked Damian, "What about you? What're you gonna do?"

Damian waved the note around. "What the fuck do you *think* I'm going to do? I'm going to be in the center of it all. As usual."

"Okay... but it's obviously a trap," Hill said. "I don't like it."

"I don't give a damn if you do. This'll be a cinch for me. Find a tunnel or an air duct or something; just take that fucking store back."

"On it," Aria said, grabbing Hill's shoulder.

Hill jerked his shoulder out of her hand, still facing Damian. He said to him, "I'm sorry I let him get away."

"You should be. Dumbass." Damian added, "When you get to that hypermarket, try my way for a change."

"I'm a cop, Damian. There're rules." Looking at him now, Hill wanted to ask him about the 'Boss.' He wanted to interrogate the little shit. If what Drake told him was true, that would mean everything that's happened was Damian's fault. Hell, maybe he could get the name of an accomplice. There seemed to be someone else working in the shadows, or else Damian wouldn't be here trying to prevent the outcome.

Or would he?

"Right, that's what stopped you from slaughtering forty men in that basement. Get the fuck off my back." Damian grabbed Hill's collar and yanked him close, his voice a furious whisper. "With this much at stake, there *are* no rules. I know you can already see that. You're already letting go. Do us all a favour: let it go. Also, go."

Hill stared at him, not quite sure what he meant.

"Why are you still standing here?"

"Huh?"

Impatiently, Damian yelled, "GO!"

"Oh!"

"Go! Go! GO!"

Chapter 038
Clearance Sale

Mackey's Market

9:35 PM.

Parked on the curb outside of the police cordon was the cyborg Drake's black Sedan, and Cyborg Drake himself watched the gun battle unfold from the comfort of his back seat. "Fucking glorious," he said, turning to the two video screens installed in the back of the front seats where two different live broadcasts covered the siege.

In the vents, Aria led the way down to the hypermarket with Hill following close behind, his eyes helping themselves to the view in front of him. He couldn't help but compare it to Jenny's photos. "So, uh... you're *actually* related to Jenny?"

"Yeah, actually, I am. Why?"

"Weird coincidence."

"How so?"

Hill almost mentioned Drake's 'theory' about Damian being the boss. He could see the family resemblance between Jenny and Aria almost instantaneously. Their fiery red hair and blue eyes were a dead giveaway, along with their tomboy characteristics. Hell, he found them both extremely attractive. Still, he knew he couldn't say it, even though he built it up. They would probably kill him if they became aware of how much he knew. So instead he said, "You, uh, have a great ass, just like your sister's."

"Wow," she said sarcastically, "I was almost flattered for a second there."

Hill chuckled.

"Do me a favour," she added, "mention my sister like that again so I can kick your face out of your asshole."

"I'm good."

"Yeah, that's what I figured."

A terrified young couple were crouched together in the frozen foods aisle. On the other side of the aisle, a mother and her son huddled together on the floor, keeping their heads down as one of the terrorists stomped his boots down on the floor like a drill sergeant, threatening everyone he came across with an Uzi. "Nobody moves an inch, not *one* fucking inch from their spots till all this shit is over! Are we fucking clear?" He turned to the mother and son, who trembled under his vicious glare. "I said, 'are we clear'?!" He straightened, stole an uncaring glance at the couple. They cowered from his gaze. Grinning with approval, he said, "Goody!" He slipped an Optimus Prime mask over his face and trotted off.

Aria watched silently from the vent above as Optimus Prime disappeared around the end of the aisle.

The charity Santa dashed down the frozen foods aisle with his shotgun waving in the air above his head. Several hostages cowered in fear, huddled against the glass doors as he passed them. "None of you bitches move! Santa knows when ya'll boys an' girls be naughty or nice!"

He stopped in front of the mother and her son huddled together, poked the son with his shotgun, causing the boy's mother to pull him away and shield him. "Santa Claus *knows!*"

Aria was ready to drop down and kill Santa Claus in a matter of seconds. It was risky, but doable. She wasn't about to sit around and watch another kid get orphaned just a couple days before Christmas.

Then the Santa moved on, chuckling to himself and twirling his shotgun around.

"What's going on?" Hill asked behind her.

"The place's swarmin' with these bastards."

"Great," Hill whispered, "now what?"

"Now we wait," Aria responded calmly, eyes fixed on the departing Santa Claus.

In the parking lot, a news reporter pushed her way through to the front police line with her cameraman in tow, stopping beside an empty police caravan, explaining the situation to her audience as quickly as possible: "It's a war zone down here. Terrorists have taken hostages in the Manharttigan Mall. We are currently caught in an intense gunfight with the police. This has stretched on for roughly forty minutes now and the robbers have foiled every attempt the police have made to infiltrate the building. The number of casualties is increasing every minute—" she ducked instinctively as the caravan's sideview mirror burst apart above her head. Despite this, she brushed glass bits off her hat and continued, speaking over the thunderous staccato of gunfire. "Cryo City faces yet another bloody evening, when a similar situation occurred just less than a week ago—"

FWOOSH!

Something hit a cruiser in the front line and burst it into the air in a cascade of fire. Police units scrambled for cover as the cruiser collided with the concrete. Almost immediately, a second detonation flipped another cruiser like a coin; it came up tails on a nearby caravan.

"Jesus—" the reporter sputtered, using her arm to shield herself from the heat of the flames. She looked at the cameraman in terror and shouted, "Fuck this! The Pulitzer isn't worth this shit! Let's get the fuck outta here!"

Inside, another maniacal assailant giggled with glee as he lifted a rocket launcher onto his shoulder and sent the rocket screeching across the lot. It smashed into the side of a third cruiser and blasted it apart, hurling police officers that were more flame than man away from its blazing skeletal form.

Almost instantly, another cruiser went up in a gout of fire— nearby police officers doubled over and scattered for cover as it flipped over their heads—and crushed yet another caravan.

"Goddamn it!" Carver roared with dismay from behind the third line, watching helplessly as a third caravan exploded. "No! We just got those re-painted!"

The front line, now mostly reduced to nothing but burning wreckage. A few persistent officers remained squatted behind bullet-ridden vehicles, pumping more rounds into the store with their pistols and assault rifles whenever the opportunity surfaced, assuming the worst for the hostages.

"Son of a bitch!" Carver snarled. He snatched up a radio. "Where the hell is our cavalry?!"

Fairman calmly responded on the other end, "Just another minute."

COBALT CHRISTMAS: A COBALT ROGUE STORY

"Hurry the fuck up!"

Goalie, officially known as Mr. Lake, raised his mask up as he approached the fifth checkout counter, which had a huge mountain of cocaine piled on the disabled conveyor belt. He sloppily grabbed a handful of coke and dumped it up his nose. He snorted most of it before wiping his face with the same hand, covering his dark-skinned face in white, shaking wildly, and shouting at the top of his lungs, "Goddamn, I said, *goddamn*, that's good! WOO!" A newfound rush of adrenaline tore through him as he yanked his mask down over his face and, still hollering, emptied his Magnum into the parking lot. Then he ducked back down between counters five and six, and reloaded as he retreated to the canned goods aisle.

A gangster in a plastic chicken mask rollerbladed by the checkout counters dual-wielding two pistols. He hopped expertly over the bodies of dead shoppers and cashiers and weaved nimbly around shopping carts. Nine gangsters were still lined up at the front, shooting their firearms at the cops. Mr. Lake was snorting more coke from the conveyor belt of counter six.

The chicken-headed gangster called out to Mr. Lake, said, "Hey, who's watching the hostages?"

"Hunh?!" Mr. Lake asked, his dark face reappearing from a mountain of powder, pale as a ghost, eyes unusually wide.

"The hostages, nigga. Who's watchin' 'em?"

"They ain't gonna start shit. Too scared. Relax, Mr. Gobble. If you're worried about 'em, then by all means, go check on 'em."

The chicken-masked Mr. Gobble rollerbladed down the frozen foods aisle whilst waving his pistols around. He pointed them at each hostage as he wheeled past them. "Alright, you miserable fucks, listen up! Any o' you bitches wanna start shit, ya better come to me, you hear! I'll put ya back in your—"

The vent cover hit the floor in front of him. Aria landed in a squat. Too close for him to dodge. Too fast for him to shoot.

He skated by her, stunned. She leaped up, grabbed his arm, and used his momentum against him, swung him head first through the glass door of a refrigerator, crashing into the shelves. Hill dropped down on the other side, grabbed Mr. Gobble's other arm, twisted it around with a sickening *snap*, jammed his own pistol into his ribs, and let loose a three-round burst through his chest. Mr. Gobble jolted before going limp in Aria's arms. Aria dropped him and took Mr. Gobble's pistols and whatever ammo she could find, and gave it all to Hill. "Here. You need these a lot more than I do."

"Thanks."

Aria glanced at the mother and child sitting across the aisle from them. "It's alright," she said. "We're the good guys. We'll get you outta this in time to open up your presents."

A pair of Afrókrema hovercopters on stealth mode descended from the polluted skyline like silent angels of death. The hypermarket rooftop seemed abandoned; nothing but domed skylights, air conditioning units, steam vents, and triangular banners that proudly waved the *Mackey's Market* brand logo.

"This is Sky Shark TC-12," one of the pilots said into his helmet mic, "Keep your eyes peeled for hostiles."

"Thermal readings show negative," the hovercopter's scanner computer stated.

The hovercopters eased toward the air conditioning units in slow-motion dives. Moving in for the landing. The hatch doors slid open as infiltration elites prepared their lines for an abseiling drop. The soft-whirring anti-gravity boosters in the hovercopters' angular wings spun up small whirlwinds that whipped across the rooftop.

On the rooftop, something flickered. A brief spark. Then, a distortion in the air—a piece of it impossibly moved out of place like a jigsaw puzzle. A face materialized from the shadows, followed by a thick set of shoulders, burly arms, a body, legs, feet... and downsized .50 calibre machine guns serving as prosthetic substitutes for hands. The anti-gravity rotor wash flickered around the strange assailant as his cloaking projector powered down. Ruby red bug-eyed goggles focused on the hovercopters.

Sky Shark TC-12 shouted, "Where did—"

KAPOWPOWPOWPOWPOWPOW!

The assailant's machine guns lit up the sky. Pelted the hovercopters with explosive .50-calibre needles. The pilots screamed as the assailant's fire shredded the cockpits. The abseiling elites cut their lines before they could be slung away to certain death. Dropped to the rooftop. One of them fell too high; his body plummeted into an air conditioning unit, which shredded him, grinding his bones, stalling... exploding.

The other elites opened up on the cyborg assailant, punching his eyes out with lead. The cyborg's computerized, high-pitched shriek hurt their ears until one of the elites' shotguns blew his head into space.

The hovercopters came down. One of them drifted over the domed ceiling of the hall between Mackey's Market and a shoe store—into the shoe store it went, diving through the ceiling, blowing apart. Mercs scattered as a rush of fireballs cleared everything out of the store in a blizzard of glass and footwear, filling the hall by the main exit and the parking lot. The impact shattered a few panes of glass in the main entrance.

The second hovercopter spun through the dome and twirled through the hall. Its tail sliced through a Christmas tree right before the rest of the aircraft came down on a small glass block 'ice fortress' maze for the kids, scattering it all over the place. *Boom.* It came apart, hurling plates from its exploding hull into surrounding stores.

Mr. Lake looked up from the conveyor belt, glanced toward the far end of the hypermarket. "You guys hear gunshots?"

"No shit!" Mr. Pork yelled over the gunfire, still firing his assault rifle into the lot.

"I meant from the *inside*, you jackass!"

"I can barely hear *you*!"

Mr. Lake muttered with annoyance, took his magnum, and headed toward the frozen foods aisle. "I'm gonna go check it out."

"What?" Mr. Pork asked. "What'd you say?"

But Mr. Lake was already gone.

Aria and Hill quickly gathered the hostages that shared the aisle with them and guided them through the produce section toward the deli at the far corner of the hypermarket at the end of the aisle. They instructed the terrified shoppers to hide behind the counter until backup came in. The indoor exit lined with free-of-charge turnstiles to avoid cart theft leading to the rest of the shopping mall was located on the far left, just beyond the produce section and the indoor shopping cart corrals. A quartet of mercs charged in from there, firing at Aria and Hill.

Hill ducked, rushing the screaming civilians to the deli as a flurry of produce exploded around them.

Aria drew two machine pistols and mowed them down, splintering the glass panes that made up the corrals' walls and bordered the exit. The mercs went down screaming, assault rifles shooting upward, taking out an electric WELCOME sign. It boomed like thunder as it exploded like a group of New Years fireworks.

Hill returned to her side. "They're in the deli."

"Let's split up. One on each side. Watch your ass."

"Gotcha."

The pair started running through the hypermarket, each picking a side.

Hill remained in the produce section, dual-wielding his pistols.

BANG!

He ducked; the apples beside him exploded. Hill whirled around and opened up on a shotgun-wielding werewolf, put five shots in his chest. Split the werewolf's mask in two with a sixth, sent him sprawling onto a cluster of bananas.

Hill rushed over and stuffed one of his pistols into his jacket pocket in favour of the dropped pump-action shotgun. "Now we're talking," he said.

He heard screaming from the frozen foods aisle and turned back to where he came from. He rushed to the deli and found a lizard man smacking the counter with a machete, laughing as he terrorized the hostages.

"Freeze!" Hill shouted, pointing the shotgun at him. "Police!"

The lizard man turned his plastic googly eyes on him and immediately charged around the produce between four rows of ice boxes, machete raised. "Bring it on, you son of a bitch!"

Hill narrowed his eyes and pulled the trigger.

Jammed.

Alarmed, Hill looked at the gun and tried the trigger again. "Damn." Then he paused, laughed at his own stupidity. Pumped an empty shell out. *Today is not your day, friend.*

The lizard man was on him. Hill dodged a machete swing and thrust the shotgun into the thug's ribs, then lifted him over his head, slammed him on the glass cover of an ice box. "Cool off!" Blasted the lizard man's body into a pile of packaged ice cubes. Hill flinched from the flying bits of glass and flesh that briefly fluttered through the air.

Afterwards, Hill breathed a sigh of relief as he peered into the bloody mess he'd created inside the box: the thug's arms and legs loosely hung over the sides, innards filling in the spaces like snakes. Hill fished around and extracted the machete from the thug's hip. He examined the blood-soaked blade, otherwise undamaged, and tapped the edge of the ice box with it. "Thanks, I guess."

Bang-bang!

More produce exploded near Hill's head. The gunshots were coming from behind him. He turned toward the bread aisle and blasted a crouching witch against the shelf.

Yet another thug in a Darth Vader mask appeared on top of the shelf like a prowling cat, Uzi rattling in his hands.

Shit!

Hill dived under another produce display, skidded beneath it as his enemy's bullets tore up a bushel of apples over Hill's head. Hill appeared on the other side under the shelf, just out of Lord Vader's field of vision.

Until he leaned forward.

That's when Hill blasted the top shelf into his face, splintering the mask, sent him sprawling backwards to the floor in an avalanche of packaged baguettes.

Aria went through the snack aisle, staring at Santa's back as he threatened a young woman with his shotgun. "You want some? Ho-ho-ho, bitch! Ho—"

"Yo!" Aria shouted.

The Santa whirled around, shotgun pumped. "NO—"

Aria's pistol delivered a deafening beat that sent the Santa crashing through a stack of eggnog cartons in a wild blood spray.

Hill didn't have any more trouble until he got halfway through the hypermarket, in the pet supplies section. An abominable snowman fired his Uzi at him; Hill retreated behind the shelf, sprayed by cat food. The snowman shouted an alarm for his companions over the rattle of his Uzi. "I got 'im, he's over here!"

Click!

"Shit!"

Now! Hill jumped back into the open with his shotgun and

blasted Frosty against the shelf. The snowman collapsed under a downpour of dog kibble.

Almost immediately, a ghoul appeared from behind the shelf and fired his dual pistols at Hill, who ducked and rolled into the pet supplies aisle. Pet food popped over Hill's head as he rolled across the floor.

The ghoul's pistols kept barking as bullets chased Hill through bleach bottles and other cleaning supplies on the other side. The ghoul screamed with manic rage as he pursued his target. He was barely at a safe distance; at risk of cleaning fluid splashing through the eye holes of his mask. He unloaded from one end to the other—

BLAM!

Laundry detergent splashed in his face, causing him to drop his guns, fly back against a crate of no-name bathroom supplies, tearing his mask off his face as he rubbed his watering eyes.

Hill circled around the shelf, now with the last thug's Uzi strapped over his shoulder. He tossed his empty shotgun away and drew his machete, raised it high, only for the ghoul to kick him in the stomach. Hill slammed into the shelf, wind knocked out of him. He dropped his machete to the floor. Still screaming, the ghoul tackled him against the shelf; he was a giant compared to Hill, thrashing wildly, nails cutting through his skin. The massive ghoul had his bulging hands around Hill's throat, still shouting in his face.

Hill's ears rang. His hand groped around the shelf, settled on a bottle of drain cleaner on the second shelf from the bottom. Then he desperately hit the ghoul over the head with it, battering the flinching fucker's face and left ear with it before thrusting the cap end into his eye.

The pain caused the screaming ghoul to retreat, grasping his throbbing eye, granting Hill the opportunity to curl his knuckles and drive his fist into the ghoul's nose. Blood erupted from his nostrils as he stumbled, not quite conscious, but not unconscious either. He threw a wild swing at Hill, who dodged the blind punch and launched his heel upward, connecting with the thug's jaw with a loud *snap*. He fell hard, making an awkward swan dive into a box full of no-name bathroom supplies. His legs bucked and he twitched occasionally, but even that died down after a few seconds as he drifted into unconsciousness.

Hill was quick to cuff him, wincing as his aching neck began to stiffen. He muttered, "Damn," and massaged his neck as he watched the ghoul's legs twitch.

"Where is he?"

"I dunno."

"Find him, shithead!"

Hill looked up from the ghoul in the bargain bin to the shelf across the aisle. He could make out three figures standing on the other side. He stooped down, picked up his machete, ran around the crate and dashed toward the shelf, and threw himself against it. The shelf creaked, tipped over. The thugs on the other side shrieked as the shelf came down on them with a deafening *crash*, causing a domino effect that toppled the next seven shelves toward the front. While it was falling, Hill climbed up to the top, using the shelves as ladder rungs. He followed the shelves as one after the other crashed into the next like giant trees. *Now this is insane,* his thoughts screamed.

More deafening crackles rang out from the alcoholic beverage section, which stretched along the outer wall. The Predator pursued the toppling shelves, his MAC-10 putting out ceiling tiles and fluorescent lights as he tried to get Hill, who scrambled across the shelf tops, keeping his head down.

Aria ran out of the snack aisle just in time to see the next set of shelves collapse, and the unbelievable sight of Hill running along the tops, keeping his head down to avoid bullets coming from the alcoholic beverage aisle. She raised her pistol as the shelves came down, revealing the Predator standing on the other side in front of a wine rack with his gun tearing up the ceiling.

She fired twice through an opening in the collapsing shelves. The first popped the Predator's Adam's apple. The second scored a head shot, which propelled the thug's body into the wine rack. He collapsed to the floor in a sparkling cascade of red and white.

Hill was still half stumbling, half running along the tops of the shelves with his Uzi in one hand and pistol in the other.

Aria rounded the corner just as a Xenomorph-wannabe down the aisle dived into her path to escape the domino effect. He rolled to his feet, shotgun locked on Hill.

Aria reacted first and drilled a tunnel through the Xenomorph's phallic head.

COBALT CHRISTMAS: A COBALT ROGUE STORY

*

A gun-toting turkey lifted a rocket launcher onto his shoulder, ready to fire. As his companions cover-fired on either side of him, he aimed for a caravan that was flying across the lot to provide extra cover for the cops—most likely an attempt to rescue the injured woman curled up in the middle of the parking lot. He wasn't going to let that happen; not just because he wanted to kill as many people as possible before this was over, but also because he liked to blow things up. Especially things that moved.

He giggled with glee and fingered the trigger as he aimed for the approaching caravan.

Hill bounded over the shelves toward the front as the last shelf came down against the row of checkout counters and crushed a screaming Optimus Prime. Aria watched Hill with surprise and quickly followed him. "Christ, it's like I'm fighting with Damian again."

Startled, the other gunmen whirled around to see Hill charging toward them on the overturned shelves, already in the process of cutting them down with his Uzi. Four thugs hit the floor screaming; the one in the turkey mask took five to the chest, crumpled on his knees and fired his rocket into the floor.

BOOM!

A flaming tsunami uprooted the checkout counters and blasted chunks of the ceiling into the air as a raging fireball ripped through the store. Hill took cover behind a fallen shelf. Mr. Lake screamed as the explosive force hurled him over counter six in a white cloud of coke. Burning thugs were blown out into the lot by a secondary explosion. The woman lying behind her shopping cart tucked her arms and legs in and let out an ear-piercing squeal as hot hail came down on her. Ceiling tiles and lights spilled onto the floor in a thunderous storm of sparks. Bits of the rooftop—and a portion of the giant neon letters reading 'MACKEY'S MARKET'—were launched into the night sky. The rest of the sign spewed a dazzling array of sparks over the lot as if New Year's had come early. Police and news crews scrambled for cover as debris crashed down all around them. The big sparking 'A' from the sign caved in a cruiser's windshield next to a shocked Carver's head.

Only three thugs remained standing in the open, their backs

turned to the parking lot cops, stunned by the sudden blast. They shouted their surprise, unable to do much else before the outside cops gunned them down.

Mr. Lake crawled between counters seven and eight, snatching an abandoned submachine gun off the floor as he did so. He rose to a crouch when he reached the part of the aisle that wasn't blocked by a fallen shelf, hidden from view.

Aria was coming out of the aisle, alert but unaware of Mr. Lake's presence. She turned to Hill, who was crawling out from behind a flaming pile of canned goods. "Jesus Christ, dude. That was probably the craziest thing I've ever seen a cop do."

"Yeah?" Hill said as he brushed debris out of his hair. "I don't plan on making a habit out of it..."

Mr. Lake peeked out from behind the checkout counter and spotted his next target.

Hill got up and looked around. "Is that all of them?"

Mr. Lake ground his teeth and aimed his gun at Aria and Hill. "Eat this, pigs."

Hill spotted him and reached for Aria. "Get down!"

It was too late. Mr. Lake's gun rattled. Bullets ripped through Aria's back. Her head snapped back; her body arched forward. A pained moan peeled through the air as she stumbled forward on crumpling legs. Mr. Lake didn't stop until she collapsed out of his field of vision.

"Shit!" Donald screamed.

Mr. Lake stopped shooting and laughed triumphantly. "Gotcha, bitch! Shoulda stayed in the fucking kitchen, eh?" The giggling thug hastily got up to his feet and scrambled down the aisle, ducking when the police reacted to the shots by firing another volley into the store.

Hill fired his pistol in hot pursuit of Mr. Lake, who dived through the entrance of the employees-only storage room and disappeared as the double doors swung shut behind him.

Hill crawled toward Aria, already in the process of picking herself up off the floor. "Aria! You alright?"

"Jesus Christ. I'm fine. Ugh." She sat herself up against the side of an overturned shelf. "Fuck, I'm tired. I think I'm gonna sit this one out."

"Seriously?"

"Go get 'im, tiger." She handed him another pistol.

He took the gun. "Will do." He stood up to his feet and stomped toward the employees-only doors. He kicked the doors open and leaped out of sight as a deafening rattle pounded his ears. Rolled behind a nearby crate as Mr. Lake hosed the entire area with his gun.

Click!

Mr. Lake swore and threw the Uzi away. Retreated in the opposite direction. Hill relentlessly pursued, his Uzi clawing after Mr. Lake like a rabid wolf out for blood until it ran out of bullets. Tossing it aside, Hill brandished the two pistols; his own and the one Aria gave him.

Mr. Lake entered a clearing and reached the loading dock—mostly empty with plastic strip doors at the end of the platform. The shutter doors beyond the small loading bay were sealed shut. Mr. Lake frantically looked around for an alternate exit, found none, and continued running for the strip doors.

"Freeze, motherfucker!"

Mr. Lake drew his backup pistol and whirled around to face Hill and the two pistols Hill aimed right at him. The two men froze under the bright orange fluorescent lights, muscles tense. Mr. Lake He snickered nervously through the holes in his goalie mask and said, "Well?"

"'Well' what?" Hill asked with a low growl in his throat.

Mr. Lake threw his gun to his right. Then he raised his hands and grinned. "Not gon' shoot a brother, are you, cracker?"

The fury in Hill's eyes intensified as his vision narrowed.

Mr. Lake chuckled. "Whatsamatter, nigga? Too scared o' me to read me my rights?" He let out another mocking chortle. "I don't blame ya. I'm so scary I make that Voorhees guy look like a pussy."

The rage was starting to take over. But then something Damian said crept into his mind: *'My way is better than yours.'* That's right. Maybe it is, maybe it isn't. So Hill shoots him, Hill might face the consequences of straight up murdering him and those guys in the basement, and so on. He couldn't even begin to imagine the body count he'd raised today. Damian truly was a monster. An influential monster, driving people to do things they thought they would never do. Before today, Hill rarely killed people for the sake of it. Before today, he was able to keep himself in check. There was torture behind the scenes, the odd incident where he was excessively forceful on someone in order to get information that would lead to a break in a case. Sometimes he took bribes. Sometimes he used blackmail. But in his mind, the ends always justified the means. Could that be said about what he was doing here, too? Or was he turning into another Damian Warkowski? Or another Drake? Or another psycho cop?

Damian *did* have a point, though. Hill knew if he spared this guy, just arrested him, he would be put on trial, sentenced, maybe given bail if he got himself a good lawyer and behaved himself. He'd be back on the street in a few years, and then the deaths of more innocents would be on Hill's hands—

Fuck it, Hill thought.

Hill snarled in disgust, "You have the right to remain silent, 'Mr. Voorhees.'"

Then he opened fire. His pistols blazed as he punched countless holes through a shocked Mr. Lake's body. His blood splattered on the plastic strip doors as he backed toward them. His arms jerked from the bullets impacting him He screamed in agony. One of Hill's pistols locked empty. Hill threw it away in favour of his spare, and ripped into Mr. Lake's body with his last two guns. The other clicked empty as Mr. Lake's back touched the bloodied strip doors. Hill dropped the empty gun, now left with his last one, which still bombarded his screaming victim.

Mr. Lake staggered through the strip doors, his right heel on the edge of the platform. "Oh... Christ. My shirt—"

One final burst from Hill's gun caused blood to erupt from the cracked hole in the center of the mask's forehead, but Mr. Lake was still standing, a raspy moan pouring out of his mouth, eyes bulging through the eyeholes of his mask, blood gurgling through the mouth holes and trickling down the mask's chin.

Hill dropped the empty pistol, drew the machete and hurled it into Mr. Lake's forehead, splitting his mask in two, revealing a face covered in sugary white and dark, glistening red. Mr. Lake only stood for another second before falling over the edge of the platform and disappearing into the loading bay with a *splat*.

Hill stared at the plentiful blood smears on the plastic strip doors. His rage continued to boil within him. Even after the brutality he dealt his victim, Hill's anger hadn't simmered down.

He crossed a line. Oh, shit. He crossed *the* line. Maybe not now, but today, he crossed it.

BLAM!

Another startling *pop* bounced off the shelves as someone behind him ran Hill through with a red-hot spear. The 'spear' came and went, poking a hole into a plastic strip door through which it disappeared. Strength left Hill's legs. He fell on his knees, staring down at the patch of red spreading across his shirt, just below the left collarbone. Then his head dived into the cold concrete floor.

Mr. Pork lowered his pistol, gripping his bloody shoulder with his free hand. "An' people call *me* a pig. You killed my buddies—"

BRRAAPP!

Aria riddled his back with a Micro-Uzi, still sitting against the shelf, hoping she wasn't too late. She looked away only for a second—

Hill got it. The backup. He rolled onto his back and emptied an entire clip at Mr. Pork with his own personal Walther. Mr. Pork convulsed as Hill and Aria's bullets ripped him apart. Tried to shoot back, only for his head to snap to the right, his blood streaking a crescent shape across the floor behind him. Mr. Pork unleashed an ear-piercing shriek. He dropped his gun and spun to the floor. Stone dead.

Aria grunted as she got up to her feet and rushed over to Hill's aid. When she finally reached him, he was nearly passed out. "Jesus Christ. Shit, man. I'm sorry. I looked away for a second. Just one second—"

"It's... okay." Hill weakly held his hand over his bleeding chest, grunting. "I guess I had it coming."

Aria ripped his shirt open, revealing a flak jacket that failed to save him. The bullet had passed right through. "He was using cop killers."

"Fucking typical," Hill groaned.

"Keep pressing on it, man." Aria saw a pool of blood expand from under him. A feeling of dread took over. "Shit. Shit. Shit."

Hill spat a mouthful of blood over his front. More of it dribbled over his chin.

"Shit!"

"Aw, man," Hill gurgled. "I think I'm dyin'."

"Oh, come on. Don't say that. I was just starting to like you."

Hill made a wheezing laugh. "You bitch."

Aria chuckled. "Take it easy."

Hill coughed up another mouthful of red. He looked at it. He was going numb. Barely had the strength to raise his head anymore. Aria had to support him with her arm. "Yeah," he gasped. "I'm not gonna make it."

Aria didn't say anything.

"Something's been... bugging me for a while."

"What's that?"

He looked at her. He fought his heavy eyelids, struggling to keep them from closing. "Is Damian really... the 'Boss'?"

Aria stared at him, taken aback.

"What was all of this for?" Hill hacked up more blood and bile. "Was it... all... lies?"

"No," she said. "Just not the whole truth."

Hill gave her a weak, but expectant look.

"Damian hasn't been the same since the Konnerd incident. Says the little girl he couldn't save still haunts him. He was just trying to appease her spirit or some crazy shit like that. Anything to get her to stop tormenting him. Damian wasn't exactly the sanest patient in the hospital to begin with, but you knew that already." She leaned back, sitting crossed-legged with Hill's head resting in her lap. "Damian wanted to get him before. In Central Congoria. But... Colonel Fairman escaped."

Hill's eyes widened. Why didn't he realize it before? "Fairman...?"

"Fairman was behind it all along. Damian drove him into a desperate corner before when he stopped all of his operations in Central Congoria. When Fairman came back here to keep his elite force running, Damian tried to sabotage that too, and sort of succeeded."

"Damian started the Konnerd fire?"

"Oh, no. No. That was a crazy situation. He just wanted to get the hostages out before Fairman could. Fairman's attempts to negotiate cost us all those hostages." Aria paused, heaving a weary sigh. "Her name was Lisa."

Hill blinked. He recalled a few times when Damian said the name, seemingly out of nowhere, out of context.

"He watched that little girl burn to death in his arms. There was nothing he could do. And if you're a narcissistic piece of shit like Damian, you'd know the biggest mistake you could ever make is remind him that there are things that he just... can't do. And he couldn't save her. And it fucked him up."

"What's all this...?"

"This was the plan gone off the rails."

"How?"

"Fairman lost the last thing he couldn't afford—state funding. Damian created an alias—a mysterious crime lord known as the 'Boss.' Making it all real was easy enough, I guess, and eventually he managed to convince Fairman into wanting to become his greatest asset. Imagine the rewards you could get from a powerful man no one thinks exists. A man rich enough to do anything undetected. Fairman needed someone like that. Then he could go on and rebuild. *This*, Hill, was a trap. Fairman took the bait, big time, but he complicated things when he seemingly resurrected Drake, or whatever the fuck he did to bring that prick back from the dead.

"The plan was simple: orchestrate a crime wave. Make the city so desperate that it *needed* something more than the cops could provide—it *needed* Afrókrema. Fairman would swoop in. Save the day. Get his funding. And when Fairman reached the peak of his new success, when life couldn't get any better, that's when we were supposed to expose him. Damian didn't just want to kill him. He wanted to *ruin* him. *Break* him. See, all the evidence from his past exploits were destroyed in the raid. We needed something new, and damn it, we had to *make* something new. So we did. It turned into this. We fueled the fire and then it burned beyond our control. Now we're fucked."

Hill rasped, "'Poetic justice.'" Beat. "You dumb motherfuckers."

"Yeah, I guess we deserve that, and worse."

"Thank you, Aria."

"What for?"

Hill gagged on his own blood. Turned his head and hacked onto the floor. He looked up at her with watering eyes. A weak smile formed on his pale face. "Now I can die in peace... knowing that you guys are *so much worse* than I am." He coughed. "You guys are worse... than assholes."

Aria frowned. "Fair enough."

"But... I'm kinda... glad I met you guys. I could almost think of you as friends... ain't that fucked up? Please." His hand wobbled around her lap, latched onto her pant leg. "Please at least... end this the way you intended. I hate Fairman. He's an even bigger asshole than either of you."

"We'll get him. I swear on it."

"You're still assholes, though."

"Okay." She couldn't help but smile.

"Please also... forward my apologies to your sister."

"Why?" she asked, perplexed. "What'd you do?"

Ah, shit. He just ruined this heartfelt moment. He said, "Nothing."

"What'd you do? Hey!" She shook his head.

"Okay, okay. I'll tell you."

"Well?"

"So, you see... I may have... uh." His head suddenly rolled to the side as air hissed from his mouth. He went limp in her arms.

"May have what? Hey." She shook him gently. No reaction this time. "Hey!" She shook him a bit harder. Nothing. "Oh, nice cliffhanger, you dick! Fuck what you say! *You're* the biggest asshole here!"

She stared at him. Shifted out from under him and set his head down on the floor, almost affectionately. "Still, though... I guess you did good." She planted a small kiss on his forehead. "Thanks, pal. Rest easy."

Chapter 039
Moving In

Mackey's Market Parking Lot

10:12 PM.

"Jesus Christ," Carver muttered between cigarette drags as a fresh wave of ambulances and police caravans came pouring in from the street. The aftermath of the Mackey's Market siege wasn't pretty. Cars had been shredded and gutted by bullets and explosives. Cops and coroners picked up the multitude of dead, and whatever pieces of them they could find, and hauled them off to the side and draped sheets over them. Paramedics loaded the wounded into ambulances. News crews from every channel filled the sidewalks. Camera flashes and cherries lit the parking lot like a rave without any dancers.

The front of the west wing was reduced to smouldering rubble. Firefighters sent jets of water through the blown-out windows to calm the flames within as their colleagues dragged out blackened corpses across blankets of debris. An Afrókrema squad with full-face respirators lined up in front of the barrier. One of them approached Carver. "Ready, sir. We have another group entering the main entrance there." He pointed at the four-door entrance made up entirely of wall-to-ceiling windows, most of which had been disintegrated by the confrontation.

Carver looked at him. "What about the hostages?"

The squad leader showed him a 3D overhead graphic of the entire mall. In the center of the cross-shaped image was a big red blot that resembled a kidney. A smaller red area could be seen in the back of the Mackey's Market. A few other dots were scattered around the complex. "Heat signatures are showing that the majority of the hostages are in Santa's village. There's another group here in the back of this store. Not sure what those are yet. Could be civilians that managed to escape and hide. Could be more hostiles. Not sure yet."

"What about all these other dots?"

"Additional gunmen or civilians. The scanner provides us with an update every thirty seconds. We got three movers for sure. A faint signal over here near the loading bay of the store here. Other than that, it looks like our biggest concern is behind this supermarket and in the center of the complex."

"You didn't really answer my question."

"Yes, sir. We've got tactical teams on every exit. Already received a report from the south wing about a trailer with an assortment of armaments left by the waste management sector. Probably backup supplies, but I don't know why they wouldn't just store it *inside* the building. They left the door wide open for us—literally. I can't tell if we're dealing with professionals or amateurs."

"Fairman's already laid out a plan: we enter every wing, silent as ghosts. We got another team on the roof; they'll come raining down on the bad guys once our ground troops are in position. Then it's silent night, deadly night for the big, bad terrorists."

"Just don't let the hostages die this time. Their safety is our top priority."

"Ours as well, of course. That's why we're gonna trap 'em first."

"Be careful when you're trapping animals. We haven't so much as received a single ransom demand from them yet. They've lost the west wing and if your scanner is anything to go by, they're making their final stand in Santa's village. It's most likely a trap. Hell, I *know* it's a trap."

"All the more reason to box them in further."

"Are you even listening to me?!"

"Look, sir. These guys are crazy, but they ain't suicidal. No bomb jackets to be found here. They want something, else they would've blown themselves up with the hostages hours ago. If we corner 'em into a negotiation, they'll *have* to trade us something. The hostages for a plane to a non-extrajudicial country or somethin'."

"Christ. That's insane. They're more likely to start capping off hostages before they start listening to us. I'm not itchin' to repeat that Konnerd fiasco anytime soon."

"You an' me both, pal. That's why there's no time to waste. You have my word, first sign of shit hittin' the fan, we're pulling out."

COBALT CHRISTMAS: A COBALT ROGUE STORY

Carver tossed his cigarette butt despite only using up half the stick. "We do this, we do this my way." He shouted at four scores of freshly arrived tactical units from the Cryo City Terror Unit, telling them to get ready and cover all the exits. As they jogged single-file in groups of four, splitting up to enter every wing, Carver pulled a respirator over his face and grabbed a shotgun off the hood of a nearby cruiser. "Hostage safety first. Obliteration of the culprits second. This place burns down, we're going down with it." He pumped the shotgun. "Let's move in." Carver headed toward the hypermarket, having failed to realize he'd been talking to a smiling Drake copy the entire time.

The copy whispered into his earpiece, "We're moving in with Carver and friends. Get ready."

In the black Sedan, the cyborg Drake got the message through an internal receiver. He reached over to the video screen adjacent to his spot and opened a top down menu. Selected 'HELMET CAM.' A live private feed from an Afrókrema copy's helmet cam came up. The cyborg Drake leaned back and enjoyed the show.

Chapter 040
Assault on Santa's Village

Manharttigan Mall—West Wing
10:19 PM.

After some navigating through the employee-access halls, Damian entered the back of the electronics store he'd scouted earlier. The store was empty save for a gangster with a bad purple Mohawk protruding from his head standing guard out front, bopping his head to aggressive synth-pop blasting through the headset he wore around his neck.

Damian unplugged a CRT TV and lifted it off its display. He snuck up behind the gangster, raised it, smashed the screen down on the gangster's head, shattering his skull. *KRUNCH!* Crumpled in a flat heap on the floor.

Damian looked the corpse over and remembered Clark the Clerk's rant about how much safer CRT TVs were and had to stifle a laugh. "'Buy a CRT TV, save a life.'" He noticed an AKM assault rifle on the floor, gripped by the gangster's lifeless hand. "Ooh. What's that? Take it? Well," he said, snatching it up. "Don't mind if I do." He checked the chamber, then the magazine. Satisfied, he looked out into the hall. The river ran between the walkways, its Plexiglas bottom allowing its light through to illuminate the potted palm tree hall under it. The river water rushed over the waterfall overlooking the pool and the food court—the waterfall was edged on both sides by two sets of multi-parallel escalators; beyond that was Santa's village in plain sight. Drake sat in Santa's chair with a kid no older than six on his lap. Gangsters in elf costumes bordered the village and the food court, boxing in dozens of hostages huddled on the floor. Two scores of gangsters in their normal outdated studded leather and chains were dividing themselves amongst the four halls with heavy machine guns and other handheld artillery. They appeared to be setting up machine gun nests around Santa's village, covering every one of the four ways in. A bridge arching over the river just above the waterfall made for a sniper's paradise.

COBALT CHRISTMAS: A COBALT ROGUE STORY

It was too good to be true, and Damian knew it. He scanned the storefronts stretching across the other side of the river. Nobody in sight, but that didn't mean someone wasn't there.

Holding the AKM, Damian stepped out into the hall, glancing both ways. Hovercopter spotlights probed through the giant domes running across the high-ceilinged complex. Neon signs flickered above cracked or shattered window panes. The static hiss of the waterfall and the occasional shout or jeering laugh from the gangsters in Santa's village were the only sounds to betray the stillness for now. Damian couldn't even hear gunshots anymore and figured the confrontation at Mackey's Market had ended, for better or for worse.

It was too damn quiet.

Damian figured they already knew where he was and what he was doing. Drake's been one step ahead so far; why would that trend stop now? Someone was lurking in at least one of these stores. Maybe the Virtreality arcade behind him. Maybe the clothing store on the other side of the bridge, or the jewellery store beside it.

Had to chance it. He moved out, hunched over, head low, ducking behind potted palms and hologram platforms with the AKM aimed at the floor, keeping his footsteps light. Every object he reached, he pausebehindd just in case there was a sniper trained on him. If it was an amateur—and most of these guys were definitely amateurs—it might throw them off. More experienced snipers, however... that was a different story.

After passing three potted plants and a holographic projection of Santa Claus swinging his sack around; Damian was now beside his end of the bridge. He peered around the glass block parapet. Nothing on the bridge but a corpse splayed out on the floor, legs stretched in Damian's direction. An assailant in disguise? Damian squinted as he crept toward the body. At five feet, it became more than apparent that the body didn't have much of a head left. Definitely dead.

Fine by me, Damian thought as he set himself up in the center of the bridge, squatting behind the glass block parapet. The waterfall roared beneath him as neon water crashed into the pool. Damian peeked over the top of the wall. The other side was a crescent-shaped embankment lined with candy cane posts and gangsters involuntarily dressed in elf costumes. Drake himself was in a Santa suit, doing a bad Santa impression as he spoke to the terrified little girl on his knee.

Aria mentioned a bomb. Damian didn't need to think too hard to make an educated guess. He looked up at the digital clock that ringed the base of the giant Christmas tree—the countdown till Christmas—just a few more hours. Fitting readout for a powerful explosive—fitting hiding place for one, too. The lifeless nutcrackers guarded it with blank faces, bayonets raised high.

He saw Drake reach behind the chair and bring up a carton of eggnog. No logo; bland as hell, just like the ones in the convenience store. Despite the loudness of the waterfall, Damian could hear Drake ask the girl: "Hey, you want some eggnog?"

That motherfucker.

Damian ducked back down. Set the AKM on the floor. Shrugged off the RPG-7 and loaded it with a rocket-propelled grenade. He took a deep breath. Stood up straight, aimed the rocket at his enemy. "DRAKE!"

Startled, but not surprised, Drake glanced up at the bridge above the waterfall. As he did so, a dozen of his men pointed their guns at Damian. "I see you got my invitation. What're you gonna do with that RPG?'

"What do you think I'm going to do with it?"

"Bluff and nothing more."

"Yeah? You underestimate me, Drake."

"I'm not so sure about that. You shoot me with that thing, and this little girl dies. I know how cold and calculated you are. You're a mean son of a bitch. A nasty piece of work. But you ain't a child killer."

"There's a flaw in that little plan of yours, Drake."

"Oh, yeah?"

"I know where your bomb is."

"Oh, really?"

"You can't bullshit me anymore."

"Or *can* I?"

"I shoot this thing, you, me, and *everyone* here will die, and I won't have to live long enough to regret killing any of the kids you've got stashed around here. What the fuck do you think about *that*?"

It was enough to wipe the smug grin off Drake's face. He

rested the carton on the arm of his chair. "Okay, Blue. You win."

"Let the girl go."

Drake released the girl. She ran off the set into her crying mother's arms. Drake watched in disgust as the mother showered her daughter in kisses, crying tears of relief. "Fuck off."

The mother hurried off to join the rest of the hostages, holding her child close as two gang members kicked at her heels.

Drake looked up at Damian. "Happy?"

"I'm pretty fucking far from happy at this point in time."

"Shame. What're you gonna do now, huh? I have the bomb. I'm not at all surprised you figured out I had *two* of those things, let alone *where* it is. But... you have nothing but that rocket launcher."

"Wrong, dickhead. I have your balls *and* Fairman's in a sling."

"Hey! Shhh!" Drake glanced over at the hostages, then back at Damian. "Loose lips sink ships, goddamn it."

"Fuck your lips and fuck your ships," Damian snapped. "Release the fucking hostages."

"You're not making this very easy."

"Good. Release the hostages."

"I'm afraid I can't do that."

"You don't have a choice. I have the power to fuck up your entire operation."

"More than you already have, you mean?"

"Damn right."

"Okay," Drake said, smiling. He rose from his chair, stood there, puffed out his chest. He spread out his arms. "Then do it."

Damian's eyes narrowed. Motherfucker was calling his bluff.

"What're you waiting for, huh? Christmas? Ho-ho-ho."

Damian's face hardened.

Drake prodded his enemy a bit more. "In less than two hours, it won't make much of a difference anyhow. So do it. Blow us all up early. Incinerate us. Let's see if you can survive a *second* wave from one of these things. Somehow, I kinda doubt it. You're a termite. A fucking cockroach. Just when I think I killed you, you pop right back up. Although, something tells me... something in my gut tells me that not even *you* could live through another close-range detonation. It drained you of your powers."

Damian's jaw tightened.

"Oh, you thought I didn't notice you using all those guns? Usually you make your own weapons. Unless, of course, you can't." Drake laughed mockingly. "You ain't got shit on me!"

"Wrong, *suka*! I got a fucking *rocket launcher* on you!"

"And I got two dozen guns aimed at *you*!"

"Guns don't scare me!"

"Not even if you don't know where they all are?" Drake asked, grinning.

Damian looked at the men below. Then he glanced left and right. Nobody there. Behind him?

K-chak!

Yup. Kettle stood behind him with a shotgun muzzle brushing through the hair on the back of his head. Kettle was sure to stay out of the exhaust tube of Damian's rocket launcher to avoid the backblast. "Don't move, motherfucker."

Two gangsters on either side of the bridge surfaced from behind potted palms and flanked him, machine guns poised.

Damian sighed. Of course it was a trap. No surprise there.

"Did you really think you could sneak up on us in that shirt?" Kettle chortled.

Drake tilted his head, smirking. "Oops!"

Damian slowly brought the RPG-7 down, pointing the rocket grenade at the floor. He turned it sideways, gripping it by the handle. "Alright," he said. "It's going down." The men flanking him were too dumb to realize just how fucked they were. "Just like you."

KACHOWWW!

Both ends of the RPG-7 erupted. Backblast ripped through the gangster on his left, sent him flying while the rocket-propelled grenade pierced through the ribcage of the other man. The Rocket Man screeched through the air like a shooting star, ripped into the jewellery store. Boom.

The bark of the RPG stunned Kettle for just the right second. Damian whirled, swinging the empty rocket launcher into Kettle's arms, batting his shotgun out of his hands. Then he hit Kettle's jaw with the back end, sent him back a step, but far from reeling.

The men down below started firing. The ice block parapets screamed as bullets reduced them to a blizzard of crystalline chunks.

Fireballs turned the jewellery store inside out, scattering across the walkway and over Santa's village a shower of glass, gold chains, watches, rings, pendants... with a thunderous roar that shook the complex.

Damian and Kettle doubled over as bullets and glass filled the air. Damian heaved the rocket launcher into Kettle's stomach. Kettle grunted, kicked Damian in the shin. Damian almost fell, dropped the rocket launcher, which Kettle kicked to the end of the bridge. Damian grabbed onto one of Kettle's broad shoulders and drove his fist into his face. Blood erupted from the mercenary's nostrils and dribbled over his mouth, off his chin. Kettle's eyes burned furiously. Obviously a man of superior strength over that of a normal human being.

Still holding the eggnog carton, Drake hopped off the set and ran over to a cardboard footlocker. Opened it. Pulled out the magnum loaded with FATE rounds.

Damian and Kettle tackled each other, spinning in a flurry of glass block pieces and whistling lead.

Gangsters carrying heavy machine guns and artillery ascended the escalators, using the moving handrails as awkward support for their heavier weapons, chipping away at the bridge's ice block parapet, getting a better vantage point every second.

A bullet ripped through Damian's aloha shirt and grazed his hip. Like getting slashed by a red hot poker. Damian grimaced and caught Kettle's fist in his jaw. Staggered, head spinning from the impact, the satchel of rocket grenades at his waist throwing his balance even further. Kettle advanced, keeping his head low as bullets continued to fly over them. Grabbed the back of Damian's shirt, pulled him back, and punched him in the ribs once, twice, three times; then a *pop* against his knuckles and a pained snarl from Damian rewarded him.

Damian whirled, backhanded him across the face, clutching his broken rib. He kicked Kettle's left knee to the side, not at the right angle to break his leg. Damn. Kettle buckled all the same. Damian slugged him. Grabbed his head. Smashed his face against a jagged-topped row of partially shattered ice blocks. Did it again for good measure. "*Pizda!*" He threw him over the parapet into the water.

Kettle splashed into the river, legs kicking up as the current launched him off the ledge with the waterfall. Kettle screamed, plummeting to the pool below.

Drake unsympathetically watched Kettle flail his arms helplessly in the torrent right before it slammed his body against the bottom of the pool. The roar of the water almost completely drowned out the sound of Kettle's spine breaking against the concrete floor beneath the raging waters. Kettle never resurfaced, pinned to the bottom by the pressure. "Hm." Drake turned to Djimon standing on his left, one of the few gangsters who had successfully refused to put on an elf costume. "Care to live up to your name and ice that little shit up there?"

"How the fuck're we gonna get outta this, Drake?" Djimon fumed. "There's enough explosive here to wipe this whole fuckin' mall off the face o' the earth, man!"

"More than that—the whole *district*! It's all part of the plan, my man. All part of the plan."

"Yeah, I bet it is."

"Look, you wanna see your side bitch and your side daughter again, I suggest you cooperate, or I might have to cap both their asses right in front of you."

Djimon's eyes burned. He sucked in air, face contorted in a half-snarl.

"Here," Drake said, handing him the magnum. "Take this gun. It'll stop any Dehue dead in his tracks. Put a bullet through his skull. Then your troubles are over. You'll get to go back home with your side dishes and your main course intact and forget this whole thing ever happened. That's my Christmas present to you." Drake glanced up at the digital readout crowning the bottom of the tree. "Oh, but I suggest you hurry. We only have about forty minutes left."

Djimon looked up at the clock. "But it's only 10:30..."

"It'll take us about a half-hour to get to a safe distance on foot," Drake said. "Now will you kill that son of a bitch like I fucking asked?"

Djimon looked at the magnum in his hand, then at Drake. "So long as you keep your end of the deal... I won't kill you, too."

Drake scoffed. "You ain't in any position to threaten me, boy. Get going."

Djimon cocked back the magnum's hammer as he hopped off the stage in the direction of the escalators on the right side of the waterfall.

Five gangsters reached the center of the escalator with their armaments ready—three jogging up the down escalator, two standing on the up. They looked at the six on the ascending escalator parallel to them on the other side of the waterfall.

On the bridge, Damian crawled across the floor, still clutching his fractured rib. He grabbed Kettle's shotgun and checked the chamber. Loaded. He knew they were coming up. He kept himself doubled down as he dashed toward the burned-out jewellery shop. Reached the top of the multi-parallel escalators. The descending stairs were closest. He could hear their feet pounding up the steps, racing against the escalator's function.

Just a few feet from him was the RPG-7. He crawled out, snatched it up, and returned to his spot. Loaded a fresh rocket grenade into the tube. Lifted it on his shoulder. Jumped up, aiming at the first man he saw on the down escalator—the man stopped what he was doing when he saw the RPG pointed right at him, light machine gun rising in his hands, eyes going wide.

KAPOW!

As soon as he fired, Damian threw himself down to the floor to avoid a hail of bullets from the ascending escalator. Both parallel down escalators were blown out of commission, ripped in half by the rocket, its occupants sent sailing through the air in flaming tatters.

An elf with an M60 reached the top of the up escalator. Damian's shotgun tore his head off before he could even adjust his aim.

Damian dashed to the other end of the escalators, reached the top of the ascending staircase, where one final gunman with a light mortar in one hand and a case of three-inch bombs in the other. Damian dropped him with two blasts from his shotgun, almost failing to notice—

Djimon on the ground approaching the escalators in a semi-circle path toward a double-storey thrift store. Eyes on the top. He squinted, trying to make out the shapes behind the thick smoke column rising from the flaming down escalators. Magnum pointed at the ceiling. His view of the top of the staircase was becoming clearer with every step.

The steps carried the artillery man's corpse up to within Damian's reach. Damian noticed Djimon. Fired shotgun pelts at him. Not quite within range...

Djimon aimed the revolver. Fired. *KAPOW!*

The FATE round blew through the end of the rail and disintegrated the shotgun in Damian's hands, tearing skin from his fingers and burning a gash across his left forearm. Damian shouted in surprise and pain, diving to the floor, hugging his burning arm, clenching his bloodied fist. "FUCK!" he roared.

Elves were crossing the bridge with light machine guns. Damian heard them coming. He grabbed an M60 from a dead goon. Rolled into action away from the escalators, out of Djimon's view. Waited for them to surface from behind the middle where the bridge crested. Then he peppered them with the M60, dropping four out of six before one of his bullets hit one of their packs of three-inch bombs, igniting them.

BOOM!

The bridge crumbled under a blossoming fireball, raining bodies and debris into the water below and cleaving through one of the panes of glass that bordered the pool.

Damian looked at his burned hand. It trembled. Fingers red with blood and slightly melted flesh. "Motherfucker," he groaned. Every time he clenched his fingers, it felt like the skin on his knuckles would rip open again.

Down below, Drake roared in anger from the set. "Goddamn it! Fuck!" He growled at Djimon as he stabbed an index finger at the second level. "You're invincible, for fuck's sake! KILL HIM! KILL! KILL! *KIIIILLL!*"

Djimon jogged up the escalator, gripping the revolver with both hands.

Damian would have to stomach it for now. Luckily he was right-handed. He took the M60 in his right hand and supported the ammo belt across his left palm. He winced at even that. The gun was heavy—not *too* heavy, but awkward to carry singlehanded. He opened up on the escalator as he approached it, unleashing hell. Bullets raked across the railings, filling the air with sparks.

Djimon squatted against the railing, eyes reduced to narrow slits, revolver aimed at the top. The escalator slowly brought him up to what was sure to be instantaneous death...

Damian gritted his teeth. Every muscle in his body contorted; every vein bulged as he blasted the rails. Overkill would be an understatement when he was done with this fucker.

Djimon didn't waste a second. As soon as a blue hair entered his sights—

BLAM!

The magnum bucked in his hands. Another FATE round blew the railing to pieces as it shot its way to the top. The M60 fell apart in Damian's hand. The ammo belt recoiled against Damian's chest. The FATE round tore a huge chunk of flesh out of his right shoulder, taking the entire sleeve of his shirt with it.

Pain was excruciating. Damian hollered at the ceiling. It was feral, bloodcurdling. His entire right arm was already covered in blood that wouldn't stop gushing out. He scrambled for cover, burned left hand clutching his shoulder under the mushy, smoking dent where the rest of it used to be. "FFFFUUUUUCCKKK!"

Djimon reached the top and saw Damian running madly across a carpet of gold watches and rings and anklets, passing the blazing jewellery store. He raised the magnum, following his prey. Fired.

Damian leaped behind a pillar as the marble floor erupted under his feet. He sailed through the air, tumbled behind the pillar, shouting in agony. The bag full of rocket-grenades tangled themselves around his right leg.

Drake shouted from below, "You got three shots left!"

Djimon slowly approached the pillar. Bits of glass crunched under his boots.

Damian panted heavily, shuffling to the other side of the pillar, watching Djimon's reflection in a cracked pane of glass in the thrift store's front. Right arm had gone cold. Left arm hurt like hell, and the skin was warped from the heat. But he could still move that one. Right arm was almost completely useless. "Fuck. Fuck." Damian searched himself for any guns. Found one tucked in his sock. Hard to tell anymore; he'd been wearing some of these weapons for so long he'd gotten used to them being there. He drew the pistol from his sock, gripped it tightly in his slippery left hand. Every movement hurt. He fired two shots around the pillar.

Djimon leaped back as a Rolex exploded and the now broken links from a gold chain flew up into the air. He fired another shot through the pillar.

The bullet came out the other side. Grazed Damian's head. Disintegrated a window pane across the walkway. Another inch and he would've been dead.

"Two shots, asshole," Drake said. "Stop dickin' around! Fucking *kill* him!"

"I'm workin' on it!"

"Don't you screw this up."

Djimon's patience had worn out. He shouted over the parapet, "Shut the fuck up, you fuckin' goddamn two-bit immortal cracker-jack piece-o'-shit motherfuckin' cockeyed shit-suckin' jive-ass bitch! I said I'm fuckin' on the motherfucker! Fuck off!"

Despite the intense pain, Damian laughed at that one. He slid up the pillar to his feet. Fired another shot around the pillar. Backed toward the storefront, popping away at Djimon, who retreated, took cover behind the escalator railing. Damian stumbled through the window frame into the thrift store, pushing over a mannequin on display, boots crushing glass shards into sparkling dust. He fired another shot at the railing. Tripped. Fell on his front. Shoulder blazed. He grunted, bit his bottom lip. Stopped himself from screaming. Fired another round over the mannequin as he crawled around a shelf lined with dusty used books.

No sense wasting a limited, rare type of ammunition on blind return fire. Djimon drew a backup pistol and fired blind, shooting out all the windows. His target had disappeared behind the bookshelf. "Shit. He's in the thrift store!"

Exasperated, Drake clapped his hands. "Boys! Gather round! Just you Campturn guys; if you're one o' mine, you stay where you are."

One of the gangsters asked, "What about the hostages?"

"Fuck the hostages. My boys'll deal with 'em. I want that little shit's head on a pike. Come on, get over here! Get over here. Come on." He waited until the remaining elves left the mercenaries to their posts around the food court and gathered on the set. Drake looked them over, counting twelve in all. "That's it? Only twelve?"

"The rest of us are guardin' the halls, man."

"Your mercs could help us out."

"No, it's fine, whatever. You guys get in that thrift store and weed that motherfucker out. Kill him if you have to. If you can, get 'im alive. If that's possible."

"*Is* it possible?"

Drake shrugged. "Dunno. Never tried to catch him alive before. Should be an interesting experience. Now, you cocksuckers, get in there and bring me that fucker alive and barely conscious, or just bring me his head. Whichever works! I don't care at this point! Christ." Hands akimbo, he looked at them impatiently as they all stared at him, obviously waiting for a follow-up of some kind. "*GO*, you fucking idiots! Go get him!"

The gangsters rushed off the set and charged toward the main floor entrance below Djimon.

Chapter 041
Shell Shock!

A Few Blocks Uptown

10:33 PM.

The streets were utter chaos. Jenny had to push her way through a sea of panicking civilians and law enforcement desperate to maintain peace and order without much success. People were scared for their loved ones, pushing forward against the barricades like swarms of shoppers waiting for the stores to open on Black Friday morning. News teams that decided to play it safer than other channels reported on the panic riots swallowing up the streets of downtown Cryo City—behind police lines, naturally, to avoid becoming casualties should things get violent.

Jenny slipped into an alley and found a stairway leading down into a cellar with a steel door. She knew it wasn't a cellar—it was one of Cannertunken's secret underground arms depots. She didn't have the key card or the passcode. "Sorry, Tunk." She kicked the door down. Ten inches of solid steel slammed onto the concrete floor. She followed it inside the dark room and lit a flame on the tip of her thumb to light her way. She scanned the gun racks and ammo shelves. Once she got a good bearing of her surroundings, she shook the flame off her hand. Didn't need too much considering the four pistols she had tucked in the waistband of her pants from the trunk of the car. Grabbed two Mini-Uzi submachine guns with shoulder straps and draped them over each arm; snatched up six box magazines and stuffed them in her coat. Then she spotted a Browning M1919A4 machine gun mounted on a bipod on a nearby table with a compatible belt of ammunition draped underneath it. *Perfect.*

She emerged from the depot and pulled the steel door back up, propped it against the door frame as best she could. No normal person would be able to push it down too easily, and she suspected Cannertunken didn't let too many people in to this particular secret, but it was better to be safe than sorry.

COBALT CHRISTMAS: A COBALT ROGUE STORY

Now to get these weapons into the mall... but how? The streets were crawling with the law—and far too many civvies.

Think, goddamn it, she thought, looking around as she moved into the middle of the city block with the Browning in her hands and the ammo belt slung around the back of her neck like a scarf. She glanced up at the night sky. The snow assaulted the streets in thick sheets. She reached a crossroad in the alleys and cut a right, jogging in the direction of the mall. Her boots splashed through wet patches of winter sludge. A dog barked behind a tall wooden fence covered in vulgar graffiti as she passed it. Her breath plumed in front of her face as she made for the street.

And stopped short of the final passageway. She could see people rioting in the street, failing to notice her, too focused on trying to overwhelm the cops. She looked at the building on her left. She recognized a small logo beyond the NO TRESSPASSING sign: CHARLIE'S SNOW REMOVAL. A garage. Looked like it'd been a fire hall at some point before it was converted into a snow removal service depot.

Perfect! She followed the back of the building until she found a door with a glass panel, which she punched in. Reached through the opening and unlocked the door. Let herself in. The garage was pitch black, prompting her to light up another thumb-flame to guide her through the blackness. A small office with glass partitions all around. A key rack by the door. She took key #3 and exited the office, entering the garage. Found three winter service vehicles parked alongside each other. She hit the unlock function on the keypad, listening through the muffled chaos outside. Heard a set of doors click two trucks down, the furthest one away. Of course they would park in order of their numbers. She went over to the third truck on the other side and climbed into the cab. Set the Browning on the passenger seat, barrel on the dash. Shut the door and went around to the driver side. Hopped in and started it up. She remotely opened the garage door. The shutters rose like a stage curtain, revealing a scene of chaos and sheer panic.

She punched the horn, startling the crowd, easing her foot down on the gas. The truck taxied out of the garage, amber lights flashing. People cleared a path. Not fast enough. "Come on!" Jenny shouted, slamming the horn in frustration. "Move it! Get outta the way! Emergency services comin' through!"

COBALT CHRISTMAS: A COBALT ROGUE STORY

Somebody threw a brick over the plow frame into the windshield, splintering it.

"Motherfucker," Jenny hissed, honking the horn. The second she had the whole truck out of the garage, she remotely closed the shutters behind her. A man with a baseball bat hopped onto her side of the truck, smacked his bat against the door, shouting at her. He smashed the window.

Jenny shielded her face from flying glass. Temper rising. The man shoved his bat inside, trying to hit her. She grabbed the bat, pulled it in, shoved it into the man's face, breaking his nose. The man pivoted off the foothold. She honked the horn again, moving at a snail's pace toward the police barrier. Another man clambered up to the window with a knife. "Get out, bitch! This is *my* truck now!"

"Fuck you, cunt!" Jenny nailed him in the face with the business end of the bat. Sent him flying into the crowd.

The passenger window shattered. Jenny turned just as someone's arm reached for the Browning. She brought the bat down on the intruder's elbow, making them yowl in pain. The arm retreated. She heaved an impatient sigh. "I hate this city." She honked the horn again. The police barricade was just a few yards ahead. Civilians made a greater effort to get out of her way as the cops took action, drawing their pistols at the approaching truck. "Ah, shit," she said. Honked again. "Outta the way!"

The cops started firing. The shrieking civvies dispersed. Jenny ducked behind the wheel as bullets punched little stars across the windshield. "For Christ's sake! I'm on your side, you assholes!" The gunfire didn't let up. *Well, of course it didn't.* She floored the gas. Now it was the cops' turn to disperse. The truck blew through the barricade, swiping two cruisers aside. News reporters behind the barricade scattered as the truck came bearing down on them. The gunfire didn't let up. Bullets chased the truck, pinging against the chassis. Jenny looked over the steering wheel just as she rear-ended a news van, sent it slewing across the ice-slicked sidewalk and smashing into a car parked on the curb. "Oops."

Manharttigan Mall

Carver led the team out of Mackey's Market into the hall. They marched toward Santa's village. Stepped over a field of corpses. Went around the flaming helicopter wreck. Separated—

some went down the escalators and handicap ramps into the lower level while the rest stayed on the main floor. Carver said into his earpiece, "Advance, advance... four hundred yards away from Santa's village."

West Wing

The gangsters had set up shop behind an 'ice castle' made up of paper snowflake banners and glass block parapets, guarded by a lifeless snowman statue. A machine gun nest and a handheld mortar fit for trench warfare manned by just seven elves. They stayed low, keeping an eye on the halls. They could see the cops filing toward them, hiding behind concrete pillars, independent kiosks lining the middle of the hall, and inside storefronts on the sides, advancing steadily. Almost *too* quickly.

The machine gunners were ready. Two gangsters prepared the mortar—one held the Stokes mortar while the other cradled a three-inch bomb.

One of the elves screeched, "Attack!"

The machine gunners hosed the cops. Streams of hot lead levelled potted palms, chopped down Christmas trees, raked across the floor in an unfocused frenzy. Pillars cratered. Windows crashed to the floor, some with police bodies pivoting through them.

The first three-inch bomb dropped into the Stokes' muzzle. Popped out a second later, whistled as it traced an arc over the gap, coming down, down...

KABOOM!

A magazine stand beside a group of tactical units blew apart, propelled the screaming units through the air.

"Contact! Contact!" a Drake copy shouted, staying in character. "It's show time, boys an' girls!"

The cops took cover behind pillars and an elevated platform. Returned fire as another three-inch bomb destroyed the front end of a cell phone shop and a pair of plainclothes cops. Machine-gunfire from the ice castle ripped a table covered in homemade blankets to shreds. The infiltration team focused their fusillade on the ice castle. A machine gunner's brain and skull fragments splattered the six-foot snowman behind him. A three-inch bomb blasted a floating holographic platform out of the air, brought it crashing down on a trio of Drake clones. A dying cop pulled a potted palm to the floor with him.   Another cop rolled down the stairs, back behind the embankment.   The embankment itself erupted in a ball of fire, showering the surrounding area in a hail of flaming debris.

A regular police officer huddled behind the embankment shielded himself with his arm as hot debris pelted him. He shouted into his radio, "We're gettin' killed out in the west wing!" He flinched as a concrete pillar just a few yards behind the embankment was reduced to dust and flying chunks.

Aria emerged from behind the ice castle with an AA-12 automatic shotgun in each hand. She scaled the back of the castle, reached the top. Blinked as the snowman's head exploded into plastic fragments. Toothpick in her mouth, pitch black eyes fixed on the backs of the remaining six elves operating the mortar and the machine guns.   Without so much as a cold-hearted quip, she unleashed an explosive barrage into the group. Ripped them and the ice block parapet to pieces. Ignited the rest of the bombs, which launched the entire front half of the castle into the ceiling in gouts of fire and shrapnel. She leaped back behind the castle to avoid the searing gales that blew the snowman and the rest of the castle to pieces.

Before the cops knew what happened, she was gone.

Chapter 042
Jenny's Foe Removal Service

10:46 PM.

Jenny stole a fleeting glance into the alley she'd parked the car in and saw Molly looking out from the back seat for a split second. *Good girl,* she thought as she reached the street that edged the shopping mall's parking lot. The Sedan was still parked there. She aimed for it.

Inside the Sedan, Cyborg Drake looked out the window at the incoming truck. "Jesus Christ! What the—"

Jenny floored the gas right before the truck's blade hit the car and sent it flipping over the sidewalk into the parking lot. Like a rolled dice, the Sedan somersaulted across a row of cars left in their parking spaces before careening into the driveway. Jenny pushed the truck over the lawn, edging the parking lot, front blade tearing the bumpers off the cars. Bumping over the sidewalk, slewing into the driveway. She hit the Sedan again. This time it didn't flip. The blade splintered from the impact and the Sedan broke through it. Pinned against the front of the truck, its tires squealing across the pavement as the truck pushed it down the driveway.

"WHOOO!" Jenny hollered. "Gotcha!"

Police, saved civilians, firefighters, and paramedics alike stopped what they were doing in the Mackey's Market parking lot to watch the spectacle Jenny had created. They were stunned.

Jenny ducked as she sent the truck barrelling through the main entrance. Glass panes shattered as the metal frames came apart like matchsticks against the rampaging vehicle. The Sedan was still stuck to the front, dragged across the hallway floor through a blanket of corpses and debris. Jenny wasn't concerned about the flaming helicopter wreck ahead. She plowed through it. A sheet of metal ripped through the passenger side of the windshield and sheared through the headrest. Jenny blinked as she pushed the truck through the blazing hull. Lost the rearview mirrors on both doors.

Up ahead, Carver and the cops whirled around and looked at

the truck, now covered in a sheet of fire, as it hurtled toward the first set of escalators in shock. The Drake copies perforated the cab.

Jenny kept her head low, shooting down the handicap ramp. The front of the pinned Sedan sliced through the glass block parapet along the side of the ramp, spilling a cascade of frosted glass into the empty lane below. She reached the bottom of the ramp. Crossed the gap. Went up the second ramp. A hailstorm of lead pelted the truck from every side. She vaulted over the top of the ramp, now following the river toward Santa's village. Jenny laughed maniacally.

Drake heard it before he saw it. Still standing in front of Santa's chair, he looked up as the snow removal truck ripped through the railings at the top and sailed over the multi-parallel escalators at an awkward, sideways angle. A flurry of questions filled his head as he watched the truck and the Sedan rotate through the smoke-filled air, mainly: "What the actual *fuck*?"

KSSSSHHH!

The truck landed on its side, bounced back onto its wheels, rocking violently, axels screeching. The Sedan tumbled across the floor and blew through the front of the thrift store. The truck zigzagged toward the set. Drake screamed and dived into the pool as the truck smashed through candy cane posts and a pair of nutcrackers, sent one of them through another pane of glass. Broke the base of the pool, unleashing water onto the floor. Grinded through the set, crushing gift-wrapped boxes and a cardboard cut-out of a cartoon elf; finally slowing down in its violent ascension to the throne. The bumper touched the arm of the chair. The chair teetered onto its side. The engine block burst into flames under the massive, towering Christmas tree. The tree's branches and ornaments caught fire.

Drake jumped out of the water, gasping for air, looking at the truck lodged in the demolished stage in disbelief. "What the hell is going on?"

A dozen and a half mercenaries stationed on the pool's border inched toward the wreck.

Suddenly the passenger door flew open. Jenny, perched on the side of the passenger seat, sprayed them with the Browning, able to hold the barrel without her hand getting burned. The perks of being a pyrokinetic.

COBALT CHRISTMAS: A COBALT ROGUE STORY

Drake fell back underwater as Jenny cut his men in half. Every remaining window pane surrounding the pool spilled into the water. The hostages beyond the pool screamed in terror at the sudden explosion of violence near them. Bullets whistled high above them. Overhead Christmas banners came apart and fell into the crowd. Chaos erupted. They all scrambled for cover. Only a small handful of mercs left available to try and control them to no avail. They got trampled under the stampede as the hostages made their way up the handicap ramp in the direction of Mackey's Market. These people knew full well it was their best chance to get out without confronting further resistance.

And they were right. They ran into Carver and his group, including the Drake copies, all of whom helped evacuate the area in a more orderly fashion.

Once she'd killed the poolside mercenaries, Jenny jumped out onto the destroyed set with the Browning.

Drake drew a pistol and fired at her from the pool, screaming with rage.

Presents exploded around her. Jenny ducked behind a candy cane post and let it absorb Drake's bullets. Waited for a break in his fire, then stepped out and nailed him to the pool floor with the Browning until the belt ran out. She discarded the machine gun, watching the water turn crimson from the overabundant gore. She shrugged the straps off her shoulders. The Mini-Uzis slipped into her hands.

There was still gunfire to be heard on the other side of the tree. She leaped off the set into the vacated food court and ran around the tree. A mercenary popped up from a nearby booth and opened fire with his AK. She bobbed her head down as the merc's fire pursued her, streaking across a cardboard house. She returned fire, splintering the table, killing the merc behind it. She looked around, checking every food counter for hidden enemies.

Drake rose up from the pool, his face a distorted nightmare of blind, demonic rage. A merc corpse floated on the water in front of him. He took the man's assault rifle and kicked the body out of his way. It floated toward the leak, which was getting bigger by the minute. He trudged through the knee-deep water toward the food court. Hopped up onto the ledge. It only took him a second to spot Jenny on the other side of the court by a sub counter, looking over it for more of his goons. He hissed through gnashed teeth, "Foxy bitch." Opened fire.

A startled Jenny hit the floor as Drake's bullets skipped across tabletops toward her. The sub shop's neon sign exploded above her. She rolled under a booth, gripping the Mini-Uzis. She peeked around the booth. Drake spotted her and fired again. She retreated as his bullets chewed up the back of the booth. "Thought I killed you already..."

A merc nimbly hopped over a Chinese food counter. Light on his feet. He drew a pair of pistols from his belt, eyes fixed on Jenny's back. He crept toward her, taking aim—"

BRRRAAPPP!

Jenny gasped. Adjusted her aim for the other side of the tree and saw Aria standing by a *Bill's Burgers* counter with a blazing submachine gun. Jenny whirled to see the dual-wielding merc just a few feet behind her.

Drake adjusted his aim toward Aria. "Goddamn bitches!" He hit Aria with a barrage, slamming her into the counter.

Jenny leaped up from her cover and riddled Drake with her Mini-Uzis, pushing him back into the pool. She rushed toward her sister. "Aria! You okay?"

"Ow," she groaned, leaning against the counter. Her healing factor pushed Drake's bullets out of her torso. She scowled at her younger sister. "You coulda been a little faster, Sis. Save me the stomach ache."

Jenny chuckled. Shrugged. "Sorry. Thanks for the save."

"Nobody kills you but me," Aria said with a wink and a smile.

"Now why would you wanna do that?"

"Dunno. I'm sure you'll give me a reason eventually. Speaking of which, what'd you do with that girl? Molly?"

"She's in the car."

Aria fixed her with a stern look. "*Why* would you do that?"

"Hey, don't give me that. It cost me a whole hundred dollars, man."

"A hundred dollars?"

"Told her I'd take it back if she left the car."

"Okay, and?"

Jenny hesitated. "I also, uh... kinda-sorta threatened to put her in a sweat shop and make coats in my basement until she died of malnourishment."

Even Aria was surprised by that one. "*Jesus*, Sis. Why don't you stick a loaded shotgun in the poor kid's face while you're at it?"

"I'll admit it wasn't my finest moment..."

"You've been listenin' to your boyfriend too much. I think you could use a break."

"That's what he said." Jenny offered her a hand. Aria took it and let her sister heave her to her feet. Jenny asked, "You know where Damian is?"

"No idea. Ain't seen him for about an hour now. I know he ain't dead, though. Drake's still pissed."

"Drake? That's the guy I just shot, right?"

"He'll be back. Trust me."

"That's the immortal, right?"

"Right."

"What a pain in the ass."

"I know, right?"

Jenny looked around the empty central area. Nothing but bodies and debris. "Now, where do you think my boyfriend is?"

They heard explosions coming from the south wing beyond the food court. "There?" Jenny asked.

Aria shook her head. "That would probably be the last of the elves defending Santa's village from the law."

"Oh." Jenny looked at the blacked-out thrift store. Right on cue, she heard gunshots and saw muzzle flashes briefly light up the interior of the clothing section. "How 'bout that?"

Aria saw the muzzle flashes, too. "A gunfight in the dark." She scoffed. "Sure fits his style, doesn't it?"

Chapter 043
Divine Intervention

10:48 PM.

In the clothing section of the thrift store, Damian emptied his backup pistol into an elf's torso, saving the last bullet for the gangster's face. As the elf collapsed, Damian switched out his empty pistol for the MAC-11 in the gangster's hand. He wouldn't need it anymore.

Then he heard the ruckus outside as Jenny made her big entrance. He heard a thunderous *CRASH* and peered through the storefront windows right before Cyborg Drake's Sedan cartwheeled through the windows and flipped through two aisles, flattening shelves, flinging merchandise everywhere.

Scared the Christ out of him. *"Blyat!"*

He saw beams of light probing the dark aisles deeper in the store. Counted maybe nine or ten of them. At least. And they were all alarmed by the racket.

I see going downstairs was a bad idea. He winced as he checked the ammo capacity in his newly acquired MAC-11 with his right hand. He could barely lift his damn arm. Left hand was the best way to go.

He switched aisles, hiding behind a row of shelved footwear of all kinds as the other gangsters converged on the clothing section. Like insects to a flame. Damian crept down the shoe aisle. Paused as an elf walked into his view on the other side of the shelf. Waited until the elf passed him to join the other gangsters as they checked out the car wreck and the body Damian left.

"That bastard got Mickey!"

"Fuck! Spread out an' find 'im!"

Gunfire erupted outside. The gangsters looked out, watching as Jenny mowed down the mercs guarding the pool. Damian couldn't see anything from his point of view, and assumed it was Aria hard at work thinning out the herd.

Damian slinked out of the aisle. Back to the staircase in the middle of the store, climbed the stairs to the second floor. A minute later, an elf trotted up the stairs with a flashlight and a pistol. Damian quietly set the MAC-11 on the rim of a trash can and waited by the entrance. Left hand trembled as it drew his fighting knife out of his belt sheath. Twelve inches of serrated steel gleamed in the darkness, reflecting the pink light from an emergency exit sign hanging from the other side of the floor.

The punk reached the top and caught Damian's blade in his stomach. He wheezed, doubling over the hilt as Damian stepped into view, still gripping the knife. The punk dropped his pistol on the floor. Damian gave the punk a cold, empty look before kicking him back down the stairs. The punk landed flat on his back at the bottom, loud enough for the whole store to hear it even with the gunfight continuing outside.

The racket didn't go unnoticed. Djimon emerged from behind a used winter wear shelf and fired his backup at the figure near the stairs. Damian flinched, dropping his knife. "Shit!" Another gunshot. Damian snatched the MAC-11 and fled the scene, returning fire, burning through a whole line of used goods near Djimon, who kept firing after him, blowing up a pair of lamps Damian zipped past.

Click-click!

Djimon swore and retreated behind the shelves to reload.

Damian returned from behind the lamps, shooting at Djimon's shelf, blowing it to splinters. Djimon crawled across the floor. Smacked a magazine home. Held the gun over the shelf and fired back. Damian didn't bother trying to dodge Djimon's blind retaliation. He sprayed the whole area with a merciless stream of lead, destroying the shelves and the sportswear and hockey equipment lining the wall in the back. "Fucker!" Damian shouted. "How's this? And this?"

The MAC-11 ran dry. Damian tossed it down the stairs. He looked down the tunnel and saw a small group of shadows surround the body at the bottom. He picked up the punk's gun and unshouldered the sack of rocket-grenades. Placed it on the floor.

Djimon stood up behind a decimated winter coat and fired, blowing out the electric STAIRS sign above Damian's head.

Damian whirled and replied with a three-round beat, forcing Djimon back down to cover. Damian looked back at the first floor.

COBALT CHRISTMAS: A COBALT ROGUE STORY

The shadows moved erratically as the gangsters took position. Damian tucked the pistol under his right arm. Squatted next to the rocket-grenades. Someone down below opened up on him, prompting him to lean further back. Someone started to ascend. Damian stopped them with two well-placed shots.

He picked up the bag. Tossed it down the stairs. Aimed his pistol at the bag.

Outside by the food court, Jenny and Aria looked at the thrift store.

"A gunfight in the dark." Aria scoffed. "Sure fits his style, doesn't it?"

Damian shot the bag and dived in the opposite direction.
KABOOM!
A fleeting flash. No more goons. No more stairs. The floor bulged upward under his feet. The stairwell belched flames, launching Damian across several aisles, sailing over the shelves, screaming as he joined the flock of flying items for sale, knowing full well the landing was going to hurt like a bitch. The second floor groaned as it rose upward; the ceramic tiles leaped into the ceiling, as did the shelves and a multitude of used goods. Flames swelled across the first floor. The entire storefront disintegrated into billions of flaming particles as fireballs rolled out from both sides. The Sedan's fuel tank ignited in the firestorm.

Jenny and Aria ducked behind a pillar as the thrift store vomited its burning merchandise across the gap between them. As the flames died down, the sisters looked out at the gutted thrift store.

"Yep," Jenny said, "it sure does..."

Damian, a curled-up projectile, smashed through a partition window and rolled across the floor of the store manager's empty office. Gnashed his teeth and groaned as glass shards bit into his arms and legs. Fresh wave of pain blazed from his shoulder wound. Almost passed out. Even the floor seemed like the most comfortable thing in the world right now.

Couldn't give Drake the satisfaction.

He pushed himself up off the floor.

COBALT CHRISTMAS: A COBALT ROGUE STORY

*

Flames from the snow removal wreck snaked up the side of the Christmas tree.

"You ready?" Aria asked.

Jenny reloaded her Mini-Uzis. "Am now."

"Let's go."

KSSSSSSSHHHH!

The mall drowned in an ear-splitting screech of glass breaking. The girls stopped abruptly. Looked up as the glass dome above the Christmas tree's gold neon star came crashing down. Two dozen Afrókrema elites swooped in like acrobats on cables, abseiling down the pillars over a shimmering blanket of burst window panes that sprinkled the giant tree in pixie dust. A billion tiny glass daggers crashed against the floor, but by then the sisters had already taken cover behind the pillars.

"Afrókrema *again*?" Jenny couldn't believe it. "They got reinstated?"

"You could say that," Aria said as she began to realize just how much information Damian kept from her.

"But those guys are assholes!"

"You can say that again." Aria drew an anti-tank rifle from her left arm.

Jenny looked at her. "Hey, wait a second. They might be bastards, but since when were they bad guys?"

"Since they orchestrated this whole thing?" Aria said.

Jenny blinked. Her face a mixture of confusion and disbelief. "*Whaaaaaat?*"

"Tell ya later. Long story short: these guys are the bad guys. So start shooting them before they shoot you!" Aria stepped out from behind the pillar and started picking them off with her anti-tank rifle. One shot reduced a Drake copy to a crimson splatter of limbs and gore.

Jenny came out of her hiding spot and strafed the descending army with her Mini-Uzis. Riddled bodies, severed a few cables; the ones whose lines were cut dropped like ragdolls into webs of Christmas lights entangled around the tree or, if they were *really* unlucky, they fell straight down into food court far below, uninterrupted by obstacles.

Deafening white noise roar as the elites returned fire, forcing

Jenny to retreat out of necessity. Aria retreated out of preference. No one likes to get shot, healing factor or no healing factor. Bullets stitched across the floor around them. The pillars pocked, cracked, cratered; reduced to flying chunks of concrete as a dozen P90s ripped into them.

Aria tossed a high-impact flash grenade into the open. *POP!* It filled the centre with a flash of blinding sunlight, disorienting the Drake copies as their eyes failed them and finding a safe place to land became their top priority.

"Let's go!" Aria yelled. She dashed toward the thrift store, firing her anti-tank rifle as if it were just a regular shotgun, decimating heads with impossible aim.

Jenny followed, spraying the elites with dual-fired lead.

Drake emerged from the other side of the pool, glass crunching under his soggy boots. One hand held the eggnog carton, the other held up the AKM which he fired at Jenny.

Jenny ducked as Drake's bullets whistled over her head and zipped through her hair, barely missing her head. She dived behind a pillar.

Aria whirled, anti-tank rifle aimed at him. Hesitated. He stood in front of the bomb concealed in the base of the tree. *Son of a bitch.*

Drake turned his AKM on her. Hit her with a five-round burst. Launched a grenade from the under-barrel launcher.

Aria grunted as she jack-knifed against the wall, knocking over a gumball machine next to a row of candy dispensers.

Jenny stayed behind the pillar as the copies continued their assault. A few of them touched down and unhooked their lines. They'd be overwhelming them in seconds. She stayed in their blind spot as she rounded the pillar and perforated Drake, sent him staggering backwards through the thrift store. "Fucker!" Drake cried out as the raging flames greedily consumed him. There was some satisfaction to be had with seeing that, even if she knew he was far from dead...

Aria slid down the wall smeared with her blood as the gaping hole in her stomach closed up. She couldn't breathe just yet.

Jenny looked at her with concern. Reloaded her guns. "You good?"

The wound sealed itself shut. Nothing but skin now. By this

point, her shirt had been reduced to scanty tatters. "I'm good," she said, getting back up.

A Drake clone rounded the corner the girls had passed. Raised his shotgun. Fired.

BLAM!

The sisters jumped, startled, as the candy dispensers exploded, rainbow pieces filled the air.

Jenny picked up the gumball machine and hurled it like a spear at the Drake copy. Glass container burst against his half-face battle mask and visor, scattering gumballs. His head snapped back. His body followed his head, flying several feet.

"Jenny."

Jenny turned back to Aria. "What?"

"Defense-offense." Aria held up a riot shield.

"Gotcha."

"You're gonna need a better weapon. Here." Aria handed her an FN Minimi with a six-foot ammo belt.

"Ooh." Jenny slung her Mini-Uzis on her shoulders in favour of Aria's weapon. She grabbed it and swung the ammo belt so that it coiled around her arm. She smiled as she tested its balance in her hand. "I like it."

"Good." Aria looked over at the copy Jenny had downed with the gumball machine. He was getting back up. "What the hell?"

Jenny turned and cut him back down to size. "Pretty sure these assholes are copies."

"Of what?" Beat. "Of *Drake*?"

"Yeah," Jenny said.

"But how would you know that?"

"Damian was smart enough to bring one of the fucker's feet home."

"And?"

"They multiplied. *Big* time. By the time I got back, there was an army of them in the fucking backyard! Imagine a lumberyard, but instead of wood, it's severed limbs from all the copies to create *more copies*."

"That's fucked up," Aria said.

"Yeah, I was thinking the same thing."

"Alright. Get behind me." Aria huddled behind her shield. "You got armour-piercing rounds on that belt. Might not kill the bastards, but the least we can for 'em do is make it hurt like a son of a bitch!"

A score of Drake copies bounded over the pool's fractured ledge on one side of the tree, while on the other side, seven or eight more were coming out of the food court, P90s raging.

Jenny carried the gun behind her sister and squatted. The two of them stepped out in the open, letting the shield absorb the majority of the approaching copies' onslaught. A grenade exploded a few feet away. The shield took the shrapnel spray, too. No problem.

Jenny straightened up and fired the Minimi over the shield, razing a few copies to the floor before ducking behind her sister again.

They backed toward the thrift store.

The copies advanced, cursing and swearing and shooting.

Fire spread around the lower branches of the Christmas tree and started to work their way up. Ornaments popped and melted in the heat.

Aria pushed against the shield, fighting against the copies' violent pushing and shoving.

Jenny fired over the shield again. Took out three others. Ducked.

A potted palm tree disintegrated behind the sisters as bullets strafed the wall.

Jenny resurfaced again, spitting a stream of lead through five others, shredding their legs out from under them. Relishing their screams as she retreated once again.

Aria found that standing up to their retaliations was like holding up a wooden board against harsh tsunami gales.

The thrift store was right behind them now. With a wave of her hand, Jenny commanded the flames in the displays to clear a path for them, and they bent to her pyrokinetic will. "We're almost there!"

The Drake army had doubled since the beginning of their advance. They were passing the escalators.

Aria strained against the barrage, struggling to keep the shield from flipping any which way that would make them vulnerable even for a second.

Jenny mowed down the whole front line. Slowed them down,

and made them angrier. She ducked inside the thrift store. "Watch your step."

Aria followed her, keeping the shield raised as they headed for the stairs—only to find a hollow frame where the stairs used to be.

The Drake copies stopped shooting, having lost their prey in the burning thrift store. They split up: half of them scaled what remained of the escalators while the rest of them charged directly toward the store.

Aria threw the shield out of the store like a ninja star, but didn't see it slice through a row of stomachs outside. She turned and jumped through the gaping hole in the ceiling to the second floor. "Come on, Sis!"

Jenny spotted something in her peripheral. The car wreck. A huge, hulking, metallic beast rose up from the Sedan's skeletal remains, itself engulfed in a sheet of red flames, reflecting off its chromed skull. Holographic image of Drake's sadistic grin flickered in the orange-saturated shadows.

Jenny just about dropped her weapon. Instead she opened fire. Her bullets bounced right off it. "Shit!"

Cyborg Drake's prosthetic right hand transformed into a minigun, which started to rotate...

Aria shouted from above, "Jenny! Hurry up!"

Jenny didn't argue. She leaped off the ground as her enemy's minigun roared. Bullets tore down the last of the stairs below her feet. She landed on the second floor next to her sister and bounded down the aisles with her. "There's some kinda cyborg down there!"

"Seen a few of 'em already. Did he have a laser beam?"

"Laser beam? Not that I could see. He was scary-lookin', though!"

"That's a damn shame," Aria said humorously. "Why do deadly cyborg soldiers always have to look so damn terrifying?"

BANG!

A pistol's report stopped them cold.

"Hold it, bitches!" Djimon shouted from behind a fallen shelf, keeping his pistol trained on them. "Not another move..."

The sisters turned to face him. "We don't have time for this," Aria said.

"Agreed," Jenny said.

"I don't give a fuckin' shit if you do or don't. You think *I* wanna be here? Cuz I don't. Drop your guns."

"Why? You're gonna shoot us anyway," Jenny replied. She squinted, trying to get a good look at him. It was a little too dark to make out his features, and he was black, so that made it a bit harder, and she felt horrible for thinking that his skin colour could be a key factor in why making out his most basic facial features was so difficult. She hadn't found Djimon Ice yet. Figured she'd take a shot in the dark. "Look pal, I got a little girl waiting for me to take her dad home from all this. Either shoot us or get the fuck outta my way."

"Got a kid myself. Don't make me no difference at this point in time. We got an hour, maybe less. Then we all die."

Jenny and Aria exchanged looks. Jenny asked him, "Your kid's name... wouldn't happen to be Molly, would it?"

The gunman didn't say anything for a moment. Then he said, "How do you...?"

"AHA!" Jenny cheered. "Fuckin' *aced* it! Yeah! *YEAH*!"

Aria cocked an eyebrow. "What's your deal?"

Jenny asked him, "You're Djimon Ice, right? *Right*?"

"Uh... yeah," Djimon said. "What's it to ya?"

"We got your kid, dude. *DUH*!"

"Bullshit. Drake has my kid. *And* her mom."

"Uh," Aria said, "actually, her mom's dead. But the kid's okay." She nervously asked her sister, "Right? She *is* alive, right?"

"Yeah, she's fine. She's in the car, like I said. Like, three minutes ago."

"I forgot."

"How?"

"A lot's happened since then."

"Wait, wait, wait," Djimon said. "You're sayin' her mom's dead?"

"Yeah, that's what I said," Aria confirmed. "Drake shot her. In the head. Saw the whole thing. I saved your kid, though. Then Jenny took her outta here, and *should've* taken her to a safehouse, *like I asked*. But did she do that? *Noooooope*!"

"Okay, I get it," Jenny said, annoyed. "I didn't take her to the safehouse. Oh well. She insisted I bring her back."

"She insisted?" Djimon asked slowly.

"Little bitch made me pay her a hundred fucking dollars to stay in the goddamn car!" Jenny hissed. "What the hell've you been teaching that kid?"

Djimon couldn't help himself. He had to laugh. "That sounds like Molly alright..."

"Sooo?" Jenny asked.

"What?" Djimon replied.

"Soooooooo?" Aria asked.

"*What*?"

"You gonna put down the gun now that it's obvious we're on the same side, or what?"

"Oh. Yeah, I guess. But only if you're here to make sure I get out okay."

"I promised Molly I would," Jenny said.

He slowly lowered his gun.

As soon as he did—

BKAM-BKAM!

He collapsed on the floor, on his front. Jenny and Aria whirled, guns ready.

Damian, having failed to notice the girls, leaped into the aisle with an unusual spring in his step, laughing with maniacal triumph. "GOT YOU, MOTHERFUCKER! I GOT YOU! HAHAHAHAHAHAHAHAHAHAHA*HAAAA*!" His pistol barked as he put another round in Djimon's back. "*Suka*!"

Jenny, exasperated, said, "Dude..."

Damian turned around, surprised to see them. "Oh, hey."

Aria said, "Dude."

"What?"

"You fucking idiot," Jenny said, indicating Djimon.

"*What*?"

Jenny went over to Djimon's body and knelt down beside it, checking for a pulse. "You better pray he's not dead."

"Why would I want to do that? That guy was a real pain in the ass. *And* my hands! You see this?" He held up his hands for Aria to see. "And this?!" He turned to show her the crimson groove in his shoulder. "Motherfucker had FATE rounds on him. I'd say I'm lucky to be alive, but obviously it was only a matter of time." He winced as he stooped down and grabbed the revolver out of the waistband of Djimon's pants. "I'll take that." He checked the cylinder. Only two shots left unfired.

Djimon twitched. A low-pitched moan escaped his lips.

"See? He's alive," Damian said without sympathy, giving Djimon's ribs a light kick.

"Knock it off," Jenny snapped. "You alright, Ice?"

"Why the concern?" Damian asked. He turned to Aria for answers. "I'm genuinely confused. He's the enemy. Look at my fucking hands, man."

"I've seen your hands," Aria said. "Pretty sure Mista Gangsta Rappa down there is switchin' sides, though. Aren't ya, Ice?"

"S-sure," Djimon stammered. He coughed, wheezing with his face on the floor. "Whatever you say..."

Jenny helped him into a sitting position. "Easy."

"What the fuck is happening?" Damian asked.

"The little girl we took outta here? She's his daughter, and she wants at least *one* of her parents to survive this." Aria gave him a hard look. "That good enough for ya?"

Damian shrugged. "But my hands—"

"You already shot me, man," Djimon said. "Give it a rest."

"Fuck you. I just might actually shoot you anyway, kid or no kid." Damian waved the magnum. "With *this* gun! Then you'll see how fucking painful it is."

Drake's copies rushed the walkway on the second floor. They lined the storefront. A row of P90 muzzles searching for their prey in the thrift store's dark, smoke-filled interior.

"Oh, get over yourself already," Aria said with a roll of her eyes. "You'll live."

"With scars."

"You'll still live."

"With *scars*!"

Jenny sighed. "Sometimes I wonder why I love you."

"Uh," Aria said as she glanced over her shoulder. "Maybe we should—"

"LIGHT 'EM UP!" The Drake copies filled the store with lead.

Chapter 044
Blockade

Mackey's Market Parking Lot

11:11 PM.

Hill jolted awake when the paramedics bounced his stretcher against the ambulance's bumper. He groaned, feeling his wounds' invasive burning in his flesh. Like drills that continued to spin in the cavities.

"I'm here, kid," Carver said, leaning into his view. "You're gonna be alright. We got this."

"The... the mall," Hill wheezed. "The hostages..."

"It's all under control. The hostages're out. We got Afrókrema back on our side. They're cleaning out the vermin as we speak."

"Afrókrema?!" Hill gasped weakly. "But... those guys are assholes."

"Every other department was swamped with this recent crime wave. Whole city's in shambles. Didn't have much of a choice. Had to cut a deal." Seeing the dismay on Hill's face, Carver said, "Yeah, yeah, I know. I don't like 'em much either. In the meantime, try not to talk. You did good in there. Now you gotta rest. You earned it."

"Bomb..."

"What?"

"There's... a bomb... like in Monterey."

Carver's face lit up like a jack-o-lantern. "What? A bomb? Where?"

Hill could barely get the words out. "Santa's... village. Counting down to midnight."

"Ah, shit. Anybody else in there besides Afrókrema?"

Weary of the nearby paramedics, Hill whispered, "Damian... and... some other girl. Jenny's sister."

"Anything else I need to know?"

"She has a great ass."

Carver rolled his eyes. "See you at the hospital, kid. You're gonna be just fine."

"But what about Damian?"

"What *about* Damian?"

"Aren't you gonna do something?"

"Like what? Save him? Why the hell would I wanna do that?"

Hill gaped at him.

"What? If he goes, it'll solve all of our problems, son. We won't have to worry about him trying to kill us, and we can take our money back. We'll be doin' the world a favour by ridding it of that freak. Come on. Don't look at me like that. You don't owe him a damn thing."

If Hill could slug him, he would have.

Carver pulled one of the paramedics to the side and slipped a pair of hundreds into his coat. "Keep him under till I get there."

"Dr. Miller?"

"Dr. Miller. Or Fisher if Miller isn't there. We need him to stay quiet."

"Sir...?"

"What?"

The paramedic hesitated. He said in a low whisper, "That's the Sergeant..."

"Your point?"

"He's on our side..."

"I'm not so sure about that anymore. Lookit 'im. He's a changed man, and it ain't for the better. Understand?"

"Yes, sir..."

"Now get him outta here fast. Get on the radio and tell your boys to do the same. I need a full evacuation of the area, and I don't wanna see a soul within fifteen blocks of this place twenty minutes before it blows. You got me?"

"Yes, sir!"

"Good." Carver waited until the paramedics put Hill under and loaded him into the ambulance. They closed up and headed out. Other emergency crews were just getting the news about the bomb and were following suit post-haste. Carver got on the police radio. "Attention all officers, this is Captain Carver. We need an immediate evac of all personnel and civilians within a fifteen-block radius of Manharttigan Mall. We only have till midnight." He hung up the radio and called Fairman.

The thrift store was turned completely inside out by a relentless hailstorm of fire and lead. Damian and the others fled through the rear exit and entered a corridor. Aria was the last one in. She kicked the door shut and put a torch to the door handle.

Sensing her linger, Jenny turned. "Come on, Aria!"

"Relax. Go on ahead. Should be a lounge we can barricade ourselves in."

"Barricade? Isn't there another way out?"

"Yeah," Aria said nonchalantly, glancing up from her work. "Knowing Drake, he blocked it off. Or not."

"Doesn't hurt to look," Damian said from a crossroad up ahead. "I can see the lounge over there." He looked to his right and saw a door leading back into the shopping centre. He looked to his left and saw, at the very end of the hall, a small beach ball-like device with a big red bow on it, situated on a red-and-white platform. *Shit.* "No other exits."

Djimon approached him. "There has to be another way out. Fuck you mean 'no other exits'?"

"I mean there *are no other exits*, fuckwad. Look!" Damian pointed at the bomb as Djimon reached the corner. "You know what that is?"

"Looks like a high-tech air balloon model t'me."

"Wrong. *Dead* wrong. It's a motion-sensitive, tamper-proof explosive. You step within five feet of that thing, and these halls are going to get really hot *really* fast."

Djimon's eyes bulged when he gave the device another look. "Shit."

"Yeah, 'shit' is right," Damian said, looking over at Aria. "What the fuck are you doing, woman?"

"Just think of how painful it'll be for whoever grabs this handle." Aria snickered.

Jenny scowled at her. "Fuckin' seriously? Petty warfare this far in?"

Damian heard a bang at the door down the corridor on his right. Another one. Someone was trying to ram their way in from the shopping area. "Aria, we need some shields. Aria! Get the hell away from that door and start passing around some shields!"

"What kinda shields?" she asked.

"Bulletproof!"

"Oh, okay." She created shields and distributed them amongst the other members of the group. When they all had a shield for themselves, Aria went back to torching the door handle.

"What is your obsession?!" Jenny asked impatiently.

"Ain't no way out with that explosive down there. Best start using every little thing you got in your bag o' tricks."

"This isn't *Home Alone*, bitch!" Jenny yelled, tearing her sister away from the door. "Let's go!"

"Whoop!" Aria stumbled, extending the blowtorch to keep from burning herself with it as Jenny yanked her down the hall. "Hey!"

"Come on!"

KABOOM!

The door vanished in a sudden concussive blast, knocking Jenny and Aria off their feet. The cinderblocks around the door jumped across the hall and slammed into the opposite wall. Smoke filled the corridor, as did Drake's copies. They opened fire on the group. Jenny and Aria raised their shields in the nick of time as a wave of bullets slammed into them.

The second door around the corner came down. More Drake copies burst in. Damian and Djimon blasted two of them with their pistols, hurting them, but not stopping the charge. They came with bats, knives, machetes, poles... but no guns. Not *these* guys, anyway. They were weary of the bomb down the hall. The Drake copies rushed them, slammed into their raised shields, pushing the Dehue and the gangster into the crossroad. A machete blade sliced through the narrow opening between their shields and cut across Djimon's shoulder, making him hiss.

Jenny and Aria retreated under fire, letting the shields do most of the work. They rejoined the men in the intersection, A Drake copy attacked Aria's shield and tried to climb over it. He swung a combat knife at her head. Missed. Aria burned his face with the blowtorch. He shrieked and reeled back. Aria shoved the shield forward, smacking him in his melting nose.

The narrow halls echoed with a deafening cacophony of battle cries and screams; clanging, banging, smashing as the two Drake forces advanced.

Damian and Djimon regrouped with the girls. The bomb was behind the men. The empty corridor to the lounge was behind the girls. Damian shouted, "Lounge! To the lounge! To the—"

A Drake copy cut him off as he climbed over Damian's shield, fire axe raised. Damian drew his knife and sliced the copy's fingers off the top of his shield. The Drake copy gasped, falling awkwardly on the shield. Damian stuck his blade through the copy's throat. Pulled it out. Blinked from the sudden gush of red that hit his face. The Drake copy slid down the front of his shield as more of them rushed forward, smearing the wounded copy's blood down the shield and then trampling him into the floor.

Djimon strained against the overwhelming force. Another one crawled over the top of his shield. Djimon's pistol sent the copy's left cheekbone flying into the ceiling.

Even more of them flooded in from two sides as a screaming mass of limbs and weaponry. Damian and the others squeezed into the only available corridor, backing up, shields rattling against each other. Damian ducked to avoid a flying lamp. Chair legs and appliances from the thrift store flew over them, thrown by the clones, crashing into the floor behind the defending quartet.

Aria fired a shotgun through the gap between hers and Jenny's shields, rewarded with arterial spray. She spin-cocked the lever-action rifle. Fired again. More blood. Another scream.

Djimon gasped when he noticed a Drake clone's head popping up under his shield. Fucker was trying to sneak under their defenses. Djimon slammed his shield down on his head once, twice, three times, four times, loosening the copy's skullcap. He kicked the clone's pulpy head out from under his shield.

Damian grunted as he shook another copy off the front of his shield, slicked with blood. "Aria!" he yelled.

"What?" she yelled back right before splitting another copy's face in half.

Damian squinted as muzzle flashes lit up in front of him. His shield absorbed an entire magazine from an Uzi. "Think you can hit that bomb from here?"

"No sweat!" Aria asked Jenny, "Think you can handle two shields?"

"Probably not."

"Well, try." Aria relinquished her shield.

Jenny had to drop her gun to take it. "Hurry up."

Aria jogged a few feet down the corridor behind them, dodging debris and appliances thrown by the clones. A grenade sprouted into her hand. She yanked the pin, keeping the spoon attached in her fist. She went behind Damian. Hurled the grenade over the moving blockade. It sailed over the heads of three dozen Drakes, some of whom tried to catch it. It flew into the intersection. Hit the corner. Spun into the empty corridor where the bomb laid dormant. It arced down, bounced across the floor toward the bomb. A Drake copy broke away from the crowd, chasing after it, hoping to grab it before it landed within the bomb's perimeter. He reached out, dived, succeeded.

The bomb didn't go.

But the grenade did, shredding the copy in a burst of shrapnel. The shrapnel flew within the bomb's perimeter.

Now the bomb went off.

BOOOMMM!

Fireballs rushed through the corridors, devouring everything it touched, blowing out into the shopping area, blasting a hole in the outside wall and scattering debris across a vacant parking lot. The flash-fire slammed into the quartet's shields, flattening them. In seconds, the flames dissipated in the rafters, leaving a thick fog of smoke in its wake—and a whole lot of burned clones piled up on the floor.

Damian was sprawled on the floor. Ears ringing. He coughed. Turned over. Reached for his shield, only to find a Drake copy with third degree burns lying on top of it. He murmured, "Get the fuck off." Kicked him against the wall. Reached for his shield. Another copy's arm jumped out from under a stack of four and latched onto Damian's wrist. Yanked him to the floor. Damian drew his knife and severed the hand at the wrist.

Aria cleared her throat and picked herself up off the floor around the same time Jenny recovered. Wincing as her eardrums screamed at a high pitch. "You okay, Sis?"

"What?" Jenny yelled.

"Are you okay?" Aria yelled back.

"Yeah. Yeah, I think so," she said, right before a Drake copy got up to his feet behind her. Eyes red with murder. Machete rising.

Aria splattered him against the wall with a magnum, startling

Jenny.

Jenny whirled and watched the machete-wielder slide back down to the floor on top of his companions. She turned back to her sister. "Thanks."

"What?"

"Thanks!"

"*WHAT*?!"

"*THANKS*!"

"Oh."

Jenny looked around for Djimon. Found him lying unconscious under his shield. She pulled him out from under it and dragged him toward the lounge at the end of the hall. She lifted him over her shoulder. "Let's go!"

The Drake copies were coming to. Their burns were starting to heal. A sea of blackened would-be corpses rising from the floor.

Damian broke another copy's face with the edge of his shield and stabbed yet another in the eye, then the throat.

Yet another copy tackled him against the wall. Stole his shield. Damian shoved his knife up through the soft tissue under his jaw. Twisted. A torrent of blood dribbled over his knuckles and trickled down his arm. Damian pulled out the knife and swung the whole blade through the clone's neck.

It was getting hard to move in this writhing river of bodies. Damian staggered out of the crowd. One of them grabbed his leg. He fell forward on his face and snarled as he felt himself being pulled back into the mass. Aria assisted with twin magnums, blasting apart a cluster of Drakes that had him surrounded. Damian kicked the now limp hand off his leg and scrambled away.

"YAH!" The machete-wielder was back. Damian whirled and blocked the swinging machete by the hand that gripped it. Right shoulder wound burned. He gritted his teeth and ignored it. Jabbed the copy's torso with the knife. Twisted his hand, causing it to release the machete. He caught the machete in midair and lopped the copy's head off its shoulders.

He darted for the lounge, still falling behind Jenny and Aria. Another Drake copy with a baton was catching up. Damian turned to face him. Dodged a thrusting baton. Slashed his newly acquired machete threw the copy's stomach, sent him spinning against the wall. The others were getting up. Starting to pursue. Damian turned and ran again.

"Come on, squirt," Aria yelled from up ahead. She pressed herself against the wall. "I'll cover ya!"

Damian shifted his dash to the left to avoid getting in her field of fire.

Three of them were beating their feet after him. Aria's magnums burned the flesh off their legs.

Jenny reached the lounge first. The double swinging doors were flanked by half-glass partitions. Handle bars were on the insides. That was something, at least. She laid Djimon down on a tabletop, checked his pulse. Definitely alive. Relieved, Jenny went to the doorway. "Move your asses already!"

"Yeah, yeah, yeah," Damian grunted as he passed Aria.

Aria followed him through the lounge entrance. Jenny eased the doors shut and slid a broom through the handle bars. She snapped off a table leg and slid it in on top of the broom. Did the same with a mop. "Help me out here."

Aria helped her sister barricade the door while Damian took in his surroundings. A few sets of tables and chairs; a kitchenette, three skylights running a straight line across the middle of the ceiling. No other exits. Lots of floor-level windows. Helicopter sounds above the skylights.

Not so good. They were coming. Yelling, feet pounding, weapons clapping against the walls; getting louder. Damian sighed as the girls tied steel chair legs around the door handles.

"Twist it!" Jenny said.

Damian said, "We're just about finished, you know."

The girls looked at him.

Damian fired up a cigarette. "Drake played us right into his hand."

"It isn't like you to admit defeat like that," Jenny said.

"Who said I was admitting anything? Not me. I admit nothing."

Jenny approached him. "Don't think I didn't catch the implication."

"Didn't imply anything either."

She touched his jawbone with her finger and moved his face in her direction. She got a good look at the bloody cuts and bruises. His healing factor was slowly undoing the damage—a lot slower than usual. She looked at the groove in his right shoulder. It was still fairly deep, slowed almost to a stop due to exposure to FATE rounds. "You really should cover this up."

"No time."

"Did you clean it?"

"No time," he said again, void of emotion.

She sighed. Planted a gentle kiss on his cheek. "Don't be so negative, 'kay?"

He scowled.

She flashed him one of her winning smiles, eyes glowing in the golden light cast by the skylights.

With a smile like that, Damian couldn't stop himself from smiling back.

Chapter 045
Head Cheese

11:32 PM.

The partition windows exploded inward. Limbs and weapons burst through. An orchestra of screams, threats, and weapons clanging and shooting without pulse or rhythm. Just violent, chaotic noise. The doors bent inward but the items in the handlebars kept them from breaking open.

Aria whistled. "Lovebirds!" She tossed Damian and Jenny a pair of combat shotguns.

They caught them and fired into the Drakes that tried to climb over the partition. Their motions in perfect sync with each other until an Uzi sputtered from the hall. They ducked behind a table. Bullets raked across the tabletop and slapped into the wall on the other side. They leaped back up and unleashed another hell storm of blazing bismuth into the intruders.

The windows on the other side of the shuddering doors were handled by Aria. She went to work on them with an electric buzz-saw; severed arms and heads, deflected weapons. She had to put on a full face mask to keep the resulting torrent of gore and arterial spray out of her eyes. Bodies were growing from the limbs she'd severed. In just a matter of seconds, more Drakes were rising from the floor until Aria noticed them and cut them short. Sent their heads rolling. Only thing that seemed to keep them down for good, minus total incineration.

Wielding her shotgun with her right hand, Jenny started throwing fireballs into the hall with her left. Blasted clusters of Drakes into the ceiling and the opposite wall. A few of them tumbled into the lounge. The corridor blazed gloriously. The Drakes writhed within the hellish, pulsating inferno like shrieking demons. Their bodies reduced to spectral shapes that lurched and shifted inhumanly in the flames. A score of them were regurgitated by the inferno, vaulting over the partition, bloodthirsty howls filling the room. Damian and Jenny blasted the lot of them back into the hall.

Jenny made the flames hotter. Sections of the partition snapped and crumbled from the intense heat. Pieces of the ceiling collapsed. Electrical outlets sparked.

Drake #66 leaped from the fire, himself a burning wraith soaring over a table, a pair of P90s spewing lead at the pair. Damian shot him out of the air. He landed flat backwards on a table. Still gripping his shotgun, Damian drew his machete and brought it down on #66's neck. Drake #66 blocked the blade with his P90s raised. His foot shot up, kicked Damian in the side of the head. Dropping the machete, Damian staggered against the partition where a dozen arms shot out from behind him, wrapped around him, tried to pull him into the flames. #66 tossed the empty P90s and drew a knife. Approached Damian. "Hold 'im still!"

BLAM!

A five-round beat from Jenny's shotgun sent #66 flying over another table.

Damian grunted, lunged forward dragging three other copies into the lounge with him. More tried to follow, but Jenny's shotgun dictated otherwise.

Damian and the copies rolled across the floor. Hot as hell. Three bodies caked in flames, flesh cooking under cracked battle gear. Damian leaped away from two of them. The other one went after Jenny with an axe, which he brought down on her head.

She blocked it with the shotgun and kicked him in the balls. He buckled. She shoved him back. Adjusted her weapon. Blew a hole through his chest. He was down, but not out. She dropped the shotgun on the floor in favour of his axe, which she wrested out of his hand and split through his neck as if it were a log of firewood. Kicked the head across the room.

Damian and the Drake #42/#67 duo traded a flurry of blows with Damian caught in between them, somehow managing to hold his own against them. Damian popped #42's kneecap under his foot, temporarily crippling him long enough for him to focus more on #67.

#67 charged him. Damian leaped back, whipped a chair out from under a table and pummeled him with it, swinging the back end into #67's shoulder, slamming him across the table. #42 was getting back up. Damian hurled the chair into his face. Knocked him back off his feet.

#67 hit the floor on the other side of the table. He kicked the table, sent it scooting across the floor toward Damian, who hopped off the floor and hitched a ride on top of it.

#66 came up behind Damian, snarling viciously. Damian whirled as #66 thrust his knife at his chest. Damian parried with his arm, grabbed the arm, spun him around, throwing him off the tables.

#67 turned and saw Djimon resting on the table nearest the doors. Reached for him—

Jenny pounced on him, booting #67 across the room through the partition, back into the hall.

#66 jumped to his feet and roared at Damian. "I'm gonna fuck your mother!"

Damian bounded off the edge of the table. "Fuck *this* instead!" His heel hit #66 square in the face. #66 flew back and hit the wall.

#42 emerged from between the tables with Damian's machete in his burning fist. He reached the end of the table behind Damian before Jenny's shotgun dropped him. He collapsed on his chest, smashing his chin over the side of the table. "*WHUUFFF*!"

Damian turned and kicked the machete out of #42's hand. Picked it up as #42 started to rise. Damian spun on his heel, swinging in an upward arc, clean through #42's neck.

#66 pushed off the wall, dazed. He didn't know Damian had already killed him in the same breath as he killed #42 until he found himself lifelessly watching the floor rise up to meet his face. His body from the shoulders down fell back against the wall.

The double doors heaved against their restraints. Aria was done with the buzz-saw. Now she had herself strapped to a flamethrower, shooting a bright stream of flaming napalm out of her designated windows, engulfing all who stood on the other side.

Djimon came to. He looked around, stunned, confused, horrified. Surrounded by fire and burning bodies. Reintroduced to the waking world by an overwhelming sensory overload of battle noise and screams. "What the fuck is going on?!"

"Oh, you're up," Jenny said calmly from beside him, blasting her shotgun into the swarm outside.

"I'm in hell!"

"Welcome to the party, pal!"

Aria laughed maniacally as she filled the corridor with napalm. "Smell that? Smell that?! How d'ya like my cooking?" Three Drake copies tried to retreat up the corridor. Aria chased them with another load of napalm, scorching them in seconds. "HAHAHAHAHAHAHAAA!"

KSSSSSSHHHH!

One of the skylights collapsed. A hulking black beast with a sinister gleam came down in the rain of twinkling glass. Damian and Jenny whirled, startled by the sound to see—

—Cyborg Drake, already in the process of blasting a wrist-cannon at the valve of Aria's napalm tank.

"Shit," Aria said, turning. The valve popped off. Napalm shot out, caught fire. Aria muttered, "Well outta the fryin' pan and—"

Cut short by the flaming jet of napalm rocketing her into the ceiling.

KABOOM!

The tank blew apart, tearing down the partition wall, bringing down the ceiling and light fixtures, destroying the doors; dousing her end of the lounge under a plume of fire.

Djimon dived over another table for cover. Jenny could take the heat no problem. She screamed her sister's name, searching frantically for her in the blaze. Her eyes found Cyborg Drake. Worry turned to rage. "MOTHERFUCKER!" She pounded him with a fusillade of bismuth that harmlessly glanced off his breastplate.

Damian opened up on Cyborg Drake's head with his last pistol. No dice. Cyborg Drake's holographic smile remained unfazed. Drake's *face* on that thing made his skin crawl. "What the—"

Cyborg Drake's wrist-cannon opened up on Jenny. She ducked low and sprang forward. Bullets whistled over her head.

Damian yelled, "Jenny, *NO!*" Dashed after her.

Cyborg Drake's right hand transformed into a long, serrated blade. Swung it at her. She dropped to her knees, skidding across the floor. The blade sliced through the air just an inch from the tip of her nose, cutting a few strands of hair. She launched herself up from under him. Slammed her knuckles into his breastplate, crumpling it. Cyborg Drake kicked her in the hip, sent her twirling to the other side of the kitchenette, bouncing off the wall, sending cracks through the concrete.

"JENNY!" Damian screamed.

Cyborg Drake seemed to be ignoring him. It turned toward Jenny—

—revealing the main Drake in his Santa outfit and satchel strapped to Cyborg Drake's back with a live chainsaw sputtering in his hands. Damian stopped himself dead as Drake swung the chainsaw at him. Felt its oiled teeth slash across his check. He cried out in pain as he stumbled back. Lost his balance. Fell on his backside.

"Ho-ho-*no*, you don't!" Drake hopped off Cyborg Drake's back, revving up the chainsaw. He stalked toward Damian with the chainsaw raised. "You an' I got some unfinished business, freak!" Seeing Damian's apparent worry for Jenny, Drake added, "Oh, don't mind them. Let the man have his fun. He ain't seen a gorgeous woman for a while."

"What the fuck *is* he?!" Damian asked.

"You oughta know! *You* made him, fucker!"

Damian gasped when he saw the cyborg uproot the refrigerator from its spot and carry it toward Jenny. He made a move to go around Drake. Drake hopped between them again. "Uh-uh!" he said. "You're *mine*!"

Damian gripped the machete handle in one hand and his fighting knife in the other. "Get the fuck out of my way!"

Drake's chainsaw blade nipped at him, keeping him back. Damian's eyes lit up with fury. Drake cackled, making threatening jabs. "Go get her, freak... if you can!"

Blood pumping. Rage exploding. Damian bellowed a deep war cry as he charged him. Blades hurtling toward Drake. "DRRRAAAAAAAKKE!"

Drake blocked his attack with the chainsaw. Metal shrieked. Sparks exploded from the edges as the chainsaw's teeth clawed against Damian's steel. Chipped a piece off the edge of the machete. Damian hopped back. Drake lunged forward, slashing the chainsaw down on his enemy. Damian's machete deflected it, leaving Drake wide open for his knife—he plunged it into Drake's throat and twisted it as sadistically as possible, trying to get all the way around for a quick, messy beheading—

Drake, gagging on the blade, blood spewing, kicked Damian in the chest and fell on the floor.

Damian hurled his machete after him. It sliced through his chainsaw-wielding arm. Drake gurgled, taking the knife out with his free hand. Damian pounced on him. Drake stuck him with his own knife. Damian felt it invade his stomach, cutting arteries, flooding him from the inside. He gnashed his teeth, trembling with rage and pain. He drove his fist into Drake's face, hammering his head into the floor. He grabbed the chainsaw then—

Drake had grown a new hand. Both his hands reached up and pulled Damian's Santa Claus hat over his eyes. Damian dropped the chainsaw's blade on his enemy. He couldn't see, but he knew he hit flesh because the machine sputtered and a fresh wave of warm blood splashed his front and dampened his hat, and best of all, he heard the familiar sound of bacon grease cooking on a stovetop frying pan— except it wasn't grease, it was Drake's organs getting blended together by the chainsaw's stirring blade. Drake's hands were still pulling his hat down on his face despite his suffering. Damian pulled the chainsaw out of his enemy and cut his arms off. He yanked the hat off, still with Drake's hands clinging to the brim, and tossed it aside. Looked up.

Cyborg Drake loomed over Jenny with the fridge raised high. He brought it down on her, shattering the floor under her. He did it again. The whole lounge shuddered. Jenny cried out.

"NOOOO!" Damian screamed.

Another impact from the fridge shook more panels out of the ceiling.

God, he's killing her!

Drake laughed.

Rage surging, Damian carved the chainsaw through Drake's head like he would an electric knife through a turkey and leaped off his body, bounding straight for Cyborg Drake. "Hey! Hey!"

Cyborg Drake paused.

"It's me you want, motherfucker! Kill *me*!"

Cyborg Drake kept the fridge suspended above his head. His chromed skull shimmering under the holographic image around it. Bulging eyeball fixed itself on Damian.

Damian smiled now that he had taken Cyborg Drake's attention away from Jenny. She's had worse. But that didn't mean Damian wanted the beating to go on. "You got an upgrade since last time. You remember? I killed you. It was *easy*. Now, you're back, with all this hardware, and you know something? I don't think killing you this time will be any harder than it was last time."

"Oh yeah?" Cyborg Drake hissed, stepping up to the challenge. He turned around. "How typical of you. What makes you think Central Congoria wasn't a fluke?"

"Because," Damian said, reaching under his tattered aloha shirt, bloody fingers wrapping around the handle of the magnum tucked in his pants. "I've got *FATE* on my side!"

The hydraulics in Cyborg Drake's prosthetic muscles whined as he *threw* the fridge at Damian.

Damian banked sharply out of its path, rolling across the floor as the fridge zipped by like a cannonball. It slammed into Drake, carried him to the other end of the lounge, plowing through tables. Damian came up in a squat, leveling the magnum with Cyborg Drake's torso.

Cyborg Drake's holographic face became a fever dream mask of dread. "Oh."

KAPOOOOWWWW!

The FATE round was a lightning bolt, streaking across the room, burning a hole through Cyborg Drake's armoured torso like it was paper, destroying vital components of his life support system and tunneling through the wall behind him. Homerun!

The other copies went berserk. They rushed into the lounge, barging through the doorway and the partitions.

Damian fired the last FATE round and decimated Cyborg Drake's neck. His Plexiglas-enclosed, chrome-skulled head tumbled through the air, image projection flickering around it. Damian threw the magnum at the oncoming army and caught the cyborg's head. "*OOF!*" Thing weighed a ton. He almost dropped it.

The beheaded machine started to power down. It pivoted forward, falling between Damian and the copies.

Damian ran into the kitchenette. Spotted the microwave. Fucking. *Perfect*. If he was going to die, he was going to do it in style. He popped open the door and shoved the head in. Slammed the door shut. Set a timer for thirty minutes. The microwave came on. The head started to rotate. It was screaming in the microwave's red interior, heating up.

The copies froze. Eyes bulging. Hands gripping the sides of

their heads. They started to moan and writhe. Mewing like cats that'd been beaten almost to death. Flesh *melting*. Wax dolls under a heat lamp.

The head shrieked. Eyes smouldering, glazing over as its chromed skull began to sparkle and pop beneath its Plexiglas container.

Damian watched. Backed up against the counter as the copies inched closer, shambling, trying to power their way through this unspeakable agony.

Drake #1 himself had managed to crawl out from behind the fridge, gripping the satchel, pushing toward Damian with more willpower than any of the others could summon for themselves. Festering burns. Blond hair turning white and falling out. Skin bubbling and peeling off...

"F-fucker," Drake moaned, getting closer.

"Yeah, that's right," Damian said. "I *fucked* you up for the *last* time, motherfucker!"

"Until... the next time!" Drake fell on one knee. "Right?" Reached into his bag. Seemed to be holding up pretty well considering his head was shriveling beneath a thinning layer of liquefying, paste-like flesh. That flesh dribbled over a sizzling layer of muscle tissue. His fat tissue glistened and crackled like bacon grease.

Cyborg Drake's brain caught fire. Its chrome skull glowed ominously in an aura of flames, electricity coursing unstably across its surface. The Plexiglas coating drifted apart, oozing off the skull's gleaming surface. The eyes withered and turned to fizz and dripped from the sockets like marshmallows over an open fire.

Drake persisted, even when his copies began to collapse. With their eyelids halfway down their faces, their eyeballs rolled out of their sockets, dangling from smoking optic nerve muscles.

Jenny came to in the corner, and immediately wished she hadn't. The sight of the rapidly degrading Drakes made her blood run ice cold. She screamed in terror and scrambled away from them as they continued their stubborn, zombie-like advance. "JESUS FUCKING CHRIST, WHAT THE *FUCK*?!"

Damian grabbed onto her, wrapping his arms around her shoulders. "Relax," he said, as calmly as he could manage. His voice trembled despite his best efforts to conceal his horror behind a fearless facade. "I get the feeling this is almost over."

Jenny gripped him tightly, watching in terror as the melting Drakes converged on them. Their battle gear slid off their bodies and crashed to the floor. They started to turn black, charring.

Drake #1 pulled out the last carton of eggnog from his satchel. His fingers seemed to flatten against the sides of the carton. He looked at his arm as the last of his skin slithered off his wrist. He knew he didn't have long. "Drink it, fucker," he wheezed. "DRINK—"

His jaw fell open. Nothing left to hold it in place. "—*IIIEEEE!*"

Damian snatched the carton out of his hand. He opened the top. "Have a taste of your own medicine." He shoved the business end of the carton into Drake's gaping mouth and squeezed the carton. Tainted eggnog shot down Drake's throat. He choked and gagged, reeling back. Crumpled to his knees. Shaking violently. His muscles charred. Seeped through his bones. He looked up at Damian with a pathetic look in his eyes, right before they lolled out of their respective sockets. He groaned. Then his innards erupted from every opening in his body. Intestines snaked out of his mouth as his torso ruptured and dumped everything else onto the floor. A congealing mass of organs spread across the kitchenette floor in a pool of microwaved bile.

Damian and Jenny moved away from Drake's innards. Their immortal enemy collapsed forward, head splitting apart when it hit the floor. Body convulsing its last.

The chrome skull sparked. The microwave burst into flames, then blew to pieces. Damian and Jenny ducked to avoid shrapnel flying off the countertop.

The other Drakes' heads came apart. They fell in chunky, shapeless, soup-like heaps.

Silence. Nothing but the crackle of the inferno in the corridor and the small fire on the countertop; the hissing mounds of black flesh in the middle of the lounge as sickly green veils of smoke rose into the ceiling in thick wisps.

Damian and Jenny stared at Drake's corpse, panting heavily. Injuries aching, throbbing. Bodies soaked in layers upon layers of gore. Clothing tattered and damp, sticking to their bodies. Damian looked at the pieces of chrome scattered across the counter before he tossed the empty carton onto Drake's remains. "Now you know what a TV dinner feels like."

Chapter 046
Escape from Manharttigan Mall

11:45 PM.

The Christmas tree was completely aflame. Neon rings of peach and teal surrounded it like a dozen halos running up to the skylight dome. The star at the top became too much for it to handle. It snapped off a large section of the tree's top and plummeted into the food court. The digital countdown was badly damaged by the fire, but it still worked. An automated female voice announced on the PA system, "Only fifteen minutes until Christmas, shoppers!"

The Lounge

Damian's legs wobbled under him, getting weaker by the second. He slid down the cupboard to the floor with a heavy sigh. "I'm beat."

Jenny knelt down beside him. "We're not finished yet."

Damian scoffed. "Says you."

"That's right. And how often am I wrong?"

"Often."

"Wrong answer." She leaned closer, eyes filled with determination. "This ain't over yet, soldier."

"Yes, it is."

"Fifteen minutes to get out of range of an explosion that equals half of a nuclear bomb is more than enough for your dumb ass. Get up."

"Don't feel like it."

She pursed her lips. "Get. Up."

He looked at her. No arguing with her when she had that look in her eyes. "For fuck's sake, woman. Even if I wanted to, I couldn't get up by myself."

"Why not?"

Damian showed her his burned hands. "They might be healing at an extremely slow rate, but goddamn, the energy's sticking to me like fucking glue. It's draining my stamina. Or did you forget that?"

"Alright, alright."

"Dumbass."

"I forgot, okay? Jesus. I just *might* leave you here if that's the way you're gonna act."

"Help me up."

Djimon popped up from behind a table. "Yo! Is it over?"

"Yeah," Damian said as Jenny helped him to his feet. "And so are we." He grunted when Jenny gave his ribs a light jab.

"How long till it goes?" Djimon asked.

"Less than fifteen minutes," Jenny said.

"So that's it, then? We're screwed."

"Hell, no, we're not," she snapped.

"How *aren't* we?" Djimon asked.

"Woman's intuition." Jenny slung Damian's arms over her shoulder and started dragging him toward the exit.

"Bitch, please!"

"Just come on!" Her pyrokinesis cleared a path in the flames. She also doused the sheet of fire draped over Aria who, in under a minute, was back like nothing had ever happened, hacking and coughing back to life.

"Whoa, now!" Aria exclaimed when she saw what remained of Drake and his copies. "What the hell'd I miss?"

"A horror show," Jenny said. "We have less than fifteen minutes to get the hell outta this mall and out of range before that bomb goes off."

"Oh, so, what you're saying is... we're screwed?"

"That's what I said," Djimon chipped in.

"No," Jenny said stubbornly. "We have all the time in the world."

"No, honey. We're screwed."

"Seconded," Damian said.

"*I* seconded it," Djimon said.

"I seconded it *first, suka*!"

"I ain't no third, cracker!"

"You're *last*, bitch!"

Jenny made an exasperated snarl. "GUYS! We don't have time for this!"

"Thought we had all the time in the world." Damian smirked.

"Oh, fuck off and follow me." Jenny darted out of the lounge with Damian's arm over her shoulders, and Damian struggling to keep up with her. Djimon and Aria followed her down the corridor to the intersection. Jenny glanced to where the motion sensory bomb had once been. Instead of a dead end, she saw a huge cavity leading out into the parking lot. "Look!"

The others looked.

"Well then," Damian said unenthusiastically.

Aria shoved Djimon aside and made a mad dash for the parking lot. "Race ya!"

"Hey!" Djimon ran after her.

Jenny pursued them, still dragging Damian. "C'mon, baby. Come on."

"I said I can't feel my legs. Just leave me."

"What was that?"

"I'm just dead weight at this point. I can't feel my legs. My hands are deformed. I'm a fuckin' cripple. My dick probably doesn't even work anymore. I'd rather die than be a cripple."

Jenny stopped at the opening and set him down. She turned him so that he had no choice but to look her right in the eyes. "Hey. I love you. I love you no matter what."

"I love you too," he said.

She kissed him. Then she slapped him unconscious. It only took one strike. "That oughta shut you up." She gathered him off the floor and heaved him onto her right shoulder. Leaped out of the hole into the winter wonderland beyond. Feet landed on freshly fallen snow next to Aria and Djimon's footprints. Abandoned cars cloaked in white filled a few parking spaces. She sprinted after Aria and Djimon toward the west end.

Two android snipers occupied the eleventh floor of an evacuated office building overlooking the parking lot. They watched the foursome make their way along the side of the mall. One of them contacted Fairman through an internal channel: *"Sir! I've just spotted four possible bogies in the northwestern parking lot heading west."*

In his office, Fairman checked his desktop monitor, watching the android's live POV feed. He zoomed in on the video, squinting. He made out Aria's distinctive form despite the quality, and he could see Damian draped over his girlfriend's shoulder. "Persistent, aren't you? I suppose this means Drake's dead..."

"Sir?"

"No survivors."

"But sir, what if they're discovered?"

"No survivors, goddamn you! The whole area's evacuated for several blocks. And when that bomb goes off, there won't *be* any evidence of them left to spark an investigation. Now kill them!"

"Yessir!"

Down below, Aria reacted with lightning reflexes as soon as the androids' rifle reports reached her ears. "DOWN!" she yelled, diving behind a sports car as the asphalt erupted under her boots.

More rounds skipped across the parking lot toward Djimon and Jenny. They scrambled behind a van parked across the aisle from Aria's sports car. The van's engine block blew apart, flipping the hood into the windshield. Two more rounds ripped through the side of the van near Jenny's head as she was setting Damian on the ground. "Shit!"

"Goddamn, god*damn*!" Djimon yelled.

The rifles crackled in the distance.

Aria scowled as her sports car buckled over blown tires. Its windshield splintered. A bullet left a hole in the passenger side door. "Fucking snipers, man! Just what we needed. They're *really* adamant about making sure we're dead."

"Ya think?!" Jenny yelled.

"Don't let your panties get all twisted, Sis. I know where they're shootin' from." An anti-material rifle grew into her hands. "Go! I'll cover ya!" She stood up. Raised the rifle over the car, leaning her body against the side. Peered through the scope at the office building, running up its glass-and-steel face until she spotted the androids. They fired, each blowing out a window on either side of her, skimming the tattered edges of her battle-damaged top. She fixed one in her crosshairs. Fired.

KAPOW!

Her target's head disintegrated beside his companion.

Jenny picked up Damian and closed the gap between her and her sister with Djimon close behind. They squatted behind her as another gunshot rang out.

Aria's right elbow came apart. She screamed into the sports

car's roof. "FFUUUUUUCK!"

Jenny pulled her down from the sniper's sights. The sniper kept firing, shredding the sports car's upholstery. "You okay?"

"Fucking *FUUUUUCK* it hurts like a son of a bitch!" Aria howled, holding her right hand and arm a few inches away from the bleeding stump. Her healing factor got to work on creating a new elbow. "That guy's *dead*, man! *DEAD*!"

Fairman contacted a different group on a separate frequency. "Air support: how many gunships do we have left?"

"Four, sir."

"You seeing the feed?"

"Yessir. Four bogies, one unconscious."

"Send the gunships! Send *all* of the gunships! Destroy them!"

"Aren't we on a limited budget, sir...?"

"Why the fuck is everybody questioning me? I gave you a direct order!"

"Yessir. Of course, sir."

Aria's arm had healed. The sports car was a smoking heap warped by bullet holes.

Djimon hugged the ground, eyeing Damian enviously. "At least *he* won't feel anything when he dies."

"Oh, shut up," Jenny snapped. "We're not dying today. Aria?"

"Way ahead of ya," Aria said. She stood behind the rifle, looking at the office building through the scope. She took a bullet through her stomach. "*HAAUUNNGGH!*" she moaned, staggering back. Didn't fall. Still looking through the scope... finger snaking around the trigger. Searching, searching... found the son of a bitch. She grit her teeth. He fired again. She fired back a split second before his shot tunneled through her chest and laid her flat on the ground.

A combination of grey matter and biomechanical circuitry exploded out the back of the sniper's head.

Aria retched and heaved on her hands and knees, spitting blood on the ground as the bullet holes closed.

Jenny grabbed her by the shirt and lifted her to her feet. "Up! Up! Up!"

"I'm comin', I'm comin'!"

Djimon lingered behind them. "Yo!"

The girls turned.

Djimon approached a pickup. Rammed his elbow through the driver side window. "Save some time, bitches. How's *this* for a *pickup* line?!"

The girls exchanged looks. Aria shrugged. "Beats walkin'."

Djimon got to work on hotwiring the pickup. By the time he got it started up, Jenny had Damian strapped into the passenger seat. He was still unconscious. She stared at his face, heart racing. Doubts began to surface. They were taking too long. She kissed his cheek.

Djimon pulled the door shut. Didn't bother with the seatbelt. He looked at Jenny. "Get in!"

"I'm going in the back!" Jenny shut the door and hopped into the bed with her sister.

Djimon scoffed, shooting a spiteful sideways glance at Damian. "Fuckin' typical. Two hot babes but I get stuck with the *asshole*." He threw the truck into gear and pushed it out of the parking space, whizzing by abandoned cars.

Jenny and Aria sat with their backs against the cab. Aria pricked up, alarmed. Sensing the disturbance, Jenny asked, "What? What is it?"

"Ya hear that?"

Jenny couldn't hear anything except the truck's engine. "Hear what?"

A FIM-92 Stinger launcher grew out of Aria's arm. "Stay beside me." She got up, aiming the stinger into the dark, cloudy sky. First, all she saw was snow.

Then the gunships came, banking in from over the mall, coming in low. The four of them fanned out above the parking lot and didn't waste any time—they started carpet-bombing the parking lot, destroying it row by row while their wing-mounted machine guns and missiles fired at the pickup.

Aria locked onto one and fired a missile straight at it. The gunship banked sharply, trying to evade—and failing. The missile pierced the cockpit's windscreen.

BOOM!

The gunship turned into a fireball. The wing-mounted rocket

launchers provided secondary explosions that seemed to rip the air around it asunder. The flaming hull dived into the asphalt.

"Whoa!" Djimon yelled, glancing at the flames filling the rearview mirror's sight. "*DAAAYUUUMMM!*"

Jenny screamed at Djimon: "STEP ON IT!"

Another gunship moved in, spitting dual incendiary streams after the pickup, raking across the parking lot, about to cut off the truck—

The asphalt jumped in front of the pickup. Djimon cut a sharp turn in the opposite direction the bullets were heading and slewed between two parked minivans. A rocket screeched after the pickup. Hit one of the minivans, sending both of them sky high behind the speeding pickup.

Aria fired another missile—it missed! "Shit!" It streaked between two gunships, spiralling out of control behind them and disappearing in the inferno left in their wake.

The carpet-bombing was so extreme it was saturating the grey night clouds orange.

"Damn!" Aria spat.

The two gunships flew overhead and parted ways ahead of the pickup. The third hung back, drawing a bead on the pickup. "Target locked..."

Jenny thrust her hands up. Flaming projectiles exploded from her finger tips and engulfed the front section of the third gunship. The pilot jerked on the stick, throwing off the targeting system. Two rockets traced strange, asymmetrical arcs after them.

Djimon looked in the sideview mirror and nearly shit himself. He spun the wheel left, right, left—the pickup fishtailed around more cars. The rockets took the plunge. The pickup sideswiped a station wagon as a rocket obliterated it, knocking the girls flat on the truck's bed floor. Pieces of the station wagon chased them, glancing off the side and rear of the fleeing pickup, punching out one of the taillights.

The other rocket was bearing down on them...

Jenny focused on its exhaust fire and magnified its power until the rocket's tail burned up and the fins flew off. The rocket spun out and blew apart in midair.

Aria launched a missile at the third gunship.

Suddenly the gunship *dipped* forward. The missile blew the rotor blades off its top, setting it aflame, sending the blades spinning out in all directions, whipping through the northern face of the mall, slicing through a shoebox light post, shearing rooftops off a row of cars. The gunship dropped like a mountain, crushing its landing gears. It *chased* the pickup on its turf, skating across snowy asphalt in hot pursuit of the much smaller pickup, which was breezing through parking spaces and between parked cars with a lot more ease. The grounded gunship plowed through the cars Djimon passed, wings clipping others parked a little more out of the way, snagging them on its wing-mounted ordnance and dragging them along with it. Fire, smoke, sparks shot out from under its belly.

"Jesus!" Jenny exclaimed, watching the blazing wraith pursue them in astonishment.

The pilot couldn't see a damn thing with the windscreen covered in fire. He lit up the miniguns, shooting blind—

—and igniting the fuel tanks in the vehicles caught on the wings.

KABLAMBLAM!

The vehicles burst into flames. The wing-mounted rockets were next to go, decimating the wings in two bright orange fireballs. Flanked by them, the gunship started to go, disintegrating from the sides. The pilot shrieked as the searing heat rushed the cockpit—

KAPOW!

Up it all went; violent tremors shook the ground as gouts of sunset yellow fanned across the parking lot.

Aria could feel the heat in the pickup. "Whoooaaa!"

Djimon had to squint from the explosion reflecting in the rearview mirrors. It brightened up the cab like a sunset. "Gettin' hot up in here!"

"Get used to it," Aria said as she turned and leaned over the roof of the cab, staring straight ahead, "cuz we got two more o' these persistent pricks after our puckered little asses." She brandished the anti-material rifle again, eyes darting across the skies, probing the clouds for them. She could hear them rumbling under the cover of snow and darkness despite the parking lot's electric lighting and the orange hue from the flames behind them.

The gunships descended from the clouds like dragons, spitting fire. The row of cars just ahead of the pickup blew apart in a fiery conflagration that cut off their escape to the west end. To Aria, it was an inconvenient wall of fire. To Djimon, it was blinding, terrifying. He floored the brake and spun the wheel. The truck slewed, tossing the girls from one side of the bed to the other.

The gunships moved in for the kill. Aria opened fire from the truck bed. Jenny threw her hands out. The firewall before them dispersed, leaving a smouldering trench. She banged her fist on the roof, denting it, shouting, "Go, Djimon! GO!"

The gunships fired all of their ordnance at the truck.

Djimon looked straight ahead. Inhaled sharply. Floored the gas. The pickup bolted for the gutted shoe store on the west-northwestern corner.

Rockets and incendiary rounds uprooted asphalt around them.

"Where the hell is he going?" Aria yelled.

The truck peeled out of the gunships' path of fire. A pair of explosions decimated the tailgate seal and lifted the pickup's rear tires off the ground. The girls grappled onto the sides and squatted, bracing themselves for the few seconds they remained airborne, then the truck fell on all floor wheels again. Djimon bounced in his seat. Head hit the ceiling. "Ow!"

The impact shook Damian awake. "Huh? Whaa—?" Confused, he looked around frantically at the flaming wrecks all around them, jumping at the sounds of war outside of the cab. "What the fuck's going on?!"

"Morning, sunshine cracker!" Djimon exclaimed.

A gunship descended directly behind the pickup. Aria's anti-material rifle barked at it while Jenny peered over the roof of the cab. Gasped when she realized Djimon had set them on a collision course with the shoe store. "What the hell're you doing?!"

"Trust me, I got this!" Djimon replied, accelerating. "Heads up! Er—*down*!"

Damian said, "The windows are already broken, dumbass, why're you driving a truck through the fucking store? Did your seven relatives run out of basketball sneakers?"

"Hold up! That is *racist*, man! Downright *racist*!"

"Blow me."

The pickup speared through a sea of burning shoes and vaulted through the windows into the shoe store's blazing interior. Passed the hovercopter wreckage in the middle of the store and burst out of the storefront into the western parking lot. As the pickup roared up the road toward the street, Djimon felt the overwhelming urge to gloat: "You underestimated me, bitch. I ain't no shoe thief."

"That doesn't mean you're not an idiot," Damian replied.

"An idiot who saved your life!"

"You didn't save shit! I did most of the work."

"Unconscious?"

"Obviously not, dumbass. I wasn't unconscious the whole time. Hence, *most* of the work."

Jenny and Aria looked up and watched the gunships coast over the shoe store and rotate in their direction. "They're gaining!" Aria declared. "Floor it, Djimon!" She blew a co-pilot away with her rifle. The gunship on the left, now with a giant hole in its windscreen, pulled back and banked sharply toward the vacated lot in front of Mackey's Market. The other one loosed another stream of incendiary rounds, tearing up a row of fake cedars dressed up for the season along the median.

Djimon swerved away from the cedars. The road was *right* there.

Aria drew a cylinder shotgun, pounded the front section of the gunship and destroyed the cockpit. The pilotless gunship careened through the air toward them. Hit the road, folding its wing against the asphalt. The ordnance blew, launching the gunship into the night air in brilliantly coloured fragments, rotor blades flying every which way. A rotor blade chased after the pickup, straight for the sisters, who hit the bed's floor as it sliced through the cab's rear window and the middle seat between Damian and Djimon, and plunged into the radio.

Damian and Djimon almost jumped out of their seats, staring at the blade in stunned silence. They looked at each other, eyes wide as saucers.

Damian looked ahead.

Lisa stood in front of them, illuminated in the headlights; skin shining, piercing eyes glinting in the high beams.

Instinctively, Damian lurched across the cab and grabbed the wheel. "LOOK OUT!"

Djimon screamed, "Yo, what the—"

Lisa stood fearlessly as the truck fishtailed around her and slewed out of control across the ice-slicked street. Tires screeched. The sisters bailed just seconds before the pickup slammed into the side of an abandoned Cadillac and flipped over top of it. It tumbled over the sidewalk and pinwheeled across the street. Six rolls, then it landed one final time on its roof and grinded to a halt against the curb opposite the mall's parking lot.

Chapter 047
Countdown Till Christmas

11:54 PM.

The sisters got up to their feet and looked over at the wreck. Jenny raced to it. Aria stayed behind, watching the gunship drift over the Mackey's Market parking lot.

Damian kicked the door open and crawled onto the road. The ice's cold, impersonal touch stung his burned hands. Limbs like jelly under a body filled with lead. He collapsed on his face. Rolled over, gritting his teeth.

Lisa stood over him, her eyes burning with a hatred that the rest of her nonchalant facial expression failed to show. A true mask of youthful indifference.

"Why?" he gasped.

"You're going to die here," she said. "You're going to burn alive. Wither away, like me. I withered away. And it's all your fault."

"Shut up," Damian said. He tried to get up. Pressed his hand down on the ice. The ice turned black, then green, then red. It cracked and fell away, dropping him into a bottomless pit. He floated helplessly, surrounded by writhing walls of red-and-green-striped vines with suction-cupped tentacles sprouting forth from their scaly surfaces. The tentacles reached for him. He drew a blade from thin air and sliced through them. Twice as many grew from the bloody stumps. He kept cutting; they kept multiplying until they overwhelmed him, slithering around every limb, making him their prisoner. More of them wrapped around his body and squeezed the air out of his lungs. He screamed and looked up. Lisa's face was all he could see above him, filling the entire sky. Her face expanded outward like a balloon, her vengeful grin blown up in a fisheye lens, descending upon him.

The tentacles dragged him deeper into the abyss. The walls transformed into warped caricatures of Lisa until she was all he could see. They booed and jeered, chanting, "BURN! BURN!

BURN! BURN! BURN! BURN!"

Damian pulled his arms forward, fighting against his restraints. Fists fanned out, fingers rigid. He watched his fingers extend like knives, stretching up and curling over his head. He howled in terror. His skull throbbed with its own pulse, cranium expanding, threatening to burst. His clothes disintegrated as spikes stabbed out from under his skin, covering his entire body before falling back under his flesh. His eyeballs popped out, rolled laps around his head and traded sockets.

The tentacles held on with steel-like grips as he flailed desperately, transforming into... *something*. He didn't know what he was turning into.

He looked down, found out where the tentacles were *really* coming from—a bottomless pit in the floor. The black floor around that pit turned into a mottled painting of Lisa's face, her gaping maw slurping him in. The back of her throat burst into flames, burning brighter the closer he got to her lips.

"BURN! BURN! BURN! BURN! BURN! BURN!"

THWACK!

A white flash. The fever dream went away. The tentacles released him and disintegrated. Lisa's face vanished with a petrified scream. He fell into darkness. Landed on ice, head spinning.

Djimon stood over Damian's unconscious form, gripping the pistol he'd whipped across his skull. He'd sustained a bloody cut across his right brow from the crash, and felt a bit dizzy himself, but hell, he was doing better than Damian. "Don't have time for your shit, you fuckin' weirdo!"

Jenny skidded to a stop beside Djimon. If she hadn't seen Damian hallucinating on the floor beforehand, she would've reacted much differently to Djimon pistol-whipping him.

Djimon looked at her, panting hard. "Your boyfriend's a fuckin' psycho, lady."

"I know," she said as she hastily heaved Damian off the road and over her shoulder again. "C'mon. We don't have much time left."

"Where's Molly?"

"Just up the road. Don't worry."

"Nah-nah-nah-nah. I'll stop worryin' when me an' my daughter are outta harm's way."

"Fair enough. Aria! Let's go!"

Aria stole one last tentative glance at the gunship before she crossed the street and joined the others in their hasty retreat up the sidewalk. The street was clogged with abandoned cars. "Where's the car?"

"First alley up this street. How much time do we have left?"

Aria glanced at her wristwatch. "Less than five minutes."

"Shit."

They entered the alleyway and found the Shelby Cobra parked right where Jenny had left it. Jenny looked inside and found Molly curled up in the back seat, fast asleep. She breathed a sigh of relief and whispered, "Good girl." She took her keys out of her pocket and unlocked the doors, opened the driver side.

Startled, Molly shot upright, eyes wide.

"It's okay, sweetie," Jenny said quickly as she threw Damian into the passenger seat. "It's just us."

The passenger side door flew open. Djimon leaned in and flashed a smile at Molly. "Hey, gorgeous."

Molly lit right up. "Daddy!"

Djimon leaped into the back seat with her and hugged her tighter than he'd ever hugged her before. "Oh, man. Oh, man. Oh, man. You got no idea how scared I was..."

Aria squeezed in behind the driver's seat and pushed the reunited pair aside. "Shove over, will ya? And close that door!"

Djimon shut the passenger side door.

Jenny climbed in behind the wheel and got Damian's seatbelt for him. Then she did her own. "Buckle up! It's about to get rough." Started up the car, shifted into reverse and backed the car out of the alley and into the street, hitting the broad side of a news van in the process.

"Watch it!" Molly said.

"Shaddap, kid," Aria snapped.

Jenny shifted gears again and floored it toward the mall. Hit the next corner, turning right and driving by Mackey's Market. She glanced out the window at the gunship as it dipped its nose and headed straight for them. Wing-mounted rotary cannons blasted away, shredding every car sitting between it and the speeding Cobra. Jenny squinted as debris sprayed out from the line of disintegrating vehicles and pounded the car.

COBALT CHRISTMAS: A COBALT ROGUE STORY

The gunship gave chase. The pilot grinded his teeth as Fairman roared through his earpiece to "KILL THEM, GODDAMN IT! TAKE THEM DOWN!"

The gunship's incendiary hail dug across the street, cutting abandoned cruisers and civilian cars to pieces in a vain attempt to catch the Shelby Cobra. Two rockets screamed from their ports.

The Shelby Cobra's passengers instinctively ducked and Molly shrieked when two explosions rocked the street and sent cars somersaulting off the curb in flaming pairs. Jenny swerved hard right to avoid a flying car. Heart pounding. Eyes fixed on the road ahead.

The Shelby Cobra flew off the peak of a small slope running down to an intersection, all four wheels airborne for a few seconds. A roadside marquee sign blew apart. Another rocket whistled past the windshield, tailfin scraping across the hood, leaving the Shelby Cobra soaring through its exhaust trail. The rocket landed in an empty park and blasted a swing set and a row of monkey bars into space.

Touchdown. Everyone's heads hit the ceiling. The Shelby Cobra fishtailed dangerously on the ice, tires squealing, threatening to careen out of control.

"You sure you got this?" Aria asked.

"I got this!" Jenny wrenched the wheel and retook control. Set the car on a clear path for the intersection. Glanced at the digital clock. 11:58 PM. She gunned the accelerator and cut a clean line through the intersection into Downtown Cryo City, leaving Manharttigan Mall behind them for good.

The gunship shot over tangled webs of power lines and streetlights. Hot pursuit. Rotary cannons spitting with buzz-saw roars as the gunship tried to get a missile lock on the fleeing Shelby. Power lines sparked and transformers burst into flames.

Gunship's targeting system locked on. Two more rockets chased the Cobra down the street, zipping past a palm tree-lined median. The Cobra weaved through a frozen traffic jam, sideswiping cars and ripping off sideview mirrors in its desperate flight for the other side. A rocket slammed into the trailer of a commercial semi, spraying flaming cases of *Broweiser* beer all over the street.

KAPOW!

The other rocket hurtled through the downpour of shattered beer bottles and continued its reckless pursuit for the Cobra, narrowly dodging an overhead sign.

Another intersection backed up by an abandoned police barricade. The Cobra blew through it and pressed forward. The rocket followed close behind, gaining... gaining. Aria and Djimon looked through the rear window. The scratches on the nose of the rocket were becoming more prominent the closer it got. "Turn, Sis!"

"What?"

Aria lurched between the front seats and jerked the wheel to the left. "*TURN!*"

The Shelby swerved wildly into the glass walls of a corner store and exploded through a pair of magazine stands and an ATM machine. Rumpled paper and glass shards showered the sidewalk as the Shelby crossed it to the curb and clipped the taillight off an ugly beige Volkswagen on its way into the street.

The rocket followed, slicing through clouds of glass and glossy magazine paper, smashing into the Volkswagen's bumper.

KABOOM!

11:59 PM.

Jenny took the next left turn and floored it. Stole another desperate glance at the clock. Sweaty palms practically soaking through her leather biker gloves and moistening the steering wheel. She shook in her chair, blood running colder than the wind outside, heart slamming, every muscle contorted.

Djimon squeezed his little girl against his chest, dark skin glistening under a thick layer of perspiration.

Aria clung to the back of Jenny's seat, black eyes locked on her sister's reflection in the rearview mirror. "Hey, Sis..."

"What?"

"I love ya."

Jenny scoffed. Her gloves squeaked as her grip on the steering wheel tightened. "Don't talk like that."

"Doesn't hurt to say it."

Jenny breathed a shuddering sigh. "I love you too. Now shut up. We'll make it."

"Doubtful," Damian said, startling everyone in the car.

"You're awake?!" Jenny asked.

"Name *one* person who could sleep through the past three

minutes, bitch."

"He has a point," Aria said.

"Well why didn't you say anything?" Jenny asked.

"She has a point," Aria said.

"Because my head hurts and I'm gonna die a cripple."

Jenny took the next exit onto the freeway. A few abandoned cars lay scattered across its otherwise empty lanes. Electric signs and holographic ads gestured and solicited to a dead late-night commute.

"What happened to Hill? I must know before I die," Damian asked Aria.

"He's dead."

"Really?"

"Unless he's immortal."

"Doubt it."

"Then yeah, he's dead."

"What a damn shame," Jenny said bitterly. "I wanted to kill that pig."

"With that in mind," Damian said with a smirk, "I guess he was *duned* from the start." He laughed. Alone.

Djimon groaned. "I wish the fucking bomb already killed us."

"Me, too," Jenny said. Nevertheless, she gave Damian's chin a loving stroke with her index finger. "I love you anyway."

"Okay," Damian said.

"Anything you wanna say to me before midnight?" she asked.

"Where's my bike?"

She sighed.

KAPOWPOWPOW!

The lane beside the Cobra jumped into the air. The gunship's incendiaries raked across the freeway and the roof of the Shelby in a last-ditch effort to ensure the Cobra's destruction. Dents streamed across the ceiling and the windshield spiderwebbed. The car's reinforced materials could take it, albeit not for much longer. Jenny gritted her teeth, shouting angrily as she swerved left, right, left, right; trying desperately to avoid the gunship's fire. "Persistent motherfuckers, aren't they?!"

"That's Fairman for you," Damian said. Then he yawned.

"Oh, is this too boring for you?!"

"It's the FATE energy. Although, come on. We do this every

other week. Oughta be used to it by now." He looked ahead and saw that they were approaching an overpass. "Stop under that."

"What?"

"The overpass! Don't leave that overpass."

"Why would I stop now?"

"Trust me on this—"

Santa's Village

12:00 AM.

The digital countdown reached zero. A chorus of bells chimed on the PA system. Santa Claus's jolly *HO-HO-HO*'s filled the cathedral-high halls—halls that were torn by war and littered with corpses both innocent and anything but. Patches of microwaved gore, formerly Drake copies, littered the floors among the bodies.

An AOL voice started to announce, "MEEEERRRRRY CHR—

Then everything went white.

It wasn't a sudden crack of thunder like most explosions. This one started as a low rumble that rose up several decibels until the whole earth vibrated. Night turned to day as the world's fieriest heat wave swept through Downtown Cryo City. Manharttigan Mall was instantly vaporized, its parking lots devoured by a white-hot ball of fire spreading to the surrounding city blocks like a hungry tumour, rising to the heavens, creating a halo in the clouds around it. A raging firestorm tossed cars and abandoned kiosks down the streets. Office buildings, shops, banks, strip malls—all uprooted from their foundations and pulverized into nothing as the ball's light greedily consumed them. An eerie, deafening howl followed every shockwave rippling from the fireball's base—a choir of angels were announcing the end times.

It reached the freeway in seconds. Flaming cars dive-bombed into the lanes. Jenny fought the wheel, keeping her foot pressed down on the accelerator. The overpass was just ahead. A burning pickup exploded in the gap between the Cobra and the gunship. Meteorites crashed into the freeway. The white-hot ball of destruction drifted to the edge of the embankment, edged the freeway.

They reached the overpass. Jenny slewed to a stop.

COBALT CHRISTMAS: A COBALT ROGUE STORY

The gunship pilot knew he was fucked. He dived in low, landing gear scraping pavement as he hurtled straight for the Cobra. He almost reached the overpass—but too late! The white-hot light was on him, filling the gunship's cockpit. Windows blew. Controls melted. He shrieked as his face burned off his skull. The gunship, swept away by flaming gales, blew apart.

Both sides of the overpass were windows to an apocalyptic event. Nothing but raging fires and cars and debris rolling with the violent orange waves across the lanes. Then it became too bright for the Cobra's occupants to keep looking as the fireball rolled on top of the overpass, trying to tear it out. The overpass's concrete pillars cracked. The bottom of the bridge splintered, crumbling, threatening to collapse on the car. Portions of it crashed down. The earth trembled, feeling like it might give way. Another deathly howl filled the space beneath the overpass. The screams of the damned peeled across the skies.

And then nothing.

The white light faded. The howling died down. It all seemed to end as quickly as it began. The overpass was barely functional, but it hadn't fully collapsed. Ahead of the Cobra sat a gigantic, half-melted chunk of Santa Claus's head embedded between two outer lanes, its sizzling eyeball fixed on them, its jolly grin warped, distended in anguish. A fog of smoke filled the air. The night was no longer lit by electric signs and lampposts, only glowing patches of fire.

In the car, everyone was fine. Shaken, but fine.

"Everybody okay?" Jenny asked.

"Meh," Damian said.

Djimon said, "Yeah... yeah, I think so. You okay, Molly?"

Molly, eyes wide with terror, simply nodded.

Aria said, "I've been better."

Jenny exhaled slowly. "Jesus... damn... that... I don't think— that's not something I'll be rushing to experience again anytime soon."

"Agreed," Aria said.

Jenny looked at Damian. "Where to now?"

Djimon said, "I wanna go home, man. I could use some sleep."

"Me, too," Molly said.

Damian looked at Jenny, then at Molly and Djimon. "We'll take you two home first."

Campturn District

2:43 AM.

Djimon gave them directions to his apartment complex, and after a bit of searching, they eventually found it and parked the Cobra on the curb. As Djimon stepped out, he muttered, "Man, I dunno *how* I'mma 'splain this little girl to my wife..."

"That's your own damn fault, shithead," Damian replied through the rolled-down passenger window, ignoring that it was minus ten degrees.

"I'm gonna get divorced for sure..."

"How long have you been married?" Damian asked.

"Four years, man."

"Just tell her she's an illegitimate child or something. Conceived with some other bitch before you got married. Problem solved."

"If that doesn't raise alarm bells in my head," Jenny began, "I don't know what does."

"I'm loyal to you, baby." It was Damian's turn to flash her a winning smile.

Djimon maintained doubt. "Yeah, I guess..."

Molly started to cry.

"Hey, now." Djimon hugged her. "S'alright, kiddo. We'll make it work."

"I'm gonna ruin everything," she sobbed.

"It's Christmas, kiddo. It's the time o' miracles. And you know what you are?" Djimon thumbed her tears off her cheeks. "You're *my* little miracle. We're gonna make it work. Ain't nobody gonna leave you alone again."

"Promise?"

"Pinky promise." They locked pinky fingers. Djimon scooped her up with his left arm and turned to face the others. "Uh... thanks, you guys. Hey, if you ever need anything, just holler."

"Will do," Aria said.

"Take care of yourselves," Jenny said, beaming. "I gave you my number, right?"

"Yeah," Djimon said. "We'll talk about. Over beer or

somethin'."

"Fuck off, faggot," Damian said.

Djimon approached Damian's window. "Hey, man... I thought we was on bad terms, alright? It was nothin' personal. I'm uh... I'm sorry about your hands. But ya know... family comes first, you know?"

Damian looked at Molly, then at Djimon. "I understand."

"Truce?"

Grudgingly, Damian said, "Truce. Now fuck off."

Djimon laughed and followed the path of cracked pavement up to the apartment complex's gate. Molly yelled from over her father's shoulder and waved at Damian, Jenny, and Aria. "Bye! Thank you all for everything! Don't forget about me, please!"

"We'll come visit sometime," Jenny replied.

"Merry Christmas!" Molly said, right before they disappeared behind the gate.

Jenny sighed and sat properly behind the wheel. "Doesn't that just warm your heart?"

"She's a sweetheart, that's for sure," Aria said. "A tough nut to crack, too. She'll do fine."

Damian grunted.

Jenny punched his arm.

"Ow! What?" He glared at her. "Alright, fine, it's a little heartwarming. Big fucking deal. I'm just excited to go on that vacation."

"Got a few things to wrap up first," Aria said.

"That we do," Damian replied, nodding slowly. "That we do..."

Chapter 048
Rise and Fall

Christmas Day—2:54 PM.

A press release at city hall with the mayor addressing the events that had taken place at Manharttigan Mall was broadcasted nationwide. He commended the police force and Afrókrema for their valiant efforts to thwart the terrorist plot conducted by the thought-dead Damian Warkowski and his cohorts, and for putting the people's safety before their own. He gushed over their handling of the situation for a good ten minutes before he started giving out medals to Captain Carver and Colonel James Fairman—the latter of whom the mayor personally congratulated for going above and beyond and finding redemption in his swift efforts to end the terror plot. He even promised a bigger budget come the new year over lunchtime negotiations the following day. Things were looking up.

As the press release ended amidst an epileptic strobing of camera flashes and a flurry of interview requests from flocking reporters, Fairman and Carver slipped off the stage and entered an empty hall. Fairman pulled Carver toward him and whispered, "Has Hill woken up yet?"

"Not yet," Carver said. "The injuries he sustained were pretty severe."

"He might know too much."

"Why do you say that?"

"He was with them longer than I would have preferred. The risk is too great. They told him something. I'm sure of it."

Carver scoffed. "You're being too paranoid. It's a party. Relax."

Fairman sighed.

Carver adopted a more reassuring tone. "Look, when he wakes up, I'll ask him about it. He trusts me."

"And if my suspicions are realized? What then?"

"Then... then we'll have to shut him up."

"Assassination?"

"Not if I can help it. He's still a friend. A bastard, but a friend. With a little persuasion, I think he might come to see reason. Perhaps with a considerable sum of hush money."

"And if that doesn't work?"

"Then we do it your way. There's already a little Christmas parcel in his mailbox. Got a guy on standby to take it out if he agrees to our terms."

"What about Warkowski?"

"'Donovan,' you mean?" Carver smirked. "You showed me the footage, remember? They never made it out of the blast radius. They're gone. No longer a thorn in either of our sides. All the money we paid them has been taken back out. It'll be returned to us in no time, once it goes through the hoops a few times. Everything has been taken care of."

"Hm." Fairman nodded, but he didn't look pleased or reassured.

"Hey." Carver give his shoulder a friendly pat. "I'm sorry about Drake."

"He was a good soldier."

"Indeed."

"There's nothing left of him to bring back this time."

"I'm going to go check on Hill. Go back inside. You earned that party. Celebrate. Live a little. Maybe woo a nice lady, hmm?"

Fairman smirked. "Maybe."

Carver patted his shoulder a few more times before he headed for the foyer. He stopped and turned on his heel. "Oh, and Colonel?"

Fairman looked at him.

"Merry Christmas."

Fairman nodded. "Same to you."

Maple Hospital

"So, you're awake," Carver said as he entered Hill's room.

Hill was sitting up in his bed, looking like hell. "I feel dead," he croaked.

"You were lucky." Carver took a seat beside him.

"What'd I miss?"

"The bomb detonated. Don't worry, we got everyone out of range. And it's all thanks to you. The mayor said he'd like to have lunch with you sometime."

"Cool," Hill said, voice crackling. "What about Damian?"

"Gone."

Hill stared at him.

"Don't tell me you're upset about that. The guy was a walking disaster. Totally delusional and psychotic, just like the rest of them. Those girls you mentioned, too. Jenny and her uh... sister? They were all crazy."

Hill said nothing.

"They didn't get to you, did they? Come on. Tell me they didn't."

"No," Hill said.

"Did they say anything?"

"No."

"Really? Nothing? Nothing at all?"

"About what, exactly?"

"Oh... anything, really. They were a very anti-social lot, as you know. Only God knows what they were talking about half the time. I don't even think *they* knew what they were talking about. They had a real hate-on for Fairman especially, it seemed."

Something cold gripped Hill by the gut. Something crept into his mind: *Not you, too.*

"They didn't say anything about him, did they?"

"No... no. Mostly just 'kill them all' this and 'destroy the enemy' that. The usual bullshit."

"Ah. Figured." He stood up and pushed his hat down on his head. "Well, I'll let you get some more rest. I expect a full report on my desk sometime before the new year. No rush."

"Hell of a way to spend Christmas, huh?" Hill said.

"Yeah, I'll say. Just call Miller if you need anything. He should be in tonight."

"I will."

"G'night, kid."

"Good night."

Carver went home and turned on the TV. He'd ordered Chinese takeout a few minutes before he got home, so he made sure his wallet was within his reach as he tuned into the news.

"—Manharttigan Mall, where the infamous terrorist known as

Damian Warkowski, or as some people know him, the 'Dead Blue,' took hundreds of hostages—"

Click!

Carver switched to the movie channel. *Lethal Weapon* was on. He leaned back in his comforter and watched for about five minutes before the doorbell rang. He got up with his wallet and met the delivery girl, a woman with red bangs over her black eyes. She got his payment, wished him a Merry Christmas, and skipped down his front steps to her car.

The smell of Chinese filled his nostrils. His mouth was watering when he returned to the living room with his takeout bags full of fried rice and lemon chicken. Passed his comforter and set the food down on the coffee table. Turned around and met Damian Warkowski sitting in the comforter, ice blue eyes fixed on him with cold calculation.

Carver just about shit himself. "You—" he choked.

"Me," Damian said quietly.

"But you're... you're dead..."

"Again," Damian said. "Just like I was when you and Hill 'accidentally' found me in that restaurant all those months ago. You were pretty quick to throw me that proposal of yours then, weren't you?" Damian chuckled. "'Work for us or we'll blow your secret. The whole world will know that you're still alive.'"

"I'm an opportunist."

"Don't bullshit me. We both know that wasn't an accident."

Carver didn't say anything. His mouth hung open.

"Sit," Damian said, indicating the couch on the other side of the living room. "We have something to discuss."

"Our business is concluded," Carver said firmly.

"You took my money. You tried to kill me. Our business is anything *but* concluded."

"Is that all? You want your money back? Because I-I can give it back," Carver stammered.

"It'd be a good start."

"I can do it right now," Carver said, reaching for his phone.

"Later. Hands where I can see them."

Carver laughed nervously. "Why so hostile? I know we've had our differences in the past, but..."

"You and Fairman were real clever. I'll give you that."

"I don't know what you're talking about."

"Yes, you do. Fairman needed a budget increase after the Konnerd incident slashed his funds. No one would take him seriously. Not the cops. Not the drug cartels. Not the gun merchants. What better way to save face than to be the one to succeed in *really* killing the infamous Dead Blue? Me. Someone long considered to be invincible... unkillable. It'd be *some* feat, wouldn't it? Everybody would want your help then, right? They'd all want a piece."

Carver stared at him.

"My question is... once Fairman gets what he wants, what do *you* have to gain from it? More money? Drugs?" He scoffed. "Don't fucking tell me if was for your country! Fairman already tried to feed me that one."

"What the hell do you want?"

"Satisfaction."

Carver tapped his knees, anxious. "Look... whatever it is, I can pay it."

"This isn't about money. Not quite."

"What, then?"

"You're going to sell out Fairman."

"Why the hell would I do that?"

"Because if you don't, I'm going to kill you."

"But if I do, my life will be ruined."

"You should've thought about that before you started consorting with a genocidal piece of shit like Fairman."

Silence between them. Murtaugh was getting information out of Hunsacker about a heroin shipment on the TV.

"Well?" Damian asked.

"I'll do it."

Damian's eyebrows shot up. "Really."

"Just give me a day. I... I'll do it." He was lying. Damian could see right through him.

Damian stood up from the comforter. "Give me your phone."

"What?"

Damian stretched his hand out. "Phone."

Carver tossed it to him.

Damian caught it and sent Hill a text message: 'Pier 5.' He hit send, then erased the message on his end, and tossed it back to

Carver. "Good man. I'll be watching you." He headed for the door. Stopped. Whirled around. "Oh, and Carver?"

"W-what?"

"I want my money in the next five minutes."

"O-of course..."

"And if anything happens to Hill, I'll personally hold you responsible."

"What do you care? For all you know, he could've been in on this from the very start."

"I know better than that." He cocked his head. "Merry Christmas."

He left Carver alone. Carver waited a few minutes, rooted to his seat in a cold sweat. When he finally got up, he transferred the funds back into Damian's 'Donovan' account. Then he rushed into his bedroom and packed a bunch of clothes and other essentials into a suitcase. He emptied his secret cash stash from under his dresser and stuffed it all in his coat pockets. He was ready to leave in five minutes. He carried the suitcase to the foyer, stealing a glance at the food in the living room. It'd be a waste to leave it uneaten, and he was starving. He sat back down and lifted a box of chicken from one of the paper bags. Opened it.

Found a package inside with Hill's home address written on it, with 'RETURNED TO SENDER – ENJOY YOUR MEAL, WITH A SIDE OF POETIC JUSTICE' written in bold across the top. Confused, Carver stared at the package. He gasped when he realized what it was. It slipped through his sweaty fingers. Hit the floor.

BOOM!

His house went up in flames. Damian casually walked down the sidewalk, never once turning to watch Carver's home smoulder at the top of the hill. He fired up a cigarette

Maple Hospital

8:35 PM.

Hill woke with a start. He realized he wasn't alone in his hospital room. A nurse with a face mask hovered over him, black eyes staring at him like empty pits, crimson hair peeking out from under her white cap. He squinted. "Aria?"

"Shh." She placed a forefinger against his lips. She whispered, "The dogs are sleeping."

"Are you here to kill me?" he asked.

"No," she said. "I'm your guardian angel."

He fought back a laugh, only because laughing hurt right now. "Some guardian angel."

"We survived the explosion."

"I figured."

"The lovebirds will be migrating shortly. But I'll be right here. Right next to you, every step of the way."

"But why?"

"Because you're in danger, Hill. They know you know too much."

"You told me..."

"That's right." Telltale lines formed in her mask, showing off her smirk without really showing it. "Carver was in on the take."

Hill groaned and pressed his head back in the pillow. "Oh, Christ... that's bullshit. That can't be true."

"It's true, my dear."

"Where's the proof?"

"In a warehouse on Pier 5. It's a storage unit containing the last of Fairman's drugs, weapons, high-tech equipment, and a certain substance from Indania. And files."

"What kind of files?"

"Accounts. Invoices. Assets. All tangled up in a financial clusterfuck. Fairman's overseas operations and local bank jobs provided the cash. Kartovski provided transport. Carver provided protection from the law. All they needed was someone to filter all that cash through 'legitimate businesses.' Somebody with a lot of money..."

"This doesn't make any goddamn sense..."

"It'll all make sense when you check out Pier 5. Carver will have sent you something.'" She winked slyly. "His death ought to scoot the investigation right along."

"What? Carver's—?"

"Shh." She pressed her finger against his lips again. "He was dirty, love. You were better off."

"But why?!"

"They were both going to kill you."

"You killed him..."

"No, I didn't. We tried to save him."

"Bullshit!"

"It's true. We were gonna get him to testify against Fairman, but that fucker was already one step ahead of us. He sent a package to his house..."

"Oh, my God." Hill rolled over on his side away from her, clutching his eyes. "Why? Why?"

"Sent one to you, too," Aria said. "Don't worry. It's been diffused."

"What do you people want from me?"

"We want Fairman. And you're gonna get 'im for us."

Chapter 049
Go with the Flowrami

December 28th, 2031.

A fancy high-rise suite overlooked the wavy sandbar and the sparking ocean dotted with colourful sails and a multitude of swimmers under the hot summer sun. On a cantilever balcony, a blue-green swim shorts-clad Damian lounged in a lawn chair with a sparkling rocks glass full of vodka in his scarred right hand. The sun's heat was a refreshing change from Cryo City's bitter cold. His solid chest muscles glistened with sweat. A pair of mirrored wrap-around sunglasses protected his eyes from the sun's blinding rays. He was resting them under his eyelids anyway, listening to the gulls, the children playing in the water, the TV playing in the suite...

"—following the death of Captain Jimmy Carver, a thorough investigation led to the discovery of what some might call an 'orgy of evidence' in the warehouse district early this morning. Police have not yet gone into specifics, but they have hinted that what they've uncovered could be damning for a few important public figures. In other news..."

Damian smiled. "They're playing my song."

"Hey."

He looked up to see Jenny smiling down at him from the screen door. He sat up to get a better look at her. A straw hat shaded her face; aviator sunglasses hid her blue eyes behind shimmering brown lenses rimmed with gold; a white towel draped over her shoulders and a red two-piece bathing suit that could barely contain her sensual form. Her hair was still damp from her shower. Her skin shined radiantly.

"Whoa," he said, awestruck.

She held up the half-empty bottle of vodka. Smiled playfully. "Care for a refill?"

"*Dā*," he said, even though he didn't need it.

"Come inside," she said coyly, slipping back into the suite. She let the towel fall to the floor behind her.

COBALT CHRISTMAS: A COBALT ROGUE STORY

He followed her, bare feet sinking an inch into the soft pink carpet. She let her hips sway with a slight exaggeration as she went over to the bed. He didn't let her get that far. Snatched her by the waist and pulled her against him. She gasped and giggled, grinding her shapely backside against his front as he ran his hands all over her body. He brushed her hair aside, lifted her hat off her head, and applied gentle kisses on the nape of her neck. Tossed her hat aside as her body tensed up under his warm breath. Her chest heaved as a moan escaped her lips. She took one of his hands and planted a wet, mushy kiss on the back, leaving a red lip print on one of his FATE scars.

He snatched the bottle from her and pushed her on the bed. She laughed and rolled over, leaning back on her elbows, feet hanging over the end of the bed. She pulled one knee against her chest, her seductive smile peeking through a veil of damp, dishevelled hair hanging in front of her face.

He threw back some vodka and wiped his mouth, eyes never leaving her.

"What're you waiting for?" she asked as she undid the front clasp on her bikini. The cups fell from her breasts, not entirely, just enough to really get him going. "Come open your present."

He dropped the bottle on the floor and approached her. His fingers touched her ankle and glided up and over her knee, tracing the curve of her thigh... he climbed over top of her, kissing her, pressing her down into the bed.

And for the next few hours, they were enjoying themselves— and each other. Their neighbours could attest to that.

December 30th, 2031.

Last call at a tiki bar settled on the edge of the beach, lit mostly by tiki torches bordering the stilted balcony the bar was situated on, with the exception of the bar itself, which had a net of Christmas lights strung over it. A small TV played on a ceiling mount. The dark ocean waves gently rolled in, splashing under the balcony floor.

Damian and Jenny laughed drunkenly on a stool. She draped herself on him, sitting on his lap, using the bar as unsteady support.

"Hey, uhhh," Damian slurred, struggling to remember the bartender's name.

"Donn," the bartender said, in good spirits.

"Donn, right, Donn... give me another beer, will ya?"

"Sure thing. One more, just 'cuz I like ya."

"I like you too, Donn," Damian said, chuckling.

"So do I," Jenny said.

"Oh," Damian said, eyebrows raised. "Making the moves on my girl, are you?"

The three of them shared a laugh.

"What'll it be?" Donn asked. "*Broweiser* again?"

"Sure—"

"*EH*," Jenny snapped. "Let's try somethin' different."

"Something different?" Damian belched.

"*Yuuuhhhhh*, somethin' different."

"Like what? What the fuck is there besides beer... and... and vodka?"

Donn made a suggestion: "Ever try a zombie cocktail?"

Damian laughed again. "Never had a cock before."

Jenny giggled all over the bar counter.

"A zombie," Donn continued, "is just a bunch o' fruit juices, liqueurs, and rums all mixed together an' served on the rocks."

"I like fruit," Jenny moaned. "That sounds yummy."

"My treat," Donn said.

"Wait a sec," Damian said, squinting. "Where's the cocks?"

Jenny broke into another giggling fit.

"There aren't any actual cocks in any cocktails I know of," Donn said, grinning.

"Why the fuck is it called a cocktail if there aren't any cocks in it?"

Jenny's giggling became uncontrollable.

"I mean, I'm not complaining," Damian added, "I'm straighter than a bullet fired true, alright?"

"Okay," Donn said, chuckling.

"I'm fucking *straight*, comrade."

"I gotcha," Donn said.

"There are no cocks in it?"

"Just fruit."

"I won't find any dicks poking out of my glass if you serve it to me?"

Jenny laughed so hard she fell off Damian's lap and crashed on the floor.

"What the hell are you doing down there?" Damian asked her.

Jenny couldn't stop laughing.

Damian looked at Donn. "You're a cool guy and stuff, but," he burped again, "but I don't want any penises tonight. Or *any* other night."

"You have my word," Donn said patiently. In just under a minute, he had everything mixing in a shaker with ice, whistling an old melody that neither Damian nor Jenny could place. Then he filled their glasses with crushed ice and poured the shaker's contents into them, topped them each with a red-and-orange cocktail umbrella, and slid them into his patrons' hands. "Voila. I give you two lively love birds... two zombies."

"Not even a testicle," Damian said. "Impressive."

Jenny snorted, almost choking on her drink.

Damian tasted it and let it sit a moment.

"What d'ya think?" Donn asked.

Damian nodded with approval. "Not bad." He threw it back, guzzling down half the glass before something on the TV screen caught his attention. He set the glass down, staring at the TV. "Turn that up, will you?"

Donn cranked up the volume.

"—series of indictments in the Warkowski Terrorist Case, as new evidence has been uncovered. Billionaire Lawrence Manharttigan, owner of the shopping complex that was destroyed in the incident, is now ironically facing charges of insurance fraud; while his son, Lawrence Manharttigan Jr., now *former* CEO Chairman of the Spraggurn International Bank, is himself under investigation for allegedly providing funds to overseas terrorist and organized criminal operations, and for laundering millions of dollars into the country." The news anchor continued her narration over footage of Fairman being escorted out of Afrókrema Headquarters by Hill and half a dozen cops fighting off the mob of reporters. "Colonel James Fairman, head of the elite law enforcement division Afrókrema, is once again under fire for his alleged involvement in a conspiracy to justify illegitimate funds from illegal operations overseas. Whether or not the incident that took place at the Manharttigan Mall prior to its destruction was a deliberate act conducted by these men has yet to be specified, but there has been speculation surrounding the official statements given by Colonel

Fairman and Captain Carver prior to his death. More on this story as it develops..."

Damian laughed so hard he almost passed out. "You see that, baby?"

"Huh?" She looked up from her glass, as if snapping out of a trance.

"You see that? Look at that. That is... fucking beautiful. Fucking... *beautiful*! Just like you." He sloppily kissed her head, making her chortle. "Mwah, mwah, mwah..."

January 1st, 2032.

He heard muffled droning. An electronic hum filled his senses every time someone spoke through muffled speakers.

Damian awoke with a start. "HUH! *VAFEL*! The fuck?" He looked around, dizzy, head fuzzy, vision blurred. Head felt like it was four sizes too big and about to explode. Assaulted by lights dangling from the ceiling, a widescreen TV sitting crookedly on its wall mount with a katana stabbed through the side, and at least a dozen dead bodies in aloha shirts and white suits with large lapels—they either wore one or the other. All of them were riddled with bullet holes, and their Uzis weren't too far off. Jenny, drizzled in blood, chocolate sauce, and sparkles, lay naked on a deflated cushion that used to be filled with water before it sprang a few leaks from some carnage-filled night that Damian couldn't remember for the life of him. Phrases were written across the bullet-pocked walls, reading, 'THE WORLD AIN'T YOURS' and 'FUCK THE SYSTEM' and 'ALOHAAAAAA.' The carpet was soaked and already smelling like mould. The ceiling fixtures had been torn out and the tiles were mostly scattered on the floor on top of the bodies. The mirrored wall to the far right was smashed to pieces. The severed head of a stuffed bear was impaled by a dildo suction-cupped to one of the walls. The toilet was overflowing in the bathroom.

Damian checked himself. He wore a strap-on next to his penis, along with a cowboy hat with its top sliced off, and psychedelic splashes of paint all over his naked body. "*Khristos*. What the *fuck* happened in here?" he asked, exasperated. He ripped off the strap-on and hurled it across the room. It bounced off the head of a dead gangster slumped under the TV. He waddled over to the bathroom, stumbling over the corpses, muttering, "Don't even know who these guys are." When he reached the overflowing toilet, he lifted the lid and looked inside. Discovered a crocodile staring up at him. He jumped. "*GUH!*" Upon closer inspection, however, he realized it was fake. Without even bothering to unclog the toilet, he took a piss right in the crocodile's gaping maw, flushed, then waded through two inches of toilet water back into the room to wake up Jenny. "Jenny." He shook her. "Jenny." No response. He slapped her shoulder. "Wake up, you lazy bitch!"

Jenny bolted upright, gasping. "FUCKIN' GET SOME!" She looked around, confused. She looked at Damian, then at the gangsters, then at everything else, herself included. "What the *fuck* happened last night?!"

"No idea." Damian looked at the TV, watching Donald Hill get interviewed on the news.

"—Fairman has disappeared from our radar right before his hearing. Seems we scared him off."

"Can you tell us anything else, Sergeant?"

"Yeah, if you see him, bring him back here. Might even put up a bounty for this son of a bitch! He's wanted on charges of treason, conspiracy, trafficking of all kinds; Christ, the list is endless..."

Damian grunted. "Of course he would run away..."

"Huh?" Jenny rolled out of the deflated ruins of the water cushion and needed to use the wall to support herself back on her feet. "Whoa, boy." Indicating the corpses littering the suite, she asked, "Who the hell are these guys?"

"No idea," he said again, eyes glued to the TV.

"I think we might have a problem..."

"What's that?"

"I can't remember what we did last night... can you?"

"Nope."

"So we might have a drinking problem, don'tcha think?"

He turned to face her. Beat. "Nah."

The TV fell off its mount and shattered on the floor. Damian sighed, not even bothering to turn and see what the commotion was. He already knew. "We don't have a deposit on this room, do we?"

Chapter 050
Frozen Grave

December 24th, 2032.

He'd taken five androids and retreated to an old cabin up north in the pines, and stayed there for a year. No communication with the outside world. No technology besides an old TV set and a radio that couldn't reach a single station way out here.

Colonel James Fairman went out to collect firewood for himself rather than getting the androids do it for him. Big mistake. A blizzard struck when he was in the woods. All he'd managed to collect was a small bundle of chopped cedar from a stack the androids had made two acres due south. Dressed in a thick fur coat and woolen mittens, he was protected above the waist, but his track pants were so useless he may as well have been wearing nothing. He shivered in the harsh winds as they tried to throw him off his feet. If he collapsed and injured himself, he was done for; food for the blankets of falling snow to devour. He didn't wither from the storm. He kept his balance.

Eventually, he reached the clearing. Nothing but a pickup truck and a log cabin; and to his far left: a long, winding driveway that cut a wavy line through the pine forest and eventually led to a back road. A wind chime on the front porch swung and spun on a single nail, howling its hollow cry without end. An android sat on a lawn chair at the far end of the porch next to a scenic window with the blinds pulled shut. Even in this weather, these types could sleep. They could sleep through anything. But even then, their settings would make them notice the lightest step applied to the porch's stairs. It looked up at Fairman, gave him a quick nod as the Colonel kicked snow off the bottom of his boots, and then went right back to sleep.

Hugging the firewood with one hand, Fairman opened the door. A sudden gust of biting wind jerked the door knob out of his hand. The door swung wide open and banged against the wall. Fairman sighed and went in. Dropped the firewood on the floor without care. Fought against the wind to shut the door. Heaved, and won. The door shuddered in its frame. Fairman locked it and tended to the firewood. Tossed a piece into the burning fireplace and set the rest to the side of the mantle. He undressed from his winter coat, shuddering as a chill went up his spine. The air was cold, too cold. He could feel it in his core. Discomfort. A presence lurking...

He pretended not to notice, facing the fireplace as he tossed his coat over a wicker chair. He kicked his boots toward the doormat. Set his mittens down on a small table beside the chair. He prodded the flaming log with the poker, leaning against the mantle. Sighed. "What do you want?"

The intruder said nothing.

Gripping the poker, Fairman turned around.

Damian Warkowski sat on the couch in the corner next to the window. The amber light flickering from the flames cast dark shadows on his face and body. His shadow throbbed on the wall behind his head. It was darker in that one corner than anywhere else in the cabin, as if he brought part of the darkness with him and threw it about the place. Despite the poor lighting, Damian's cobalt blue eyes shimmered brightly, like diamonds in a white room. How eerily they glowed... fixed on him with a sense of condescension a cat might give its owner.

"I suppose it was only a matter of time," Fairman said quietly.

Damian nodded. "True."

"How did you find me?"

"I watched *Breaking Bad* recently and made an educated guess."

Fairman leaned the poker against the table. His eyes never strayed from Damian. "Why?"

"Because it's a great show?"

"No, why *this*?"

"Oh." He shrugged. "Why not?"

"You've already ruined me."

"Yes, I did," Damian said, without emotion. "But you and I still have some unfinished business to attend to."

"What 'business'? What more could you possibly take from me?"

"Your life, Colonel."

"Why not leave me to suffer? After all you've done to me,"

Fairman growled. "What are you trying to prove?"

"I'm not here to prove anything. I'm here to wrap this up." Damian adjusted his position, placed a foot on the coffee table in front of him. "You want an ulterior motive?"

"What difference does it make?"

"It's what separates me from you."

Fairman looked perplexed.

"During the Manharttigan incident, you said you and I were the same."

"I can't remember much of what I said. It's been a while."

"You strongly implied it if you didn't explicitly say it. So, 'hero,' how's the new life treating you?"

"You fucked up everything."

"I get that a lot." Damian smirked. "But to be fair, *you* were the first to fuck it all up."

"How?"

"It was all going according to plan until you involved Drake. Drake, a man you somehow managed to keep alive till I gave his brain a taste of Hiroshima. He was never part of the equation. He turned a simple black operation into a total clusterfuck."

"What are you talking about?"

Damian chortled. "Christ. You're an idiot. Even Drake had it figured out. Ever since you took control of Afrókrema, I was already playing you like a harp."

Fairman's face was a sad mixture of confusion and disbelief. "But... the jobs, the... how? Why?"

"Central Congoria, Fairman. I don't like the way you do business. That was the trigger. Then Konnerd... you blew it there. But that wasn't how I wanted it to go. It was supposed to build you up. You were supposed to become top dog for saving those hostages. So, I *had* to find another way... and I did. Manharttigan. The crime wave. The city had to get desperate. They had to look *somewhere*. And you were the one who would jump at the opportunity for a second chance. Because that's what you are, Fairman. You're a man of opportunity. Aren't you?"

"You son of a bitch," Fairman gasped.

"And when you would finally succeed, when you finally became the state-funded hero you wanted to be... when you finally had *everything* you could have wanted... that's when I would tear you down and ruin you. *End* you."

"Konnerd... *You* set the fires. Those arsonists were—"

"Scapegoats. And *you* were supposed to put it out. That was the day your time as the city's golden child was supposed to begin. But that's not what happened, is it?"

"Those people... those people died... because of *you*!"

"Wrong, Fairman. They died because of *you*! Because *you* were spineless! Because *you* couldn't think of a proper solution! I gave you *every* opportunity to be a hero, goddamn you, and you fucked up! Those people died because of you." Damian's voice rose to a furious sneer. "A little girl died in my arms because of you!"

"No, fuck you!" Fairman shouted. "They died because of you! Don't you dare paint me as the reason for your misery! Don't you fucking *dare* use my failure to hide from your guilt. It was *your* responsibility!"

Damian drew an energy pistol out of thin air. "Shut up."

Fairman jeered at him. "I suppose I ought to thank you."

"For what?"

"You've given an old man some clarity... and you've assured me that the biggest coward in this room... sure as *hell* isn't me."

Damian didn't move. Didn't say anything. Blue-hot flames raged in his eyes. "Fine." He raised the gun.

The door flew open. In walked the android from the porch with a submachine gun.

Damian blasted him against the door. "Five-kill streak!"

Fairman bolted for the kitchen in the back. Damian cursed under his breath and fired two energy pistols after him, burning holes through the walls, setting the place on fire.

Fairman dived into the kitchen and scrambled behind the wall. Threw open a cupboard and took down a loaded Marlin 336C hunting rifle and a spare box magazine full of six .30-30 Winchesters right before a deafening report from Damian's energy pistol dropped him instinctively to the floor. The overhead shelf where the rifle was stored exploded; a stack of .30-30s blew across the kitchen and out the back window. Fairman blinked as he cocked the lever. Fingers trembling. Hands shaking. Heart pounding.

"Get the fuck out here, Fairman. Die like a man!"

Fairman obliged, leaping into the doorway, muzzle level with

Damian's head.

POW!

The top of the mantelpiece exploded next to Damian's face. Damian recoiled, shielding his eyes from flying splinters. Disoriented.

Fairman spin-cocked his rifle.   Blasted a hole through Damian's stomach, sent him jack-knifing through the window onto the porch, entangled in the blinds. Now he made him mad.

Fairman made a run through the kitchen for the back door. Kicked it open. Stumbled onto the deck overlooking a backyard that sloped down to a shed by the frozen lake.

With an impatient grunt, Damian burned the shades off his body in a burst of black fire, incinerating the fabric instantly. The hole in his stomach closed rapidly. He looked through the window and found an empty cabin. Snarling, he kicked through the wall. What was once a window was now a door. A ball of compressed energy formed in his hand. He threw it across the living room.

KABLAM!

The entire kitchen was concussively blown out into space; utensils, appliances, splinters from the wall sailed flaming over the backyard. The sheer force of the explosion sent Fairman flipping over the balcony railing. He plunged screaming into the snow and tumbled down the hill, losing a few spare shells in the process, but he never let go of his gun. The oven slammed into a pine tree just a few feet away. He readjusted his roll, landing on his feet, using the momentum of his fall to bolt for the shed in knee-deep snow. Wasn't easy. Slowing him down. Like walking through mud. He knew Damian was right behind him. The shed was too far. He looked at the overturned fridge embedded in the snow. Took refuge behind it. Had to reload anyway.

Damian stepped onto the porch, surrounded by black-blue flames.   He scanned the backyard littered with the kitchen's appliances and pieces of all four of its decimated walls for any sign of Fairman.

No coat. Just slippers. No gloves. No hat. The cold was starting to set in. Fairman shivered as he pushed the last of his spare shells into his rifle.

Damian held out his hands and concentrated.   Every large appliance and chunk of debris Fairman could hide behind turned black and rose up from the snow, hovered in midair. The fridge was among them, revealing a startled Fairman. Damian grinned. "Peek-a-boo, motherfucker!"

Fairman squatted, aimed his rifle—not at Damian, at the barbecue under the deck. The red flame label on the propane tank—

KAPOOOWWMM!

A sudden rush of fire ripped the deck out from under Damian's feet and sent three quarters of the cabin up in the air in a bright orange fireball. The flames consumed him, searing through his clothes. He was more flame than Dehue, engulfed in it, flailing in a blazing cloud.

Fairman scrambled for the shed, dodging appliances raining from the sky. Cleared the steps to the wraparound porch and ran halfway up the jetty till he reached the shed's side door. He kicked it in and leaped inside. It wasn't any warmer in here. The wood creaked against the wind whistling through the openings. A motorboat lay dormant in six feet of ice. A snowmobile sat on a platform at the top of a ramp beside the boat. Fairman snatched a key off the rack and plugged it into the ignition. Strung his rifle over his shoulder. "Come on, come on!" Revved up the engine.

Fire carpeted the backyard. Damian charged out of the flames, bellowing   wildly,   like   a   feral   beast. "FFAAAIIRRRRRMMMAAAAAAAANN!" Two blades extended from his hands. He hurled one after the other at the shed.

Fairman accelerated. The snowmobile roared toward the ramp.

The first blade sliced through the wall behind him, sheered through a gas pump—

Fairman took off, rocketing straight for the lake as—

BOOMM!

—the whole shed leaped skyways. Fireballs bloomed rapidly from the fuel, the boat, the kerosene supply... the wraparound deck and jetty were reduced to clouds of sawdust as the shed's walls burst outward, as did Fairman, the rocketeer on the Ski-Doo, streaking across the sky above the frozen lake, leaving a trail of fire behind him as burning gouts of fuel gave chase.

Damian's second blade shot out of the inferno like an arrow and clipped the snowmobile's rear, disintegrating the treads, igniting his fuel tank, knocking him off kilter. An awkward shooting star.

COBALT CHRISTMAS: A COBALT ROGUE STORY

Fairman screamed as the snowmobile burned up between his legs. He bailed, tucked his arms and legs in right before he landed on the ice. Banged his left knee up pretty bad. The snowmobile flew a few more feet ahead, arced down, plowed into the ice, blew apart. Fairman rolled after it. Threw his hands out, trying to get a grip, sliding across the lake's slick, solid surface. Could barely feel his fingers now.

A telekinetic shockwave through the burning jetty cleared a path for Damian to walk along. His wounds were healed. His winter gear had been telekinetically repaired. His eyes locked on his prey.

Fairman groaned as the numbing pain in his knee intensified. "Shit!" He positioned himself in a crouch on his good leg, shrugged off his rifle, cocked the lever. Aimed. Fired.

Missed. Damian didn't even flinch. He was walking on the ice now.

Fairman cocked the lever. Aimed. Hands shaking. Bones rattling. The harsh winter wind was unkind today. He fired.

The round burned a hole through the Dehue's left side. Damian grunted. Didn't falter much. The wound started to close almost as quickly as it opened.

"Shit! *Shit!*" Fairman struggled to cock the lever again. Getting harder to do that. Losing strength. He aimed. Fired.

Bullet whistled by Damian's right ear. Boots stomped across the ice. He watched Fairman push the lever forward, trying to cock it again. His energy manifested into a Model 500 with a 4-inch barrel—an old favourite of his—and he gripped it tightly. Fairman cocked his rifle. Could barely raise it. Never will again. Damian shot him through the rifle, splitting it in half, ripping a hole through the old man's stomach and out his back. Pounded him against the ice.

Fairman gurgled, shrieked to the grey, unforgiving heavens. He moaned in agony, rolled on his side, clutching his bleeding, steaming guts as they began to slither out. "Ugh... no. No. No. No."

BANG!

Damian blew his good leg apart.

"AAAGGHH! GODDAMN YOU, WARKOWSKIIII!" Fairman howled. Tears streamed down his cheeks, face distended in agony. "Fuck you! Fuck you! *Fuck* you!"

BANG!

Damian shattered his other leg.

Fairman whined, drawn out, like a siren. He started to crawl for his life, leaving both his legs behind, jagged blood trails smearing behind him.

Damian reached him. Stomped his heel on Fairman's spine, fracturing it, pressing all the air out of his lungs. "Look at me, bitch." He kicked him onto his back. Fairman was choking on his own blood and bile, sobbing pathetically. Damian sneered at him. "'They say your life flashes before your eyes when you know you're going to die.'"

Fairman groaned, writhing under Damian's unblinking stare.

"'Sometimes the killers see it. Don't ask me how we see it. We just do. Something about the way their eyes look at you; it's something that will never, and I mean *never* leave your brain.'" Damian pressed his foot down on the edge of the cavity he burned through Fairman's stomach. Fairman grunted. Looked up at him. Gagged. "'You look a man in the eyes when you kill him, and what you see in his eyes is forever burned into your memory. There's no washing it out.'" Damian scoffed. "'A man in our profession'd go *crazy* if he looked into the eyes of every man he killed. It adds up fast. All those eyes.' Do you remember when you said that? I remember that." Damian peered into Fairman's mortified gaze. Fairman stared up the barrel of Damian's revolver. "Tell me, Colonel James Fairman... what do you see?"

BLAM!

He didn't know how much time he'd spent standing over Fairman's liquidized corpse. Until it froze over, perhaps, or until the rest of him—what very little Damian left intact—became stiff enough to break like glass if he were to disturb it. The snow squalls were merciless, assaulting Damian from all sides.

He looked up, suddenly. Cobalt eyes pierced the hail.

Lisa stood a few yards away, watching him. A faint, yellow aura surrounded her small form.

"Satisfied?" he asked.

She didn't answer. The gales intensified. She disappeared in the snowstorm.

COBALT CHRISTMAS: A COBALT ROGUE STORY

Damian shivered. Stole one final glance at his last kill of the day before he pulled his hood up over his head and headed for land, whistling *It's the Most Wonderful Time of the Year*. The tune carried across the lake's frozen surface by the winds, until eventually, it faded into the night.

And he faded with it.

END

AFTERTHOUGHTS

(CONTAINS SPOILERS—DO NOT READ TILL YOU'VE FINISHED THE NOVEL)

Well then... that was an interesting go.

Believe it or not, *Cobalt Christmas* was a lot more violent in its first draft, before I started chipping away at it. Damian had a few more bodies to *propel* through (haha) during the airport raid; I originally described a scene in which Damian and Jenny actually look at the convenience store clerk's head in the toilet, and in Dexter's office when they were getting the files from him, Dexter originally tried to make another break for the window once Damian untied him from the chair, prompting Damian to shoot him in his other leg and say, "You never learn, do you?" These are just two examples.

Just about every action sequence was shortened and/or toned down to some degree. Damian would've been closer to something like Jason Voorhees (if Jason Voorhees had a sense of humour, or even talked) by that point, which I guess would be amusing if it were in a different setting, but who knows. I have this strange fascination with unstoppable boogeyman-type killing machines like Voorhees from the *Friday the 13th* films, or Kaiser Corbane from my own *Tea Party Affair* novella, among others.

The most difficult moments for me to write were probably the scene where Jenny manages to get those photos of the dead bank robbers from Hill by appealing to his sleazy desires, and the sex scenes, because, well... *those* are kind of fucking awkward (LOL).

There were a couple of sequences I deleted, mainly because the story changed and rendered them pointless—two of which, strangely enough, were on separate occasions intended to introduce Molly Todd to the story. The first takes place during Drake's grotesque army-building in the backyard of Damian and Jenny's abandoned safehouse with the ax and the wood chipper. The next door neighbour is tired of the noise and for the sake of his wife and children, takes a bat with him to ask Drake to stop. This would have taken place at around six in the morning (Drake starts doing this around 3 or 4). Naturally, Drake kills him, and then invades the house, from which Molly manages to escape. I didn't like that scene, so it was omitted, seeing as how I was probably pushing (or crossing) the boundaries of good taste as it was. I decided I would make that neighbourhood a simple cottage area for the summer, so the number of witnesses would be greatly minimized.

The second, and originally planned sequence, is what I call 'the orphanage sequence'—by far the hardest scene to write. I might not like children, but I can't say I'm a fan of mass child death, even in fiction. Drake's party send shipments of poisoned dairy products to two places: an orphanage and a police precinct during their Christmas party. Suffice to say, almost every cop in the precinct dies, and the 'donation' at the orphanage turns out to be the last donation they'll be getting for a while. Molly is the only one who survives simply because she's lactose intolerant, a pitch-black joke of some kind almost equal to Holocaust jokes at the Jews' expense. Which, yes, I'll admit, I think can be kind of funny. I'm a sick person. Sorry. Anyway, Molly comes stumbling out into the road as Jenny is biking to the hotel, so that's how they were originally going to meet. It turns out I didn't even need the orphanage sequence, but I found that putting her in the shopping mall would be a better (and I guess more tasteful) alternative.

Alas, it's still pretty violent, which I'm okay with on some levels. Much of it was necessary for the type of story I wanted to write: something dark, angry, and upsetting—but also something that, as of this writing, earlier *Cobalt Rogue* stories in *The Final Apocalypse Saga* lack. And that's a sense of hope for the future; salvation, redemption, and of course, a bit o' the ol' holiday cheer, given that it takes place during Christmas.

Because you just gotta have that holiday spirit in there *somewhere*.

I mentioned inspirations without going into too much depth in the Author's Note. If you're reading this after you've read the novel, and you're familiar with the works of Shane Black, then it wouldn't be much of a surprise that he was a major influence. *Lethal Weapon* and *The Long Kiss Goodnight* are primary inspirations for the plot and structure, as well as the first two *Die Hard* films and *Gremlins*. Of course, I wanted to make it my own thing, and I think I did, but I guess that really is up to the individual reader to decide.

The Mackey's Market sequence was in my own personal 'development hell' for years. Originally it was supposed to provide the opening for a novel I never finished, called *Donut Shop Brothers*, about a New York cop (a *super* early Donald Hill prototype, in fact!) who gets caught up in an armed theft ring in the eighties, and after losing his partner in the Mackey's Market situation, he's motivated to transfer to Texas to take down the ring at its source. The story was extremely flawed, and after multiple revisions and drafts, I could never decide on what to do with it, so here I was with 300+ pages of material and nowhere to put it. Eventually, I found a use for the Mackey's Market opening, which itself has been written, edited, and rewritten about ten times now. Its history is even lengthier than *Donut Shop Brothers*, which is strange for an action sequence. Or maybe it isn't. I'm not sure.

The sequence was then changed for a *Cobalt Rogue* opening sequence, changed when *that* project fell through, and revised *again* for a different *Donut Shop Brothers* draft... three or four times. Then that one also fell apart, and I was left with what I thought was a terrific action sequence left up in the air until I started writing *Cobalt Christmas*. It's funny how it once again became a *Cobalt Rogue* set piece after all that time, and in the end, it involved Donald Hill anyway. First it had robots and cyborgs and superhumans, then it was a gritty, stylized 80's-style action set piece, then it turned back into a futuristic action sequence with the cyborgs and superhumans put back in. The inspirations for this one stemmed from the likes of *Predator 2* (a sequel I find is grossly underappreciated, especially considering how well *Predators* did critically and financially, for some reason...), *Cobra*, John Woo's *Hard-Boiled*, and several others. It's one of my favourite action sequences ever written, and by this point, I've written a lot. Perhaps I've gone overboard with it, but I'll leave that for the reader to decide.

One other thing I wanted to talk about was my thoughts on social satire. I was going for something with a *RoboCop* edge, making society look almost... inept in its pursuit for glory and materialism and consumerist needs. I like to think that the little commercial snippets throughout that film were made as examples of news broadcasts put to the extreme—you have the horrible goings-on in the world being told to you, most likely not even in a straightforward way. Sometimes they could be twisted or bent to show a different side depending on political or corporate stances. *RoboCop* is like that, in a way, only blown up and exaggerated to a live-action Saturday morning cartoon, with commercial breaks that pose as distractions from the carnage.

The mall sequence, as Damian enters various shops while he scopes out the place, are dedicated to *RoboCop*, and I'm sure it's pretty obvious why I did that, given the time in the story. I'm not going to analyze every detail; I think I'll stop here and just let it sink in how unsubtle a writer I can be. LOL.

Cobalt Rogue in general is two things: a character study of the deeply disturbed/flawed Damian Warkowski, and a celebration of comic book excess over an 80's action movie backdrop with tints of 80's and 90's anime here and there. Mostly cyberpunk, because nothing inspires me more than a good, stylistic cyberpunk anime thriller like *Ghost in the Shell* or *Akira* (to name obvious examples), or *Battle Angel* or *Cyber City Oedo 808*. Check those out if you haven't already.

This was only going to be 200 pages... somehow it's about 320, and adjusted for paperback form, it's 478! Wow. Wasn't expecting that. Because of this, I'm over a month late in getting it out there! I'd intended to have this out by December 10th! Sorry! I'm not sure if I'll write more of these spin-offs... I have a lot of work to do on *The Final Apocalypse Saga*, Damian's earlier years. That's gonna take a while... and I have a bunch of other projects I'd love to share, too. Hope to see you there!

Stay tuned...

COBALT CHRISTMAS: A COBALT ROGUE STORY

<u>Works by Alexander Engel-Hodgkinson</u>

Clockworld (One-Shot)

The Tea Party Affair

I Keep My True Love in the Basement (One-Shot)

Reality Glitch ('Jumping for Charlotte' segment)

No Bounds ('Cranston & Layman' segment)

I Keep My True Love in the Basement/REMIX

Cobalt Christmas

She Watches Me Bury Her

<u>The Final Apocalypse Saga</u> (First two volumes previously published as 'Dark-Boy')

Cobalt Rogue, Vol. 1: The Dead Blue

Cobalt Rogue, Vol. 2: Sky Japan Welcome Party